"I don't  ny
voice was n ly
too close an
didn't want him to know the things. My
pride was too strong. I'd been this way for so long, I didn't
know how to give in. I didn't know how to trust.

He opened his mouth, like he wanted to say something
else but stopped, and his eyes drifted down to my mouth and
held. My breath caught in my throat.

Before I could think to even push him off, his mouth
claimed me. He kissed me hard enough that my head pressed
back into the wall. His hands slid back to cup around my jaw
to keep me from pulling away. His lips pressed down, mouth
parted.

I kissed him back. I don't know what came over me, but I
wanted to feel those promises. I wanted to believe, for the
moment, that maybe I could just let go, like he said, and trust
that I could be accepted for who I was. Was I just like him?
Could I be like that? Could I find a place just for me among
these guys and waltz in and be with them? I opened my
mouth, inviting him in, just a little.

Like opening the gates, his mouth claimed me again. In
every possible place I could think to hide, he found me. My
mind blanked out. I didn't have room for anything else other
than him and his kiss that told me everything would be all
right. His kiss sank into me over and over again. Lips pressed
against mine, tugging at my skin, at heart strings, at my core.

When he finally released my mouth so I could breathe,
his lips trailed over my face, across my eyes and my brows.

"Why did it have to be you?" He breathed out as he
whispered against my face. "I was hunting a thief, and I
found a beautiful wreck."

The Academy

The Scarab Beetle Series

Thief

Book One

Written by C. L. Stone

Published by

Arcato Publishing

ISBN-13: 978-1496017222

ISBN-10: 1496017226

This book is a work of fiction and any resemblance to persons, living or dead, or places, events or locales is purely coincidental. The characters are productions of the author's imagination and used fictitiously.

Thank you for purchasing this book. Keep in touch with the author to find out about special releases and upcoming events, including spoilers, author chats and swag.

Website: http://www.clstonebooks.com/ - Sign up for the newsletter - It's the best way to stay up to date with the latest from C. L. Stone.

Twitter: http://twitter.com/CLStoneX

Facebook: http://www.facebook.com/clstonex

For that group that found me when I was lost
For feeding candy canes to lions
For believing in a complete stranger
For showing a young girl how to trust
For the very first Academy members

♠

I AM A THIEF

*M*en are brilliantly stupid.

For one thing, guys carry the most cash with them anywhere. Didn't anyone ever tell them cash was dead?

I nestled myself in one of the side branches of Citadel Mall. I picked my way through a Claire's but the lights were too bright reflecting off the sparkling plastic and crystals of the teeny bopper jewelry and handbags. I ducked into a shoe store where the lighting was dimmer and the window wasn't as obstructed. Waiting was the hardest part.

My favorite place to find dumb guys with lots of cash was the mall. Always fairly crowded on a weekend; I could count on at least a couple of twenties for every wallet I temporarily borrowed.

I never kept all of it. Forty to sixty dollars at the most. Not enough to bother reporting to the cops. I didn't mess with credit cards, or bother with selling ID cards. That's the kind of crazy stuff that gets you sent to prison. I always left the wallets and the rest of the leftovers tucked away in the food court and on benches where management would see it and find the owner. That way, the people wouldn't have to get new ID, which is a huge hassle.

And they never suspected a thing. All they saw when I accidentally bumped into them was batting eyelashes and as much cleavage as I could muster the absurdity to expose without dry heaving.

It was even better if one of them had a girlfriend on his arm, because the girl would smack the tar out of him, causing an even better distraction with his head turned the other way. Too bad the next place they walked into where she gave him the doe-eyes to buy her yet-another-pair-of-shoes, he'd be out of a wallet, and she'd be on to the next boy toy.

If I could easily distract a guy when he had a decent girl hanging off his arm, he probably deserved to get his wallet picked and the girl was better off. Loyalty was a big deal to me.

This Saturday had, so far, been a bit of a letdown. Only two hits for me, and I only got forty between them. I handled the cash inside my pocket. The money felt like it was burning between my fingers, partially from the guilt. I wanted to release it, but I'd worked hard for it, and didn't want to let it go.

Forty dollars wouldn't be enough to cover the rent for next week, let alone food. I only had about an hour or two left before ...

A target came into view, walking around the corner. He was alone, and wore a dark red jacket. It was kind of early in the fall for it, but I wasn't going to start complaining; no wallet bulge in his pants pockets and jacket picking was easy. Easier still when he shoved his hands in his jean pockets, and the jacket bulged out on the sides, making my job even easier.

I waited, watching from inside the shoe store, pretending to study pairs of spiky slut shoes. When he stopped and hovered in front of the cookie shop, I figured it was as good a time as any.

I left the shoe store, taking the long way around the corridor, keeping to the middle potted plants, benches and other mall shin-splitters between us. I looped around casually, moving toward the cookie stand.

My Doc Martin boots and jeans were casual enough to blend in and be forgettable later. I tugged the hem of my white tank top lower down my body, exposing just a slip of the gray material of the bra underneath; I'd give him a bonus for being an easy target.

I steadied my pace, trying to give him room and without staring; a skill I'd perfected. I aimed for the right pocket, which was hanging slightly lower than the other, hopefully the sign of a full wallet. If I was wrong, there wasn't much chance I'd get the other one without attracting notice. Dipping into an empty pocket is a lost target.

I stalled as he bought his cookie, watching to make sure I'd been right about the pocket with the wallet. Sure enough, his hand reached in and pulled it out to pay the teenager behind the counter. I stopped and bent over to tie my boot, another stalling tactic, following him by watching out of the corner of my eye to where he stood off between two stores, digging the cookie out of the bag and stuffing it into his mouth. He was at least a couple of heads taller than I was. Not a problem, but I preferred people more my height, which made picking more natural. He had a wide jawbone and deep-set eyes. He was looking curiously around, as if trying to pick out which direction he wanted to go next.

He caught my eye briefly on his glance around and I froze. I'd learned early on if I looked at the face, it became harder to make the move.

This was a real person. I was a thief.

I usually picked a scruffier type that didn't look like a nice person. With the jacket, however, he was too easy a target to miss, and I was out of time to pick another.

I spotted the closest trash bin and waited him out.

It didn't take the guy long to finish his cookie. He aimed for the trash bin I'd picked out.

I started walking, pretending to decide not to buy a cookie. From my pocket, I dug out a crumpled piece of paper to throw away.

The next few moments slowed for me, as it did every time. My heart thundered. I questioned again for the millionth time why I did this.

I prayed I wouldn't get caught and that if I did, this guy wasn't the type who would beat me to a pulp.

With every step I took closer, I thought about changing my mind and running away. This was wrong. I was a criminal. Every wallet I took added up into some kind of unseen karma debt, and one day I'd strike out big time.

Except my brother and I wouldn't have a roof over our

heads if I gave up now.

One more. I promised myself this would be the last. I'd find a good job soon. We just needed to scrape by this week.

I focused on the jacket.

I aimed, and increased my pace to match his stride.

Bump.

My left hand brushed against his jacket at the heavy pocket.

My right hand released the trash, tossing it away. I caught the strap of my tank top that slid down my shoulder. Practiced moves I'd done dozens of times.

Big brown eyes flashed, focusing on my face. Instead of lowering to my breasts, they remained, studying.

That alone caught me off guard. Targets never did that. Not holding my gaze for so long, as if he was disinterested in the body and instead wanted to see the person. See *me.*

At least his eyes were up instead of down at waist level. It was enough. My hand was already in his pocket, curled around the leather wallet, lifting. All I had to do was blush and apologize, tuck the wallet under my arm and out of sight and turn ...

"Hey! You! Girl!"

The shout was so desperate, so commanding, my whole body started to quake and I stopped. My target and I broke our locked gazes and sought out the voice.

It came from across the corridor at the pretzel shop. A guy behind the counter wearing a folded paper hat and blue and white print apron stared us both down.

And pointed right at me.

"Come here," he shouted, in a tone that had my knees jolting into motion. The power was undeniable.

But I was clutching a wallet that didn't belong to me. Rattled now, I realized too late that I had hesitated. I returned my focus again on the target, meeting cool, brown eyes. Eyes that lowered down to my hand that was holding his wallet between us.

I popped my mouth into an innocent 'o' shape. "You dropped this," I said in a quiet voice, holding up the wallet toward him.

My target frowned. He tugged the wallet from my hand and shoved it back into his pocket, zipping it up. I turned away quickly. My mind whirled, trying to figure out the closest exit. I needed to get out of there before he put two and two together and ...

"Girl!" The guy shouted again from behind the counter. He whistled, a sharp, high pitch, snapped his fingers and pointed again. "You. The pretty one with the brown hair."

I scoffed, turning around and spotting the guy focused on me again. He was drawing so much attention that I wouldn't be able to make another target here for hours, if not for days. I glared at him, and closed the distance to his pretzel stand. Maybe if I ate his stupid sample pretzels, he'd stop drawing attention to me.

"What?" I seethed.

When I finally met his gaze, my body froze.

Two different colored eyes blinked back at me. That made me think perhaps I was dreaming. One blue and one green. That didn't seem possible.

His soft brown hair was a little longer on top, brushed to one side at the crown, and cut close around the nape of his neck. The style reminded me of a rock star I'd had a crush on a couple of years ago. He had broad shoulders under the blue T-shirt he wore beneath the apron, and a black cord around his neck with a silver-encased sand dollar. His left wrist was covered in tiny bracelets made out of braided thread and some were plastic like you'd get out of a quarter machine. He wasn't as tall as my target, maybe just a head taller than I was. It was hard to tell, since he was behind the counter. It seemed as if the floor dipped a little on that side.

His lips curled up in a brash smile. "What's your name?" he asked. His voice, when he wasn't shouting, actually had an amused tone, like he was incredibly curious and needed to know.

My jaw's hinge didn't seem to want to work to close the gap of my mouth hanging open. Was he serious? "Pardon?"

He planted his palms on the counter, leaning over it. "I

was asking your name. You know, the thing on your driver's license."

"I know what you mean," I said quickly. "Why do you care?"

"Do you want a job?"

I huffed indignantly. He called out to me from across the mall to ask if I wanted to work for him at a food stand? He appeared to be my age, about eighteen at least. Maybe a little older. It was hard to imagine him as a manager. "No thank you," I said. Not that I didn't need one, but the way he was asking me was too odd to comprehend. Plus, I didn't like the way he was looking at me. I simply didn't believe he was being genuine. He'd call some random girl over to his food stand and hire her? And, he'd called me pretty…

I started to walk off but he called out, "Wait!" It was that commanding tone again and I found myself pausing to obey. "Just tell me your name."

I grunted and turned to meet his mismatched eyes. "Bambi."

He cocked his head at me. "That's not your real name."

My lips parted, my heart pounding. "How would you know?"

"You're not a very good liar."

It was usually one of my better talents. The only other person who could tell was my brother. I turned away from him, too rattled to talk any more.

"Wait," he said.

I ignored it this time, my ears filled with the sound of my pounding heart and masking his tone. I wasn't sure what disturbed me more: the fact that he knew I lied so quickly or that I was impressed he could.

Before I could get past the window of the next store over, I tilted my head casually to check behind me. I caught him jumping the pretzel stand's counter. He tore away the hat and the apron, dropping them to the ground and started after me.

I leapt into a half jog so as to not look like I was running away, but simply trying to get somewhere. I started to turn back to see if pretzel boy was still chasing me when I crashed into what felt like a brick wall and started to stumble. I caught myself on the wall to stop from falling.

A pair of deep-set eyes stared down at me. My target with the red jacket. His serious face focused on mine, recognition setting in.

I pushed myself off of him. In full panic mode, I dashed down a corridor to the left. This time when I looked back, I had two pursuers. They jogged together after me. Their feet moved in unison, something I'd only seen in movies about the army. They knew each other? It was too much for it to be a coincidence.

I cut my way between two women walking babies in strollers together. One of the best things about being a girl is to be able to weave around and through areas and be excused, even if it was rude. Guys can't get away with that, not in South Carolina. Any other guy passing by would chase them, which I was kind of hoping would happen.

Unfortunately, they didn't take that risk, and were stuck lolling behind the strollers, which was almost as good.

I took a turn down another corridor, finding a wide courtyard with a center fountain. I spotted a guy by himself on his cell phone, standing in the corner. He had short cropped, sun-kissed blond hair. Tall, maybe even taller than my target, wearing a black T-shirt with a Zelda Triforce logo from the video game. Nerdling.

I stepped up next to him and wove an arm around his, which was hard to do, because now that I stood next to him, I realized he really was towering over me. "Sorry. Can I borrow you for a second?"

The guy choked on whatever he was about to say into the phone and fixed his eyes on me. They were a very nice cerulean blue. His face was a touch unshaven, almost unnoticeable with his blond hair. His skin had a gorgeous tan as if he'd spent a lot of time outside. "What ... uh ... Can I help you?" he asked.

The smile sliced right through me, catching me off guard with the sincerity. His voice was strong and appealing, with a

7

hint of amusement. "Yes," I said when I pulled myself together. "Could you pretend I'm your girlfriend for a minute?"

The skin at the crest of his high cheekbones tinted. "Any particular reason?"

"An ex-boyfriend and his buddy just spotted me. I wanted to get away before they try to corner me, or at least dissuade him from coming over. He's not a good guy."

"Oh?" he asked, tapping at his cell phone and dropping it into his pocket. "He's not a big guy, I hope."

I liked him. He was quick and willing to play along. If I hadn't been in panic mode, I would have kissed him. "Can we just go into a shop and pretend to make out or something?"

"Sure," he said with a hint at a smile, like he didn't believe I really meant the making out part. He pointed at the closest store. "How about that one?"

"Perfect," I rattled off, without actually looking at where he had pointed. We just needed to get going.

I followed him inside a Love Culture store. I couldn't spot anyone tailing us, which was good, but I wanted to make sure. If they were still trying to find me, I wanted to be out of view for a bit. I'd backtrack and find an exit when I was sure they had passed us by.

I clung to the nerdling's bicep, surprised to feel a bulge of muscle. He had a fit body underneath his T-shirt and corduroy slacks. I noted the confident way he carried himself into the store, and how eager to please he seemed to be.

Nerdlings weren't usually my type. They were usually "yes men" -- you could tell them to jump off a cliff and they'd do it and beg for another order just to make you happy. Some girls liked that, but I hated it.

But I tried not to presume based on looks, or fashion choices.

He headed toward the back, and picked a spot behind one of the clearance racks. He nudged me beside him, so we were both hidden from the front of the store. "How's this?" he asked, a blond eyebrow going up.

I nodded, and then stopped short when I realized we were in a section of bras and ladies' underwear.

He followed my gaze and studied the displays. His cheeks tinted again. "Sorry," he said. "I was just ... didn't mean ..."

"It's fine," I said quickly. I wanted to make him comfortable since he was being such a good sport about the situation. "I hadn't noticed either."

"What's your name?" he asked.

I hesitated. "Bambi," I said, going with my initial lie. I wasn't sure why I did it. I was just sure I wouldn't see him again. A shame, but really, it was for the best. I wasn't his type, or anyone's type, for that matter.

"I'm Corey," he said, oblivious to the fact that I'd just lied. That brought back some confidence. I wasn't that horrible at lying.

He held out a hand, and looked expectantly at me.

I took it quickly, shaking it and hoping he didn't notice me rattling from leftover panic. "Sorry to inconvenience you."

"Not a problem. I wasn't in a hurry." He tilted his head, focusing on my face. "Did you try telling him to back off?"

"Who?"

"Your ex-boyfriend. The one we're hiding from."

"Oh," I said. "Yes. He doesn't listen very well."

His eyes flicked up as if checking to see if anyone was paying attention. He returned his focus on me and smiled sympathetically. "And I'm sorry."

He seemed so sincere about his apology that I had no idea what he was saying it for. Because of the place he picked out? "I said it was fine."

"Not that," he said. "I mean ..." and he angled his head to indicate I should look behind me.

I turned, surprised to see pretzel boy leaning against the wall. His bicep muscle bulged as he put his weight on his hand. His smile played on his lips as he cocked his head toward me. "Hey there, pretty girl."

I tumbled backward in a panic, flat into the rack of bras.

A space between the top and base of the rack allowed for an escape. I weaved through quickly to the other side. I stumbled forward and shot between two sales racks and hauled it to the exit.

My target in the red jacket had parked himself by the entryway. He weaved, his arm outstretched to catch me by the elbow. I diverted, turned and ducked out of range. He probably wasn't expecting me to get away from his pals.

This time I didn't stop for any more games. I was going to find an exit and run home. Mall security must have caught on to me.

I had to cut through two more crowds before I found the entrance to a small service hallway. I launched myself between a couple, breaking their hand holding, and made a dash for the hallway.

I started to slow when someone from the other end of the service hall came out of a side door. I combed my fingers through my hair, away from my eyes, to try to look presentable, like a tired employee going home.

As we closed in on each other, I thought my eyes were playing tricks on me. He looked almost exactly like the nerdling, except his clothes were different, wearing a red T-shirt depicting the local college football team, jeans and Nike sneakers. He also carried himself differently, with a swagger. It was like the nerdling had managed to get all cool in a blink.

I slowed, staring, sure I was going crazy.

The guy, once he caught my eye, stared right back at me. His head tilted, a curious smile played on the side of his mouth. When we got close, he slowed. "Hi."

"No time," I said, trying to sound apologetic. "Have to get home." I turned my body sideways to squeeze by him.

His hand shot out toward the wall, right next to my head, blocking my path. His blue eyes focused on me.

These were different than the nerdling's too. Same blue shade, but dimmer. Sad. Wounded. Embedded so deep inside him that it seemed overwhelming and I wanted to tell him I was deeply sorry for whatever hurt caused his otherwise incredibly handsome face to look so down.

Those eyes stilled my lips as well as my legs. His gaze seemed to penetrate through me, right to my core, begging me to find what was lost in him, wanting to fix him, so the smile on his lips actually reached his soul.

"You don't have to run," he said in a tone that was soft, deep, and suggested deeper meaning.

The sound of a door crashing open behind me told me otherwise. "I have to ..." I said. I inched to move under his arm.

His arm slid down, until his fist was against the wall, at my chest height. His eyes were still sad, but he masked them somehow with a teasing glint. "Stop it, sweet pea. You aren't in trouble. Yet."

My eyes widened at him. I turned my head, catching pretzel boy, my target, and Corey, the nerdling coming down the hall. My panicked heart was unrelenting against my rib cage. Despite what the cool guy was saying, this was clearly a security team, obvious in the confident way they approached me. Pretzel boy had taken the lead over the other two following him. His mismatched eyes zeroed in on me, the smile on his lips smug, satisfied. He'd caught his prey.

But I had one more last trick. A dirty girl trick.

"Rape!" I screamed at the top of my lungs.

The entire group of boys stopped dead, except Corey, who jumped a short step back.

I took my chance. I ducked under the cool guy's arm.

"Wait," pretzel boy called. "Bambi!"

I didn't stop. I felt the brush of the cool guy's fingers swiping at my back, but he wasn't fast enough. I darted down the hall toward the exit.

An alarm didn't sound. I was out in the parking lot and weaved amid the cars. Losing my breath. Losing my mind. Losing the boys.

For now.

♠

BETTER THAN
A CARDBOARD BOX

*T*he short walk to the extended stay hotel was almost as terrifying. I was going nonstop to get there. Every couple of minutes, I checked over my shoulder at every passing car, any shadow, every bit of noise. My senses were in overdrive, paranoid that pretzel boy and his gang were following me.

That was too close. Way too close. Someone must have noticed me hanging around more than usual, and had been ready for me. Now that I was away from the situation, I realized my mistake: the red jacket. The easy target, when it was still warm for early October.

I'd been too greedy and too eager to hurry and get out of there. The setup should have been obvious, but I'd never been caught like that before. I'd been getting too lax with my targets. Maybe one too many wallets had been lifted at that mall in the last few weeks. I didn't think I'd done that many, but there might have been more pickpockets there than just me.

The problem was I only had the forty dollars, still short of what I needed. I only had tomorrow morning to find the rest or we'd get tossed out into the streets. The Citadel Mall had been an easy spot, full of tight corners and distractions. It was also close to the hotel we were living at, and closest to the Savannah highway in West Ashley. I wasn't sure I had time to scout a new area, like one should do, when picking a new place to haunt. I needed time to figure out cameras and security routines.

I turned the corner down the street, walking through the parking lot of the extended stay hotel, where rent was over two hundred dollars a week, and the place was usually always packed.

A white utility service truck pulled up just as I crossed through an empty parking space. It took a spot near the staircase I was heading to. The window rolled down on the passenger side. An old man with a grizzly beard stuck his head out and catcalled at me. "Hey there, pretty girl. Staying here? Need a free room?"

Ugh.

I ignored him, and rushed for the stairwell. I skipped the steps two at a time and took my key out for Room 221B.

"I'm home," I called out the moment I had the door cracked open.

"Kayli!" my brother called. He could usually hear when it was me.

"Wil!" I called back, like I always did. I locked the door behind me, and turned from the short corridor to the wider hotel room.

Wil was in the kitchenette. He waited by the coffee maker and emptied a packet of oatmeal into a coffee mug. "Where have you been?" He looked up, his green eyes covered by a pair of glasses meeting mine. His thin lips pursed as he studied my face. "You okay?"

"Yeah," I said, trying to slow my breathing and look casual. "Those jerk construction workers were just bugging me."

"Work ran late?"

I checked the time on the clock over the microwave. Six was pretty late to get back if I wanted to be here before our old man got up. If I wasn't, he'd root around for money, sometimes breaking things and sometimes finding our stash and taking it to go drink at the bar. "Yeah," I said, avoiding his eyes by pretending to be engrossed with a crack in the tile on the counter.

"How's Tasty's?"

Tasty's was the name of the Chinese restaurant where I

worked part time. It was the only place within walking distance that would hire me. The owner paid me barely minimum wage under the table and it wasn't enough for the outrageous rent required by the hotel. "Busy," I said. "You wouldn't believe the line of customers."

"Liar," he replied. He sighed. "No leftovers for us today. Damn. I was hoping for something else besides bananas and oatmeal."

One of the few benefits to living in a hotel was it served free breakfast in the morning. Unfortunately, it often consisted of oatmeal, bananas, apples and a few pastries. And lately there hadn't been any pastries. To save money on food, we picked up more than our fair share of breakfast staples to last throughout the day. Occasionally I got rice from the Chinese restaurant, and if I was really lucky, I'd get someone's order that didn't get picked up.

The coffee maker beeped. Wil poured his hot water into the coffee cup, and started stirring the oatmeal mix. For being the younger brother, he was taller than I was, with the same eyes, and the same dark brown hair. His was cropped really short. Mine was straight and reached midway down my back. From that point, our looks differed. He was gruff, wiry and usually had a playful grin that seemed permanent to his face. Meanwhile, I hardly ever smiled. There isn't much to smile about when you live in a dump hotel and scrounge for food and pick pockets to make the rent.

A snore broke through our mutual silence. I turned my head, spotting Jack in the bed closest to the wall. Daddy, Dad, Papa and other father names never really fit well between my lips and his ears. Jack was the thing we'd settled on. And those moments he wasn't cursing at me, he sometimes remembered my name was Kayli.

Wil and I were more like roommates to him. He stayed up all night, drinking my hard-earned money away at the local bar, while my brother and I tried to catch some sleep before he got home. Most of the time he came back alone, but every once in a while he bought enough beer for one of the barflies to believe his promises about drugs, money, or

more beer at the hotel room. He'd shoo us o
escape to spend the night in the hotel l
overstuffed sofas, or by the pool that was
repair. Management only hassled us every once in a while. If
that happened, we'd break in and sleep in the hotel's laundry
room, cramped up together in the overheated space.

The lump in the bed shifted. I groaned internally, rolling
my eyes and turning away from him.

Wil didn't say a word, but looked at me, asking me
quietly about money.

I yanked out the twenty-five dollars I had earned
working too few hours today. I also dug out the forty dollars I
got at the mall.

Wil sighed. "I didn't get that much either," he said. He
pulled out thirty dollars and a few ones.

I counted it again just to be sure, but including the
money we'd made earlier that week, we still didn't have
enough for the rent that was due tomorrow. Jack had broken
into our stash this week. I could have shot him for spending
nearly seventy dollars on a barfly and himself.

"I should just quit," Wil said. "School isn't that
important. It takes up too much time."

"No," I said. "You have to finish high school. Mom
would have wanted it."

Wil grunted. "Do you think she'd care at this point?"

I didn't respond. He knew the answer to that. If I didn't
think it was important, I wouldn't have objected. But I
managed to get us this hotel room after our father had a
scrape with one too many landlords and we couldn't get
another rental apartment within city limits. We were one step
away from a cardboard box.

"How did you get the money anyway?" I asked. "You
went to school, didn't you?"

"I got a quick job helping mow someone's lawn on the
way home."

I scrutinized him. Unlike how Wil could read me, I
couldn't tell when he lied. I think it was those big eyes and
the way the smile tripped in the corner of his mouth almost

onstantly. A goofy type of smile, and I was always a sucker for goofy smiles.

"But I should do more," he said.

"You should get through your senior year with those good grades and get a scholarship into college."

"We don't have the money for college."

"Colleges give you the money. And you can get loans and stuff, too."

"The last thing anyone would give me is a loan." He dipped his spoon into the coffee mug and took a bite of oatmeal. He grimaced. "I think he put out the expired packets again."

I groaned, but shooed him out of the way to take one of the bananas. "The point is, you'll be able to go to class and eat campus food and maybe even pick up an internship that will pay you. You'd be set for like four years. Maybe even longer if you decide to become a doctor or something."

"Do you want to tell me which classes to take, too?" he asked, ending his question with a smirk.

"No, dummy. I want you to go to class so we don't have to live here anymore. Not with him." I nodded toward Jack.

Wil's eyes narrowed. "We can just leave him here," he said. "No one will say anything."

"They did last time. He may call the cops on us again and tell them you're a runaway. Finish school." I stuffed pieces of banana in my mouth and chewed and swallowed. "You can't leave mid-term anyway. And if we left and you continued going, your school is the first place he'll come looking for us. There're only a few months left. This is your last year. And you can start applying to colleges in January. Maybe you can get in on the summer semester."

"There's fees."

"I'll figure it out," I said. "We'll get Jack to buy the cheaper whiskey."

Wil pressed his fingers to the edge of his spoon, smoothing over the metal. He started shoveling the oatmeal into his mouth. I ate my banana and took a glass of water. When I was done, I cleaned both the coffee pot and the glass.

With nothing better to do with my time, cleaning room helped.

Wil settled into the second double bed. Textbooks were stacked neatly in the corner and he picked up one. The room had a television, but since Jack slept during the day, we rarely ever turned it on. The hotel had a complimentary business nook, with a single old computer with internet access and printer. Late at night, when everyone else was mostly asleep, Wil would go down and do whatever homework he needed. If he didn't need to use it, I sometimes used it to look for jobs.

I left to steal newspapers from the front lobby. I returned, sitting on the floor, scanning for jobs I could do, hoping to find one open close by.

After a while, I gave up. Most of the jobs listed were repeats. Some I'd tried before and failed. Most were out of my skill level.

I told Wil I was going to bathe. I pilfered through one of my two book bags for clothes and locked myself into the bathroom. I ran the shower as hot as I could, undressed and under the spray with my arms crossed over my body until I could adjust to the temperature.

While I did, I thought about pretzel boy. How had he spotted me from across the mall? They must have caught on to what I'd been up to for a while. Maybe they hadn't been sure who I was, but they knew how I operated. So they set up the tall guy to be a target? And their plan was to corner me?

Why did pretzel boy offer me a job? What was that about?

And how was it I managed to run smack into the nerdling who was part of their team? And then his doppelganger, his brother most likely, in the hallway?

It made me wonder if they had a whole team of people working every section. One thing was for sure, I had to switch stomping grounds for good. This made it harder, especially with rent due the next day. It couldn't be another mall, as they'd likely cover any of the others now. There weren't many crowded places with people carrying full

nd. People rarely used cash these days
d credit cards. The mall had been my

ruined. Why now? Why when we
this the right way? I only took what
ever had the extra money to spare, I'd dump
every last dollar I stole into some donation box for orphaned
kids.

I swallowed back a thick lump in my throat, letting the
stream of water wash away my tears. I hated pickpocketing. I
hated feeling like a thief. I hated living in a hotel, where men
traveling on business stayed. I hated their lecherous eyes and
their catcalls. I hated the constant nerve-wracking worry
about needing to make rent, and always being a dollar short.

I hated cringing every time I heard a siren passing by in
the night. I always assumed they were coming for me.

When I couldn't stand the self-pity any more, I washed,
shaved and shut off the water.

I changed into to a pair of old pajama pants that belonged
to Wil once, but had gotten too short for him. Since I was
smaller, they were still snug but comfortable. I put on a black
T-shirt. The pajama pants stuck to my skin, which was
already itchy from the old, worn blades that liked to nick at
the crevices behind my knees. I wasn't sure why I bothered
grooming at all, outside of trying to blend in at the mall.
There was no one to impress. I couldn't date anyone. I simply
did it because I should and it wasted time.

Holding the thin blue men's razor made me think of my
mother's pink razors before she died. Back when I was little,
maybe around six years old, I would sneak into the bathroom,
and tamper with pink razors, and tampons, and other girl
items she kept in a drawer away from everyone else's
toothpastes and washcloths. I didn't have much to play with
as a kid. Rocks and sticks weren't allowed in the house, so
I'd used the razors and the tampon box to build a pretend
mansion, where little Molly and Polly Tampon lived in
luxury with horses and breakfast cereals I saw on television,
and toys overflowing from every closet.

My mother had caught me and laughed at my imagination. "You're my little storyteller," she'd said, braiding a strand of my brown hair, the same color as hers. "Always something interesting. You don't need a toy when you've got such vivid ideas of your own."

I sighed at the fogged hotel mirror, blinking away the memories. It was still too hard to think of her back then, because inevitably, I started thinking about the day she died.

And that was something that made me angry at Jack. I was so tired of being angry, feeling a weight in the pit of my stomach that never went away. When Wil had his diploma, and finally settled into a college, I'd be able to strike out on my own. Then we'd leave Jack to his fate. He wouldn't be able to come after us. I'd stay for Wil, but not a second more.

A grumbling old voice, muffled through the bathroom door, broke my thoughts. "Where is she?"

I made a face, and then drew a frowning face into the fogged up mirror that I thought mimicked my own. I didn't really want to deal with Jack now. I hung my towel properly to let it dry and yanked open the door.

Jack was leaning against the wall, his arm up ready to knock. His scruffy face was in dire need of a wash, with grime darkening the crevices. His teeth had yellowed. He had thread veins and a drinker's nose. "What are you doing in there?" he asked, his question full of suggestive intent.

"Nothing," I said, trying to duck around him, and holding my breath as I did. I wasn't sure how he managed to lure women to the hotel room. Probably on a promise of a twenty dollar bill he'd nipped from me. His heady armpit smell surely wasn't what they were after.

Jack coughed thickly, as if he had a fur ball. "Your brother told me you haven't made rent."

"It'll be here tomorrow," I said. I bit my tongue to the fact that if he didn't require me to be here when he was awake, I could probably get a better job and make enough for a better place.

"It better be. How am I supposed to teach you responsibility at your age?"

19

"By setting a good example and getting a job, yourself?"

"Don't you start that snippy attitude with me." He shoved the bathroom door open. "Now go clean up the room before I get out."

I moved slowly until he grunted and shoved me aside. When he was behind the bathroom door, I made a face to mock him. Not that there was a point, but at least it made me feel better. A little.

I got to work changing the bed sheets and getting fresh ones from the dresser.

Wil got up from his reading. He picked up one of the pillows and changed the cover.

"You should study," I said.

"I have time to help you change the sheets."

Since we lived in a hotel, technically we could have had a maid come in. Jack had already irritated the maids enough that I'd promised them I'd clean the room and change the sheets regularly if they'd leave what we needed outside the door. They were more than happy to leave it to us, since they knew they'd never get a tip anyway. I ran a powerless sweeper over the thin carpet and Wil replaced the bed's blanket. The worst part was the mess Jack made: collections of bottles, crumpled Kleenex tissues and occasionally a pair of ladies' underwear of unknown origin.

Jack slept for most of the day. I was convinced he only woke up and worked just hard enough to be presentable so they'd let him into the bar. I checked my stash of money, counting to make sure he didn't take any. I don't know where he got money if he didn't get it from me, but I thought he might have made a few friends at the bar who occasionally gave him the fifty-cent shot specials.

The phone rang on the nightstand between the two beds. Wil and I both stared at it, silently urging the other to answer and deal with it.

"I've got homework," he said, crawling back onto the bed and snagging his textbook.

I sighed, and picked up the receiver. "Hello?"

A woman's voice replied. I recognized her as being the

front desk attendant though I forgot her name. "This is Kayli Winchester, right? Do you have a minute to come down to the front desk, please?"

"I'll be there in a second." I slid an evil eye at Wil, who wriggled his eyebrows at me and grinned. I was stuck facing off the questions of if we would be staying another week.

I was hoping they'd believe my lie. I wasn't sure if we'd make it.

♠♠♠♠♠

I walked barefoot down the steps and toward the hotel lobby. The maroon walls and the brown and black striped carpet irritated my eyes, not to mention made the hotel lobby look like it catered to hookers. The front desk was empty. I didn't want to wait and knew what this was about anyway, so I found the short hallway on the other side that lead to the manager's office.

Colby was inside. Colby was a black lump with legs and a shiny bald head and wrinkled neck. If he wanted to, he could look mean, and often needed to because of people the hotel usually catered to. The rest of the time, though, he was just a lump.

His feet were up on the shaky oak desk. He stared at the large screen TV hanging on the opposite wall that had the football game playing. When whatever play was finished, his dull eyes broke from the screen and focused on me. "Oh, hi Kayli."

"Did you need something?" I asked. "I was called ..."

"Margaret wasn't at her desk?"

"Nope."

He frowned. "I just wanted to see if you'll be staying another week."

"I've told you ..."

He held up his hands. "Sorry. We have to ask. The higher ups have us do this thing, you know?"

"And it's due tomorrow," I said. "I know that."

"It's not just that. We've had complaints."

Not again. "What kind of complaints?" I asked, trying to make my voice light, like I had no idea.

"The neighbors hear the shouting and the banging late at night. They say it sounds like people beating each other up. They were wanting to call the police."

I stared off at him, not wanting to confirm or deny anything, just wanting to listen. This was one of the reasons we got kicked out of the last apartment we lived in.

He sighed, shoving his fingers through his thinning hair. "Well, just try to keep it down, okay?"

"Okay."

He pursed his lips, as if my answer wasn't enough for him. What did he want me to say?

"By the way," he said. "The weekly rates have gone up this week."

My mouth dropped open. "How much?"

"A hundred dollars."

"A hundred?" I cried out. "Don't we get the same rate because we've been here for a while."

"It doesn't work like that," he said. "This isn't an apartment. It's a hotel. The rates go up whenever the big guys tell us."

"Isn't there something you could do? You're the manager."

"I don't control the rate. I'm giving you a head's up. I'm sorry, but maybe you should be looking to live somewhere else."

I glared at the wall just so I didn't have to look at him anymore. "Thanks," I said, unable to prevent the slip of anger in my voice. I wanted to hit something, but was afraid he'd kick us out sooner, so I settled for stomping out and slamming the door behind me.

♠

THE PRICE OF
A GOOD NIGHT'S SLEEP

I woke up right around three in the morning and stared at the ceiling, waiting. Wil was in the bed next to me, curled up on his side and staring off at the opposite wall. There wasn't much point to sleeping now. The bars had closed an hour ago. Jack would stumble in at any moment.

I hadn't told Wil about the rent increase. I could barely sleep as it was, and only went to bed because if I didn't, Wil would ask questions. I'd have been up all night conspiring with him and it wouldn't have done any good. He'd insist on not going to school, and I knew there were a few big tests he was preparing for. There was no need for both of us to have a sleepless night. Neither of us ever slept well as it was.

Rattling echoed from the doorway. My teeth ground together. The door opened, and I held my breath, preparing.

Jack left the door open, and lumbered inside. He swayed on his feet, the floor below creaking as he rocked. I didn't need to watch. He did the same dance every night when he didn't score a woman.

He stumbled forward, hitting his shin on the corner of the low dresser. The television set rattled on top.

"Go to bed, Jack," I said, hoping my tone was strong enough to convince him to avoid a fight. Oddly enough, I felt I was mimicking pretzel boy's tone from earlier.

"Shut up, Kay," he said. He felt for the side of the dresser, using it to steady himself as he slid his foot along the carpet. He made it to the corner of his bed, sitting up on it and staring off at the wall. "Wil, come help an old man out."

"No," Wil said.

"What's this?" Jack's voice boomed. "Listen, Son. When your father speaks to you, you ask how high."

"Keep it down," I said.

"And you, Miss Snooty. I'll have you know, you're not too old for me to take you over my knee ..."

This was a critical point. I tried to keep calm. When he was drunk, he walked the line of about to pass out and ready for a fight. "Keep it down," I said. "The neighbors are complaining."

"Fuck the neighbors!" he roared.

There was a sliding of leather against pants, and I knew what was happening. I shot up, moving faster than Wil, practically rolling on top of him.

The first whack of the belt against my back was padded by the blanket. The second hit caught me on the edge of my chin, and I had to bite my tongue to stop from crying out.

Wil shoved me, launching me off of the bed and onto the floor. This time, I was too tangled in the blanket to pop up quickly.

As I yanked myself out of the blanket, Wil tackled Jack. Jack managed to get a good couple of slaps of the belt against Wil's shoulder before he fell onto the bed.

Wil landed on his chest, holding down Jack's hands, trying to catch the one with the belt. "Kayli," Wil called.

I snapped up, finding a pillow and tossing it over Jack's face. I planted my knees on Jack's hands, forcing them down, and shoved down on his chest as he bucked and writhed underneath our combined weight. He tried kicking, too, but was uncoordinated, and never managed to hit Wil.

There was wild mumbling and cursing under the pillow.

I held my breath again, waiting. He must have hit the whiskey harder tonight. After a moment, there his legs slid off the edge of the bed with a thunk. Wil and I jumped up off of him. Jack continued to slide, and landed on the floor. I picked my head up, leaning over the edge to check.

Jack was sprawled out on his back. His shirt had rolled

up his stomach, his pants hung down around his knees, revealing the splotchy boxers underneath. His gut hung over the waistband. His jaw was slack, drool pooling in the corner of his mouth.

The fight was over early tonight. He was out cold.

I jumped from Jack's bed to ours, and crashed onto my back. I touched at the spot where the belt had got me. Now that the fight was over, the pain felt fresh and throbbed. I was too tired to go grab some ice.

Wil sighed heavily, crossing over Jack and gathering our blankets. He fixed them, fluffing them over before sliding into bed beside me. "I hate this place."

I squinted my eyes closed, swallowing back the emotion in my throat.

He didn't know he might soon be free of it.

♠

HARD BARGAIN

*J*ack was still on the floor at five a.m. when Wil had to leave to get to school. He took a series of busses via the TriCounty Link system that headed into Goose Creek. Spending two hours on a bus route must have sucked, but it was better than the trouble of transferring to a closer school, which would have been nearly impossible without Jack getting involved. Not to mention the closest school was scary dangerous, as far as schools went for the area.

I woke up early to snag breakfast from the hotel lobby while Wil showered up in the room. I was surprised to find a couple of boxes of Krispy Kreme doughnuts, that were probably yesterday's batch, out along with the usual packets of oatmeal, fruit and coffee. I grabbed four of the plain glazed doughnuts, along with extra packets of oatmeal, just in case we later were evicted. At least we'd have something to eat while we looked for cardboard boxes.

I wasn't sure why I bothered. If I didn't have a hundred and fifty dollars by noon, Colby would be at the door, or send in some security bully to kick us out. I could just imagine waiting for Wil to come back and having to tell him we were moving again. I racked my brain for the millionth time to figure out where we could go, but if I had a plan B, I would have used it by now.

I just needed money for one more week. Maybe then I'd find a better job. Or the Chinese restaurant would let me work more than enough hours. Or the apocalypse would happen and then it wouldn't matter anymore. It would save me a lot of trouble.

At the thought of the restaurant, though, I dropped my

shoulders. Even if I went in when they opened at eleven, he still wasn't going to pay me over a hundred dollars for an hour's worth of work. I couldn't even beg him for an advance.

As I entered the hotel room again, Wil was collecting his text books and shoving them into his book bag. "Anything good?" he asked.

"Doughnuts," I said. I planted the tray on the counter.

"Finally," he said. He walked over, grabbing a glazed, and shoving the entire doughnut into his mouth in one bite.

"Eat a banana," I said.

"I'm tired of bananas." He took another doughnut, shoving half in his mouth before he reached for one of the coffees to wash it down. His gaze finally settled on my face as he drank coffee and he paused. He lifted a hand touching at my chin. "You've got a mark."

I brushed my fingers across my face, feeling the tender spot. "I'll cover it. I've got some of those makeup samples leftover."

The corner of his mouth dipped, but he caught it. "Yeah, just don't go looking like a cake face. There's a bunch of girls at school that do that. Well there's one that doesn't—" He cut himself off.

When I looked at his face, he was blushing.

"You never talk about girls at school," I said. "What's up with this one?"

"Nothing," he said, but too quickly.

"Liar," I said, grinning, glad to have finally caught him in something. "You've got a girlfriend."

He snorted, shaking his head. "Geeks don't get girlfriends. We die old and alone."

I rolled my eyes and popped him on the arm. At the same time, my heart lifted. I hoped this girl had some common sense. I'd never heard my brother talk about girls at all before. For a while, I thought maybe he was gay or didn't know what he liked. It wasn't something I wanted to talk about too much, but was glad he was showing interest in something other than schoolwork. "Stop talking like that. Go to school."

He hiked up his book bag and headed for the door. "Don't forget," he said.

"Yeah, yeah," I said, waving. "I'll get the money to him."

Wil stood in the doorway a moment, staring in at me. He nudged at the edge of his glasses, where the left side frame was bent and didn't fit well on his face.

I stared back. "What?"

"Don't do anything stupid," he said.

His comment made me flinch. "Will you shut up and go to school?"

"I'm serious," he said. He shut the door behind himself.

I rolled my eyes, shaking off the fact that my younger brother was telling me to stay out of trouble. Wasn't I supposed to be telling him that? Except he didn't get into trouble. He was the smart one. I shoved a doughnut into my mouth and downed the coffee, leaving the last doughnut for Wil for when he got back from school. It was a hard decision to leave food behind when we rarely got such treats, but I felt like being nice since after that, I would have to tell him about the eviction.

I stared at Jack for a moment, disgusted that he was still on the floor. I yanked the blanket off the bed to cover him, mostly so I wouldn't have to look at him and it kept the smell down to a minimum. I made up my bed, and cleaned up the bathroom a little.

I picked up my two book bags, one with my supply of clothes, and the other with everything else that belonged to me. There wasn't much to the second bag: a couple of old paperbacks Wil found left around at school, a collection of freebie makeup and other samples I picked up while at the mall. Near the bottom was an old photo album, one of the few things I still carried from our past life, the life before mom died. I hadn't opened it in years, but still kept it with me.

I tugged out a pair of shorts. It had been a bit warm for October and I had a ways to go if I was going to find a new place to target. I didn't like wearing shorts while doing this sort of thing, but I didn't have much choice this time. I only had one pair of jeans because they were too thick to carry in a bag containing everything I owned; shorts took up less space. I stretched the hem of my shorts down on my thighs, but they were still pretty short.

I found the same bra I wore yesterday, and a dark gray tank top. I pulled on my boots, wishing I had sneakers.

I smothered my face with foundation to try to cover the blotch of purple on my chin. Just so I didn't look like a colorless monster, I swiped on some mascara and some lip gloss. When I wasn't picking pockets at the mall, picking up free samples were the next best thing. Makeup came in handy if I needed to go talk to a manager about a job.

Today, I just needed to look human enough to blend in.

♠♠♠♠♠

A half hour later, I was on a bus, heading for downtown Charleston. It was a long shot, because tourist season didn't last through early October. Since the mall was no longer an option, and Tasty's wouldn't help me earn enough money, the only place I had left was Market Street.

Market Street was the home of an old slave trade building, a brick structure with wide open archways welcoming the weather in. I couldn't imagine what it looked like in the old days, but it was filled with vendor stalls now. The building split up the middle of a street, and nearby on either side of the brick market were two story shops, the old kind with apartments on the second floor.

When I was in grade school, there was a field trip downtown and we had to write essays to try to explain how historical and romantic this downtown Charleston area was. To me, it was just an outside market, filled with expensive knickknacks people stuff on shelves and never look at again. People who didn't realize how much money they were wasting. The price of a sweet grass basket, a painting of the old district homes, and a few useless key chains could have fed our family for a month or two.

As the city bus stopped in front of one of the hotels along the street, I climbed off, scanning the neighborhood. Only a handful of stalls bothered to open during the week when tourists were less likely in early fall.

I started my way up along one side of the street, with the brick building that was the market to one side, and the rows of stores not yet open on the other. I kept to the sidewalk and away from the vendors. I was unsure of this territory and didn't want to look too familiar if I had to cross in front of them a few times.

It didn't take long to find my first target. He was an older man, with white hair combed over on his head, blue eyes and age spots, like freckles, kissing his cheeks. He weaved around stalls at a slow place, occasionally bending over to examine a trinket. I followed casually behind him. I didn't like how close together the stalls were, or the fact that the place wasn't as busy as a mall. It was too difficult to blend in.

I hated the fact that he was older, too. I didn't like pickpocketing girls, or older people or kids. Not only were they more difficult to distract with a flash of cleavage, but it just felt worse to be doing something that was already wrong. I didn't want to be the person who stole old ladies' handbags.

The only relief to the guilt I had was that he was wearing brand-new clothes, or so it looked to me. His was well-groomed, with a gold ring on his finger. If he was strolling around downtown in the middle of the week, he was more than likely someone well off enough he didn't need to work or retired. With his nearly white hair, he appeared older at a distance, but up close he could have passed for perhaps fifty, so maybe he still worked. Maybe he didn't need a hundred dollars.

The old man strolled with ease through the center of the market. It became more evident that we were heading the same direction, and he had plenty of opportunity to catch me out of the corner of his eyes, although he didn't particularly seem interested in me. I pretended to pause on occasion at vendor stalls, fingering through faux silver jewelry and admiring yet another painting of a beach scene.

He paused in front of a sweet grass basket stall, making me think he might have been a tourist. Normally during the tourist season, local African American women sat along the edges of the shops, on top of cloths spread out along the ground. They weaved baskets made from sweet grass grown locally. Now, a couple of women merely sat along the edges of the displays, showing off the leftovers woven during the summer.

The old man turned sharply, redirecting his attention. He crossed the street, and ducked into a candy shop.

It had been a while since I'd been downtown, but I was fairly sure that shop was pretty massive. It had sections that were completely out of view of the front register. That meant there were cameras in there. I was hoping the cameras weren't taping. It was still early in the day and without crowds of tourists, I was hoping the attendant would be very bored. If no one noticed, maybe it could still work.

I took my time crossing the street, not wanting to catch my target just inside the door and bump into him too soon.

When I entered the shop, I needed to stop and let my eyes adjust to the dimness. The store was almost cold with the air conditioner on full blast. I tucked my arms around my stomach, trying to recapture some of my own body heat. That was the sucky part about the weather in early October in South Carolina. A tad too warm in the sun, chill in the shadows. It usually gave me a headache.

The shop had shelves starting at stomach level and reaching up over my head. Displays were covered in packages of candy and gift baskets and little trinket toys to capture the attention of kids. The scent of sugar and nuts and chocolate was heavy.

My stomach growled. I nearly growled back at it for drawing needless attention. One doughnut hadn't been enough. I should have followed my own advice and eaten a banana, although I was as sick of those as Wil was. I should have eaten another doughnut. I should have taken the whole box. I could have eaten them all. My hunger validated our needs. I had to make this pull. I had to run home with whatever I could get. I needed something other than oatmeal tonight.

The old man hovered over a display that had several bowls of hard candies, with plastic scoops and a scale for measuring out amounts. He stuck his hand into one of the bowls, and picked out a red cream hard candy and ate it. He tilted his head, his mouth moving as if he'd never tasted that flavor before and was considering it.

Must be nice to have so much money and free time to linger in a candy shop on a work day. I pretended to do the same thing, lingering over a couple of bins of chocolates, trying to find something that sparked my interest. I picked out one, a chocolate truffle. I cast a glance around and popped it into my mouth.

I nearly forgot my plan to pick up his wallet, because the mix of flavor, of sweet soft center, and milk chocolate set my stomach into turning. I'd had plain oatmeal and apples and bananas for so long that the sudden shift in flavors was overwhelming. Why couldn't I work in a candy store?

Reluctantly, I pulled away from the chocolate displays. I would have picked out every single one to 'taste' and probably would have gotten chased out by the store clerk if I'd been spotted.

As if reading my mind that I was hoping he'd hurry, the old man collected a bag of the red cream candies, and a gold box from a chocolate display. I tracked him out of the corner of my eye as to not alert him I was paying attention. I lingered by the door, as if checking out a candy display before leaving the store. He pulled out his wallet within my eyesight. He exposed it, showing me the ample amounts of cash inside. He paid for his purchase in the little alcove where the attendant was.

This was perfect. I'd never taken more than sixty from a wallet before as a general rule. I felt this time I might break my own rules. He had plenty, and I needed to get back.

This is the last one. I made myself promise to not do this again. This was it. After, I'd find something else to do. I'd check with the local bars again for a job. I'd beg on the street. I just had to keep Wil in school. I told myself my reasons over and over again, as if that could ever make me feel better. I wasn't selling my body. I hadn't been that desperate yet. I didn't want to get to that point.

The old man approached, and time slowed to a crawl. Questioning myself. Asking the old man silently to forgive me. Hoping he really was well off and this wasn't *his* rent money I was stealing.

He passed by me, and I swayed.

Bump.

I dropped my hand.

I hipped bumped him as I turned, lifting at the same time.

"Oh!" I said softly, faking a laugh. "Pardon me." I turned my body toward him, masking my hand behind my back as I slipped his wallet in the spot between the small of my back and my underwear in my shorts. Easiest place to hide a wallet without looking like you've got a wallet bulge yourself.

The old man focused on my face, his lips curled into an instant smile, which made me feel worse than ever, but glad he was willing to be distracted by my face and not my breasts. "Pardon me, young lady." He bowed his head politely, and headed out the door, packages in tow.

My heart thundered, and I stared at a jar of candy to count off a couple of seconds, giving him ample time to create some distance from us.

When I counted a full minute, I pretended to check the time and dashed out the door, heading in the opposite direction. It didn't matter where I was heading, now, as long as I got out of eyesight of everyone who could have possibly spotted me.

I swallowed back the wedge of emotion in my throat. The aftermath of stealing was always the worst. Guilt really started to settle in then. Fear, too. It was a crucial time. At any moment, my target could check for his wallet, and put two and two together with my face. I had to get out of the area.

At the mall, there were easily a number of corridors and

bathrooms and places to wait out time until I was sure things had calmed down.

Since I wasn't familiar with this area, I dashed down the street as quick as I dared without drawing attention. The first spot that caught my eye as a good place to hide was an alleyway between two shops. I turned into it, pretending to be familiar and ran down it. There was an old dumpster near the back fence that separated this street from the one behind it. I was hoping for an intersection, but a place to hide would do.

I crouched behind the dumpster. I recoiled at the smell, and held my hand over my nose as I backed down the alley, checking to make sure I wasn't followed.

When no one appeared, I patted the wallet through my clothes at my back. I was eager to get home. I wasn't sure where I'd leave the wallet this time. Weren't you supposed to drop lost keys into a post office box? Did that work for wallets, too? I didn't want to leave it on the street. Maybe I could keep it just for now, and find his address, maybe even stuff it in his mailbox later. A risk, but I'd rather do that than put it somewhere unfamiliar to have it stolen by someone else.

Maybe I could do it before he got home.

I dipped my fingers into my shorts, tugging out the lump.

I pulled out a folded piece of newspaper, made square into the shape of a wallet.

I stared at it, confused. I blinked heavily several times, sure I was going crazy. Nope. Still a newspaper.

What did I just do? My heart raced as I retraced my steps. I snagged the wallet. I was sure. I felt the leather.

"You're amazing," said a male voice.

My body erupted in a tremble, startled, and I landed on my butt on the gravel. A sharp rock stabbed itself into the flesh at the back of my thigh and I yelped.

The old man stood above me. His blue eyes twinkled with amusement. "There's only one other kid I've seen be able to make a pull like that. You definitely have the advantage though."

"What?" I asked, not really asking anything at all, only

panicking out of my mind that he had already called the cops. I started pushing myself off the ground, ready to run.

He held out a hand to me, offering to help me up. "I think it's that pretty face. Most thieves try to turn attention elsewhere. You draw it right to you. You command it."

I blew out a sigh, not wanting to knock an old man over to throw on top of my list of horrible things I'd done. I let him take my hand, and dragged myself up. He wasn't berating me. Was he not mad that I'd tried to steal from him? I guess technically I didn't succeed, since all I had was a newspaper. What I really wanted to know was how he knew. "Sorry," I said. "It's nothing personal."

"I'm sorry to say it is," he said. "At least for you. You're not exactly a blind thief."

"Blind?"

"You're not sticking guns and knives in people's faces. You're not taking on old ladies, who probably would be easier targets. You pick targets that can defend themselves. Not to mention you don't even bother with keeping all the money. No. Something tells me this is personal, or you wouldn't be trying so hard to go unnoticed. A thief with morals."

I flinched again, taking a step back and holding up my hands. "How do you know about--"

"You're hard to find, Kayli Winchester. No, I take that back. Hard to keep tabs on is more like it. Slipping past four of our best guys. That's something."

My body rattled and I took another step back. "You know me? And those guys?"

He held out a hand, motioning to the open end of the alley back toward the street. "Can you trust me enough that we can talk to you without slipping off again? We won't hurt you."

A black four-door truck appeared at the front of the alley. It was too much of a coincidence. It had to have been waiting for a signal from him.

"I don't think I should," I said. I'd seen enough mob movies that started out like this. I didn't want to end up wearing concrete shoes tonight. "Besides, I really need to get going."

"You mean your rent is due? That's why you tried to steal my wallet, wasn't it?"

I stilled, not wanting to answer one way or another. I didn't know who he was, and this could be my ride to jail from an undercover cop. Or worse.

The old man smiled. "We just want to talk. And if you come with me, I'll make sure the rent gets paid for a month. You don't have to do anything. You just have to listen."

My eyes widened. He had to be crazy. "I'm not having sex with you."

He tilted his head back, laughing softly and shaking his head. "My god, no. Thanks, but I'm married." He held up his hand, showing me the gold ring I'd noticed before. "Very happily, by the way."

"You're going to pay my rent for a month and all we have to do is talk?" I asked, suspicious.

"You don't even have to do the talking." He motioned to the car again, dug his hands into his pockets and started heading toward it. "Or don't and go back to picking wallets. But you should know that there's a team of cops on to you. You're on a list of suspects they're looking to pick up."

"How do you know?"

"Who do you think called us?" He kept walking to the car, not waiting for me to respond.

My heart raced. I wasn't sure if what he said was true, but if he was part of the police department in some way, he'd know more than I would. I'd already known from the day before that I was running out of luck.

I was also sure that this was more than some simple cop setup or mall security team.

I shifted on my feet, unsure.

Until I saw the door of the truck open as the old man approached. From inside pretzel boy leaned out from behind the steering wheel. His mismatched eyes looked right at me. He beckoned with those eyes and his hand, with the same commanding tone as if he'd spoken it out loud.

36

I started walking toward the truck. If I was going to get kicked out of the hotel anyway, if I was going to go to jail anyway, I might as well see where this rabbit hole led to.

Morbid curiosity.

When I got to the truck, the old man held the passenger side door, and ushered for me to get in.

"I can get in the back," I said, feeling awkward taking the front seat when he was older. There was some politeness code in the South that you simply didn't mess with.

"I'm just here to direct you," he said. "I can't stay and play. I've got work."

"Work?"

"The hospital should be in chaos right about now."

From inside the truck, pretzel boy leaned over the middle console. He waved shortly at the old man. Longer locks of brown hair crossed over the start of his brows, dipping into the blue and green pools of his eyes. "Hey, Doc Roberts."

"This is the one, isn't she?" Dr. Roberts asked him.

"Yup. Nice work. Thanks."

My jaw fell. "You're not a cop?"

Dr. Roberts's head tilted back and he laughed. "No, sweetie. I'm on your side. Get in the truck."

"But what about …" I didn't want to say it out loud. It felt like begging.

"I've got it taken care of. Don't worry. Your little hotel room isn't going anywhere." He gestured again.

I sighed, and wedged myself into the passenger seat. Dr. Roberts started to close the door, stopped and then picked something out of the paper bag he had gotten at the candy shop. He handed over a gold box to me.

"And here," he said. "Thought you might like these."

I took the box from him and he shut the door.

Pretzel boy started down the road. I used the side mirror to glance back at Dr. Roberts, who remained on the sidewalk. He looked after the truck for a moment and then turned away, walking the opposite direction.

Traffic was slow since we were still downtown and pedestrians dominated the streets in this particular

37

neighborhood. When pretzel boy stopped, he looked curiously at my lap. "What did he get you?"

I undid the ribbon and opened the box.

It was filled with chocolate covered truffles, the same kind I'd tasted at the candy store.

♠

THE TYPE OF GROUP THAT REQUIRES A THIEF

I'd put the box of candy on the floor, folded my arms around my stomach, and sat back in the seat, glaring out the window. My heart raced. I was nervous, worried about making the biggest mistake and was on my way to prison.

"Relax, *Bambi*," pretzel boy said. "You're not in trouble."

"Sure feels like it."

He grinned, and reached to fiddle with the air conditioner. "Cold? Warm?"

"No."

"Change it if you are," he said. He sat back, one hand on the wheel, the other raking through his hair to pull locks away from his eyes. He wound his way through downtown, heading back toward I-26. "Glad we found you. I had a hunch you wouldn't try the mall again, but had to leave a guy there just in case. We're going to go pick him up, and then meet the others."

"He knew my name," I said. "Dr. Roberts did. Do you?"

"Yup," he said. "Kayli Winchester. Eighteen. Born and raised here in the tri-county, mostly in North Charleston, but the last few years hovering between Goose Creek and West Ashley. Your school record's a mile long, too. I didn't know they let kids graduate when they skipped so many classes."

I closed my eyes tightly and pressed my fingers to my temples. "Why are you stalking me? Who are you?"

He steered with his left hand, and held out his right in

offering. "Marc."

I stared at his hand.

"I don't bite, sweetie."

I slipped my hand into his, and he easily enveloped it. He squeezed mine gently, shook it once and pulled his back.

I stopped playing coy and stared at his face, especially at the eyes. "Is that your real name?" I asked.

"Yes."

I squinted at him. His hair was rich brown and soft-looking and his skin had a nice tan. And the dark brows complemented his two-toned eyes. He wore a deep blue collared shirt, unbuttoned to reveal the white ribbed tank shirt underneath. His fine-sculpted chest was more defined as the tank shirt was snug. Around his neck was a black cord, and hanging from it was a sand dollar encased in silver.

I glanced away, not liking where my thoughts were going staring at his body. Even his face was incredible, with a day's worth of unshaven gruffness and high cheekbones. "Do you really want me to work at your pretzel stand that badly?"

He broke out into laughter, twisting his hands at the wheel and leaning forward. "No, no, I don't work there. They make a pretty good pretzel dog though."

"How do you know who I am?"

"Followed you home last night and talked to the manager at the hotel. He's not a really nice guy but for a hundred bucks, he was willing to tell me a few things."

"Is that why he was anxious to get us to move out? You spooked him?"

"He's not going to kick you out. You're a solid gold star compared to his other tenants. Which reminds me, why are you living there, anyway?"

"Oh so there's stuff about me you don't know?" I shoved my arms over my chest and sat back. "Well, at least I get to keep some secrets."

"Come on, Bambi. Don't be like that. I'm trying to do you a favor here."

"Stop calling me that. And why?"

He stared hard out the windshield and his hands tightened on the wheel. "You just don't seem like the type that really wants to steal. I saw how you hesitated. You really didn't want to. That wasn't greed on your face. That was desperation."

"Why does that matter to you? You don't know me."

He twisted his lips, staring off at the cars in front of us. "Do you want a shot or not? I won't force you into this."

"Is that why you practically had me kidnapped?"

"I just want you to hear us out before you make a decision. Unless you really like being a thief or in jail. Because that's where you were headed."

I mumbled a little, not wanting to admit he was right and not wanting to pretend to be in denial about it. Every time I stole, I was spinning the barrel of the gun one more time in a twisted bit of fate, hoping the bullet never caught up with me. Now it had, I supposed. What kind of police force was this though? He still appeared my age, so he couldn't have been a detective or something similar.

"I'm taking a chance on you." He turned his head, meeting my gaze. There was an edge. A wild, unforgiving stare, daring me where I was sitting. Like his command, it rocked me breathless. "Tell me I'm wrong. Tell me there's no chance in hell you'll stop stealing."

I narrowed my eyes at him. He didn't know me. I didn't want to admit to anything. "I didn't ask for a chance."

"None of us do. But you don't throw away one when you get it."

I stared off out the front windshield. I didn't mind having a chance, I just wasn't so sure I wanted one from him.

I sensed a movement and turned my face to see what he was doing. He poked at the bruise on my chin. I winced, covering it, and smacked his curious finger away.

His eyes narrowed on me. He slowed the truck, pulling off to the side of the road. My heart roared into a panic. Traffic sped onward to our left as he stopped in the grass. What was he doing? We were on the interstate!

He turned fully to me. His hands clenched into fists.

"What happened to you? You didn't have that yesterday."

I kept my hand cupped around my chin. He could tell? Did the makeup wear off? And why did he care?

"Who touched you?" his voice was full of the command he'd had the day before. How did he do that? "Is it that brother of yours? Was it Wil?"

"No," I snapped at him. "Don't worry about it."

"That manager said there were complaints about a fight and yelling every night. Does that dad of yours beat you?"

"Not if I can help it," I said, and realized too late what I was admitting. "Don't give me any crap about it. Once you hold him down long enough, he gives up the fight and falls asleep. And it's none of your business ."

He stretched out, popping my hand to get me to drop it. He caught my chin. His eyes begged me to allow him to do what he needed. I grasped at his forearm, not pushing away, just holding it in warning as if to say I would.

Time slowed. My breathing slowed. My heart thumped hard against my eardrums, and my mouth was dry. He leaned forward, the silver sand dollar dangled from his neck.

He cupped his hand at my jawline. Rough skin of his thumb traced over the bruise. He massaged slowly as if doing so could erase what he was seeing. He tilted my head, gazing at it from a different angle.

His mismatched eyes never left my face.

"You've got a scar," he said. He traced over a spot on the underside of my chin. It was an old one, at least a couple of years. "Did he do that, too?"

"No," I said.

He narrowed his eyes at me, studying. He frowned. "Liar."

I yanked my face from his grasp, shoving his arm away. I hated that he was right. I couldn't answer him, and glared at the dashboard like I wanted to glare at him, only I couldn't. Those eyes made me feel too weak. I pinched hard at my thigh, trying to tell myself to calm down. This was way too close. Been down that path one too many times, too. When someone discovered too much about me it always ended in disaster.

"Can we go?" I asked.

The silence lingered. I sensed his stare. He hovered like he wanted to move closer but wasn't sure. He'd already started probing, asking the questions most of my old boyfriends never dared, but I always worried they would eventually. If I thought they were catching on to who I really was, the life I had, I usually ended it. No one could understand me.

Now here was Marc, who already knew the details of my life I tried to keep in the shadows. He didn't seem angry. He wanted to know more. I had no idea how to respond. This was the worst place I'd ever been and even that didn't scare him. I didn't know what to do with that. My first instinct was to bail; run home and avoid him. Only I couldn't now.

Or could I? I supposed if I really wanted to, I could have opened the door, walked out, run off, disappeared forever.

What stopped me? Outside of knowing I'd possibly never see Wil again, and even that may have been a good thing, for all the trouble that I was in.

Marc grunted and leaned back in the driver's seat. "I know you don't know me, and you don't have a reason to trust me, but I swear if you give me a chance, you'll never have to see that old man or that hotel room again." He jerked the gear shift and pounded on the gas, racing to get back onto the road.

Why did my heart have to surge at that promise, even as I didn't believe a word of it?

We rode in silence, which I almost hated as much as him talking. Marc pulled up to the curb at the mall. I stared at the glass swinging doors nervously, knowing that if what they said was true, I was probably safest never showing up at a mall again. Even being outside the doors made my spine tingle, itching to run. I didn't want the cops to see me and arrest me. I sunk into the seat.

Marc wedged his cell phone out of his back pocket, punched in a text message and planted the phone on the console between us. "He'll be here in a second."

"Who?"

"Raven."

I raised an eyebrow. "Seriously?"

"His last name is Ravenstahl. Everyone calls him Raven."

"What's his first name?"

Marc smiled, and his eyes lit up. "He'd kill me if I told you."

I gazed out the front window as we waited. I started watching people coming and going from the mall. It'd been a while since I'd visited the place when I wasn't having to rush to find a target. I watched kids with their parents, teenage boys rushing to get inside, a group of girls giggling as they shadowed the boys and whispered to each other.

When I was stealing, I avoided contact with everyone. Attention was the last thing a thief really wants. Now that I wasn't targeting anyone, the people seemed so oblivious to me. I spotted purses exposed and bulging pockets in places I could pull from without having to touch someone at all. Easy marks, but they were the wrong marks. Women. Kids. I wanted to chase them down and tell them to do better. Don't let someone worse than me steal your wallet. You'll never get it back.

A palm dropped on the back of my head, nudging. "What are you doing? Spacing out?"

"Shut up." I tried to karate chop him in the arm, but he dodged and then swooped in and popped me on the head.

"Too slow," he said, with a teasing grin on his face. I grunted, hating that he was being cute. It made it difficult to stick to my initial plan to not like him.

He glanced around my head. I turned in reaction but slowly, worried he was going to distract me and pop me on the head again.

My side door opened, and a face leaned in, gazing at the both of us. He had thick brown hair, cropped short, but left a little long in the front near his face so he had a little bit sticking up. Brown eyes, a couple of days' worth of unshaven growth around his strong chin. His black tank top revealed heavily tattooed arms, one covered in tribal marks and the other an ongoing art depiction of roses, one of a knife and barbed wire, and a few more things blended in I couldn't see yet because it twisted to the other side of his bicep. He had two earring studs in his left lobe, and a lip ring.

He took one glance at me and smiled big.

"In the back, Raven," Marc said.

"Scoot over, little thief. It's tight in the back." His deep voice had a gruff tone, like he talked a lot. He had an accent. It almost sounded Russian.

Marc sighed and lifted the middle console. I harrumphed but slid over. I tried glaring at the dashboard, not wanting to be noticed, but despite my being irritated, Raven was pretty hot. The black tank shirt was tight to his body, and he wore dark blue jeans and boots.

Did the secret police somehow just happen to recruit the best looking guys? I wouldn't admit it out loud, but I kind of didn't mind this. What really drove me crazy was they knew more about me than I did of them.

Marc pulled out of the lot. Raven stabbed his seatbelt into place and then planted an arm around my shoulders, holding onto the side of Marc's headrest.

"So this is our thief?" Raven asked. "I expected someone ..."

I turned my head, meeting his dark eyes and dared him to say blond or with bigger boobs ... or that he expected me to be a boy.

He smirked, his lip ring protruding. "Uglier," he said, thickening the accent.

"I could show you ugly if you'd like," I said.

Raven huffed once. "With that face? I doubt it."

I didn't have a comeback for that, but my insides were squirming. "Where are we going now?" I asked.

"We'll go meet up with the guys," Marc said. He picked up his cell phone, and started poking at the screen. "Let me wait to talk about it there so I'm not repeating myself."

"You need to call the boss and wake him up," Raven said. He nudged his side into mine, leaning a little into me, more than he needed. "He wanted in on this."

"Who's the boss?" I asked. "You mean that old man?"

"Dr. Roberts," Marc said, still poking a text message while he was driving. He didn't seem to struggle with handling both, but it still made me nervous.

"Do you mean Dr. Roberts? He's your boss?"

"No," Marc said.

"Is it the tall guy?"

"Huh?"

"The guy who wore the red jacket yesterday?"

He poked at his phone more. "Nuh uh."

I glanced at him and then the road. I wasn't sure he was paying attention to me or the road. He was following another car way closer than I was comfortable with. Since he was still playing with his phone, I snagged it from his hands.

Marc grunted. "Give it back, Bambi."

"Stop calling me that. And I'll text for you. Keep your eyes on the road." I glanced at the screen. "Who's Jenny?"

Marc scowled at me. "Ex-girlfriend."

Jenny: I want to talk to you.
Marc: I don't want to talk.
Jenny: I just need to know.

"A clinger, huh?" I asked.

Raven laughed next to me. "All American girls are like that. Even a few of the boys."

"How would you know?" Marc asked.

Raven lifted his arm, reaching across my shoulders and leaning into me to ruffle his fingers through Marc's hair. "Come on, pretty boy. Give the girl the boot already."

Marc waved Raven off. "Stop it."

"You've got to cut this off," I said. "Clingers stay for as long as you talk to them."

"I didn't want to hurt her feelings," Marc said. "She's a sweet girl, but she's a pain in the ass. Calling all the time to see where I'm at. She's always claiming someone's hurting her and she needs to be saved. She's kind of crazy."

"Is that your type? Sweet and crazy?" I asked.

Marc pulled a face but didn't respond.

I could sympathize with him. I once dated a guy who tried to cut himself to get me to come over. Those types start out really sweet, but end up being psycho when you try to get rid of them. "Here," I said. I typed in a response and sent it.

Marc frowned. "What did you do?" He snagged the phone out of my hand, checking the message.

"I just told her you're out on a date."

"What? I told her I was at work."

"A date will make her mad."

"I don't want her mad."

"Mad is good," I said. "If you want a girl to go away, you've got to piss her off."

Marc stopped at a red light and turned his head to me. "Is that how you treat people? You must be a fucking barrel of peaches to your boyfriend."

"Yup. I tell him where to go and he goes," I fibbed. Ha. Boyfriend.

Marc squinted at me. "Holy shit. You're single."

"Aw," Raven said. He planted a palm on my head and massaged my scalp. "Little thief, don't worry about it. I've got you now."

I reached out, popping him on the chest with a loose fist. "Stop touching me."

He hooted, laughed and dropped his hand from my head and rubbed at the spot where I'd hit him. "I like it. Feisty."

"Back off, Raven," Marc said.

"You make the claim or she's fair game."

I waved off Raven and pointed to Marc's phone. "Why don't you just tell her you didn't like her."

He sighed. "It's not that easy. I feel horrible. I mean she felt so strong about it that I was wondering why I didn't feel anything at all. I thought something was wrong with me. She's pretty and she's sweet. Isn't there supposed to be a spark or wiggly feelings or something?"

"You were waiting on wiggly sparks?"

He brushed a palm across his face. "Forget it. Why am I

telling you all this? I don't even know you." He shook his head. "Anyway, I guess it doesn't matter now."

"She may be mad for now, but she may try to weasel back. If she comes back, you'll have to be mean. You can't backtrack or she'll keep doing this."

He sighed heavily enough that his broad shoulders lifted and fell. "I don't know if I can do that to a girl."

"You do a pretty good job making me mad. What's the difference?"

He made a face. "I think you barely qualify as a girl."

I harrumphed.

He waved his hand in front of himself. "I don't mean it in a bad way. Don't take things so seriously."

"We'll see if you feel the same way when I start calling you Mary instead of Marc."

He smirked and karate chopped me in the corner of my neck and shoulder, causing me to cringe. "Shut up."

I grunted, running my fingers through my hair to get it out of my eyes. "Can't we just get this over with so I can say no and go home?"

"Almost there," Marc said.

Marc pulled into a parking lot of a tall, dull brick building on the southern edge of the Charleston peninsula, really close to the river and the bay. I'd been by the place a few times, but never really took a good look at it. It appeared to be an office tower, so it wasn't interesting to me before. "What's this? Is this where you work?"

"This is home," he said. "Welcome to the Sergeant Jasper."

"It's an apartment building?" I asked. It appeared so plain from the highway. Weren't apartments a little nicer looking? Like with gardens and fountains? Or at least a brick front office with a sign out front that told people what it was?

"Go Detective Kaylie," Raven said. He opened the door, unfolding himself to step out. I followed. He grabbed the gold box that was on the floor. "What's this?"

Before I could answer, he had the box open and picked out a piece of truffle. He sniffed it, and took a bite. "Not bad," he said, licking his lips.

"Hey," I said. "Save me one."

"*Kto ne uspel - tot opozdal*," he said.

"Huh?"

"You snooze, you lose," Marc said. "Give her the box, Raven."

"Don't worry. I'm just carrying it for her. It's not my type. I prefer a steak." He smirked as he passed by me. "Or a nice bite of a good-looking bird."

I waited until he had turned around before I gulped.

I let the guys walk ahead of me. I could smell the ocean breeze from where we were. Part of the bridge that crossed the Ashley River and headed to John's Island stuck out in the horizon. I guessed that people on the upper floors could possibly see more of the bay and a good portion of the water. I sensed the water was just beyond where I could see.

I'd have given up my left eyeball to live in such a place. This close to the islands and downtown? With a view of the water? Sign me up.

I followed the guys to the lobby, where a security guard was perched at a desk. She glanced up, nodded quickly, smiled at the two boys, and shared the same smile with me. I pretended to be dazzled by a painting on the wall and avoided eye contact. Felt bad about it after. It was an instinctual reaction to anyone wearing a security uniform.

At the elevator, Raven smacked the buttons and the boys loaded in. I stepped in beside them. Raven held open the door as a couple of guys I didn't recognize hurried down the hallway and got in.

"What floor?" Marc asked.

"Eleven," one of the guys said. Marc punched the button, but the guy kept his head turned, looking at me. "Haven't seen you before. You new?"

I felt an arm sliding around my shoulders. Marc leaned in on me, tilting his head toward mine. His hand squeezed my arm, tucking me into his body. "She's just visiting."

Disappointment crept across the guy's face, but he nodded and turned to stare at the doors.

What a jerk! He didn't give me a chance to talk myself. As if I needed help letting a guy down. I elbowed Marc in the gut. Marc made a noise that sounded like a smothered groan and eased his arm from around me, but still hung on loosely around my shoulders.

We got off on floor seven. When the elevator doors closed behind us, I pulled away from Marc and got some distance between us. "What was that for?" I asked.

"Don't flatter yourself," he said, starting down the hallway. "I just didn't want you distracted."

"I can tell a guy no. Or not. Maybe I wanted his phone number."

"You wouldn't have asked."

"How do you know?"

"He's not your type."

"How would you know my type?"

Raven pressed his palm against his forehead. "God. You guys sound like you're already married. This is going to be a disaster."

"Shut up," Marc and I said in unison. I glared at him. And he had the audacity to stare right back, smiling like he was enjoying this!

Marc paused in front of Apartment 737. The door was unlocked and he and Raven walked in.

There was a small living area, with a hallway on the left and right The dining nook had several desks around the wall and a couple of computers on top of each. There was a tiny kitchen, with a dingy electric stove, and a worn fridge. For the rest of the apartment, the walls were a hideous off-white and the floors were wall-to-wall with an old beige carpet that was maybe white once. There was a large brown faux leather couch that took up most of the living room, facing a large flat-screen television.

The space also had a heavy smell of coffee and sweetness. I could have mistaken the place for a coffee shop, it was that strong. It made it difficult to ignore, and my stomach wanted to growl.

The only window was high up, the sill above my chest.

And took up all of the upper level of the apartment wall on that side. There were vertical blinds that were closed, but there was bright sunlight seeping in between the slats.

I wedged myself between Raven and Marc to cross to the living room. I wanted to snoop. Their fault. They let me in.

"Yeah, sure," Raven said. He planted the gold box on top of the kitchen counter. "Make yourself at home."

There was an old wall style heating unit, much like the ones at the hotel. I planted a boot on the top of it, using my palms on the wall to balance myself as I climbed up. It might have been rude, but they were the ones kidnapping me; I felt I could at least poke around where I wanted.

I felt the chill of the wall against my thighs as I leaned against it and inched my way up until I was high enough that I could see out the window and look down.

"Hey," Raven called.

"Let her look," Marc said.

"She's going to break that thing. Or break her head."

I tried pulling the slats out of the way, but they were the sort that were tied down on both the top and bottom. I glanced around, and found a control pulley that adjusted it. I jumped down off of the heater, grabbed the rope and yanked as hard as I could.

The slats opened up, sliding all the way over. I climbed again, pulling myself up on my elbows on the window ledge to look out.

The view was incredible. At my hotel room, the best I got was the parking lot and an abandoned building that was busted up. This apartment had a view of the water. The edge of John's Island and homes built up next to the river stood out in the distance. The water lapped and swayed with the current.

Jealousy swept through me. I wanted this.

Raven materialized next to me. He scanned the view and then stretched to look down. "The bridge kind of ruins the view."

"Have you seen it at night? It looks kind of cool," Marc said. He came over, standing underneath where I was. "Scoot over, Bambi."

"Nu uh."

"I want to see." He grabbed hold of my arm, using it to help pull himself up onto the heater with us.

We stood together, looking out across the water. "You mean you guys live here and haven't looked out the window?" I asked.

"If I wanted to go see the fucking water," Raven said, "I'd go outside. It's right there."

"The view's not bad though," Marc said. "Too bad the window is so high."

"What about other apartment buildings?" I asked. It shouldn't have been important to me right then, but now that I was here, and could see this, I really wanted to daydream about one day managing to afford a place like this. I'd lived in a lot of cruddy places. Once I got rid of Jack, and I didn't have to worry about Wil, I wanted something close to the water. A girl could dream, right? "Do they have a better view? Or at least lower windows?"

"This is the only one on the peninsula," Marc said. "At least the only apartment tower. The other apartments are closer to the college. Or the downtown carriage houses."

"Do you guys go to the college?"

They both laughed.

"What's so funny?" I asked.

"Long story," Raven said. He dropped down and then snagged me around the waist, dragging me down to the floor until I was standing. "Get off that thing before you break your ass."

"Ugh." I slapped him hard on the arm, right on one of his rose tattoos. "Stop telling me what to do."

Raven opened his palm and smacked me right back on the arm, no hesitation. This was different than Marc's, who did it lightly enough. Raven's strike was just as hard as I did it to him.

I gasped at him and raised my arms up defensively. "Did you just hit a girl?"

"Don't give me that double standard bullshit." He raised

his hands, making fists and hovering them in front of his own face in a blocking motion, mimicking me. "I let you get away with that first one, but if you're going to keep hitting me, I'll get you right back."

"Bambi, Raven, cut it out." Marc bent his knees, and climbed down off of the heater.

"Stop calling me Bambi."

"You should have picked a better name," Marc said. The corner of his mouth lifted, lighting up his blue and green eyes. "I think it's adorable. You totally look like a little baby deer."

"Bambi is a boy deer," I said.

Raven laughed. He lunged at Marc, catching him around the neck, and swooped in, pecking him on the cheek. "'Cause he's got a thing for dick."

My heart did a flip. A tattooed hunk just kissed tough Marc on the cheek. That was actually kind of hot.

Marc wrestled himself away from Raven. "Don't make me sic Bambi on you."

The front door to the apartment opened. My tall target walked in, followed by the nerdling Corey, and the cool looking one. Now that Corey and his doppelganger were next to each other, they were clearly related. Brothers, if not twins.

My target took one look at me, and went straight for the couch, landing his butt into the corner. He sat back, folding his arms over his chest, waiting. He wore a gray shirt that almost matched his eyes, and his jeans were dark.

Corey's cerulean eyes lit up as he came in. His T-shirt was black, with Mario Bros written in orange blocks. He did a small wave at me and then addressed Marc. "Where's bossman?"

"His door's closed. Guess he'll come out when he's ready."

There was shuffling as the space became crowded with all the new bodies. I circled the coffee table and then got turned around as Raven tried to get past me to get to the kitchen. I backed up and Raven walked away, but another pair of hands clasped me by the waist.

I sucked in a breath. "Sorry," I said, trying to sidestep since I didn't know where to stand.

"Watch where you're going," said the cool-looking brother. He kept his hands on my hips, guiding me sideways until I was out of the way. He locked his sad blue eyes on me. "You're going to get run over."

"You either need a bigger apartment or to get rid of this coffee table. It's too big for the room."

"I like the table." He released my hips and headed to the kitchen. He redirected his attention to the group. "We downgraded mall security," he said. "All wallets were accounted for. Found them at the food court."

My insides vibrated. This was awkward enough, but he was just rattling this off as if I wasn't standing here and didn't have anything to do with it. I crossed my arms over my chest. "Why am I here?"

"Right," Marc said. "Have a seat, Bambi."

I wanted to stand, but my target made to scoot over for me, even though he was already in the corner. I felt obligated to sit, and did so next to him. Corey sat on the other side of me, until his brother came over, and nudged him in the leg. Corey slid down and his brother plopped down next to me.

I stuffed my arms under my breasts, glaring at Marc. Because of how close the guys next to me were, our thighs were touching. The tall one leaned over to give some more space. The cool doppelganger kept his close. I didn't want to look like a dork with my legs crossed. I ended up settling for leaning forward with my elbows in my lap. Somehow this made for less direct contact.

"Bambi, this is Corey, Brandon," he pointed to the twins. "And this is Kevin." He motioned to the tall one. "Guys, this is Kayli."

"I thought you called her Bambi?" Brandon asked.

"Yeah," Corey said. "She told me her name was Bambi. Is that her preferred name? Is it Kayli or Bambi?"

"It's not Bambi," I said, tilting my head back and glaring at the ceiling. Couldn't blame them too much. I did lie in the first place. "It's Kayli."

"Are you sure?" Brandon asked. "I don't know. Maybe. You don't look like a Bambi. Aren't Bambi girls usually blond with a lot of pink? Like Candy or Bunny?"

Raven smirked. "Yeah, that sounds like her."

I made a face, sticking my tongue out at Raven.

"Don't sport it unless you plan to use it." Raven stuck his tongue out, his eyes narrowing with intention. The ring on his lip protruded out.

"Enough," Marc said, slicing his hand through the air as if to cut off the conversation. Marc sat on the coffee table facing the rest of us and Raven joined him. "There's a house party tonight," Marc said. He pointed toward the open window. "One of the downtown homes."

I cocked my head. "You brought me here to tell me about a party?"

Marc held a hand out, palm facing me in a stopping motion. "Hang on. The guy we're looking for will be there. He's been leaving his home every night lately, coming back a little after dawn. He goes to an office downtown sometimes, but most of the time he's prowling around in some of the rougher parts of town."

"So?"

"We want to know what he's up to."

I raised my eyebrows, and glanced at Raven, who seemed more interested in tracing one of the tribal tattoos on his arm. I slid a glance at Corey, who had perked up and was listening. His brother had his arms crossed like mine, attentive. Kevin was in the same position. No one was objecting? "Why?" I asked. "Why do you care what he's doing?"

Marc shrugged, the blue collared shirt he wore bulked up, revealing the broadness of his shoulders. "We're curious."

I did another sweep, glancing around the room. "This is a job? To satisfy your curiosity?"

Marc continued. "We need to slip into his office, find out what he's doing and get out of there before anyone notices.

There's some suspicion that it might be chemical. The areas he's been traveling at night are known to be local drug-ridden territories. We need to find out why this guy is so interested."

"Why?" The guys all turned and looked at me but I couldn't stop my questions. "Why do you care? It's his business. Are you going to steal his drug business? You want to find out so you can take over?"

"We just want to know what he's up to, and make sure he's not using his wealth to develop new drugs. We think he might be creating some," Marc said. "He can do whatever he wants as long as he isn't doing things like that."

"But you don't know for sure if he's doing anything."

Marc shrugged. "Do we wait for him to start working with local gang members and causing drug wars or do we check him out now and stop him ahead of time? I vote now before we have a mob-type gang war taking over the town."

"But again, you don't really know. You want to go figure out what he's doing just to make sure he isn't doing anything illegal?"

Marc nodded. He planted his elbows on his knees, tilting in. The way he leaned in, looking up at my face, with his one blue eye and one green eye lit up and the twitching smile playing on his lips made him look like an adorable puppy. "Please?"

"You want me to find out?" I asked. I jerked my head back, shaking it. "You're crazy. What am I supposed to do? Just walk in there and say, 'Hey! Heard you've got a secret drug in your basement. Can we go and check it out?'"

Raven laughed deeply. "Could give it a shot."

Kevin rolled his eyes. "If she doesn't want to do it, let her get out of here. We don't really need her."

"She's our best shot right now," Marc said. "Did you see her? Even you didn't expect it. I might have missed it if I blinked."

"Why don't we get Luke?" Kevin asked. "What happened to that plan?"

"Luke's busy," Raven said. "Something about a new girl their team's been helping out."

56

"Yeah, that should tell you something. We're not really supposed to work with a girl," Kevin said.

I shot him a glare, and he met my eyes. If he wanted to tell me to go away, he could have told me himself instead of through the guys. I had to agree with him, though. At least someone outside of myself thought this was a crazy idea.

Brandon sat forward, looking at his buddy. "Let her decide for herself. It's just one job."

Kevin grunted. "I'm just saying, we should find another guy. This isn't going to be worth it."

"Don't worry," Marc said. "We're all together on this. You won't spend a lot of time with her. Mindy isn't going to know."

"I don't like keeping secrets from her. We do that enough," Kevin said.

I pressed a fingertip to my brow, sliding it back and forth to smooth it. They'd already lost me. Kevin had a girlfriend? I got that. But did he have to be mean about not letting me work for them? And they worked for someone, he just admitted it. If they weren't supposed to work with girls, it meant someone established the rule. Who established the rules around here? The pieces were in front of me, I just needed more time to process. "Let me understand this right. Somehow my pinching wallets is going to help you guys figure out what this guy's new nighttime habit is?"

"We need his security card," Marc said. "He carries it in his wallet. You're going to snag it, let us take it to his office and use it. We'll bring it back, you drop it back into his pocket and no one knows the difference."

"Wait, wait," I said, sitting up, holding my hands out. "Pinching a wallet is one thing. I'm supposed to put it back?"

Marc nodded. "In his pocket."

My mouth unhinged. "Why do I think this isn't as simple as it sounds?"

"It is as simple as it sounds," Marc said. "This is it. We go in, find out what's going on and get back out. You and Brandon will stay at the party and make sure he stays there. We'll take care of the rest."

57

"So you were nagging at me for stealing wallets, and offering me a job to steal a wallet so you can steal his drugs?"

"We just want to look at what he's doing. We don't want to touch it."

"Well, forgive me if I don't believe you. Who in the world is curious enough to break in and look at something and not want to steal it, or use it, or whatever? What kind of job is this? How does this make money for you?"

"Don't worry about that," Marc said. "All we want is information."

"What's in it for me if I do?"

Marc pursed his lips, he glanced at his companions. Raven shrugged at him. Marc turned back to me. "You do us this favor, we'll get you a job. A real one. We've already agreed to pay your rent for a month, but we'll get you a job where you won't have to steal wallets any more. You can get a real apartment, too."

"Who would hire me?"

Marc tilted his head at me, as if surprised I would ask the question. "Pick a place."

"What?"

"Where do you want to work?"

"You can't just get me a job anywhere. I have to apply. And there's interviews."

Marc leaned in on me again. He reached out, dropping a hand on my knee, and stared me right in the face. "If you do this, help us, you can name the place you want to work, and I can guarantee you, you'll have a job there. I can't do the work for you, but you'll have a job."

I couldn't believe this. I was sure I must have been dreaming. Maybe I thunked my head and was still back in the hotel room, just not having woken up yet. "How can I trust you?"

Marc flinched. He sighed, pulled out his phone from his back pocket. He dialed a number and held it out to me. "Talk to the manager at the hotel," he said. "Ask him to confirm your room is reserved."

"What?"

He held out the phone to me. I took it.

"Hello?" The voice was Colby. "Who is this?"

"It's ... Kayli," I said. Marc made hand gestures to me to keep going. "I was just calling to ask about the room—"

"Oh yeah. Yes, we got it for the next four weeks. Your room is reserved. Listen, I'm sorry I fussed at you before. I just ... you know how it is around here."

"It's fine," I said, but I lost him after he said four weeks. I hadn't even finished talking to these guys yet and they had already kept their first promise? I didn't know how to respond to that. "Could you do me a favor, Colby?"

"Sure."

"Can you tell my brother I may be a little late coming home today? And let him know that it was paid?"

"I'll leave a note under the door."

I hung up on Colby and turned back to Marc. "How did you do that? Why?"

"We told you we would," Marc said, determination settling into his eyes. He needed me to believe this. "I'm not playing with you right now, Kayli. This is your chance to get out of the gutter before something bad happens to you. You've had a rough start, I get that. You went to a shitty downtown school, and got tossed around a lot. Your dad's a drunk. Your mom's dead. That's fucked up. From what I understand, you take care of your brother, and you do your best. Well, here's fate for you giving you a leg up. Pickpocket, but this time, do it for the good side. Work with us this one time, and I guarantee you, that you'll never need to pickpocket again. You'll always have a job. I'll make sure."

My heart thundered under my chest. I had a hard time controlling my breathing to look as cool as I was pretending to be. He could have been offering me solid gold. A job. I had no idea where to start with that. I was willing to take anything before.

I still wasn't sure I believed it, but now that I could walk out of their apartment, and possibly never see them again and still had my rent paid for a month ... what would I do with the next month? What happened when Jack drank all the money I earned? Would I just start this endless cycle again? Maybe Marc was right. I didn't want to steal forever. "I just need something until Wil gets into college," I said. "If you know of anything ... I mean, as long as he can keep going to school. That's all I need. I can take care of myself from there."

Marc's once intense smile softened. His eyes lit up. Raven next to him started smiling, too. When I glanced back at Corey and Brandon, they had the same stupid look. Kevin looked pleased.

I groaned, rolling my eyes. "Will you idiots stop grinning like that? Just tell me what I need to do."

"There is no name calling on my team," a voice said, the severity and sternness catching me me off-guard.

It took me a moment to identify who had spoken, because lips around me didn't move and the voice didn't fit any of the boys in front of me. It was only when heads shifted to the second hallway, the one where the boss was supposedly busy and behind a closed door, that I realized they knew who had spoken.

The door was open, exposing a tall man, with longer jet black hair, parted down the middle, and the ends hanging around his chin. He shoved it back with his fingers as if used to his hair being in the way. He wore black-rimmed glasses on his face. He had an olive complexion which made me think he was as foreign as Raven, but more Mediterranean or perhaps Native American. He had strong, thickly muscled shoulders and a defined, tight abdomen that looked like he spent every moment flexing to strengthen it. He had a birthmark on his lower right hip. There was a trail of hair running from just above his belly button, right down to his crotch.

His exposed crotch.

Outside of the glasses, he wasn't wearing a stitch of clothing. His length was partially erect, and already impressive, as if he rolled out of bed with morning wood and wasn't even going to bother waiting for it to go away before baring himself to everyone.

I'd seen a few naked men in my life, mostly from movies and the few times I'd been exposed to the internet. There were guys at school who liked to expose their genitals to me if they thought they could get some attention. Only a handful of times did I ever get close to my boyfriends and their body parts. I thought at first I could play it cool with this new guy standing naked in front of me and divert my eyes in the causal way that I wanted to.

But I simply couldn't take my eyes off of him. I couldn't stop staring at the definition of his sculpted body, the defining lines of his collarbone and the matching indents on the sides of his hips.

Not to mention his penis.

"Dude," Brandon barked at him. "Get some pants on, will you? We've got a girl here."

The naked man inhaled sharply, and looked me square in the eye, as if asking me if I was offended. The darkest eyes, almond shaped, dragged my attention from his body up to his face, challenging me and at the same time telling me the answers to questions I was asking without saying a word.

He studied me just as much as I studied him. His eyes swept over me in the shorts, the boots, the way my hair hung around my cheeks and down my shoulders to almost chest length. His eyes stayed at my chest and hips for so long that I felt a swell in my breasts and genitals and the warm wave of a blush as if I'd been the one naked instead of him. Slowly, his eyes reclaimed my face with a determination that nearly knocked me over. He angled his head. There was the slight rise of a heavy, dark eyebrow. I wasn't who he was expecting, I presumed. However, he didn't seem displeased.

And suddenly his entire face blanked, becoming unreadable.

"She's seen one before," he said, toneless and as cool as water, and yet every syllable was with precision.

A finger poked at my temple, pulling my attention away. Marc smirked at me. "Pervert," he said.

I gasped, and made hand signals where my voice wasn't

going to work. Gesturing to the man, like this wasn't my fault. Me? He's the one walking around naked!

The nude man turned, heading for the kitchen. He grabbed a box out of the cabinet and walked back to his room. He paused at the door, and his eyes once again retrieved my attention. "You and I are going to talk later," he said, his voice now smoky and severe, and he closed the door behind himself.

The last view I had of him was his butt, and with the way the light played and the shadows, I caught a dimple.

Marc planted a palm on his eye. "For Christ's sake."

Raven only smirked and shrugged, looking right at me. "Enjoy the view while you can, right?"

I unhinged my mouth from hanging open so I could talk. "I take it that's the boss?"

Marc sighed. "Yeah. That's Axel."

I did a double take. "Did you just say Axel?"

"Yeah."

I absently rubbed at a tiny spot on my cheek. "So ... you guys live together?"

"Marc, and I, and Axel live here," Raven said. "The twins live down the hall."

"I've got my own house," Kevin said.

I glanced back at Brandon and Corey. Corey smiled, happy, his face all lit up in a pleasant way. His brother merely looked curious as to what I wanted.

"Huh," I said. I didn't mean to make my tone sound like I didn't believe him, but I'd just stumbled into this odd place. Still, I was starting to be really amused. And they'd paid my rent. And they were going to help me find a job. All I had to do was pickpocket some old guy? I didn't know what lottery ticket fate was ringing up for me, but I thought I could get used to this. And if I woke up and this was a dream, I'd be really pissed off. "So tell me who this old guy is I'm supposed to pickpocket?"

Marc lit up again. "You'll do it?"

"I guess I don't have anything else better to do at the moment. As long as you keep your promises."

"Start dreaming up where you want to work," he said. "I'll make it happen."

"And I want to know what it is we're taking a peek at," I said.

He looked at the others, who seemed to shrug in unison. "Okay."

"And I want to be able to hit Raven without him hitting me back."

"Hey," Raven said.

"Done," Marc said.

I reached out, slapping at Raven's thigh hard. Raven lifted his hand like he was going to pop me back when Brandon snapped an arm out, taking his hand and squeezing it, yanking it back until Raven twisted himself off the coffee table to ease the pressure and then writhed onto the floor. "Let go. Shit. Okay, okay."

"Hey," I said to Brandon, admiring his technique. "How'd you do that?"

Brandon released Raven and smirked.

"Stick around. You might learn something."

♠

COREY

aven collected himself off the floor and the group started to talk all at once for a moment.

A sharp ring interrupted the din, and the group silenced, turning to Kevin.

Kevin fished out a cell phone. He took one look at the screen and pressed the button. He stood quickly, rushing to the front door. "Hey. Everything okay?" He stepped out into the hallway, shutting the door behind himself.

"Mindy's calling again." Corey said.

Marc nodded. "She's doing that a lot more lately."

"Is that bad?" I asked. "Why do you guys say that like you don't like it?"

Marc shook me off. "It's not bad. It's just they've been getting really close. He's been a bit distracted. No big deal. Happens, right?"

I shrugged. I wasn't exactly sure what he was worried Kevin would get distracted from.

Marc started going over the information for me to catch me up on their plan. The location of the party was a fancy house. It was an informal party, but by informal, they also meant snooty and out of my league. They had an overview of the house, a few pictures of the place and the grounds. A photo of the target; a faded image from a security camera. The house itself looked like one of the estate properties further down the peninsula. It probably cost a million dollars.

"How am I supposed to walk into a place like that?" I asked.

"You're going as Brandon's girlfriend," Marc said. "He's got an invitation."

I turned on Brandon. "How'd you get one of those?"

Brandon shrugged. "I'm a nice guy."

"Okay, well, despite it being a casual party, they're not going to let a girl like me walk in there."

"Why not?" Marc asked.

I squinted at him, unsure how to reply. Did he want me to say out loud that I was a poor girl wearing clothes I bought on clearance five years ago? "Outside of the million other reasons why, let's just say I don't really fit in."

"We'll fix that," Marc said. "In fact, Brandon, you want to come with me? We'll pick up a few things."

"I'm going," Raven said.

"You're staying," Marc said. "Axel's busy. You need to stay with her."

"I don't need a babysitter," I said. "Where are you going?"

"We're getting supplies and lunch. You want anything in particular?"

If he wanted my opinion and was paying, I'd tell him. "Anything but Chinese." And bananas. And oatmeal. I wanted to mention those out loud but I got the impression he was talking about picking up fast food.

"Pizza it is." He pointed at Corey. "Staying?"

Corey had been buried in his phone. He picked his head up. "Yeah."

"Did you even hear me?"

"I'm staying," Corey said.

"Okay." Marc patted his pockets as if checking to make sure he still had his wallet and phone and keys, and did it while looking at me.

"I didn't take it," I said blankly.

He smirked. "I'll be back. Don't go anywhere, Bambi." He reached out, patting my cheek. I karate chopped at his elbow to get him to quit. He avoided it and chopped me back lightly on the shoulder. "Too slow." He walked out with Brandon following him.

I shifted to sit back on the couch, crossing my arms over my chest.

Raven stood up, stretching his arms over his head until the bottom of his black tank shirt stretched up over his abdomen, revealing his belly button. I tried to pretend I was just looking at him in general instead of the deep hip lines as thick torso muscles bulged. There was a continuation of some tattoos but I couldn't figure out what it was.

Raven smirked at me and walked out of the room before I had a chance to comment and defend myself. Great. I was starting to look like a complete pervert.

That left me alone on the couch with Corey. I studied him as he poked at his phone. The difference in the eyes between him and his brother was astounding. He was as tall as his brother, taller than both Raven and Marc, perhaps even Axel. The twins had wide shoulders and seemed to be lean in the torso, sturdy powerhouses. Corey's cerulean eyes were brighter by far. His whole face was friendlier, too. Softer with smiles that lit up his eyes.

I leaned into his arm on purpose. "Texting your girlfriend?" I asked.

Corey glanced up, his blond eyebrows rising. "What? No. No girlfriend."

"What's so interesting?"

He glanced around the room and blanched as if realizing he was alone with me. "Uh, nothing. Just work."

"Where do you work?"

His lips moved like he had an answer but he wasn't sure he wanted to respond.

I smirked. "I don't bite."

He laughed a little. "Are you sure?"

Did he worry I'd fight with him like I did with Raven? I tucked my hands together over my stomach and sat back, trying to look friendly. "So what are you working on?"

He fiddled with his phone in his hands for a moment before turning to me. "Promise not to say anything?"

My eyebrows shifted up. "You'd trust me not to tell? You don't even know me."

"Doesn't mean your promise isn't any good." He sat back, leaning against my arm. "I've put together a new phone app. I was just checking to see how the reviews were going."

"Oh," I said, blinking at the screen. I'd never owned a cell phone. If I ever had one on me, it belonged to a boyfriend I was dating at the time. I looked at the alien screen on Corey's. "You create phone apps? What kind of app?"

"A video game," he said. "A small one."

I leaned over him, letting my arm wedge under his so I could study his phone better, checking the title of one he pointed to. "Castle Zombie Defense?"

"It's like a castle defense game, except you have to defend it against zombies."

"You did it? By yourself?"

He shrugged, his shoulder digging into mine a little. "I had some extra time between other projects. The hardest part was learning the 3D software. After about a week, I got the hang of it though ..."

I sat up sharply. "You learned how to do this on your own in a week?"

He blinked those cerulean eyes at me. "Well, I had to learn about video game structure. The software itself has a lot of elements already in place, so there was some coding I didn't have to piece together myself."

"Did you take a class?"

He shrugged. "I mean I took some, but they didn't really dive into this sort of thing. I stopped going because it was faster if I learned it on my own. There's one I want to take next semester, but I may just attend the more interesting lectures. It's usually quicker just to pick up a book and learn."

"But that's amazing," I said. "Why didn't you want anyone to know?"

"I don't want the other guys to know," he said. "I mean I don't care if they know but ... I don't know. I just feel weird about mentioning it. They think I'm too involved in video games and that it's distracting."

"So you told me?"

He smiled a little. "Unless you want to tell me it's a waste of time."

"Who am I to tell you what to do?" I asked. I was too impressed to say anything critical. "I mean, you learned how to make them, not just play them. That sounds productive. A lot of people would love to learn how to do that."

Corey pressed a button on his phone to shut it off and planted it on the armrest next to him. "So Bambi ... Kayli. Sorry. I meant Kayli."

"Don't worry," I said. "Sorry I lied to you before. It's just I didn't really think I'd see you again."

"Surprise, surprise, huh?" He grinned and sat up. "Well, while you're here, do you want to look around?"

"You mean the building?"

"Or outside." He stood, and then turned to me. He rolled his shoulders back and forth. "I've been hunched over a computer all week. How about a short walk around the lake?"

"What lake?"

His eyes brightened and he held out a hand, palm up in invitation. "Come on and see the lake. You might like it."

It wasn't like I had much else to do. I took his hand, letting him help me stand up. After, he squeezed it gently once and released me. The move was odd to me, mostly odd because I actually felt a warmth from him I wasn't expecting. He wasn't just friendly. There was something about him I was drawn to. He made an effort that made it impossible to hold up any wall against him. He simply climbed over it and offered to help you knock it down. Instant and overwhelming.

He picked up his phone again, stuffing it into his pocket. I followed him out of the apartment and to the elevator. He walked close to me so that his arm brushed mine but he didn't seem to notice. Normally I'd shove my elbow into a guy that tried that, but I didn't have the heart. He wasn't doing it to annoy me like I thought most guys did. He just seemed so comfortable, like we were already best friends, and this was just something best friends would do.

"So were you creating your game?" I asked as I followed him inside the elevator and he hit the button for the main floor. "Is that why you were at a computer?"

"Oh," he said. He stared at the shiny doors as the elevator started to sink to the lobby. "Well, a little bit. Mostly it was tracking our target today."

"Me or the guy we're stealing the wallet from?" I asked.

His cheeks tinted and he pressed a palm to the back of his short blond hair, rubbing at his scalp. "Well, I guess you could say both. Although your information wasn't too hard to locate. We needed to dig up some details about you. You know, just to make sure you weren't a psycho killer."

I wanted to yell at him for stalking me. When it came down to it, I didn't know what to yell at him for. Or maybe I simply couldn't. His sheepish grin at admitting what he'd been up to had me smirking back. I couldn't argue with that face. How did he do that?

The elevator doors opened. I followed him out and through the back doors. We crossed a smaller parking lot, and then between tennis courts and a dusty baseball field to a road. When the traffic paused, we crossed the street toward a park on the other side.

The entire edge of the lake had a concrete structure like a giant rectangular pool. At the four corners appeared to be small areas of green lawn park space. There were palmetto trees lining the long sides of the lake, and the short sides had sprawling live oaks. The concrete walking path surrounded the entire lake, with the occasional bench facing out toward the water.

The water lapped gently at the sides of the bank. Ripples eased over the surface, soft against the breeze. From our angle, the fancy Charleston homes on the other side reflected in the water with a wavy distortion of colors.

"It's more like a big pond," Corey said. He pointed across the water to the houses lined up, picturesque at the start of autumn, decorated with pumpkins and orange and red leaves. "They usually take the horse carriages around this way. I think it's part of the normal tourist routes."

I could see why. The view was okay if you liked to look at rich people's homes, but I did like the view of the water. "Must be nice to live so close to the bay and the ocean, and then have a lake right outside to walk around."

"Just wait until you see it around Christmas. We'll take one of those walking tours then." He rushed ahead of me a little, claiming a spot on the wide sidewalk that surrounded the lake. He stopped there and turned expectantly toward me, waiting.

It was crazy adorable. He didn't even ask if I would, he simply assumed I'd be around during Christmas and would go with him. His happy nature was infectious, and I felt my own seemingly-constant inner anger ebbing away. I jogged over until I was standing beside him, allowing myself, for the moment, to get swept away.

He started walking and I followed beside him. For a while, he didn't say anything. He walked close to me again, his arm brushing mine. He let me have the inside lane, so I could have the view of the lake, but he was so tall, he could see over my head anyway.

The lake dazzled my eyes, distracting me. The mirrored city and sky made it seem like I could fall in and be a part of a reflected world. The only distinction that separated it was the soft ripples, and occasionally those ripples sparkled under the sunlight, as if suggesting that reflected world was better than the one we walked in.

When I finally drew myself from staring at the lake, I found Corey smiling at me in the silence. His cheeks bunched up close to his blue eyes. "Don't fall in," he said.

I grinned back, unable to stop myself. "I bet kids love it. Is it deep?"

"I think you can wade out a little, if you want. It's probably cold right now. During the summer, some kids usually sail little boats or use those electric ones." He snapped his fingers. "We should get some of those. We could race them."

"You haven't done it before?"

"I hadn't thought about it. I'm usually busy."

"Doing what?"

He opened his mouth to answer when a voice called out. "Corey?"

We stopped. Corey turned, scanned the surroundings and then paused, zeroing in on an older gentleman running up. It looked like he stopped his car in a no parking zone near the street and had jumped out. The driver's side door was still hanging open.

Corey darted until he was in front of me, as if to cut off my view. He frowned. "Stay behind me," he said in a suddenly deep voice.

The edgy feeling I'd been fighting all morning crawled back through me. I bristled. Now what?

The man stepped onto the sidewalk, ignoring me, and addressing Corey. "I can't believe it. I found you. We've been looking all over for you."

"That's too bad," Corey said in a dry tone. "You've been wasting a lot of time."

"Wait a second," the man said. He had dark hair, wore a fitted suit, and there were a couple of indents on his nose like he normally wore glasses but recently took them off. "You haven't even heard what I've come to talk to you about."

"It doesn't matter," Corey said. "Whatever it is, I'm not interested."

"Do you have a few minutes?" he asked. He gestured to the waiting car. "I think you'll be interested in what we have to offer. Whatever your current company is paying you, we'll double it."

"I'm not really ..."

"Triple. Really, whatever you want. If you just talk to my employers, I'm sure they could work out something."

What was this? A job offer? Triple his current salary? I thought Corey giving him the cold shoulder meant maybe the job was with the mafia, but the man who was talking to him didn't look dangerous. The suit looked expensive, and the car was shiny. The person talking to us appeared to be the driver. And his face seemed placid enough. I didn't get weird killer vibes from him. I had pretty good intuition about people.

"It's not the money," Corey said. He drew his shoulders back. "Please, if you don't mind ..."

The man coughed. "*Wenn Sie nicht möchten, dass wir*

vor Ihrer Freundin darüber sprechen, würde ich mich freuen, mich später mit Ihnen kurz zu schließen."

My eyes widened. I wasn't sure what he said, but the language sounded like German, or close to it. The fact that he felt the need to change languages at all completely changed my perspective of this seemingly innocent deal. What foreign company wanted Corey to work with it? Despite the man's eagerness, the fact that he wasn't listening to Corey declining his offer irritated me.

I stepped out of Corey's shadow. "He said no," I said. Corey eyeballed me like he didn't want me to say anything but I held my ground. "Maybe you should find someone else."

The man tilted his head down at me, the shadows under his eyes darkening, making him look worn. Maybe he really had been searching a long time for Corey. "Who is she?" he asked.

Corey, slowly, threaded his arm around my neck. "My girlfriend," he said carefully, as if testing it with me.

I allowed this, understanding. I weaved an arm around his waist, hugging him close. "Yeah," I said.

The man looked at Corey and then at me and then back at Corey. "Like I was saying, if you don't want to talk about it in front of her ..."

"She can hear anything you have to say," Corey said. "But I'm telling you, I'm not interested."

"Maybe I should come back later," the man said, turning away.

"I wouldn't waste the time," Corey said, standing firm. His fingers massaged at my shoulder. I sensed he was telling me it would be okay. I'd been wrong about him before, about him possibly being a yes-man. He was sweet, but he held his ground when he really believed in something.

The man frowned, turned, and went back to his car. He sat in the car for a full couple of minutes, as if waiting for Corey to join him in case he changed his mind. When it was clear Corey wasn't going to follow, the man turned the car around, driving off into the city.

Corey let out a slow breath. His arm loosened from around my neck. "Sorry," he said.

"Don't worry," I said. "After all, I did the same thing to you yesterday. Fair's fair."

He perked up. "I guess you did."

"Who was that? He had a job offer?"

He shook his head, his lips tightening in the corners. "It's nothing. Don't worry about it."

"He was going to triple what you make at your job now. You didn't want to hear about it? I mean, unless he was the mafia. Is there a German mafia?"

His face slowly softened and he grinned down at me. "You know German?"

"Not a word," I said. "I just recognize the dialect, or the accent, or something. He seemed to assume you did. You know German, don't you?"

"It's on my resume," he said. "I'm not fluent. I don't get to use it a lot." His face flinched and he picked out his cell phone from his pocket. I guessed it was on vibrate. "Raven's looking for you."

"What? Why?"

He shrugged, reaching for my hand, tugging once to get me to hurry along. He let go after, and I was sorry for it. It had been a while since I'd had any serious friends. I suppose after high school, after my mother died, I blocked myself off from any of my old contacts. And after I started working, started stealing, I really didn't want to talk to anyone. Corey's easygoing nature had me yearning for that connection to someone else that I hadn't realized I was missing.

I couldn't shake my curiosity about the German visitor. As we rushed back to the Sergeant Jasper and up to the seventh floor, I knew I had to keep my eyes open.

I didn't think he'd give up so easily if they put this much effort into finding Corey.

♠

RAVEN

K ayli!" Raven called from the bedroom the moment
we re-entered the apartment.

"What?"

"Come."

I glanced at Corey. He shrugged. "He's mostly harmless."

I smiled at his Hitchhiker's Guide to the Galaxy
reference. "Will I need a towel?" I headed to the bedroom
door. I caught how Corey's blue eyes lit up when he realized
I understood. That alone made my insides giddy.

Raven's bedroom was small with a tiny closet door that
was closed, and with a bed shoved over to the back wall to
make space. There was a fold-out table in the middle of the
room. The top had been partially covered by a towel.

Raven had a handgun taken apart and in pieces in front
of him on the table. He held a cleaning brush and the barrel
in his hand and was scrubbing the inside. From this view
with his shoulders exposed to me, I noticed more tattoos
along his back and up his neck. It was a picture of some kind,
but I couldn't tell what it was yet. It was too covered by his
tank top. I wondered how far down the tattoos went.

The power he held in his body, evident in his stacked
muscles was almost overwhelming, too. His shoulders were
as broad as Marc's, but he definitely had more substance in
the torso.

"Kayli," he called again.

"I'm right here," I said.

He twisted in his chair and looked back at me. He
nodded toward the bed. "Do me a favor, little thief. Sit right
over there."

"Why?"

"Marc just called me. He wants you to stay within eyesight."

"I was with Corey."

"He wants you within *my* eyesight."

I blew out my frustration in one heavy breath, marching over to the bed and sinking onto it, leaning back on my hands. "I wasn't doing anything. We were just talking."

"I don't care. I'm just following orders." He finished cleaning the inside of the barrel, putting the brush aside and wiping down the outside with a cloth.

There were a couple of other cases stacked nearby on the table, with Berretta and Smith & Wesson logos on the outside of them. The walls were covered with used targets, shots aimed at center mass or the head of a black cutout on a white background. By the wall was a dresser, currently holding two flak jackets and boxes of small arms ammunition stacked together neatly, sorted by size and type.

I scrunched my eyebrows together. I'd been around a handful of guns in my life, mostly old boyfriends who had been interested in them. This was the South, and half of the kids grew up hunting. "What's with the artillery? I thought you said this was a simple job."

Raven looked up, figuring out what I was looking at. He grunted and went back to cleaning the automatic. "Different job."

"How many jobs do you have?"

"How many jobs will you give me?" he asked. He focused on piecing together the gun again. "These are just for training."

"Training?"

His lips twitched, the lip ring protruding, while he finished assembly and put the gun on the table. He leaned forward, sizing me up. "What? You think I'm training these guys to kill? Is that what you're worried about?"

Yes. "No."

"Do I look like a killer?"

I lifted an eyebrow up. He really wanted me to answer

that? "Where are you from?"

"Omsk."

I stared at him. "Huh?"

"Omsk, Russia."

I'd thought so before, but thinking and knowing were completely different things. Now I was nervous. No reason why, I supposed. Just too many Bond and Russian gang movies.

I leaned forward, folding my arms around my stomach. His room was cold, like a meat locker. "When did you move here?"

He grunted, and planted the gun into one of the cases, opened another, pulled out a .38 and started cleaning. "You ask too many questions."

"You're the one that wanted me in here."

"Little thief, if I wanted you in here, I wouldn't be cleaning guns right now. I'd play, but I've got a lot to do before tonight. I don't really want you in here."

"Why?"

"You're distracting."

"If you don't want me to talk, give me something to do."

He planted the gun on the table with a hard clatter, leaning forward again. His dark eyes focused on my face. "I didn't mean you talking."

"Huh," I said in a non-answer. I hoped the heat on my cheeks was covered by make-up enough to hide it.

He cocked his head to one side. "You're cold."

"I'm—"

"You've got duck bumps."

I raised my brows. "You mean goose bumps?"

"Duck, goose." He waved his hand through the air and then stood up, heading to the closet. He left the light off, leaning in, and pulled out a thin cotton track suit jacket. He tossed it over the table, and I caught it. "Put it on."

It felt like an order, although I wasn't really complaining. I stuffed my arms into the sleeves. "Why do you have the room so cold?"

"It's either too hot or too cold in this building. I'd rather it be cold."

"Because you're from Russia?"

He made a face, sinking back down into his chair. "Because there's only so many clothes you can take off if you're too hot. Eventually you're naked and it's still hot. At least when it's cold, there's always something else you can put on to wear and warm up."

Made sense. I watched him clean the gun. I felt kind of stupid just watching him. Maybe it was thinking ahead to what they wanted me to do, and if I thought too much, I got nervous. I wanted to keep my hands busy. "Want me to do anything?"

He twisted his lips, glancing around the room. He pointed to the dresser. "See those boxes?"

"The bullets?"

He motioned to the pile of empty cartridges on his table. "Load them up. If you can figure out how."

I gathered the bullets and the cartridges and returned to the bed, kicking off my boots and sitting cross-legged. I smoothed out the dark comforter so the boxes wouldn't spill over. I opened one. The bullet heads were a gray plastic material. I held one up between my fingers. "I haven't seen these."

"You've seen others?" he asked, not looking up.

"A couple of ex-boyfriends used to go out to the woods and shoot."

"Did you go?"

"Once, but he wouldn't let me shoot. He was more interested in having me watch."

He huffed, grinning. "No wonder he's an ex." He motioned to me without looking up. "Those are training rounds. Plastic. Cheaper. We can reload the cartridges with the bullets again and again. No need to waste the real bullets. They're getting harder to purchase these days."

"Do you have real bullets?"

"Do you really want to ask me that question? Of course there's some here."

"Who are you training? And why?"

C. L. Stone

He looked up as he stuffed a wire brush into the barrel of the gun. "We're the good guys, little thief. Stop talking like you're trying to figure out if we're not."

"Bad guys think they're good guys, too."

The corner of his mouth lifted. "Guess it depends on where your morals are, or which side of the law you're on. You've been on the bad guys' side too long."

"I'm not—" I stopped short, realizing I was falling into what I was just telling him. "I had good reasons."

"There's always a reason," he said. He finished his cleaning and started piecing the gun together again. "It's why we have training, not just shooting practice."

"There's a difference?"

He placed the gun down in the case. "Training involves psychology, not just technique. For example, let's say you had a gun." He shoved the case across the table to the corner and within my reach. "And I have one." He tugged one of the others toward himself. "Let's pretend we're at the grocery store." He opened his, displaying a Ruger, bigger than I'd seen in person and I guessed it to be a .45.

I opened up the gun case. A .38 automatic was inside, a Smith & Wesson logo on the handle. The cartridge wasn't in place, so it was clearly empty. His was, too. And since he'd just cleaned them, there wasn't anything in the chamber. Still, I didn't touch it knowing these things could kill.

He lifted his, pointing it toward one of the posters at the wall. "I'm robbing the store. I've got it in the cashier's face. You're in the line next to us. What do you do?"

I frowned, not really amused. "Run away?"

"Ernt!" He made a wrong answer buzzer noise. "I've already got my gun out pointed at someone's head. But if I hear motion …" He snapped the safety off the .45 and swung his arm until the end of the gun was pointed to one of the targets behind my head. "I'm already a step ahead of you. What do you do?"

I remained quiet, unsure.

"I'm robbing the store," Raven said. He wriggled the gun toward the wall. "I'm getting all the money. People are scared, on the floor. I'm screaming at the nervous cashier. Kids are crying." He got up, walking the long way around the table, coming to stand by the bed, the gun still pointed at his target. He loomed over me. "You've got an automatic in your pocket. You're possibly the only other person in the store with a gun. What next?"

I frowned. I had an answer, but I didn't like it.

"Come on, little thief," he said. His brown eyes were intense and unrelenting as he stared at me. "Stand up. Show me what you can do."

My heart pounded in my chest, and I rose slowly, leaving the gun on the bed. I stepped away from it so I was standing clear.

"You've left your gun," he said.

"I know."

He cocked an eyebrow. "You're not going to use it?"

"No."

The corner of his mouth lifted and he stepped closer, toe to toe with me, enough so my breasts brushed up against his chest. He angled his elbow, until I felt cool steel at my temple. I didn't have to look. I knew he had the gun pointed at me. "Why not?"

I resisted the urge to back away, staring back into his face.

"Why Kayli?" He leaned in, until his nose hovered over mine. His dark brows furrowed as he challenged me with his eyes. "I've got the gun."

"But you aren't shooting," I said, trying to sound calm even with my heart thundering. I could smell gun oil and a musky scent from his body. His chest moved as he breathed heavily, in and out, brushing against me. A reaction stirred in my nipples and I tried to ignore it. I wasn't afraid. I was excited, my skin electrified. Because of the guns, or the threat of violence, or maybe just him; I didn't want to think of why.

"I could shoot," he said, the tip of the gun pressed into my temple. "One wrong look. One little breath in the wrong place, I might just make the pull."

"But you aren't," I said. I tilted my head away from his

gun, and the gun followed until I was looking away from him at the floor. "You're not shooting. You're only pointing a gun."

"So?"

"So if I start waving a gun, you will shoot. Isn't it better if I let you take the money and leave?"

His head leaned in, his lips traced my ear. His nose shifted through my hair. "Is it? Are you sure?"

I shivered warmly. He was so close and at the same time, I sensed he was toying with me. It almost scared me how much it turned me on. I breathed in slowly to focus. "I'm sure I wouldn't start waving a gun at someone trying to steal money and run away. If I had to rob a store like that, I wouldn't shoot. I'd just want the money. So if as a bystander, I shoot, you may be so panicked, you start shooting everyone. If I stay quiet and let you leave, you might have the money, but no one's been hurt."

He backed his head up. The tip of the gun eased at my temple, and traced down my cheek, sliding further along the side of my neck. I straightened, finding his brown eyes.

The corner of his mouth lifted. "It's not often I get the right answer on the first try," he said. He smirked. "Then again, you do think like a criminal."

I grunted, rolling my eyes.

"That's not a bad thing. Training honest men to think like a criminal is much harder. No one wants to turn their minds to always thinking at that angle. Everyone wants to be the hero and find the right solution, and win all. Letting a criminal get away for now is hard for honest people to consider." He raised the gun tip until he had the barrel planted under my chin, drawing it up until I was looking back at him. "But if you've already got the criminal instinct, then you don't have to think. It becomes natural. You can't be one step ahead of the bad guys if you're spending too much time trying to figure out what they're up to, or worse, play the hero and try to save everything. The real world doesn't work like that."

I pressed my lips together as he locked me into looking

at his face. His square jaw was set. The ring in his lip glinted under the light. "Do you think like that?" I asked, although my voice was softer than I wanted it to be. "Like a criminal? Is that how you can train them? Are you one? Or did you use to be?"

His eyes narrowed into slits for a moment. He pulled the gun away from my chin, but lowered his face until his nose hovered over mine. "You ask too many questions," he said. He pulled back, hitting the safety on the gun, turned and walked around the table again. "I'm thirsty," he said. "There's Coke in the fridge."

I huffed. "Do I look like your maid?"

"Do it or I'll tell Axel you tried to take my wallet."

I grunted. Go figure. Making the low man on the totem pole play fetch. I stomped out of his bedroom, but part of me was relieved for a little break. I breathed out slowly after I left the room. Did I just let him point a gun at my head?

And why wouldn't my heart stop pounding?

♠

AXEL

I glanced at Corey on the couch, who was tuned into his phone again. I sighed, thinking it would be easier and faster to just do what Raven wanted and try to make him feel like an ass for asking by being nice.

I padded in my socks to the kitchen. I tightened Raven's jacket around my body, shivering at the chill in the apartment. It felt weird to open someone else's fridge. When I did, I paused and stared. The inside was filled with food. Leftover containers. Sodas stacked on the bottom shelf in organized bins. Fresh produce. My mouth watered and my stomach rumbled at the sight. Marc was getting pizza? He had so much food here.

A noise behind me made me think Corey had entered the kitchen. "Did you want me to get you a soda, too?" I asked.

"I'll get my own damn soda if I want it," said a voice, smoky and severe.

I turned still holding the door to the fridge open. Axel stood a mere inch behind me. I felt the need to back up, but I couldn't move. I was surprised he had gotten so close without me noticing.

He wore blue jeans, black boots and a dark button up shirt. The upper buttons of the collar were undone, revealing the lines of his collarbone underneath and the start of a black tank undershirt. His long black hair was combed back away from his face and he had removed his glasses, leaving his dark eyes unchallenged.

He cocked an eyebrow. "Who's getting you to play fetch?" he asked in a way that told me he had a suspicion but wanted me to confirm.

I wasn't too sure if I should lie. Was he worth protecting? "Raven."

"Funny. From what I've heard, Miss Kayli Winchester isn't the type to let someone else tell her what to do."

"He said he'd tell you I'd stolen his wallet if I didn't."

His eyebrows lifted. "If you manage to get that wallet, you can keep whatever's in it."

Then he nodded mischievously toward the soda bottle in my hand. "I know you're thinking it. Do it."

My heart started pounding excitedly, but I was still intimidated by this idea. I had entertained the thought, but given that I didn't know these guys very well, I didn't want to start pushing too many buttons.

But he was the boss, wasn't he? He was telling me to do it.

I started shaking the bottle, feeling the pressure bulge in the plastic. Foam started up near the top cap but settled deceptively while still contained.

"Go on," he said, as cool as if asking me to recite a passage from a textbook. He tilted his head toward Raven's bedroom.

I trailed him to the doorway, and stopped short when Axel stopped, nearly bumping into him.

Raven was bent over a gun. He had a radio on nearby playing what I guessed was Russian rock music.

Axel knocked his knuckles against the doorframe.

Raven picked up his head, turned around. He nodded to Axel and then looked at me, spotting the bottle. He put a hand out reaching for it. "Need something?" he asked Axel.

I crossed the room putting the bottle in Raven's hand, and tried to appear casual about taking a step back from his table, as if to get out of the middle of the conversation that had nothing to do with me.

"Those guns ready to go yet?" Axel asked.

"Two more to go." Raven squeezed the top of the bottle and twisted the cap. The soda nearly shook in his hands.

A geyser formed and the top popped up into his palm. Cola erupted around his hand and over his clothes, dripping to the floor. Soda splashed against his face.

"Shit, fuck!" Raven grabbed the bottle, jumping up and running to the door. "Out of the way."

Axel leaned right and left, blocking Raven from leaving his bedroom, as if pretending to get out of his way, but being completely uncoordinated. However, he did it so smoothly and with such precision that you could tell his bumbling was a farce, as if Axel would never be so clumsy.

The result was the spraying fountain of soda got over Axel's shirt and mine, including the jacket. Axel didn't flinch. I stepped back against the wall but couldn't help the grin on my face, though at the same time, felt the desire sweep through me to be as cool and as collected as Axel appeared to be.

"Fuck, Kayli. Look at the mess," Raven said.

"I expect you to clean it," Axel said. "She's not your errand boy."

"I was just teasing her!" Raven bellowed at him. He squeezed the top back onto the bottle. "Look at my floor. I'm going to need a steam cleaner."

"It'll be coming out of your budget. Your Academy training should have taught you better."

I wanted to ask what the Academy was, but my mind was reeling. I suddenly felt bad about ratting out Raven. It was a pretty big mess. And what a waste of a soda. "Where's the towels?" I asked, trying to make peace. If we had to work together today, I didn't want to do it on bad terms. "I'll go get them."

"There, Raven," Axel said. "Girls can be nice if you give them a chance."

"I know she is," Raven bellowed at him. "I was just messing with her for hitting me."

Axel shifted his intense gaze my way. "You hit him?"

I winced. "It was part of the deal."

Axel smirked. "Good."

"What?" Raven made a fist and planted it next to his temple. "It's not okay to tease her but it's okay for her to beat the shit out of me?"

"She's a girl. If she manages to 'beat the shit out' of you, you're going soft."

"Hey," I said, unsure which one of us that was meant to insult.

Axel turned on me, he opened his mouth and then stopped as his gaze lowered from my face to my shirt. I thought at first he was checking out my boobs, like most guys do when they look down.

Instead I followed his eyes. My shirt was covered in soda. Even my shorts were soaked.

Axel's mouth dipped in the corner. "Your clothes are ruined."

"It's her own damn fault," Raven said.

"It's no big deal," I said. I wiped my hand across the shirt, and then felt guilty as cola dripped to the floor. I eased the jacket off my shoulders.

Axel pinched the edge of the jacket. He passed it to Raven. "Get this cleaned. I'll get her some new clothes to wear."

"It's not a big deal," I said.

"You won't walk around in soda-drenched clothes this in this apartment," Axel said. He made a wide step to get around soda, and snagged my arm. "Come on."

Corey was sitting at one of the computer desks now. He closed a screen as we walked by, turning to us. "What happened? Do you need a hand?"

"Do your thing, Cor," Axel said with such an ease and at the same time using that stern tone, as if suggesting that he had full command of the situation and has had it all along. "I've got her now."

I swallowed.

I followed Axel to the other side of the apartment, toward his bedroom. I hesitated a moment, already stressed about this situation and now heading into the inner sanctum of a guy who barely knew me at all. It was a wild thought for me to have in the moment, because I had already followed a group of guys to their apartment without knowing much about any of them. Did I consider him separate from the others? He didn't seem older than any of us. Slightly over twenty perhaps. Maybe it was because they called him "boss".

And what was he the boss of, exactly?

Maybe I was intimidated because the first time I ever met him, he was completely naked, and I didn't really hate him for it. It didn't feel like at school when boys occasionally flashed their parts, or that he did it with any sort of malice. Rather, it felt like he didn't care in the moment.

And why did his nonchalant attitude make me feel all weak in the knees?

Axel opened the door to his room, stepping aside. He continued on and I paused, hovering in the doorway. I wasn't sure what I was expecting. Axel being naked the first time I saw him made it hard to figure out who he was. His bedroom, however, was far beyond what I imagined.

There was a single bed, barely bigger than a cot, pushed to the far side of the room. Above it and next to it were rows of shelves filled with journals, notebook and binders chock full of paper. Some pages were folded and stuck back into the binders, sticking out and baring clips and stabled notes. There were piles of textbooks in a tall floor-to-ceiling bookshelf in topics like biology and physics. There was a desk in the middle of the room, with a laptop and a printer, covered with additional notebooks and binders that were open. All of the handwriting appeared the same on all binders and paper with any writing on it, so I had to assume he wrote every bit of it.

A low dresser and several tables around the room held a collection of glass aquariums. As Axel went for his closet, I moved closer to the dresser, examining the contents. A couple were fish tanks with small fish swimming together. Two aquariums held frogs, one a scorpion and the other I couldn't see anything inside, but was filled with water and a layer of algae covered rock at the bottom like the fish tanks.

"You've got to step up to Raven," Axel said as he poked around in his closet. "If you let him walk over you once, he'll do it forever. It's that Russian blood. They figure out who the alpha is and try to establish the hierarchy immediately."

"What's in this one?" I asked. I pointed to the empty tank. "Is it hiding? Or are you going to put something in it?"

Axel leaned out of his closet and looked at me, his eyebrows going up for a moment as if he wasn't sure what I meant. His eyes followed my pointing finger to the tank. "They're there," he said.

"They?" I asked.

He walked back out, having removed his shirt, revealing his very fit, tan body. There was a little bit of hair around the crest of his chest. Probably missed seeing it the first time because he was naked and my eyes had been drawn elsewhere. It disappeared and then there was the firm formation of his upper abs. My eyes followed it to the tiny trail of coarse hair that led down toward his pants.

He wasn't as tall as the twins, but it was the way he carried himself that made him seem more powerful. Like his voice, every inch of Axel was unyielding and exuded a precise calm without having to say a word out loud.

He flicked off the light from the closet and crossed the room. He pointed to the empty fish tank and reached for the bedroom light switch. "Stand there. Don't move," he said.

Oh god. I realized a little too late he was going to turn off the light. The bedroom door was closed. My heart started to thunder and my body tensed, ready to throw punches if this was a trick to try to hurt or rape me. I didn't get that vibe from him, but I didn't want to not be prepared in case I was wrong.

He flicked off the light. The room went dark and it was the first time I realized the window that was near the bed must have been covered over underneath the blinds. It took me a moment to readjust my sight, making out just the thin sliver of light coming from around the bedroom door.

I sensed Axel moving closer. I stilled, waiting for something to happen.

Axel caught my arm, wrapping his fingers around my elbow.

Fear and distrust caused me to pull away, wrestling myself out of his grasp.

"Calm down. I'm not going to hurt you." He reached, slower this time, and wrapped his fingers around my wrist. "I know you've probably heard this before, but trust me."

I relented, letting him take my wrist. His thumb trailed over the underside, right below my palm, in a reassuring motion. If my heart could quiver and then stop and relax at the same time, that's exactly how he made me feel.

He held my arm out with his to hover over the tank, and then as if reconsidering, moved to take my hand in his, his palm to the back of my hand, intertwining our fingers.

"Here," he said, his voice as quiet and as calm as ever. "I'll do it with you."

"Do what?"

"You'll see."

With that, he lowered our joined hands into the coolness of the water in the seemingly empty tank.

A shiver went through my spine, but it wasn't totally from the chill of the water. I held my breath. Anticipating.

He stopped when both of our hands were inside. "Watch," he said.

He moved our hands together, shaking up the water.

A glow emanated from the water. It was faint, like glow-in-the-dark stickers, but it was there. Blue. Ethereal. The more violently he shook our hands, the brighter the glow became.

"Holy crow," I breathed, as if speaking out loud would stop the reaction.

"Interesting, isn't it?" he asked. He released my hand in the water. "Go ahead. Shake it up yourself."

I did, feeling the smoothness of the water passing by my fingers, and playing with the level of the glow depending on how quickly my hand moved. If I stared hard enough, I thought I could see the little things clustering against the rocks, illuminating together.

"Certain creatures have unusual reactions to different environments. The tiny creatures in that tank get that glow effect from ..."

"Bioluminescence," I said, excited by the idea he had

this in his bedroom. "Defense mechanism? That's why you have to shake them up to see it?"

Axel studied me quietly. I wondered if it was because I interrupted him. "I thought you dropped out of school," he said.

"They let me take my GED early so I could get out and take care of my younger brother after my mom died," I said. "I'm not an idiot."

"I'm sorry. I didn't mean to sound surprised. Most girls I've met usually hate it when I talk about science."

"Not all girls are the same," I said. I stopped the movement of my hand, letting the light fade in the tank. "What is this? What's the name of it?"

"*Noctiluca scintillans*," he said. "The common name is Sea Sparkle."

"Is that why you've got the scorpion?" I asked. "And the frogs? You're studying glowing animals??"

There was a movement and the light flicked back on again. Axel's face carried a softer, interested smile. "You know about those, too?"

"Scorpions glow all weird under a black light. And certain types of frogs glow. It looked like a couple of your fish started to do it, too, while the light was out. What are those? Firefish? Or... um... sorry. I can't remember the name. Are they supposed to do that? No, that has to be a genetic manipulation. Those don't glow on their own naturally, do they? Or is it a new breed?"

A dark eyebrow shifted. "Are you sure you're Kayli Winchester?"

"What's that supposed to mean?"

He held up his hands, palms up. "If you're that smart, why the hell are you picking pockets?"

I huffed, drying my hand on my shorts. "It's complicated."

"No shit." He moved back to the closet, flicking the light on. "Come here and find a shirt you can wear. We'll wash your clothes."

I grunted, but moved forward.

His closet was as big as the tiny bathroom we had at the hotel. There were boxes along the floor on either side and cartons of notebooks and folders and more textbooks on the shelves. Shirts and jeans and other clothes hung up along the two racks on either side, but I got distracted by some of the equipment in the back. "Is that a diving suit? What's that shotgun for?"

"Will you stop being nosy for a minute?" He yanked a black button up shirt off of one of the hangers. "Here. Take that shirt off. And those shorts. This should be long enough." He passed the shirt to me and then snatched another one in a deep green color, and stepped out of the closet, turning around. He started threading his arms through the sleeves.

I turned my back on him. I was wearing a pretty modest bra and panties. If he could parade naked in front of me, I wasn't going to pretend to be that modest about him seeing my back and butt.

I bent over a little, slipping the white tank top off. I inspected my bra, checking for wet spots but didn't see any so thought I could keep it on. I looked for a place to put down my shirt so I wouldn't get soda on some notebook or his other clothes.

A hand touched briefly at my shoulder blade. I jumped in my skin, and turned quickly, holding my shirt against my body.

Axel hovered over me. His firm jaw set in a rigid expression. His eyes had gone dark. "Turn back around," he said, the smoky and severe tone returned.

I lifted an eyebrow, wondering why he was telling me to turn when he was the one that poked me. I faced the back of the closet, unsure of what he wanted.

His fingers returned to my skin, and traced along a spot just under my shoulder. "Where'd you get that scar?"

My heart raced, mostly from the touch of his fingertips smoothing over my skin. It became difficult to remember what he wanted to know. "I ... elementary school, perhaps? Some kid knocked me off of a platform on the jungle gym."

"And that one?" he asked, his fingertips glided down, to

one along the edge of my ribs around the height of my elbow. He traced at the scar with the edge of a fingernail and then repeated backward with his thumb pressed a little harder, like he could massage it out.

"A fight in school a couple of years ago. Wasn't my fight. I was just walking by but got slammed into a staircase."

His fingers lowered along my spine, sending a gentle ripple through my body. I stared hard at the back of his closet, at the diving suit. At the shotgun. At the boxes of folders. At the life of someone I'd just met not an hour ago, and here he was poking into my past. I dreaded the next question, even when I could guess it was coming.

He traced the scar that was at the start of my hip, the one that continued down along my butt. "And this one?"

My eyes closed. I wanted to answer him as coolly as I had the others questions, but for some reason I couldn't find the nerve. And with his fingertips on my skin, I couldn't think of a lie. "I don't want to tell you."

Axel's voice deepened. "Are there more?"

My lips glued shut. I wasn't going to let a complete stranger rip the past from me just for showing me glowing fish.

Someone started knocking on the door. Axel grunted. "What?" he bellowed.

The bedroom door opened. "Is Kayli in here?" Corey asked.

Axel drew his hand away, and I turned to see his eyes locked on mine. His were quietly telling me I could tell Corey to go away if I wanted.

"What do you need, sugar?" I asked, willing to do anything to stop Axel from prying.

Footfalls sounded in the bedroom, and I half turned to meet him while I unbuttoned the shirt Axel had given me so I could slip it on.

The moment Corey's gaze met mine, his eyes widened then lowered down my body, walking over my breasts, down to my hips in the shorts, and the thin line of my underwear that peeked out. "Ah," he stammered, and turned, facing the door frame, but his eyes kept sliding to my body. "Oh. Sorry. I mean ... I just wanted ..."

"You're fine," I told him. I threaded my arms through the sleeves of Axel's shirt and started buttoning it. I tried not to puff out my chest at his adorable modesty on my behalf.

Axel sighed and then took my soda-stained shirt from me. I slipped my shorts off under the shirt that fell to my thighs, covering me enough. He collected the shorts, too, and my socks. He filed past Corey.

Corey only watched, his blue eyes curious and his mouth working like he wanted to comment but couldn't come up with anything. The lower hem of the shirt was long enough that if I was wearing really short shorts, it would have covered them. Did he not know girls who wore shorts like that often? I didn't imagine it was a problem for him. Despite the nerdling exterior, he was pretty stunning.

I planted my palms on my hips for a moment. "What?"

He blinked hard and shook his head, his eyes finally zeroing in on my face. "Sorry. I just wanted to ask you ... your brother takes a lot of high level math classes, and he's got this one computer course he's working on that's an AP course for college. I was wondering if he was interested in computer science."

I stammered for a moment, "How'd you know?"

"I... uh..."

I squinted at him, folding my arms. "You've got a copy of his transcripts?"

His eyebrows raised. "Don't be mad."

I wanted to yell at him, but something in that face of his stopped me. He was a computer hacker. I got that. What I wanted to know was why he was still poking around my life? And then really, it was Wil, so my instinct was to be more protective. However, was it really menacing or was he trying to find something? When the spark of anger faded, it simmered into curiosity. "Can you show me?"

"What?"

"I didn't know he was in a computer science class. Can I see?"

He nodded, motioning for me to follow him. I trailed behind him to the computers set up in the dining room. He went to the one he was working on, sitting down in the chair. He used the mouse to bring up a document that listed Wil Winchester's high school transcripts. He scrolled down, and then pointed at the screen. "There. He took a computer science last year and trigonometry. Now he's in a follow-up computer class and trig two."

I leaned over Corey, dropped my hands on his shoulders to hold myself up as I leaned over his head. I scanned the screen. Wil's transcript was a little confusing to decode because all the information seemed clustered together. Trig and computer classes topped the list. "He didn't tell me about this. Is he doing okay?"

"Best in his class. He'd be valedictorian except that there's this one little twelve-year-old girl who is taking some sort of specialized physics class. Technically I think he's earned it, but they're making exceptions for her being a little girl graduating so early."

I couldn't believe my ears. I knew he was doing well but I didn't know he was amazing. "I can't believe he didn't tell me. He only said he was taking what everyone else was taking."

Corey shifted forward so he could turn and look at me. "I was going to say, he could technically graduate right now unless he really wanted to stay and graduate with his class. If he is interested in computer science, I could talk to a professor friend of mine and the dean at the local university. If he'd be willing to work in the science lab, maybe even starting now, he'd be able to get into some early classes that start up in January."

I blinked at him. "You're not serious."

"What?"

"He could get into college now? But there's fees. And I mean there's an application process and the cost of classes."

Corey's cheeks tinted. "Well, he'd have to put some work in. I know a few people that could help."

My mouth fell open. I couldn't even begin to imagine

this was even a possibility. "You don't even know him. You'd do that?"

Corey's face lit up. "I just thought it'd be easier on you both if he got in as soon as possible. He'd be able to stay in the dorms if that's where he wanted to be. I don't know for sure if that's what he was planning to take in college, it just seemed like he was heading that direction. I thought—"

I stretched out, and took Corey's face in my palms. "Tell me you're not messing with me. I swear to god, I'll kick your ass..."

"No one's kicking anyone's ass." Raven materialized next to me. "What are you doing? What's with this shirt? And let my boy go. I do the ass kicking around here."

I slapped his bicep, right on a tribal tattoo. "He said he'd get Wil into college in January."

"Yeah?" Raven said. He popped me on the arm. "So?"

I squared off my shoulders at him, holding up my fists and ready to hit him in the chest or face or wherever I could reach. Maybe I was crazy, but I kind of liked that he fought back. Most guys played too easy, too soft. Raven was ready to go head to head to me and I respected him for it. "So none of you guys know me or him. Forgive me if I don't want to get Wil all excited by the suggestion if he's all talk and it won't really happen."

Raven cupped his palms around my fists. It made me realize how much bigger his hands were compared to mine. Not to mention the way his biceps flexed. If he'd really wanted to, he could probably take me down in one hit. He held my fists together in his hands. "If Corey says he'll do it, he'll do it."

"Yeah," Corey said. "I don't mind. I did the same thing when I graduated high school and got in an early semester. It interrupts his current classes, but when I did it, the school let me take the final exams early. So unless he really wanted to graduate with his current classmates, he'd be able to start now."

"But," I said, unsure how to put it. "I mean, I haven't even done anything for you yet. Why would you?"

Corey blinked at me, like he didn't understand. "I don't need a reason. I just didn't know about him before. But now I do, and if it's like you said, you're trying to get him into college, this will get him in quicker. He'd still have to go in and talk to them."

I yanked my hands from Raven's grasp and leaned forward, wrapping my arms around Corey's shoulders and drawing him into a hug, almost falling on top of him. "Can you? I'll pickpocket all the people you want. I'll even put the wallets back. I'll do whatever you want."

"Make her not hit me back any more," Raven said. "I get to hit her and she can't hit me back. Make her have to get sodas from the fridge for a month. No wait, I want—"

"You don't have to do anything," Corey said. He planted his arms down on the chair, trying to hold himself up while I was hanging around his neck. "I don't mind."

I cupped his cheek in my palm, drawing his head over until I could plant a kiss on the opposite cheek. "Please, please, please?" I begged. I don't know why I was still asking. I think I just wanted to play. I was so excited, and I didn't know how to say thank you for this.

"I said yes."

"Please?"

Corey laughed, and patted at my arm around his neck. I leaned heavily into him and the chair swayed underneath us. "Stop it, I'm going to fall over in this thing."

I was about to release him when I felt thick arms wrapping around my shoulders, and leaning against my body. "Please," Raven mimicked my light tone of my voice. "Please, Corey. Please?"

Corey started to teeter in his chair. I was trying to push back to let go, but Raven leaned too far forward and I ended up pushing on Corey.

Corey fell backward in the chair, and I landed on top of him, sprawled out awkwardly, with the shirt riding up my hips and exposing my underwear. Raven landed on top of me on top of Corey. My face landed smack into Corey's chest.

I started laughing, too caught up in their promises to be

angry. Wil? In school? It was a struggle before to think of him getting into college in the summer. Now it could happen as soon as a few months from now. It was unbelievable. If it were for myself, I'd have said not to worry about it. For Wil, though, I'd do anything to help him get going to a better life than what we'd had. If it meant swallowing my pride so Corey could do me a favor, I'd do it. If I had to sink deeper into this strange group to get it to happen, I'd do it.

Corey chuckled underneath me. "You okay?"

"Yeah," I said.

He dropped a hand on top of my head. "Don't hit me," he said. "I'm just trying to..." He wriggled underneath me, and held on to my arm a bit, as if trying to make sure I was okay.

"I won't hit you," I said. I tried to push myself up off of his chest but Raven sunk his full weight onto my body, crushing me against Corey. "Ugh. You jerk, get off of me." I reached around, slapping at Raven's arm.

Raven shifted above me, and a hard spank landed on my thigh close to my butt. "Girl, I swear..."

I whimpered, rubbing at the spot where he hit me. It didn't really hurt that bad, I was going to pout and then pop him back when his guard was down.

"Hey," Marc's voice barked behind us. "I leave you guys for five minutes. What the hell are you doing to her?"

"Raven did it!" I cried out, reaching around to point at his head. I had a brother. I knew how to win this, and it was whoever planted the blame first.

Marc chuckled over us. "Why are you in your underwear?"

"Raven ... Axel ... I don't know. Long story. It's their fault."

Raven planted a palm on my back, shoving himself up while squashing me back into Corey. He hopped up. "Don't look at me. If I'd taken her clothes off, there wouldn't be any left."

I crawled up until I was on my knees on the carpet, and felt my cheeks catch some heat as Marc and Brandon stood over us, gawking. I huffed, and rose from the floor, stretching the shirt over my hips. "Can we get this stupid party thing over with before one of them kills me, please?"

♠

PIECES OF A PUZZLE

*A*ll of the guys gathered around the coffee table for pizza, while Marc went over the plan again. The only one missing was Kevin. Mostly it looked like Marc was informing me, because his eyes stayed on mine. Everyone else looked like they'd heard this before. I guessed for them it might be a review.

I was only half listening. All I could think about, when food was in front of me, was eating. I inhaled three large pepperoni slices before I finally slowed enough that I could pay attention.

"We should only be gone for thirty minutes," Marc said. "We need to make sure he doesn't notice his wallet's missing during that time."

"I could plant a second wallet," I said. "Like what Dr. Roberts did to me."

"Can you?" he asked. "Have you tried it?"

"I never stuck around long enough," I said. "But it's a good idea. I wish I'd thought of it before."

Axel perked up, pointing a long finger at me. "No, miss sticky fingers. No more pickpocketing if you're going to be connected at all with us."

"Don't give me that high moral ground lecture," I said. "You're wanting to steal a peek at this guy's office. You're not telling me what you're doing with what you find."

"We're just looking at it," Corey said.

"Yeah, you've said that." I took another bite and talked while I chewed. "You're committing a felony breaking and entering just because you're curious."

Marc's differently colored eyes slid over to Axel. The

guys stared quietly at each other, as if silently debating how much they were willing to tell me about what they were really up to. That was really all they needed to do to confirm my suspicions. This wasn't simply someone's curiosity.

"Who do you work for?" I asked.

Mouths stopped chewing and glances were exchanged across the pizza boxes. They only did it for a second before they resumed, but again, it confirmed my suspicions.

I dropped my pizza on my plate and snapped my fingers at Marc. "If you aren't doing it to steal drugs for yourself, or to make money in some way, you're an investigation team. You said it could be drugs, but you don't know. Corey can hack into a high school's computer files. Dr. Roberts could switch his wallet from my hands for a newspaper. You planted people at the mall knowing I'd be there."

"I didn't know it was you," Marc said. "We didn't know who it was. We were asked a favor to flush out a thief. It just happened to be you."

"That's what's confusing me," I said. "That's a mall security job. That's maybe local police. Local police don't need to swipe a security card to break into anywhere. They just grab a warrant and go. Neither does the FBI. Not on American soil. So you're either Homeland Security that's above all the need for a warrant... I'd say CIA perhaps, because you're looking at drugs and that could be an international operation. I want to say either of those, but for some reason I don't think that's it."

Corey stared at me, open mouthed, pizza in his hand. Brandon had curious eyes. Marc was grinning, his arms folded at his chest and sitting back. Axel was smirking, his head in his palm, his elbow planted on his knee, simply watching.

Raven pointed a finger at my face, looking back at the others. "Who wanted to hire the smart girl? I told you this was a bad idea."

Brandon kicked Raven under the coffee table. "Shut up." Brandon waved a finger at me. "And you, just do your job. It doesn't matter—"

"No," Axel said. He crumpled a napkin and tossed it at his plate. He sat back and lifted his foot, crossing it over his knee, rocking his ankle back and forth. "Let her keep going."

I flitted eyes between each of them, trying to pull pieces out of the air to fit together. "I want to say CIA or Homeland Security, but if that were the case, you wouldn't be working security at a mall in the middle of South Carolina. You also wouldn't need someone like me stealing a key card. You'd have some special hacking gadget for that sort of thing. So you're either lying to me about this not being for profit, or there's some private security informant division you're working for. The Academy?" I sucked in a breath, snapping and pointing a finger at Axel. "You mentioned that. What's this Academy?"

Marc looked me in the eye. "It's a school," he said.

I stared directly at him. His face was stern, but there was amusement in his eyes still. "That trains you to do this kind of thing? Where Raven is training people with guns? They pay you and let you do your own thing, but ask you to do these special investigation jobs?"

"How do you figure they let us do our own thing?" Marc asked. "You don't even know anything about us."

"It's Axel's glowing fish," I said. "That requires a high-tech lab, and time to alter DNA on that level. Did you see his room? All those notebooks? Either he's stealing them, or if they're his alone, he's been writing since the age of negative a hundred and four. And Corey's computer science friends at the college even though you're only... what? Nineteen?"

Corey glanced at the others, as if unsure whether to confirm or deny this.

"We turn nineteen next month," Brandon said, and his mouth went slack again as he stared at me.

"And he was talking about taking perhaps some classes or at least attending lectures later. So it can't be a full time gig if he's expected to get to class." I planted my palms on the coffee table, drawing myself up on my knees and leaning forward. "You're an investigation team of some kind, but not on an official level. I want to know what this is. So either you guys tell me what's really going on, or I'm going to go find this supposed bad guy and tell him someone wants to sniff around his basement and steal his stuff. I'm not getting arrested for a felony when I stood a better chance getting a slap on the wrist for pickpocketing at the mall."

The silence after my rant lasted for a solid couple of minutes. Glances were exchanged. I glued my lips together, waiting it out. I knew I had them pegged, I just didn't know which part was true. And I wanted to believe they weren't in it to simply steal drugs, but that had been the easiest answer to believe. The other part was just the next answer based on what I'd been given, but it still seemed so far-fetched. This crew? A private espionage team of some sort?

Raven leaned over, picking up the plate with my last piece of pizza on it and sniffed. "What the hell kind of pizza did you get?"

Marc grinned, his blue and green eyes lighting up and growing wide. He looked over at Axel. "I think that's a record."

"It's your fault," Axel said. "You brought her here. I told you not to bring her here."

"I'm sorry," Marc said. "I didn't realize we were bringing Sherlock Holmes. My background check told me she was in the lower half of her grade all through high school."

"You should know better than anyone that paperwork can be deceiving on intelligence." Axel turned, directing his dark eyes at me. "We aren't getting arrested for anything. And you aren't going to tell anyone what you know about us. You're bluffing."

I twisted my lips, meeting his stare. "Fine. Just tell me who you work for and why I shouldn't worry about getting arrested."

Axel took a glance around at the other guys again and then sighed. "I can't tell you all the details, but for a broad generalization, the Academy is a private group with their own interests. Part of our work, our team in particular, handles training, and sometimes we get called in to check out what's going on in the neighborhood. That's not everything, but as far as you're concerned, that's all you need to know about."

"Who hires you?" I asked.

Axel sighed. "You ever hear on cop shows or movies where they say 'an informant told us'? That's part of what we do. Our team in particular deals in information."

"What do you mean?" I asked. "The cops let you do this? That's who you're keeping tabs on people for?"

"It depends on what it is," he said. "To keep it simple, let's talk about this case. A rumor came to us that our target suddenly started going out late at night into sketchy parts of town and talking with particular drug dealers. He's rich, and doesn't need the money, and his money sources are clean, but we don't know why he's suddenly interested in talking with these people. While the police are curious, there's no evidence he's doing anything wrong. He's just in a position that he could do a lot wrong if he's up to something."

"How did you know he was going to those places?"

"We tracked his location via his cell phone."

I glanced at Corey. "Was that you? Did you find that?"

Corey's cheeks tinted and he shrugged, wordlessly answering my question.

Marc cut his hand through the air. "It doesn't matter who did it. The point is, we keep our eyes and ears open for things like this. The guy we're looking at happens to travel the globe. We're wondering if he's considering a drug import and lining up buyers."

"And you have no proof he's doing anything wrong," I said.

"Exactly." Marc picked up his plate, planting it on top of Brandon's empty one. He started cleaning up the table. "But it would be wrong if people like us didn't at least check it out. We're not collecting pictures, or stealing his business, or trying to find evidence he's doing anything wrong at all. We're the opposite. We'll clear his name and his reputation, if he's a good guy, so someone like the CIA, or worse, doesn't have to come in. We don't care what he's up to as long as it isn't something that's going to be illegal or kill a bunch of people. Either this guy is clean and we'll clear his name off the list, or he's a bad guy and we'll start the ball rolling so someone with authority can take over. We don't collect evidence. We just make sure there's evidence enough to be collected if that needs to happen."

"If you work with groups like the police, can't they give you special tools to work with? Why ask me?"

"The police and the FBI don't know, or care, about who we are. We're informants. We leave anonymous notes and phone messages. We use our own talents, and tools we can get from any local hardware or electronics store, or anything we can make ourselves. Using anything too high tech draws attention. Using his own key card against him won't leave much information about us. He won't be able to track us."

"So how do you get paid?" I asked. "If they don't know you, the CIA doesn't pay you anything for ratting out bad guys?"

"This isn't everything we do," he said.

"But you'll do a job like this just out of the kindness of your heart?" I asked.

He huffed, glancing at Axel.

Axel shrugged. "It's complicated."

This whole thing felt crazy and I knew there was more to it. They couldn't just follow everyone in town around. How did they pick up that this guy was acting odd? They were feeding me half-truths. "Un-complicate it," I said.

"We can't," Brandon said.

"Why?"

They glanced at each other again.

Axel leaned forward, looking me dead in the eye. "I'll answer that if you'll tell us why there's a scar on your ass."

I leaned back on my heels, crossing my arms over my chest. I tried staring him down, threatening without saying anything that I'd walk out the door if he didn't give in.

Axel's brown eyes flashed with a power that had me trembling where I was sitting. He challenged me right back, and every inch of my skin felt what he was trying to relay to me in silence. He meant it. He was going to rip the past out of me if I wanted to get these details from him. He'd do it right in front of everyone.

I sighed, bringing my hands up to cover my face. I couldn't, so I had no choice but to give up my desire for answers, and settle for at least some confidence. "Just tell me who I can pin the blame to, for Wil's sake, if something goes wrong. Tell me even if I get caught, he'll never know I did something stupid, and he'll be okay."

The silence now was heavier than before. I was a stranger amid a group of friends, people who worked together for some secret organization known as the Academy. I managed to unravel this much in a few hours. I wasn't that smart, or at least I didn't feel like it. I had basically dropped out of high school, even though I got my GED, it was just a cop out. Everyone knew it. It wasn't enough to secure a job good so I could pay for a decent place to live. I couldn't figure out how to survive. What was I doing with any type of informant division? Suddenly this whole plan felt so out of my league. I'd fail. What was I doing here?

I sensed someone getting up. Arms threaded around my body, squeezing. "God damn," Raven said. "Are you crying? Stop crying."

I ripped my palms from my face, finding Raven close. I punched at one of the tribal tattoos on his shoulder. "I'm not crying. I'm pissed off."

Raven released me to grab my wrist and held firmly. "Marc, get her to stop hitting me."

"And why is Axel the boss but Marc's the one rattling off all the plans and telling everyone what to do?" I asked.

Marc broke out into laughter. Corey joined in. Axel and Brandon merely smirked, shaking their heads.

Raven grinned. He yanked me closer and held my wrists in one hand and then wrapped an arm around my shoulders. "Will someone tell her so she'll stop crying already?"

"I'm not crying!"

To my surprise, Brandon turned. His cerulean eyes took on a deeper shimmer, dulling a bit of the sadness that hovered in the back and focused on me. "Look at me, Kayli. You have no reason to believe me over anyone else in this room, but you're sitting around in your underwear in an apartment with five guys with your rent paid for a month. You aren't running out the door yet. I'm going to assume, despite what you're saying, you feel at least somewhat comfortable with us." He took one of my hands that Raven had trapped, drawing it toward him until his lips hovered over my knuckles. "Will you please just go on this one date with me and pull a wallet? You don't even have to be successful. You just have to try."

I blinked at him. "What? You mean if I fail, you'll still—"

"Everything we've promised," Brandon said. His jaw tightened in the corners, a determination washing over his features. "Just promise me you'll do what you can to help. But if we don't get this information we need, it's not the end of the world. We'll still help you get a job if you want."

"Yeah," Corey said. "And I'll help Wil get into that college program. I was going to do that anyway."

"And I promise," Marc said, "you won't go to jail. You won't get into trouble. Wil will never know. We won't tell him. And if you never want to see any of us again after this, we'll just help you with your job hunt and get Wil into college and you can be on your own from there. If that's what you want, we'll leave you alone."

"She's not going to do that," Axel said. The smirk on his face broadening. "Look at that face. She likes us."

I rolled my eyes. I hadn't been able to meet new friends since high school, so I was a little out of touch, but they were starting to grow on me. "I hate you guys."

They all laughed.

♠♠♠♠♠

Now that I was more than committed to this, Marc wanted to start getting ready.

Brandon and Corey went to change clothes. Mine were

finally dry and I slipped my shorts on but kept the button up shirt. With the shorts still being very short, the shirt hem brushed my thighs. I may as well have just worn the shirt by itself.

When the twins returned, they were wearing identical outfits, both in dark slacks, white button up shirts and loafers. They were both cleanly shaven, too.

"Well," Brandon said, motioning to himself and then his brother but looking at me. "Here's the test. Which one of us is which."

"Huh?" I asked.

"Who is who?" he asked. "Here, let me make it harder."

The twins switched places a few times and then stopped and didn't say anything.

They were dressed identically, and at first glance it was kind of hard to tell. The only difference was the eyes. I pointed at Brandon. "That's Brandon."

The twins' jaws dropped in unison. "How'd you know?"

I shrugged.

"Wait, wait," Raven said. "It's got to be the hair or something. Like ruffle it up."

"Turn around, Bambi," Marc said.

"Stop calling me that," I said, but turned around. I waited, hearing shuffling behind me.

"Okay," Marc said.

I turned, and the twins had changed places. Their hair was combed back with fingers close to their heads. It didn't matter. I could still tell.

"Corey," I said, pointing and then shifted to the other "Brandon."

There was a chorus of groans. "How the hell can you tell the difference?" Brandon asked.

"Yeah," Raven said. "I've known these guys for years. How are you able to tell them apart when I can't even do it?"

"Their eyes are different."

Corey looked confused, but Brandon stared at me in a strange way that made my insides squirm.

"Okay," Marc said. "Turn back around. This time, guys,

close your eyes."

I let them rearrange themselves and when Marc gave me the signal, I turned around. Brandon and Corey had their eyes closed and this time, I really couldn't tell. "Identical," I said.

"Great," Brandon said, opening his eyes. "We'll just keep our eyes closed the whole time."

"Were you trying to fool me and switch places at the party?"

"Corey's going to slip in and out of the party to give back the key card," Marc said. "I went over this during lunch. Weren't you paying attention?"

"Kind of. There was pizza in the way. But unless someone's really looking at their eyes, no one's going to be able to notice."

"What's different about our eyes?" Corey asked. He glanced at his brother. "No one else told us that."

I couldn't think of a way to tell them without embarrassing Brandon. I motioned to Corey. "Your eyes are prettier."

Corey's cheeks tinted, but Marc huffed. "If you don't want to tell us, you don't have to lie."

"His eyes are pretty!" That certainly wasn't a lie.

Marc squinted at me but didn't say anything.

Brandon held up his hands. "Whatever. It's your turn."

"Excuse me?"

"You've got to get dressed. You can't go looking like that."

Marc went back to the kitchen counter, picking up a couple of plastic shopping bags. He opened one, pulling out a handful of material. "Do you like pink or purple?"

"Neither," I said. I walked around the other guys to pull at the bag. "What the hell is this?"

"Dresses," Marc said. "For the party."

My mouth dropped open. "Nuh uh. No way. No one said anything about wearing a dress."

"You have to fit in," he said. He held up one of the dresses, showing me the pink ruffled skirt. "See? This is stuff that girls wear."

"Maybe your girlfriends wear that."
"Just try it on."
"I'd rather light my hair on fire."

♠

SOCIALITE

*L*ater, I stood in front of the mirror in the bathroom with my hair redone with a borrowed comb and my cheeks pinched to create a fake blush. The pink dress had spaghetti straps, and a ruffle around the breasts. It was modest, except for the skirt. I didn't have any heels. This is what happens when you let boys shop for you. They never remember things like this.

I hated dresses and skirts. They were a luxury I usually couldn't afford, and it was harder to blend into a crowd in ruffles, anyway. They were meant to draw attention and that wasn't what I wanted most of the time.

Jeans were durable. Tank tops were about as sexy as I dared to get when I needed a distraction. Boobs were easier to spot for a target because they were closer to eye level, and when I was up close, I wanted to be sure they were looking at my breasts, not lower at my hips, where I'm trying to pull a wallet from a pocket.

I was going to leave my bra on, but the straps were tacky with the pink, so I took it off. The dress had built-in bra cups anyway, but was probably designed for a smaller boobed girl, as it felt tight. The fit at the waist, however, was a little big. I hung my bra over the towel rack. I smashed my boobs with my palms against my chest, trying to stop them from looking so restrained in the gauzy material. No matter how I positioned them, though, I still felt like I was almost spilling out of the top.

I sighed, giving up, and stepped out of the bathroom, smoothing the material. It was itchy against my skin already. If I had to wear a dress, I wished they would have told me so

I could have gone with them and picked one myself. Or maybe wouldn't have agreed to this whole plan so easily.

It's for Wil, I reminded myself.

Corey was at the computer with Marc hovering over his shoulder. They both turned, staring and blinking for a moment. Corey's cheeks tinted, his mouth dropping open. Marc smirked.

A catcall came from across the room. I turned to see Raven jumping up. Brandon leaned over on the couch, his head tilted and his eyes landing on the short skirt.

Raven elbow-bumped my arm. "Now this is a Bambi."

I ignored him and glared at Marc, and gestured to my waist. "See the problem?"

Marc blinked at me slowly. "No."

"Corey?" I turned to him, trying to stifle my indignation over being in a dress in the first place. "Could you stand next to me for a second?"

Corey stepped up beside me, his fingers drumming on his thighs. "Where?"

I guided him by the shoulders to make him stand in front of me. My toes itched on the carpet. I usually didn't have anyone to practice on, so this was awkward. I spotted his wallet in his left back pocket. "Just stay still," I said. "Look forward at Marc."

Corey did. I took a few steps back, breathed slow. I walked forward.

Bump.

Hand drop.

I faked a blush as Corey turned his head. "Excuse me." I emphasized with batting eyelashes.

At the same time, I pulled the wallet, and made sure my hip stayed pressed to his as I did, lessening the effect of the lift out.

But when his wallet was out, all I had to hide it with was my back turned to him. I stepped away, with my hand behind my back and then turned to Marc. "See? Now I look suspicious. My hand behind my back is obvious, and I don't have a place to deposit the wallet. And anyone standing behind me is going to notice."

"What if I'm standing nearby?" Brandon asked. "You could hand it off to me."

I thought about it. "Come stand next to Corey," I said.

He stood next to his brother, nearly arm to arm. After seeing them like this, I shook my head. "Never mind. That won't work." I snagged Brandon by the elbow, dragging him to stand behind me. "You'll have to follow right behind me. Let me feel your pockets?"

Brandon's ears turned red. "What?"

I dropped a hand on his hip, sliding my palm down until I felt the front of his thigh and the size of his side pocket. I slipped a hand inside, feeling the inside space. "It's tight." I slid my hand back, reaching for his butt pocket. There was a button and I opened it, feeling around. "Sorry," I said. "Nice butt though."

Brandon smirked, and wriggled his eyebrows at his brother. "You might have the eyes, but I've got the butt."

Even with the back pocket open, I was having more doubts. This wasn't just lifting and putting another wallet back. This was also passing off to someone else. This was not my regular *modus operandi*, and that concerned me—I always worked alone. "It'll depends on how big his wallet is." I pointed to the corner. "Stand over there. Count off. Try to pass right by me and reach out just after to collect it. If we don't time it just right, it'll be too obvious to anyone watching what we're up to."

It took a few tries, but we timed it so Brandon walked right behind me when I made the switch. Corey felt the hip tap and then nothing, and I was there with empty hands afterwards.

"Now I just need a second wallet," I said.

Marc pulled several out of the shopping bag.

I kept practicing with Corey and Brandon. Being engaged in what I was about to do had me more nervous. The move didn't feel natural like I'd done before. Doing things on the fly seemed to be more my style, where I didn't have to think about it too long.

It was harder still not knowing more details about my target, like what he would be wearing, or seeing where his wallet was located. What if he kept his wallet in his front pocket? What if he wasn't carrying it to the party with him? I'd never worked so hard on one person, and one shot was all I was going to get. Fondling someone's butt or front pocket to find the right one wouldn't be acceptable. I worried about how busy this party was going to be, or if I'd even get a chance near the guy.

After another hour, Marc checked the time on his phone. "I guess we should start heading out."

I grimaced as I lifted Corey's wallet out of his back pocket for the hundredth time. I slipped it back in and smacked him over the wallet on the butt. "Let's get this over with," I said.

Corey chuckled. "Good, because my butt feels numb right now. I'm going to be checking my wallet every two minutes from now on."

"If you want to stop your wallet from being picked," I said, "put it in your front pocket. I'm less likely to want to target you if I have to get my hands that close to your junk."

Raven stood up from the couch, and coughed to get my attention. He pulled his wallet out and stuffed it down the front of his pants. "Maybe you should practice this," he said. "You never know."

"Cut it out, Raven," Marc said.

Raven removed his wallet, but slipped it into his front pocket. "Are we leaving?"

"Yeah. Axel!" Marc called out. "It's time!"

Axel appeared with a book bag slung over his back shoulder. His long black hair was stuffed behind his ears. He was dressed causal, but he wasn't going to the party anyway so it didn't matter. I was jealous.

He took one look at me and made a face. "Who put her in a dress?"

112

I left the apartment wearing the dress and my boots. They'd forgotten to buy shoes. Boys.

In the parking lot, the others broke away and headed for different vehicles. I trailed after Brandon.

Brandon pulled keys out of his pocket, hitting the unlock button on a fob. A gray BMW lit up.

I pointed to it. "You own this?"

"Borrowed it for tonight to fit in better," he said. "Mine's that one." He pointed to a large black SUV parked across the way.

"Huh," I said.

"You don't like it?"

"It just seems big. And expensive."

I was heading to the passenger side door but he ran around and opened it before I could get to it. I shook it off. Southern guys have certain habits, like opening doors for girls. You just let them do it. It's that moral code. "We need to pick up some shoes. I can't go barefoot."

"I'll stop on the way," he said.

He stopped at a shoe store, asked me my size. I described to him a couple of styles that would match. I couldn't go in barefoot. He came back with some strappy sandals. He showed them to me. "Will these do?"

I tried them on, and they were a bit wide but I could manage. "Not my type," I said.

"I can tell," he said. He got into the car and started up again, weaving his way through city streets.

I realized I'd forgotten something. "Pull over," I said. I pointed to the drug store on the corner.

"Why?"

"I forgot about makeup."

"You don't need makeup. You look fine."

"Just pull up to the curb."

He did as I asked, pulling close to the doors. I jumped out, rushing into the store.

The clerk was bored at the counter, and the makeup stand was within eyesight. She looked up in a mild expression.

I pointed to the makeup. "Late to a party and my

boyfriend forgot my makeup case. Mind if I do a touch up a the sample counter?"

The woman shrugged, gesturing in a way to tell me I could do what I wanted. Perfect.

I dashed to the counter, spotting the overused makeup probably tried on by dozens of people. I sucked in a breath, looking through the palettes for a sample that was close to my color.

Brandon surprised me by touching his palm to the small of my back. "What are you doing?"

"Hold this up," I made him hold the mirror and I smeared on lip gloss and dabbed my eyes with liner and mascara. A quick brush of powder, and I had a day time look going at least.

Brandon's lips twisted into an awkward smirk. "You are not the same Kayli I met this morning."

"Should we use our real names at this party?" I asked. I took the mirror from him and put it away, waving thanks to the clerk before leaving. We got to the car and he held my door open again while I hopped in. Brandon got back behind the wheel and started off once more. "I mean, if we're going in together, shouldn't we be all covert about this?"

"They already know mine. We could shorten yours. It's always best to go with something close to what you're familiar with." He glanced over at me. "Kay fine with you?"

"Meh," I said. "Want me to call you ... Brad?"

He smirked. "No. Maybe stick with pet names. I guess that'll work."

Ten minutes later, Brandon pulled in front of a downtown Charleston house. A valet service boy raced to the street and opened my door.

Despite having seen pictures of the house, the closest I'd ever been to a house like this was probably in elementary school when there was a field trip to a plantation house, the name of which I couldn't remember. Otherwise, it was passing by if I ever managed to find myself downtown, which wasn't often. Charleston homes were narrow, sprawling front to back instead of wide, almost shotgun style.

Deceptive of their actual size, they were still opulent. This house was painted bright white, almost too bright for my eyes with the sun beaming on it. Wide live oak trees towered in front, along with the lush greenery surrounding the property. They were the only things that stopped the white paint from being too eye-crushing intense.

I waited for Brandon, and followed his lead, feeling completely out of my comfort zone. I stood close enough that my arm touched his. We went up a short flight of stairs and were greeted at the door by an attendant, who told us the party was in the garden at the back of the house.

I hadn't anticipated being outside. The problem with this job was I couldn't pick and choose my target, and the location was a challenge already since I didn't know the house. I'd imagined a party indoors with crowds of people and easy reasons to bump into someone. Now we weren't in the house, but outside in the backyard. Changing the plan in my mind so quickly left me at a disadvantage.

I followed Brandon closely through the house, as we were led to the back doors. The inside of the house had a few lingering partygoers who stopped to looked at knickknacks and paintings on the walls. Several attendants stood by, offering champagne and encouraging people to move out to the garden.

My heart started to race. I realized the attendants would be watching our every move, trying to anticipate what we needed. If I was caught, there would be absolutely no place to run, either. I'd have to go through the house, or maybe run for a neighboring yard? Neither option felt like it would work.

Out on the porch, wide steps opened up to a flat lawn. The yard itself was smaller than I thought an expensive house should have, but space was limited on the peninsula, and they fit as many houses as they could. The grass yard had a few old live oaks, shared in the corner with other properties behind it. There were flower gardens and pathways nearer to the house. A stage was set up at the far end of the yard with a small orchestra playing a concerto piece. People stood around in small groups, talking with champagne flutes in their hands. There was a large buffet table. Attendants filtered through the party, almost invisible as they fetched and retrieved what anyone might need.

My hands started shaking. This was worse than I thought. Everyone seemed taller, prettier, wealthier. A few couples swayed and danced to the music. Most were talking in groups, with backs turned. Any interest in us, any look cast our way, seemed to tell me exactly who I was without anyone saying a word. I was the rat at the swan party.

As if reading my mind, Brandon pressed his palm against mine, squeezing. He leaned in, and his lips brushed against my ear. "You'll be fine."

He started to let go, but I held tight, intertwining my fingers with his. I didn't know how to say it out loud, and I didn't know him well, but he was the only one there I knew, and I needed him. I needed a connection to the real world. These were the wealthy I'd abhorred from a distance for years. And I was about to steal from one of them. They were the very people who, with a snap of fingers, could summon security or bring down the police, because they were important, and superior.

He let me hang onto him, and he led the way down the steps and into the crowd. He did it with such ease that even though I'd shared a pizza with him only an hour or so ago, I was in awe that he seemed to blend in so well. His handsome face, the casual stance, his clothes and everything about him seemed to work together. I tried to mimic him, but felt myself wanting to hide behind him instead. This made me stand closer than I probably would have otherwise, and my cheek swiped occasionally against his shoulder when I leaned in.

And he squeezed my hand on occasion. I knew he was trying to be reassuring, but the only thing I wanted at that point was to leave. I'd go back to the apartment and fetch a thousand sodas for Raven. The confidence I'd faked this entire time had been zapped.

We took our time shifting through the crowds. I picked up a champagne glass just to fit in, but realized my mistake quickly. I needed both hands when the time came. I didn't know where to put it down, and caught how another lady finished her glass and an attendant came near her instantly and took it from her.

I brought the flute to my lips and drained the glass in one gulp. I felt the light burn of alcohol on the back of my throat and coughed.

"Hey, hey," Brandon said. "No drinking on the job."

On cue, an attendant materialized next to us. He took my flute and another attendant followed, offering another that was filled. I declined this time. I was fitting in enough.

Brandon spotted our target on the outskirts of the party by the buffet table. We got close enough that I could keep my eyes on him, and Brandon positioned himself to turn to me so I could peek over his shoulder at him.

When he let go of my hand, I felt some of the remaining confidence seep out of me. We were close to other couples and groups chatting. Talking to each other, we probably blended in enough. I wondered how many people here knew each other. Would they recognize I didn't belong?

Brandon's sad eyes darted out to the crowd behind me, covering my back as I kept an eye on our target. "How're you doing, sweetie?" he asked.

"I don't like champagne.

He chuckled. "How's our target?"

I zeroed in. I remembered Marc had called him Mr. Coaltar. I couldn't remember his first name. Mr. Coaltar's back was turned to me, so all I saw was a sports coat, and smoothly brushed dirty blond hair that hung long around the nape of his neck. "Taller than I thought. This party's pretty extravagant. Are you sure he's doing drugs?"

"Some guys are so rich, they get bored. That's when they get stupid and start dealing in illegal activities."

"So you think he's a bad guy?"

His head tilted, and I felt his gaze on my face. "I get hunches about people. I'm usually not wrong."

I hoped the makeup was hiding how hot my cheeks felt as I was sure I was blushing. I met his stare, trying to feel as brave as I wanted to appear. "Any hunch about me?"

His eyes never wavered. "Yeah."

"And?"

He smirked, and then drifted his focus back to the crowd. "Probably should have left you at the mall picking pockets."

I frowned, gazing at my target. "I was going to quit, you know."

"They all say that."

"Do you want me to start picking at skeletons in your closet? 'Cause seriously, I've got the time right now. Did we go over how we're committing a felony?"

He grunted. "We've got a good reason."

I scoffed and clenched my fists. Forget about the target. I was about to pounce Brandon. "Are you saying my reasons weren't good enough?"

He turned fully now, squaring off his shoulders at me. "I'm saying if you are really as smart as all that, you'd have found another way."

"I tried," I said. "I did everything I could. I applied everywhere."

"Everywhere?" he asked, his cerulean eyes lit up. "Really?"

I pointed a fist at his face. I spoke low and through my teeth to make sure no one else was listening in. "Listen, buddy. I've got a little brother I'm trying to get into college. I've got a drunk father who steals our money or beats us if we don't have any, so he can drink it at the bar and pay for women. We tried to leave and he called the cops on Wil, and they brought him back. They didn't care. Social services didn't care. They just wanted us out of their hair. I can't leave Wil until he can safely leave on his own, and I'm not about to be sorry for doing whatever I have to do to make sure he gets a better life than me. Not like you could ever understand that. You've got a fancy apartment, and friends, and food in the fridge, and a new car."

"I earned those," he said.

"I'm trying to earn my way," I said. I held my hands out, palms up, flustered. Tears bit at the sides of my eyelids, but I silently threatened them with a thousand deaths if they dared start to fall. I wanted to spit back a thousand reasons why I did what I did, but even despite myself, I knew myself better than that. Deep down inside, I wondered, too, if there was anything I could have done, any different path I could have taken, to change who I was and what had happened to us. Could I have saved mom? Could I have stopped Jack from destroying himself? Could I have fought harder? Worked harder? Begged more?

We glared each other down. Why did it matter to me what he thought? If this had been anyone else, I would have walked away. What did I care as long as Wil and I were okay? What anyone else thought didn't matter.

Except it did just now. It did with Brandon. Maybe it was those sad eyes, penetrating through my body and magnifying every thread of self-doubt I'd ever conceived about my actions. It was like he was trying desperately to understand me, just like I needed him to believe I wasn't just an idiot, greedy girl.

I bit back the tears and forced the words out, cool and slow. "If it were up to me, my mother wouldn't have died, my father would be the way he was before she did, and I wouldn't need to be here right now. When I finally get a chance, I'll work my tail off and dump a ton of money on charity, and help whoever I can to make up for every penny I've ever stolen. And, believe me, I know every cent. I feel it every time. Now look me in the eyes again and tell me you've ever fought that hard for anything."

He lowered his body at the waist, until his face was level with mine. "I did," he said, but his voice was a tone softer now, and it threw me off, curbing the anger that had my fists ready to sail. "I've got a brother, too, you know. And if I ever needed to steal, or fight, or suffer to make sure he's safe, I'd do it. And believe me, I have."

I blinked hard, jerking my head back. "But... you... You just told me I should have worked harder."

"I just wanted to hear it from your lips that you knew what you were doing was wrong." He straightened himself again. "I think you could have done better, but I understand why you did what you did when you felt cornered. I do sympathize, but I wasn't about to stand by and let you lie to me, or yourself, about what you've done like some misunderstood hero. I won't lie to you Kayli. We're about to steal a wallet from a man who might have powerful allies, and break into a building that doesn't belong to us. We put our lives at risk to save others, but we can't ever forget exactly where we stand. In the shadows. Inside secrets that can rip us apart. If we're not honest with each other, this won't work. We'll become as bad as the guys we fight against."

My breathing slowed and my heart stilled. Somehow the party had disappeared around us. Brandon's eyes were swallowing me up, telling me things I wasn't sure I was supposed to know. "I didn't mean to lie," I said in a quiet voice.

"Don't feel too bad," he said. He turned again, focusing on the partygoers. "Sometimes you tell yourself a lie so much, you start to believe it. Sometimes when you're in the middle of shit, you need a lie to keep you sane until you can get out again."

I swallowed hard, and side-stepped into his shadow to block my face from everyone else around us. "I wasn't trying to... I didn't ..." After being so angry, and suddenly not, I was shaking. What was I doing here? Who was I? Somehow he had me questioning everything. Despite him being near me and the party around us, I felt a million miles away from everyone. I was the thief among the crowd. I was the bad apple in the orchard. I trembled, feeling lost.

He glanced back down at me and sighed. His hands slid up, catching my elbows. "I'm sorry," he said. "I need to learn to shut up. I shouldn't have started talking about this. Not now."

"You should have left me at the mall," I said, staring blankly at his red tie.

He grunted, and suddenly his arms encircled me, drawing me close. He swayed gently with the music. He was pretending to dance with me. That didn't matter to me as much, but his strong arms across my shoulders were suddenly everything I needed, that I never knew I needed.

"I meant you were probably safer there," he said. "You were probably right all along. This is dangerous and you don't even know. We know and we choose to be here. You were bribed and still don't know. I don't like that."

I clutched at the breast pocket material of his shirt. "I don't know who you are," I said. "I don't know who exactly you work for. I want to believe this is the right thing. Tell me I'm not making a huge mistake."

"I can't promise that," he said, his hands sliding across my back in a soothing motion. "Because I feel like we're making a big mistake letting you in this close. But I can tell you that this guy could be a bad guy, and we could possibly be stopping *him* from making a big mistake if that's what he's planning. Or he could have been bad all along and we're just now catching on. If that's the case, we're all in trouble. But if we get out of this without getting caught, I'll do everything I can to make sure we keep our promise to you. Because I know exactly how hard you'll work to save your brother. I probably would have done the same thing. Actually I have, just in a different way."

I tightened my face, afraid I'd cry. I was already worried I was ruining my mascara. I sucked in a deep breath, and then pulled myself away. I wanted to sink into him more, but I wouldn't allow it. "This is the worst pep talk I've ever had."

Brandon released a forced chuckle. He touched at the knot of his tie. "Sorry. Corey's always telling me I scare girlfriends off by talking too deep. I didn't mean to make you cry."

"I'm not crying." I stuffed an arm against his chest in a faux punch that lacked any effort. "Just shut up and let me do my job. You can talk to me later."

"You'll talk to me after this?"

I rolled my eyes, and didn't answer. The truth was, I didn't have one. I wondered about that, too. More than one of them had mentioned that if I wanted, I didn't have to see them again after this. They weren't bad people. If everything was true, and I was starting to believe it was, I wouldn't want to just forget a group of people who helped me so much. Whatever weird fate had thrown us together, it seemed cruel that this job would end and that might be the last I ever saw of them.

Would they disappear again and never want to talk to me? Did that matter to me?

Despite our conversation, the party went on around us without noticing our little spat, but I wasn't as nervous as I was before. When I zeroed in on my target again, he was still by the buffet table. Women seemed to flock over to him. They hovered around him in a circle. A couple of men came along at one point, escorting certain ladies away. I understood they were probably husbands and boyfriends dragging their girls away from Mr. Coaltar. He must have hundred dollar bills hanging out of his nose. I still couldn't see his face.

But I could see the bulge in his back pocket. Bingo.

A waiter trailed past us with champagne flutes. I picked one up, coming up with an idea.

"I said no more drinking," Brandon said.

"I'm not going to drink it." I gestured to our target. I sunk my hand into Brandon's back pocket, pulling out the fake wallet and planting it in my palm, pressing it against my thigh. "I'm ready. Let's go."

Brandon glanced at me once more, and then backed off, heading through the throng of people, angling himself as we'd practiced earlier. He'd walk right behind my back at just the right time so I could pass off a wallet.

Time slowed for me again. It was different though. The guilt-ridden thoughts were gone. I was doing this man the biggest favor by clearing his name or doing Charleston a favor by getting rid of a potential drug cartel. Win-win, right?

I focused on the bulge in his back pocket. I held on to the flute in my hand, ready with a new distraction.

I walked steadily as if I were going to pass him and head to the food buffet. The food buffet alone was enough of a distraction. I bit my tongue to concentrate.

Fake stumble.

Bump.

Hand drop.

I held the flute sideways to spill at the top of the pink dress, causing a wet stain. I dropped the glass to free up my hand.

I lifted the wallet, and halfway out, started dropping the new one back in.

I started in on batting my eyelashes right as he started to turn. "Oh," I breathed in the softest voice. "Sorry. I didn't mean..."

There was a commotion all at once. Two attendants flew in, offering me a napkin and picking up the dropped flute.

I couldn't turn back to look as it would be too distracting, but someone lifted the wallet from my hand. I could only hope it was Brandon. I sensed him walking away. He would head out to pass it off to someone else, giving me time to collect myself and look natural when I went searching for him.

Mr. Coaltar turned.

The world shifted.

His whole appearance was surprising, because part of me had expected him to be middle-aged, but he didn't appear much older than twenty-two or so. A dirty blond eyebrow arched up. His face was slightly unshaven, but it seemed intentional, making him even more photogenic. His dark blond locks framed his face. His cheeks were slightly sunken under high, defined cheekbones, giving his angled jawline a hardened look. Yet there was a hint of a coy smirk playing on his lips.

And, god forgive me, I paused for a millisecond to admire the view.

"Oh no, not again..." he started to say before he fully turned and even noticed who I was.

And the way he said it made me realize, to my horror, I'd probably just pulled the same stupid stunt dozens of women tried on him, only with the intention of getting into his bed or a hold of his money. Or both. Another stupid girl trick that I'd never used before because I didn't play that game, so I thought I was being clever.

And then he looked up.

His eyes dead locked on mine.

They were a stunning hazel with flecks of gold around the center. The discontent and boredom slipped away in that moment, quickly replaced with curiosity, as though he had just been presented with a new, interesting puzzle to solve.

And my heart wouldn't stop racing. I almost forgot to let go of his butt after I'd dropped in the second wallet.

I forced myself to focus and planted a hand right on Mr. Coaltar's lapel. I wanted to draw attention up. I shook off my initial fear and tried to resume my charade. "Are you okay?" I asked, trying to soften my voice. If he thought I was there to flirt originally, I could at least play into his assumption to distract him.

Mr. Coaltar's eyes danced as he looked into mine, sparkling with interest. "Sorry, sugar, I didn't see you."

"It's fine," I said. "It was my fault."

His eyes slid down in slow motion, toward my chest. I arched my back, puffed my breasts out like a pigeon. I didn't know where Brandon was or how quickly he was walking away. I wanted to protect him.

Part of me was too curious to pull away and disappear. I could see why women were flocking to this man. I tried to resist, not wanting to admit to how attracted I was to him. I wasn't the type to create a fake interest in someone just because I knew he was wealthy, was I? Was that the only reason?

But Mr. Coaltar's eyes didn't stop their slow perusal of my body. He took a step back, getting the full view. It gave me a chance to look at him entirely, too. He was a head and a half taller than me, with broad shoulders under his dark suit coat, a white collared shirt underneath, and a silver tie with a red pin. His suit fit perfectly to his body, and it wasn't hard to imagine a sculpted body underneath.

"Oh no," he said, his voice had a deepness, but with a

curious Charleston accent - Southern refinement. "I reckon the fault was mine. I'm so sorry. Did I ruin your dress?"

"Oh, this thing? No. Don't worry about it." I waved carefully. Now that a minute had gone by, I wanted to make my exit. This was too close. "Now where did he..." I started to say, ready to pretend to find Brandon, the boyfriend.

"No, please, sugar. Don't run off," he said. His hand loosely cuffed around my wrist. "Let me at least apologize properly."

"You don't really have to."

"As your host, I insist." He bowed his head. "Forgive me. How can I make it up to you?"

"Host?" I asked, not meaning to ask the question. The formality just struck me off guard. Or he did. I felt he didn't want to release me at all.

"This is my party," he said. His lips cracked open into a sly smile. "Didn't you know whose house you were walking in to?"

I glanced from side to side, wishing I had known more about what we were doing, or who I was up against. Maybe Marc had told me when I wasn't paying attention. "Oh, yes," I said. "You're ... Mr. Coaltar."

"So you have heard of me?"

"Your name," I said. "My, uh, boyfriend brought me."

His eyebrow lifted again. "Who?"

"Brandon."

"Brandon who?"

My lips parted except I didn't know what his last name was, and I wasn't sure if I should lie. If I said the wrong name, and he didn't know him, would he think I was lying and throw me out?

Mr. Coaltar's smile broadened. "Is it too personal a question, sweetie?" His tone suggested maybe he knew I lied and I didn't have a boyfriend and he was hoping that was true.

Run away. Run away. Run away!

"No, I mean, it's not that," I said. I inched my body around, angling as if I had to go. "I should probably find him."

He released my wrist but stepped around to block me as I tried to escape. "Of course, if you did say his name, I probably won't remember. I hate to say it, but I'm hardly ever at home. Half the people here I can't remember their first name sometimes. I'm over in Europe way too long these days."

I glanced around, looking to see who he might have been talking to before now. The others had completely vanished. We were on the outer edge of the partygoers. How was I supposed to get away?

Something struck me about what he'd said. It wasn't what he was telling me, it was *how* he was saying it. There was a way he held himself, the deep tan that seemed to drop down below the collar of his shirt. "Did you say you go to Europe a lot? Is that for business?" I asked, trying to sound casual, but giving a question that I expected him to answer no to. This playboy? Would he laugh at the suggestion of work?

He tilted his head in a way that suggested he was surprised at the question. "I go when I can. The most recent trip lasted maybe a month, but felt like a lifetime. I don't like to think of it as just for business. Most of my research requires my being in different locations. If I have the choice, I try to at least go to pleasant places."

I squinted at him. Did the guys even talk to him? Maybe I could get out the information they really wanted. That would show them I could do more than steal a wallet. Not that I should need to impress them, but it was an amusing thought. I wanted to grin but smothered that instinct. "What sort of research?" I asked, pushing him to talk a little more.

He paused and his eyes narrowed, suspiciously dancing back and forth with mine again, searching for something. "Oh, you can't fool me. You don't want to know about that. Girls like you don't really want to talk about science. You just want to know how big my yacht is."

I swallowed back the urge to huff indignantly. "I like science."

He sliced his hand through the air. "Bless your heart for

entertaining the idea," he said dismissively.

"I was recently doing a study on bioluminescence," I lied. "About the chemical reaction within animals."

"Oh?" He perked up, his shoulders straightening. His eyes brightened with honest interest.

"My current one is on the reaction of Sea Sparkle as a defensive response." I faked a blush. "I mean, I know it's probably silly and unimportant research."

"If you really want to do some helpful studies, you should consider forensic research. I did something similar with chemiluminescence a couple years ago."

"Really?" I asked, widening my eyes for extra emphasis. Movement distracted me from the corner of my eye. Brandon stood a distance behind Mr. Coaltar and signaled, asking me if I needed help. I cut off his distractive motioning with a slight wave of my hand. Not that I wanted to jabber on, but I had a feeling. I refocused on Mr. Coaltar. "That's the chemical reaction, right? The stuff they put in glow sticks?"

He laughed, his lips puckering at the end. He tilted in, lowering his tone as if sharing in a secret with me. "Same idea, different research. The idea was to use it on bullets as a sort of tracking system so I could better calculate distance and location of the bullet at gunfire. Something better than the tracer rounds they've got these days."

"How would it be better?"

"I was the only one who could see where the bullet was going. My targets couldn't see them coming."

My heart started to thump. So he wasn't beyond doing research on weapons. But was that illegal? "Did you manage to get it to work?"

"It helped. Unfortunately the government heard about my research and kept sending people to interrupt. They offered me a contract to work with them, but they wanted to work with phosphorescence materials instead so I turned them down. Joke's on them. They'll never get the consistent chemical reaction needed for a bullet launch. It'll be too dull a glow for the human eye to follow. And they didn't really care about the research, they just wanted another advantage

127

on the battlefield." He waved a finger in the air. "Let that teach you what the world thinks about scientists. Their only interest in us is how to use our brains to hurt others. Or worse, make a profit off of our efforts without doing any of the heavy lifting."

I sucked in a sharp breath and caught the golden flecks in his eyes as he watched me with that same curious expression on his face. He didn't like the idea of working for our own government on their weapons. Even for profit? That didn't sound like a criminal. A legitimate contract with a lot of money, anyone would have jumped on, including me. Maybe he didn't need the money, but all the assumptions of him being a rich playboy started fading.

"But you're able to do your own projects now?" I asked, wanting to get him to talk more. "Things you'd like to do?" He shifted again, raising his hand to cut me off. I got the feeling he was going to tell me off and laugh about not wanting to talk more about science. I politely touched his forearm to stop the motion. "I don't mean to pry, of course, but I have to admit, marine biology research isn't exactly something the government is interested in issuing a contract for, you know? Not a lot of demand for research on Sea Sparkle."

"There might be. Depends on who you know," he said. He tilted his head to the side. "Where are you studying? You seem a little young to be a marine biologist."

"You seem a little young to be a forensic scientist, and one good enough to be offered contracts by the government."

He smirked. "*Touché*."

"Mr. Coaltar!" A middle-aged man with a wiry frame and a wide smile called out. He waved while walking up. "It's good to see you. I didn't know you were back from Italy."

"Couldn't play for too long," Mr. Coaltar said. He stuffed his hands into his front pockets. The move made me flinch, because I thought tightening his pants may make him feel the difference with the dummy wallet in his back pocket. If he felt it, though, he never indicated it. "I was just talking too ... I'm sorry. I don't know your name."

"Kate," I said.

The new man smiled shortly and with disinterest. "Pleasure."

Mr. Coaltar straightened his stance. "We were just talking about whether or not Kate should change her research focus from biology to forensics."

"Really?" The gentleman said in a bored tone. He turned his back in a way that effectively cut me off from Mr. Coaltar. "I don't mean to interrupt, of course, but I wanted you to meet my new wife."

I almost snarled until I realized he was giving me an out from talking to him. Did he think he was saving me? No, the back turn was deliberate. He either needed to talk with Mr. Coaltar himself, or he didn't like me. Did he think I was too poor to be here? A bumbling girl flirt? Not that I should have cared, but what an insult!

And then the man glanced back at me over his shoulder and his eyes were no longer friendly. They were cold, calculating, and inquisitive. That told me too much about him in a single look. He was an older man, I would have guessed at least late forties. New wife? Married quickly over the last few months? Clearly he wasn't exactly a best friend of Mr. Coaltar or he would have met the new wife before then. So the urgency to get Mr. Coaltar to meet her was a distraction. That meant business. Business that was urgent enough to interrupt Mr. Coaltar at a social event and have to talk to him in secret about. Who was he?

I scanned the locals, pinpointing a black shirt and sun-kissed hair. I almost ran smack into him in my hurry to get away.

"Finally," I said, touching him on the shoulder. "You might be wrong about Mr. Coaltar."

"Wrong about what?" He turned, and I found myself looking at Corey instead of Brandon. His blue eyes lit at seeing me.

"Oh," I said. "Where did—"

He put a finger to his own lips, his eyebrows going up.

"Oh. Yeah. Well, remember when *you* were telling me about your hunch about Mr. Coaltar?"

"Fill me in later," he said, his eyes darting over my head.

"Are we good?" I asked. "Is something wrong?"

"The one that walked away with Mr. Coaltar is watching you."

I resisted the urge to turn around. "Who is it? He walked up and basically cut me off."

"I don't know," he said, frowning. "It may be nothing, but we're going to have to stay here in view of everyone here for a while. If we run off anywhere, it'll look suspicious."

I sighed. It didn't matter. We were done here. "I'm tired of this party."

"We've got to stay until we can return the wallet. It's not the worst job I've had," he said. "The band is pretty good. I wonder if I could put in a request. I wonder if they know any of the theme music from The Lord of the Rings."

"Oh I loved those movies."

Corey brightened. "Really? Did you read the books?"

"The first one. Meant to pick up book two but ... I don't remember. I think I got busy."

Corey's lips parted and his head tilted. "You read?"

I choked on a laugh. "Is that surprising?"

He pushed his palm across his cheek. "I suppose it shouldn't be. You just don't seem like ... I mean you're ..." He smiled. "My brother doesn't read, you know? I mean he can, he just doesn't like to for fun."

"So you thought I was like your brother?" I smirked.

His cheeks tinted. "I thought you were more his type."

"You mean moody and antagonizing?"

He laughed, shaking his head. "I don't know. If I had to picture you in high school, there would be the jock and cheerleader tables and then there's my table."

"You think I'm a cheerleader? Or was one in school?"

"More like popular, yeah. Not now though. I guess. Unless you were. It was just that first glance, you know?" He grinned. "You were pretty. I mean you still are." He rubbed at the back of his neck, and darted his eyes as he tried to save himself. Adorable.

I harrumphed. "Yeah, well, I guess I'm as bad. I thought you were a nerdling."

"A what?"

"A cute geek," I said. " I mean you are still, and not in a bad way. I didn't realize you were athletic."

He blushed deeply, all the way up to his ears. "You thought I was cute?"

I smiled instead of answering him. The truth was, he was more than cute. His strong, wide shoulders and fit body stood out among the others around us. Dressed up, I thought he resembled a few country music stars I'd seen on billboards, with the down home look — in a hot way. His brother had the same look, obviously, Corey's was just much friendlier and open.

The corner of his mouth lifted high, revealing his even teeth in a lopsided smile. He combed his fingers through the shorter strands of the hair at the nape of his neck. "So you're into sports?"

"Not necessarily all the time." I shifted on my feet, daring him to meet my eyes. "But I like to get outdoors every once in a while."

He stared at me for a moment, as if he wanted to ask me another question, but was wondering how to put it together.

"Are we allowed to eat?" I asked, suddenly feeling a pang of hunger, and catching an eyeful of someone carrying a plate of food. I leaned around him, checking out the buffet table. "Please tell me we can have some."

Corey chuckled. "I suppose."

I grabbed his arm, dragging him along. He caught up, and while heading to the table, he gathered my hand, holding it.

It made me giddy inside for some reason. I felt like the hard part was over. I'd gotten away with replacing wallets. I did it once. All I had to do now was wait and replace it again and run away. I'd won. I deserved a snack.

The buffet was a mountain of finger food: fruit tarts and finger sandwiches, tiny chocolate cakes and some fresh homemade crackers. I think the crackers were for the caviar in the goblet bowls but even I had my limits. Too squishy a thing to want to put it in my mouth.

I piled a plate and made Corey hold one, too. At first I was trying to sample a bit of everything, except for the fish eggs, but I ended up with a third plate of what I liked best: the fruit tarts and tiny barbeque meatballs speared on frilly toothpicks.

"Why didn't you tell me you were hungry before we left?" Corey asked. "Didn't we just eat pizza? Did you not get enough?"

"Look at all this food," I said. I wasn't going to waste a moment when I could eat free rich people food. Now that I was somewhat satisfied, I scanned the other people at the party feeling completely different about it now. Most of the others were absorbed in each other. Their gazes flew from dress to tie, to who was sitting with who. Heads turned. Lips flapped. It was a lot like high school. "Is this what rich people do with their time?"

"Some of them still work," Corey said.

"Why?"

He shrugged. "What would you do if you had enough money not to worry about working? Would you throw parties?"

"Never thought that far ahead," I said. Never believed it would ever happen so didn't worry about that. Surviving pretty much took up all my time.

A pair of deeply sunken eyes caught my attention as I was scanning the people. It struck me, because usually people who caught my gaze were quick to look bored and glance away. He simply held my attention longer than most. It was a younger guy ... no, he dressed younger, with a polo shirt and tan slacks instead of a shirt and tie like everyone else. He was maybe late twenties. It was hard to determine. His face was stern and lean so he could have been thirty and just appeared younger. He broke his gaze, caught Corey standing next to me, and then seemed disinterested. His attention moved on, and I followed his line of sight to Mr. Coaltar, who had taken up a position closer to the band.

"Do you know who all these people are?" I asked Corey. "I mean if Mr. Coaltar was doing what you thought he was doing, could he be considering distributing with people at his parties?" My brain wanted to start working now. I wanted to figure out this new riddle, because their prior assumptions of Mr. Coaltar didn't fit with who I'd met.

"A contact for the wealthy?" he asked. "I want to say yes, because maybe it would be a simple answer. But the rich generally tend to be more careful than to work with petty street dealers. It's too easy to get caught, and they either mask a habit with a prescription, or they fly off to Amsterdam or anywhere that it's legal to do what they want." He took up the empty plate in my hands. "Did you want more?"

I smiled. I didn't think I could stuff myself with another bite, but his offer made my heart melt. I shook my head. "I'm going to end up with a gut," I said.

"You could use one," he said, holding out the plates for an attendant to take as he passed by. "You're a stick."

An arm cut through between us. I glanced up to find the man who had interrupted me with Mr. Coaltar earlier. He stared at me. "Pardon me for interrupting you again," he said. "You're Miss Kate, aren't you?"

It was my turn for my cheeks to heat up. "Oh ... yes."

"Mr. Coaltar has mentioned you did research. Biology, wasn't it?"

I nodded slowly, glancing only once at Corey. He didn't react like he was surprised to hear this, only curious about who this man was. I was, too. "I'm afraid Mr. Coaltar didn't introduce us."

"My name is Mr. Fitzgerald." He turned, nodding his head at Corey. "And you must be..." His question trailed off with a hint of expectation.

"Brandon Henshaw," Corey replied casually. He stuck out a hand in offering at Mr. Fitzgerald.

"Henshaw? Yes. I see. I hope you don't mind, Mr. Henshaw, but I wonder if I could steal Miss Kate from you for a moment. Mr. Coaltar was asking about her."

Corey's eyes widened. "Was he?" He glanced at me, keeping his eyes big, asking me silently if I was comfortable with this. "Would you like for me to join you?"

Yes! Did he find out about the wallet in his pocket being replaced? I thought if that were the case, Mr. Fitzgerald wouldn't be asking me to see Mr. Coaltar. It would be a policeman. "I'll be fine," I said, lying my lips off. "He was telling me about how he previously did chemical research. Forensics. Really interesting ideas."

Corey nodded. "I'll come find you later," he said. His eyes told me a different story. He'd stay back, but he'd be watching.

With Mr. Fitzgerald walking so close beside me as I turned, I couldn't look back at Corey and send him pleading looks that he come find me soon and maybe plan to hightail it.

Stealing wallets wasn't my original objective when I'd started picking pockets when I was in school. Instead, I lifted all sorts of objects. Most of it was for fun, and I'd usually put it back in or around someone's book bag after a successful pull. I wouldn't know what the object was before I lifted it and I'd take a guess at what I'd find just looking at the pockets. Sometimes I was spot on. Sometimes I was completely wrong. The challenge to me was trying to guess the item. That carried with me as I spent a lot of time observing people trying to find my next target when picking pockets for actual money. I wanted to make sure I lifted a wallet and not something useless. And I'd gotten very good at it.

What I was certain about as I glanced again at Mr. Fitzgerald was that he carried a holster underneath his sport coat. Probably common since it was the South, but this was a fancy party and I didn't think there were many civilized snobs that toted guns to a scene like this.

To me, it wasn't the biggest gun I'd seen. I guessed it to be a .38, or close to it. It made sense to have a small caliber at a social event, no need to go overboard.

The fact that he had it though, made me wonder again about his relationship to Mr. Coaltar. Was he a bodyguard? I hadn't exactly walked in the same circles as Mr. Coaltar by any means, but I didn't think many kept a bodyguard around just like that. Unless he was up to something dangerous and felt he needed protecting.

As Mr. Fitzgerald escorted me to Mr. Coaltar, I suddenly realized this could mean he had noticed the missing wallet.

♠

A JOB OFFER
IS A JOB OFFER

*M*r. Coaltar sat on one of the white folding chairs on the wide back porch that overlooked the partygoers in the yard. These had been placed on the porch under wide wicker ceiling fans casting a cool breeze on some of the more elderly people who had gathered there. Some held buffet plates. Others simply chatted.

More chairs surrounded Mr. Coaltar as he talked to a couple of other men. One chortled and the other nodded his head, amused.

As we approached, Mr. Coaltar looked up and directed his attention to me. "Oh good. You haven't left."

"Nope. Still here. Did you need something?"

"Yes, actually." He nodded to the two gentlemen and then excused himself. He stood, captured my elbow, and directed me to another group of chairs. "I was thinking." His eyes zeroed in on me, and then lowered again to my body and back up. "Were you serious about making a transition from biology research to a real science?"

Uh oh. "Well, it is a lot to consider. Very tempting but I'm not sure how and..."

"You see, your studies had me thinking about that project from a number of years ago. Your research might not be too far off of where I was going with it. You did mention Sea Sparkle, didn't you sweetie?"

"Right," I said. "The self defense mechanism when disturbed..."

"Causes those pretty lights under the water. Yes, I

know." He turned, and patted the chair. "Would you care to sit down? I don't mean to be rude."

"Ah well, my boyfriend—"

"Oh. Right. You mentioned him." He cocked an eyebrow. "Not going well though?"

My lips parted. "What?"

"Oh, Mr. Fitzgerald said he noticed your little spat earlier. Seems you resolved it but you were a bit upset."

I stuffed my hands behind my back to hide my fists clenching. He rattled off the comment as if it wasn't invasive. This was some rich tycoon I was talking to! And why was he interested in who my boyfriend was? "It was nothing, really. Mostly a misunderstanding of what he was saying."

He patted the chair again. "This will only be a moment. I have a job proposal for you."

"A job?" I couldn't help it as the words slipped out of my mouth. My mind raced with ideas of what he could mean. Was he serious? "Oh, I don't know," I said, absently sitting in the chair. "I have to admit, I wouldn't know where to start with such a project."

He turned toward me, his knee grazing mine though he seemed not to notice as he focused on my face. "Most of the research is already done. It's just in the testing phase."

I resisted the urge to flinch. He was considering me based on one accidental bump with him? "Were you reconsidering the government contract?"

"I've grown beyond government grants. They want to oversee the experiments, and are never satisfied with the results, plus they'll pay you the same rate as a college intern for all the work. Usually worse. It's a free world market. I can dabble in a few of my own ideas as long as I'm not killing anyone, right?"

Maybe the guys were wrong. Maybe he's just looking at commercial work. And he was offering me a job! He was offering *Kate* a job, and I had no real experience in science. I don't know why I was entertaining the idea. Probably because he said job and I'd been looking for one for so long. I wanted to see how much he was serious. "You mean you'd want me to test the brightness levels or something?"

"If you'd like."

That wasn't much to go on. Did he expect me to guess? "Is everything you do about weapons?" I asked. "About working with things that kill people?"

He cocked a smile. "Hardly. I'm more interested in solving puzzles rather making it easier for people to create new ones. And the occasional human equation is usually the most stimulating." His hand went out, and caught the strap on my dress that I hadn't noticed had slid off my shoulder. His fingers grazed my skin as he adjusted the strap back into place. His touch sent my heart into a dizzying spin. "Are you interested in hearing more? This is probably an inappropriate time, given that we're at a party. Perhaps we should talk more in depth later."

My breathing quickened and my heart raced. The golden flecks in his eyes were distracting. His touch and invitation were clouding my judgment. Temptation swept over me, intimidating and precise.

He was testing me, I knew. He wanted to see if I was willing to play his game. Something about him made me want to step up to this shrewd challenge he was putting across to me. I wanted to figure out how far he was going to take this. "Do you mean an interview?" I asked quietly, pretending to be naïve to his seduction.

His sly fox smile broadened. "If you'd like to call it that. Personally, I'm not fond of a hiring process that's so formal. I like working with people who I connect with, which is hard to do from across a desk."

I lowered my eyes prettily, hoping to appear modest. Not usually my style, but this game was fun, albeit dangerous. And maybe that was the exciting part. "I just feel a bit underqualified."

"We all start out underqualified, Miss Kate. I just have a good feeling about you." He rose from the chair, and stretched out a hand toward me. "I'll let you return to your date, but you should call me."

Cat and mouse. He was putting the ball in my court. It

was a coy move. That alone was something I didn't expect. I had believed he'd try to win me over tonight. Most guys wanted to get to the goal right away. I had imagined he'd try to corner me and even try to sweep me up to his bedroom. Instead, he was deepening the challenge by giving me a tease and then sending me on my way like a pet. If I wanted to play with him, I'd have to step it up and show him I was willing to play.

I put my hand in his to allow him to help me to stand and then my heart stopped. He said to call him. He'd give me his card. His card would be in his wallet.

His real wallet wasn't here.

"I'll do that," I said, grasping at his hand to still it before I could think about it. My other hand went up, grasping his second hand. It was very forward, but I needed to immobilize his hands and make him know I didn't need his card. "I'm sure Brandon has your number," I said.

The corner of Mr. Coaltar's mouth twitched up. "I believe so."

"Then I might call," I said, although I hoped I sounded as cool as he did. I turned from him, not daring to look back, but the whole way, I felt his eyes on me.

My heart was thudding against my ribs, telling me that despite what I wanted to believe, he may have won that round.

♠♠♠♠♠

The party after that point was mostly uneventful. The worst part was waiting for Brandon to return with the wallet and the keycard.

I consulted with Corey about my suspicions that Mr. Coaltar had a few bodyguards. He said not to say anything and pretend as if he didn't. If they were watching us that closely, he didn't want us making eye contact in an effort to figure out if this was true.

Corey and I held hands and made rounds through the party. We would stop beside another group, pretending to socialize with each other while blending in. We repeated conversations about the weather. Corey reeled off his opinion about restaurants I'd never been to, while I made occasional comments about how interesting they sounded and how I'd like to try them.

I thought it would never end until Corey squeezed my hand hard once to get my attention. "Ready for round two?" he asked.

"I'm ready to leave," I said.

He chuckled. "There's still half a buffet of food left."

"I don't suppose they give to-go boxes."

He squeezed my hand again. "Go stuff yourself with some last minute things. Be right back." He winked and shuffled off.

I was in the middle of trying to swallow the last of one too many fruit tarts when one of the boys angled up beside me. One glance up at his eyes confirmed it was Brandon. "Did you leave me one?" he asked, eying the buffet.

"You would not believe the day I've had. I think I'd rather pickpocket."

"Well here's your chance." He took my hand and casually drew it to his waist and then slid it down toward his butt.

"How'd it go?" I asked, feeling the outline of the wallet. I gazed around, looking for our target.

"I don't know. I didn't go in. Do you want me to hang onto this until we get close?"

I tapped gently at the wallet against his butt. "Actually, just hand it over. I have an idea," I said. I found a fancy folded napkin, and smoothed it out. "Do you have a pen?"

"What are you doing?"

"Job prospect," I said. "Maybe."

"Maybe? What's going on?"

I held a finger to my lips. I didn't want to talk about it now. I didn't really want to talk about it at all except I knew Corey would probably mention the second encounter. They would probably give me a lecture about lying to get a job. It was their fault I had to do it.

And I was totally lying to myself that this was any kind of job offer at all.

I wrote down the phone number of a voicemail box I'd established on the internet for whenever I applied for jobs. I couldn't resist this game. I started it, I suppose. Maybe it was masochistic of me to find enjoyment in flirting with danger in this way.

I blew out a puff of air. Dropping a wallet was bad enough to think about before. Now that I knew his bodyguards were on the lookout, I needed to get this just right.

I waited, watching Mr. Coaltar from a distance. He was chatting with a couple closer to where the band was playing. Mr. Fitzgerald was standing by, but he was keeping an eye on the younger man in the polo I had spotted earlier who was now leaning toward one of the girls of the party, feeling his way up to her breasts. I shook off that image and focused again on Mr. Coaltar. At least Mr. Fitzgerald had a distraction. I checked back on Brandon, who was standing by and watching. It would have been too awkward if he passed by again in the same routine. Once was excusable. Two times would have been noticeable. This time, I had to do my best to switch the wallets and have Brandon come save me and escort me away. The difference was, if I was caught with a fake wallet after the exchange, I could easily pass it off as Brandon's. Getting caught with Mr. Coaltar's wallet was what I had to worry about.

I repositioned myself until I was behind Mr. Fitzgerald and walking toward Mr. Coaltar's back. At the same time, I crossed in between people, nodding a polite hello on occasion as I passed – even if they weren't paying attention to me. I tried to appear as if I was heading somewhere specific, not actually for Mr. Coaltar.

I tried not to shake too much. It was the last thing I might ever have to do. Maybe once and for all, I could leave bad girl Kayli behind. I could be someone new. Maybe even Mr. Coaltar would hire me.

Or date me.

C. L. Stone

I forced myself to take slow breaths and angled my head to make sure Brandon was hanging back. I waited until Mr. Coaltar started to turn and adjust his stance, so it was him moving into me.

Bump.

In a fluid motion, I'd traded the wallets and held the second one behind my back. This time I made sure to do it quickly so I wouldn't be distracted. I avoided his eyes on purpose.

Through batting eyelashes, I focused on his tie. "Oh, sorry," I said, being completely dismissive. I even started walking off as if not really looking at who I'd bumped in to.

"Miss Kate," he said, not allowing me the luxury of simply walking away quickly. "When I said after the party, I meant..."

"Oh, no, I'm sorry," I said, pretending to just recognize him. However, one look at his eyes, and I knew he assumed I bumped into him on purpose. Time for plan B. "I was just leaving and wanted to say goodbye."

A smooth eyebrow cocked. "So soon?"

"I had ... um..." I had a lie ready, but thought feigning awkward pauses probably sounded more natural. I floated the napkin with my number in front of him. "I know you said to call you, but I thought..."

The corner of his mouth twitched up. He captured my wrist lightly and with his other hand, gently removed the napkin. "So I have talked you into it?"

"I'd like to learn about it before I commit," I said. I pressed the fake wallet with my palm at the back of my thigh. I didn't have to hide it now that I had the fake one back but didn't want to draw attention to it either.

His head turned, gazing around the crowd once before returning to my face. "Your boyfriend doesn't seem happy about that."

I flicked a look, sighting Brandon not too far. His arms were crossed, and his brows furrowed. I was supposed to be walking away by now. He wasn't happy.

"He probably thinks I should stick to sea creatures." Or

pickpocketing.

"I don't think that's the problem." Mr. Coaltar kept hold of my wrist, and switched his position until he was dead in front of me. He clutched my hand between his fingers. He brought it to his mouth. His lips grazed along my knuckles. Our eyes locked, and he focused on me as if no one else mattered. The same spark that lit up the gold flecks in his eyes flowed through his lips, against my skin and sent a flicker of warmth through me.

He was staking claim.

"I'll give you two something to fight about on the way home," he said.

A slow breath escaped my lips. That wasn't coy like before. I realized the move I'd made just now was really too forward. It probably made him feel like I was welcoming the chance to play this game with him. His response was an aggressive attack. Challenge accepted. A whirlwind of pleasure through me that I never wanted to admit to feeling.

I was about to answer him when I felt a hand on my shoulder. Brandon leaned into me, his fingers clutching my bare skin strongly. "Haven't you bothered Mr. Coaltar enough today, sugar?" he asked, his voice deeper than before. At the same time, his other hand collected the wallet, and he pulled it from me, freeing my hand.

Mr. Coaltar squeezed my hand once before finally releasing it. "No bother," he said coolly. His gaze locked on me. "Let me know when you'd like that interview. I'm at your disposal." His head inched forward in a nod, and the start of a smirk played on his lips. He turned, walking away. Mr. Fitzgerald met up with him and they headed into the house.

"What are you doing?" Brandon asked me through his teeth.

My heart trembled, not only from Mr. Coaltar's provocation but also for Brandon having spotted it. "I'll tell you in the car."

♠

BULLYING

We picked up Corey around the block. He was walking away from the party, wearing a sports coat and trying to look inconspicuous.

When we pulled up beside him, he hopped into the back seat, grinning. "We did it? No one noticed?"

"Oh he noticed," Brandon said. His hands twisted at the wheel as he drove, his knuckles whitening. "He noticed *her*. You didn't tell me they buddied up."

"She was being a distraction," Corey said. "She was handling it."

"What was that, Kayli?" Brandon glanced over at me.

I shrugged and slumped in my seat, kicking off my shoes. "He wanted to give me a job."

Silence filled the car. Corey tilted his head. "What?"

"He said he was interested in letting me help him with some chemical research project." I spent a few minutes quickly filling them in on all the conversations, skipping over the underlying flirting.

"Oh no," Brandon said. "You're not getting near that guy again."

I sat up, planting my hand on the dash to square off at him. "What do you mean? Is he doing the drug thing? Did you find out?"

"I don't care if he's doing drugs or planting bombs, running numbers or not doing *anything*. You're not working for him."

I huffed. "He offered me a job."

"He offered *Kate* a job. What's going to happen when he finds out you lied?"

"Kate could be short for Kayli. Besides, he said the job was easy and he'd train."

"He doesn't want to give you a job. He wants a piece of your ass."

I squinted at him. I was trying to leave that part out. But maybe he'd noticed when he talked to Mr. Coaltar himself. He did seem to bristle. "Is that a problem for you?"

His mouth fell open and his hands let go of the wheel for a moment. He reclaimed it and shook his head at the road. "I can't believe you're serious."

"You're the one yelling at me to do something other than stealing wallets. Now here's a good opportunity and you're suddenly against it."

"We'll get you a job."

I didn't really care about this fake job offer with Mr. Coaltar but it was irritating that Brandon thought he could tell me what to do. I wanted to push a few of his buttons and get him to back off. "There's one right here! You won't need to look. And if he's really looking for a date, well, he's single and smart."

Brandon nearly growled. "And rich?"

"And none of your business," I said. "What? Am I only supposed to go out with people in my social status? Sorry, call me a snob, but I'm just not attracted to hobos."

"Oh my god, you're such a fucking girl. You'll do anything to justify going out with someone who can buy you whatever you want."

I grunted, turned and punched him on the shoulder. "Take that back."

The car swerved and Brandon overcorrected, obviously not expecting the hit.

"Whoa, whoa," Corey's hand shot out and captured my wrist before I could hit Brandon again. "Hang on there. He's driving. Beat him up after we get back."

"You're on her side?" Brandon said.

"I'm not on her side. I just don't want to die." Corey released my wrist. "Sorry, Kaylie. I know I don't know you that well, and I don't really have a say in who you date, but this guy is on our watch list for a reason. If it were anyone else at that party, I wouldn't say anything. He's dangerous. You should stay away from him."

I grunted and folded my arms, sitting back against the seat. "I'm not a gold digger. And I don't think I could get a job with him, anyway, even if he was serious. He knew I was with you and he wanted to get you ticked off so you'd break up with me or whatever."

Brandon's eyebrows furrowed. "So you know he's trying to get into your pants."

"I shoved my boobs into him twice. Of course he wants in my pants. Do you think for one minute if I was serious about it, I'd even be here right now? No. I'd be back there at that party trying to hook up. I'm not that kind of girl. If I was, I wouldn't have to steal in the first place."

Brandon frowned. Corey bowed his head, staring at his shoes. I sunk into myself, staring out the window. I hated that part of what I'd just said was a lie. I had been intrigued. I'd always thought rich people were stupid, in a general sense. To me, they all just lived completely oblivious lives. Mr. Coaltar seemed different. Was he? Or was I just letting myself be tempted because he was rich? Was it because I always assumed someone like him would never be interested in me?

But he really wasn't interested in me. He didn't know me. He liked Kate. And Kate probably looked like she almost fit in. It was still a lie. Brandon was right.

Suddenly I couldn't wait to get home to Wil and go back to what we were; at least there I knew where I stood and what I had to do. This job was over. If they kept their promise or not, I needed to get away and figure out what I was going to do next.

I snuck a glance at Corey in the rearview mirror. He was already looking and caught my gaze. He smiled in that way that made the wall around my heart want to crash down. He understood. He wanted to know if we could be friends again.

And that did it for me. Despite being mad at Brandon, I realized maybe he was only looking out for me. I wanted to hang out with Corey again. He knew more about me and didn't cringe. Was this my chance to finally be around people who didn't care what I came from and still liked me?

A deep part of me hated the thought that this could be over. I wondered if they did this type of thing regularly. It was tempting to think maybe I could work with them again—I had to admit, it had been pretty exciting.

But after this party, would they want to keep me around?

♠♠♠♠♠

Back at the apartment building, Brandon led the way to the front lobby. I scanned the lot, but didn't know when the others would get back. I was tempted to tell them I'd go home and take a bus back simply to avoid the awkwardness. I wasn't sure if the busses were running this late, but I would have hitchhiked if I had to.

It was Corey that grabbed my hand, odd to me because we didn't need to pretend to be boyfriend and girlfriend any more. Did he forget? "Come on, Kayli," he said. "I want to show you something."

I relented, and he continued to hold on to me in the elevator. Brandon shuffled in, and pushed the number seven button with a thumb.

"Thought you would want to check out our two bedroom. I wasn't sure if you wanted to room with Wil in something like we've got. I didn't think you needed a three bedroom."

I laughed, shaking my head. "I can't afford a place like this."

"You could," Corey said. The doors opened to the seventh floor. He tugged at my hand. "This isn't exactly Mt. Pleasant. Or Isle of Palms, for that matter."

He said it like one little job could help me manage to pay for everything. I checked back with Brandon. He followed us with his hands stuffed into his pockets, his head down.

Corey released me to grab keys and open the door.

Inside, the set-up was similar, but a little backward. The

front had a living space, and there was a couch pushed up against the wall on the left and an entertainment center on the right. In the back was a small corner dining space, and a smaller kitchen. The dining space was set up with two desks, but this time, instead of having only a couple of computers, the desks were littered with a variety of them. Desktop computers were set up in a row, side by side, underneath the desks and pushed up around the wall. On top, there were several monitors, although there were only two chairs, so it appeared to be just two workstations.

There was a door just in front of the kitchen on the right. On the left, a small hallway, and the bathroom door was open with a matching bedroom door beside it.

Corey crossed the living room, heading to the door on the right. "Come see," he said. "there's a bathroom in here, too. So two bathrooms. You wouldn't need to share."

I crossed the living room while Brandon locked the door behind us.

The moment I entered Corey's bedroom, I got distracted. The walls themselves were bare ... but instead of the usual apartment white, they were covered in a gray surface. At first, I thought it was just a color until I noticed white markings from chalk.

My fingers traced over the surface. "How did you get chalkboards in here like this? Are they bolted to the walls?"

Corey paused on his way to the other side of the room, he stopped, studying what I was staring at. "Oh," he said. "It's just chalkboard paint."

I turned, the room was covered from ceiling to floor with the stuff. The smooth gray surface had occasional chalk dust smatterings across it. There were various trays of chalk and erasers positioned at about elbow height pinned to the walls. On top of the paint, there were mathematical formulas far more advanced than I'd seen. It wasn't algebra or geometry. It had to be some sort of advanced calculus or beyond that even. I tried following the formulas, but I couldn't keep up with where he was going with them. Some sections had tacked up aerial maps and charts. Mathematics based on area location?

"What is all this?" I asked.

Brandon grumbled. "Maybe you should take her out of here. She shouldn't see this."

Corey shrugged. "If she can figure it out, she's allowed to know." Corey ventured over to the far wall, where there was a door and shoved it open. I stepped up next to him, finding a tub, toilet and sink crammed together, a lot like at the hotel. "The other one is bigger," he said. "But it's pretty decent. And if Wil wants to stay on campus, they have a few single bedrooms, too."

"They don't have as good of a kitchen, though," Brandon said. He stood in Corey's doorway, leaning against the frame with his arms crossed. "I've seen those floor plans. You'd barely have enough room for a microwave and a mini-fridge."

"We could probably get her one of those camping stoves," Corey said. "Or if she's living here, she can come by and cook."

I smirked at the sink, sliding my fingers over the counter top. "I love how you guys assume I can cook," I said.

Their heads turned simultaneously toward me, eyebrows raised. "You don't?" they asked together, the same notes of disappointment working through.

"I thought you guys didn't want me hanging around after anyway," I said. I turned, crossing my arms under my breasts and leaning back against the sink.

"Why not?" Corey asked. "You need somewhere else to live besides that hotel. That place is a rip off."

I sighed. I didn't know the answer to this. I couldn't afford it now and I couldn't leave Wil yet. "Anyway." I tugged at the material of the dress. "Please tell me I can borrow clothes from one of you? I can't stand this anymore."

♣♣♣♣♣

Later, I was on my back on the couch in the living room, watching Corey play Assassin's Creed on the Xbox. I had on a Superman T-shirt that was Corey's, and a pair of old black boxer shorts that Corey had given me, but Brandon claimed were his. I had a pillow under my cheek and was zoned out staring at the screen while Corey played his game.

I nudged at Corey's leg with a forefinger. "There's a pack of wolves after you."

"I hear them coming," he said, making his video game character dash in circles, dodging and shooting. "Are you sure you don't want to play something with me?"

"I would, but I'm brain dead. All I want is to rest here before I go home and go to bed."

"Stay here if you want," Corey said. "We'll just have to go fetch you tomorrow anyway."

They wanted me here tomorrow? I didn't say anything for a bit, contemplating. Because of all the food I ate and now being done with the stressful job, I was really feeling run down. "Where are the other guys, anyway?"

"They had to make a stop," Brandon said. He walked over with an iPad, and patted my legs. I bent at the knee, and he sat down. I wedged my toes between his back and the couch to keep them toasty. He smirked at me. "What are you doing?"

"Warming my toes."

"By putting your cold ones on me?" He nudged my legs. "I'm not your heating pad. Go put some socks on if you're cold."

I pretended I was going to pull my feet back, and instead, dodged his arm, aiming for a bare spot of skin between his shirt and pants.

"Shit," he dropped the iPad onto his lap, and captured my ankle. "You keep ice in your feet or what? Stop that."

I smirked, drawing my feet in and pushing them at the couch back. "You guys have it freezing in here."

"It's either cold or way too hot," Corey said. "Want a blanket?"

"If I take a blanket, I'll fall asleep. The cold is the only thing keeping me up."

"Sleep here," he said, and there was a note to his tone

suggesting he'd prefer if I did.

I sighed, still not knowing what to do. Tempting, but what about Wil? Not that he couldn't fend for himself for just one night. And in the moment, probably because I was tired, I didn't want to leave. One night away from the hotel? In an actual apartment? I secretly reveled in the luxury I'd missed for so long. I was tempted to ask if Wil could come, but didn't want to make things awkward. And Wil, well, it was one night. "Can I use the phone?"

Brandon leaned forward, plucking his cell phone from his pocket. He plopped it onto the space of the couch in front of me. "No calling Romeo Coaltar."

"I don't even have his number," I said. I punched in the number for the hotel and then the extension to reach the right room.

The phone rang for a good bit before Jack answered. "What?"

"What are you doing there?" I asked. He was awake? And at the hotel?

"Kayli?"

"Yeah."

"Oh," he said. "Where are you? There's not a red penny anywhere in this place."

"Good," I said. "Where's Wil?"

"Don't tell me *good*."

"Where's Wil?"

"Where are you?"

He never listens! "Where's Wil?"

He grunted into the phone. "I don't know. He's off doing homework like he does all the time. He's probably downstairs at that computer. I keep telling him to tell me where he's going."

I didn't like not hearing from Wil and asking if it was okay if I stayed away one night. I knew the answer, though. He'd be okay with it, and probably would encourage it. He probably had a lot of questions as to why the rent was paid for a month. He'd want to meet the guys. I thought he might like Corey and Axel. He may not like Raven. "Tell him I'm working late. I got a new job."

"Where's this job?"

"Downtown. Just tell him it'll be overnight and to get to school. Don't wait up for me." At least if I lied through Jack, Wil wouldn't be able to tell I was lying. I didn't want Jack knowing the truth. I'd make it up to Wil later.

I hung up, tossing the phone back toward Brandon and hitting him in the thigh.

"Who was that?" Brandon asked. "Your dad?"

"Yeah, he stayed home. Ran out of beer money." I stretched, pushing my head against Corey and my legs against Brandon. "Where do I find a blanket?"

"I'll get one," Corey said. He dropped the controller, and started heading toward his bedroom. He stopped halfway and turned. "Or do you want to sleep in the bed? I'll sleep on the couch."

"I'll sleep on the couch," I said. I didn't really care. I just didn't want to get up.

At the same time, there was a knock at the door. Brandon hopped up, ran over and unlocked it.

Marc lead the way, followed by Axel and Raven. Brandon returned to where he had been sitting. Corey came back with a blanket and tossed it at me before he sat down, but he held the controller still instead of going back to play.

Marc spotted me on the couch and an eyebrow cocked. "What happened to you?"

I turned my head toward them. Long strands of hair fell across my eyes, and I tried to shove them back. "Is he a drug dealer or what?" I asked.

Raven plunked himself down in one of the rolling office chairs next to the computer desks. "Is that hope I'm detecting in your question, little thief?"

Brandon made a noise that sounded a lot like a growl. "If he's not a bad guy, she's hoping for a date."

Eyebrows lifted on faces around the room. Raven smirked. "In that case, yes. He's a dealer. And a rapist. And a murderer. He murders babies. Girl babies. And puppies. And he rapes them. After they're dead. Sometimes."

Axel popped him on the back side of the head as he headed into the kitchen. "Just stop talking." He headed toward the fridge, opening it. "Tell her, Marc."

Marc frowned, and he crouched down close to the couch. His hand drifted up, pushing back some of my hair from my forehead. "You about to pass out? You look like shit."

"Not that," Axel said. He fished out a bottle of water and opened it. "Tell her the other thing."

"We didn't find anything," Marc said.

I got up on my elbows, nearly bumping into him. "What?"

"He didn't have anything at his office."

"You mean he's clean?"

"I mean we didn't find anything. Not a paper. Not a computer. Nothing. It was a storage unit for empty boxes, a desk, and a couple of filing cabinets that were empty."

I held my breath. That ... wasn't right, was it? Did he have it emptied? Or was it always like that? If he purposefully showed up there before he went out to talk with drug dealers, it didn't make sense to stop by an empty office first. "A decoy?"

"Yeah." He settled back onto his heels, planting his palms on his thighs. "Looks like we bothered you for nothing."

"It's not nothing," I said. "Now you know he's hiding something worth hiding, right? What's the next step?"

Marc's face lifted. "Pardon?"

"Were you going to follow him around until he did something stupid or what?"

He smirked. "Well, Plan C was probably going to be to try—"

"Hang on," I said. I sat up, spinning around, leaning forward. "You mean this was Plan B?"

He laughed. "Yeah."

"What was Plan A?"

"Try to ask him what he was up to."

I felt my eye twitch. "Plan A was to ask him?"

"We sent Brandon in to get friendly with him. That's

how he got the invitation. Only he wasn't talking, so we went with trying to break into his office. But don't worry about it. We'll think of something else."

"There might be a problem,' Brandon said. He cocked his head my way. "Miss sticky fingers here got a little too close to him. He was trying to piss me off so I'd back off and he could get it on with her."

Marc frowned.

I hesitated, unsure how far I was willing to push these guys, or myself. In the end, I couldn't resist, though. "Maybe I should take the job he offered me."

"Nu uh," Brandon said.

"What job?" Axel asked.

"Mr. Coaltar wants to give her a job working in research with him," Corey said. "Although I think it was a ploy to getting her to agree to date him."

"He just wants in her pants," Brandon said. "He was coming on to her."

"Shit," Marc said. He yanked his fingers through the soft brown locks, brushing them away from his mismatched eyes. He breathed out slow. "This is bad."

"I can do it," I said. "I'll be able to keep an eye on him. I'll scope out his house."

"No."

"But..."

"Not now, Bambi. We'll worry about it later. Right now you need to sleep. We all do."

"I want to figure it out."

He waved me off, tucked his arms around my stomach, and stood, hoisting me over his shoulder. "Come on," he said.

"Ugh," I dangled precariously over his body. I pressed my hand against his butt to pick myself up so I wasn't just limp. I punched him in the back with my other hand. "Let go!"

"Marc," Brandon barked at him. "You can't do that to her."

"I'm just taking her to bed."

"Oh no, you're not!" I punched his butt and back again. I was disoriented and the blood was rushing to my head, but I aimed for where I thought the kidneys were. Weren't you supposed to hit people in the kidneys? I thought I read that somewhere.

"Stop, or I'll drop you." He shifted me higher on his arm and walked out the door.

He marched with me down the hall to his apartment. I punched at him the entire time, and tried calling out to the others to help me, but none of them budged. Their loyalties were clearly with Marc.

Marc didn't put me down until we were inside his apartment. He stopped on the carpet in the dining room between the desks and dropped me to the floor. I landed on my side in a heap.

"Ow!" I cried out. I jumped up, and threw a fist at his chest. "What was that for?"

He smirked. "I wasn't going to have you bullying my team."

"Who's bullying who?"

"You were sprawled out, taking up the entire couch and they had a little bit of space. I saw what was going on."

"I had moved over! And I was about to go to sleep. Corey even offered his bed. Why don't you ask them if I was bullying anyone?" Somehow I didn't think this was about the other boys at all. He just wanted to separate me from the others.

Marc had opened his mouth to say something when there was a knock at the door. Finally. Someone had come to their senses and came after me.

Marc's brows furrowed. He crossed back to the door, opening it. "Hey," he said. "Uh ... sorry. I don't really have time."

"Marc," a female voice said. "I want to talk to you. Just for a minute."

Oh god. Drama queen.

"I can't, really," he said. He wedged himself between the door and the frame. "I've got a lot of work to do and ... what

155

happened to your shirt?"

"This?" Sniffle. "Oh, nothing. It was just an accident."

"Was it?" he asked, though doubt dripped from his voice.

I groaned. He was going to give in. I didn't want to see him tortured, even if he was a bastard. I marched forward. Sure, it wasn't my business, but I was going to do him a favor.

I shoved the lower hem of my shirt up and through the inside of the collar, tying it off, as if I was trying to look sexy. I captured Marc's arm, yanking on him to back away from the door, and at the same time, swung the door open.

A thin girl, with blond hair and red patches on her cheeks, narrowed her eyes on me instantly. Her shirt was ripped along her side. At a second glance, I realized it was blatantly cut with a pair of scissors, I was sure. The lines were too smooth. There was a red mark along her exposed skin. Makeup. She didn't even have the decency to actually injure herself. "Who are you?" she asked in a highly strung out voice like I was completely unexpected.

"Sorry to interrupt," I said. I turned full on against Marc. "Sweetie, come on back to bed, won't you?" For a bonus, I leaned in, and planted my lips against his, intending to give him a small kiss.

His mouth opened in response. His teeth parted, deepening the kiss. His hand drifted up, catching my cheek, and he held my head, tilting his own.

My heart fluttered in ways I hadn't felt in a while, and so strongly that it scared me. I pulled back, trying to maintain my ruse and at the same time hide the sudden attraction I felt for him that had become overwhelming. I winked at him, ignored the girl and walked back into the apartment.

Marc froze against the wall, gazing back in at me. I couldn't see the girl, but I heard footsteps running away. This seemed to jar him from his daze. "Hey!" He called out down the hall.

"Don't encourage her," I said. "And you're welcome."

He slammed the door and turned on me. "What the hell did you just do?"

"I cured her from your pussyfooting and dragging this out."

His head reeled back. "What the hell are you talking about?"

I planted my hand on my hips. "That girl out there has an addiction. All girls get it hard the first couple of times. She cut her shirt and tried using makeup to look injured. I've seen that one before. She thought if you played the hero enough, you'd see something in her and fall in love, or at least guilt trip you into staying."

His hands dropped to his sides. "That was makeup?"

"Trust me. What she needs right now is someone to hate. It'll probably end up being me, but that's okay. Giving a girl a *let's be friends* line doesn't work. They feed on that. You have to cut them off sharply. Give them something to hate, and she'll be on to someone else in a week."

His hands roughed up the brown hair at the crown of his head. "You can't just do that kind of thing."

"She'll have a hard night tonight but give it a couple of days and—"

Marc launched himself at me. I only managed a half step back before his hands caught my cheeks holding me strongly between his palms. He lowered his head and his mouth met mine.

Instinct took over, and my mouth parted as he kissed me. His lips crushed against me, and he sucked at my lower lip once before diving in for another kiss. I nearly tripped as he pressed me back, but I planted my hands against his chest and leaned against him.

When my mind finally caught up to what I was doing, I found a little strength to break the kiss and step back. His hands released me and I found myself with my butt against the computer desk. I pressed the back of my hand to my mouth, unable to figure out what to say. I had kissed him to save him some trouble. What was his about? Some weird way of getting back at me?

Marc stared at me. His chest rose and fell harshly. I willed him to say something, but his eyes never wavered and

157

except for his breathing, he didn't move.

"Marc," I breathed a whisper. This was ludicrous. He didn't know me at all. I didn't know much about him, either. Why wasn't I yelling at him about it?

Why did I want him to do it again?

His mouth slowly closed and he swallowed. "If you want," he said, his voice deeper than normal. "You can sleep in my room. I'll take the couch."

After all that, all he wanted to talk about was where to sleep? "How big's your bed?"

He walked by me, so close that his arm brushed across my body. I curbed the urge to tug him back. I gave it up to being tired. I was just having a weak moment.

He led the way to the third bedroom door. He opened it and stepped aside, presenting it to me.

He had a double bed in his room. It wasn't quite as pressed up against the wall but it was close. There were two pillows stuffed up in the middle and the bed was unmade. There was a pile of clothes in the corner, and a dresser. A bookshelf was clustered with books and boxes and disheveled notebooks. It wasn't disgusting like I'd seen some boys' rooms. It was just cluttered like he didn't have enough room for everything.

I focused on the bed again. "Its wide enough," I said. "We're both adults. I think we can manage to keep our hands to ourselves. Unless you toss around in your sleep or something." I don't know why I offered. I guess even despite what just happened, I didn't want to sleep on the couch, and I felt too awkward to sleep on the bed knowing he'd be on the couch.

"Right," he said. He turned. "I'm going to go tell the guys something. Get in bed. I'll be back in a minute."

He left the room and I hovered for a moment, wondering what door I just opened.

♠

HOW TO ASK
A BOY FOR HELP

I was half asleep, curled up on my side in the middle of the bed before I felt Marc nudge me for more space. I flipped over onto my other side until I was facing the wall.

At first just the bed shook as Marc slid in next to me. A moment, or an eon later, he pushed his back up against mine.

"You cold?" he asked.

"Hmm?" I heard him, but I couldn't answer him as I was really too far asleep. I was cold though and responded by rolling toward his back.

"Yes? No?"

"Hmm."

"Gotcha." There was movement and I felt another blanket getting tossed on top of me.

I kept waking up during the night, forgetting where I was for a moment. Each time I did wake enough to recognize where I was, I panicked, and worried about Wil being alone. I worried about why I was there. I stressed over why I was in a bed with a near complete stranger.

For a time, I stared at the ceiling, afraid of what tomorrow would bring.

Sometime while it was still dark, I woke up in a half daze to hear Marc talking.

"What do you need?"

I mumbled.

"Not you," he said. He nudged my shoulder. "Go back to sleep."

I twisted onto my back. At first, all I saw was him sitting up, his phone pressed to his ear.

And then I noticed he was shirtless. There were shadows across his back that were uneven in the dim light. I thought it strange, until I realized I was looking at scars. In my sleepy state, I stretched out a hand, feeling one with my fingertips.

"Yeah," he said into the phone. He twisted at the same time, capturing my wrist and holding it in a firm grip. He gazed at me and frowned. "Yeah. I'll be right there." He hung up the phone.

I wanted to ask him where he was going, but in my tired state, I only managed to mumble something incoherent, as I stared at him with my muddled questions through half closed eyes.

He sighed, leaning over and planting a soft kiss on my brow. "This is why I'm going to end up old and alone."

"Hm?"

"Nevermind." He got up, fished a T-shirt from out of the dresser and headed to the door.

I turned over, unsure what he was up to. Too tired and out of it to follow. Did he just kiss me on the forehead?

I heard a distinct knock from down the hall.

"Raven," Marc called. "Go stay with Kayli. Don't let her run off or anything."

I gave a tired, indignant snort and rolled over, facing the wall.

Another minute-eon later, and the bed shook again.

I yanked the blanket, stuffing it over my head. "How does anyone sleep here?" I asked.

"Hey," Raven said. He tugged at the blanket. "Get your own apartment if you don't like ours."

I kicked backward, finding his shin. His foot knocked back into my ankle in response.

"Stop," he said. "Trying to sleep."

I grunted and turned, lifting both feet until I was pressing my frozen toes into his bare back. He jerked forward, capturing an ankle.

"As cold as your heart," he said.

I stilled, and expected him to let go. I was going to turn over again and go to sleep. Raven, instead, held on to my feet, cupping them with his hands.

"What are you doing?"

"Have to warm those toes, little thief."

♠♠♠♠♠

In the morning, when the light was filtering in through the window, I flipped over, finding Raven sprawled out on his back, snoring. His shirt was off. Since he was sleeping, I was able to study the tattoos on his arms that extended on his chest. Along his chest were some Russian words I didn't understand, and on his stomach were three Russian-style towers, with what looked like upside-down dome tops. There was a rose with barbed wire twisted around it along the inside of one of his arms.

I stared at the details as I drifted in thought. It was hard to shake off the feeling that I had to get up and go. It felt like every minute I spent standing still, I was losing the little bit of headway the guys had provided for me. Did I really not have to pick pockets anymore? Would I get a job? The tingle of my life changing made me feel so alive. Different, too.

Maybe the truth was I never thought I'd stop stealing. I didn't have much hope for myself. And what sort of job could I do? I'd done odd jobs all my life. They were asking me what I wanted to do. I hadn't thought this far. I was always trying to get by, let alone get ahead.

I absently traced the line of one of the barbed wires, checking out the detail. Raven's hand made a sweep, and he slapped my fingers away from his arm. "Stop." He turned over onto his side, exposing his back to me.

His back was covered with the face of a grizzly bear with his mouth open in fierce snarl. The eyes were wide, harsh.

I grunted, planted my two feet on his back and shoved.

The sheets were cotton and smoothed out tight, leaving almost no friction. Raven slid off the edge of the bed, landing on the floor in a heap. He growled, and sat up. "*Pidorás!*"

161

I didn't need a translator to guess that he was cursing in Russian. I rolled over until I was taking up the rest of the bed, spread eagle on my stomach. I stuffed my face against the pillow, trying to hide my smirk. For having woken up several times, I did sleep better than I had in a long time. I was awake now, and ready to play.

He shoved the heel of his foot at my hip. "Scoot over."

I tilted my head away from him so I could talk to the wall. "No."

He climbed up until he was on top of me. He sat on my butt, and started dropping his full weight threatening to squish. "Crazy woman. Move."

I tried knocking my heels into his back but he didn't budge. "Go away."

"I'm supposed to stay here."

"I'm not four years old. I don't need a babysitter."

He lifted himself but still hovered and dropped a hard hand against my butt. "Marc said to not let you out of sight. This Coaltar fuck's already called for you."

I jerked up, but my movement was limited since he was on top of me. I tried shoving him off, and he rolled over onto his side next to me.

"He called?"

"Don't sound so excited."

I couldn't help it. My heart was pounding like I was a girl with her first crush. I wasn't sure if I really liked him. He was hot, yeah. A night of sleep had mangled my feelings up until I wasn't sure what I had felt at the party. I think at some point I presumed he was just toying with me and wouldn't think of me again. "How do you know he called?"

"He called Brandon's cell phone looking for you last night. I think it was on purpose to piss him off." He rolled onto his back, folding his arms under his head like a pillow. "He's a shithead, so you're going to stay here with us for a bit."

"For how long?" Not that I minded a few more hours or even another day. It'd been a long time since I felt I could take a day off. "I mean I need to get to work if I'm going to

162

be able to afford rent. And I need to call Wil."

"You can't call Wil," he said. "You're in hiding."

Somehow what he said didn't register with me at all. It didn't make sense. "What?"

"Coaltar has a big reach. You don't know. You need to go underground."

I got up on my knees, leaning over him a little. "What do you mean? How long is this for?"

He shrugged. "Could be a week. Could be a month."

"A month!"

"You're the one that got too close." He got up, swinging himself around until he was sitting cross-legged on the bed. It was the first time I noticed the sweatpants he had on. I guess I was too distracted by the tattoos before. "You need to stay with us."

"Like hell I do." I got up, crawling to the edge of the bed and put a foot down on the carpet.

Raven reached out, grabbing at a wrist. "Hang on, little thief."

"Let go," I said. I swung around, catching him in the arm with a fist. "I want to talk to Marc. Where is he?"

"He's not here." He tugged at my wrist, strong enough to get me to kneel on the bed again.

"You mean he's following Coaltar?"

"Maybe."

I grunted. "How am I supposed to yell at him if he's gone?"

"You can talk to Axel. I'll take you to him if you stop hitting me."

I pouted, and swung a fake punch with my free hand at his knee.

He caught that wrist, drawing my hands together, and held tight. "Now what are you gonna do?" he asked.

I wriggled to try to slip my hand out of his grip, but he clutched me with one hand easily. I shoved a foot at his arm, trying to pry him off.

He leapt on me, shoving his free arm around my waist until he could scoop me up and tackle me to the bed. He sat on my hips again, pinning my wrists to the pillow. His broad nose lowered until he hovered over my face. His deep brown eyes bore into me. "I don't understand you. Are you trying to tell me you don't want to talk to Axel? Is that why you're fighting with me?"

"I'm just ticked off. I don't know what I want to do." It was true. I had no idea what to think. Would yelling at Marc do any good? Axel was the boss, but if he had disagreed, he wouldn't have let Raven hold me hostage here, would he? I didn't want to believe Coaltar was a bad guy, but what did I know? They were some super spy team and I just walked in on this yesterday.

"So you start beating me up? Christ, I'm going to start calling you little demon."

I twisted and squirmed underneath him. Why was I fighting him? My heart was pounding. Raven's muscled, tattooed shoulders and attitude set something off inside me. I would never admit it in a million years, but I wanted to pummel him for making me feel like I wanted to kiss the tar out of him. "Get off of me. I'll tell Axel."

"I told you, he's not here." His eyes lowered, tracing my face around my cheek and down to my lips. His eyes shifted, as if something caught his attention, and his gaze settled on my shoulder. The big T-shirt I was wearing slid off my shoulder, revealing my skin. He poked with his free hand at a sore spot. "Looks like I left a bruise."

I twisted my head, trying to see what he was seeing and couldn't. "I get those all the time."

"No shit. Do you do this with all your boyfriends?"

I snorted. "What boyfriends?"

He released my wrists, sitting back. "Don't give me that, like you've never had one."

"I'm not saying I've never had one. You just said it like I've got a pocketful right now and all over the place."

"So Marc was right? You're single?"

I huffed, indignant. "As if I'd let you sit on top of me if I did have one. I'm not that kind of girl." I planted a palm on his stomach, shoving. "Get off of me."

He climbed off, and landed on the floor. He sat on the carpet, cross-legged, leaning with his elbows on his knees. He twisted his upper half, inspecting his arms. He poked at a spot. "Shit, you're leaving a few on me, too."

I found where he was pointing. A splotchy purple mess could be seen between the tattoo pigments. "We're rough."

"Yeah," he said. "Do I need to go easier on you?"

"No," I said quickly. "A few bruises never bothered me." I didn't want to say so, but after a while, I understood that I tended to bruise pretty easily. I telling him would make him feel like he had to go easier on me. I didn't want that. Wrestling with guys was a lot of fun.

He smirked. "I might have been wrong. Maybe other boys couldn't handle you – not like this. Not like I can."

I sputtered and then snorted.

"All right," he said. "First thing today, we need to get you settled."

I couldn't believe this was happening. Settled? I needed to get out of here. "No, first thing we need to do is find Wil."

"Kayli."

"Raven." I got on my knees on the bed. "He needs to know or he'll come looking for me. If what you're saying is true, if this guy is so terrible, help me warn him."

His lips twisted, the hole where his lip ring had been removed for the night flexed. His dark eyes squinted at me, like he wasn't sure how to do this.

"Please," I begged, in a softer tone. I thought about the day before and what I did to Corey. I hoped that worked on Raven. I stumbled off the bed, tentatively moved as if to crawl into his lap. I was ready to jump in case he was going to push me or hit me.

He sat up, and then back to lean on his hands, opening himself up but unwilling to pull me in. I was fine with that. I was the one begging. I crawled into his lap, planting a knee on either side of his thighs as I faced him, I slipped my arms around his neck, and then felt an odd thrill as his bare chest was pressed up against my T-shirt covered breasts.

"Raven," I pleaded, pressing my cheek to his. "Help me

165

get word to him. Anything. I'll stay here if you want me to. I can do it. Just help me make sure."

A wide hand dropped to the nape of my neck, cupping, warming. "You'll stay here with me?" he asked in a low, gruff whisper.

"Please," I breathed, trying to be nice. I had been rough with him for no reason but now I was being serious. Wil needed to know I was fine. I needed to make sure he wasn't looking for me, that he was safe and Jack wasn't treating him too badly.

His thumb massaged a spot behind my ear in a slow motion as if trying to make a decision. Moments passed with me pressed against his body. His thumb pressed harder, making my head tilt toward it and for the moment, I forgot I was asking. His fingers were strangely relaxing.

Suddenly, he pushed me away from him until I spilled out on the floor. He stood up, and marched to the door.

"Raven?"

He paused just in the hallway, his fists clenched. "Get dressed, little thief." He turned partially, facing the wall, but it was enough for me to see the lightning firing off in his eyes. "I'm going to do this. And when we get back, you're not going to worry about your brother, and you're not going to worry about this Coaltar. That party is the last time he'll get anywhere near you." He turned again and punched at his door to open it wider. It swung in, hitting the wall hard enough to feel like it shook the apartment.

I stilled on the carpet, my heart trembling in my chest. What on earth did I just do?

♠

THE FIERCE BEAR

I wore my old shorts and a borrowed-without-asking shirt from Marc's closet. Raven dressed in jeans and wore a black T-shirt that only partially covered his tattooed arms. He'd put the lip ring back in. He directed me to a black truck in the parking lot.

"I thought this was Marc's?"

He grunted. "I'm borrowing it."

He had a key? I shrugged it off. They shared an apartment and shared cars. For friends, I guessed that was just their thing. Most of the guys I'd known in high school wouldn't do that, but most guys were jerks anyway.

We were on the road for only ten minutes when traffic slowed us down. Raven cursed at the other drivers through the windshield. I slumped in my seat.

"Where are we going?" I asked. I mean I knew the general plan, but didn't have a clue what his intentions were.

"I'm going to find your brother and let him know you're safe."

My mouth fell open at his suggestion. One look at his hulking figure and tattoos and I had a sudden vision of how well that would go down.

He side glanced me. "What?"

"Oh, nothing. It's just you look like you're part of the Russian mafia and if you walk up to him and say 'she's safe', you're going to make him think you're holding me for hostage money."

He grunted. "What am I supposed to do? Send him flowers? Butter him up?"

"Can't I talk to him?"

"It's best if you're not seen together right now. If anyone comes asking for you, he can honestly say he hasn't seen you for a while. You should be back at the apartment but you need to stay near me."

I breathed in deep and exhaled slowly. South Carolina dampness and car exhaust filled my lungs. I coughed. It was mid-morning, so the traffic made no sense. Why wasn't everyone at work by now? "What if I left a note?"

"Where?"

"At the hotel. I could leave a note in the room."

"You shouldn't go near the hotel."

"Why?"

"Same reason. No one to say they've seen you recently."

"How would he know if I lived there?" I grumbled. They were making a lot of assumptions about this guy and what he could do. Coaltar met me yesterday. What did he know about me? Did he stalk every girl at his party? "What if I wrote a note and you took it to the room?"

He thumped his fingers over the steering wheel. "You can't tell him where you are."

"What can I say?"

He shrugged. "Tell him you've eloped with a handsome Russian." He leaned on the door, angling to see around the row of cars. He pounded at his horn but despite the effort, the line didn't move.

I snorted. "Me? Get married? I may as well tell him I sprouted wings."

He leaned forward, digging his cell phone out of his pocket. "Tell him now. We won't have to bother him later when we get around to it."

I thought he was joking so I shook it off. "Where's a pen?"

He gestured to the glove compartment while he was still buried in his phone. I found a small notebook and a couple of pens, along with binoculars, and a pocket knife. Spy stuff. I wanted to dig further but wanted to get the note out of the way so I closed it up.

I was just telling Wil in the note that I was fine when

Raven shifted gears and started cutting off to the right, driving along the shoulder. Part of the truck ended up in the grass. I gripped the suicide handle to keep from knocking my head into things. "What are you doing?"

"Going around," he said. "This goes on for miles. Out past Summerville."

"Why?" I asked. "Bad wreck?"

"Yeah, bad wreck," he said. "The police fucked up. There's a threat at one of the schools that called in the bomb squad. The responding officers cut off some people driving on the highway and there's a ten car pileup down there."

"Which school has the bomb threat?"

"I don't know," he said.

I shrugged. "Happened a lot at my old school," I said. "There's never a bomb. It's just a stupid kid calling it in to get out of class. Which was nice. Usually stalled things at school for a few hours."

"Probably lucky," he said. "In Russia, they wouldn't have called anything off. You fend for yourself. And the kid wouldn't be bluffing. He probably wouldn't have even called ahead." He pulled the truck onto an off-ramp, weaving his way around other cars also trying to get off the road. He cut in front of an old lady in a clunker and made a left onto a main road.

My heart thundered in my chest as he drove. He muscled his way between two cars to cross the street. "Did you learn to drive in Russia, too?" I asked.

"What does it matter?"

"Just wondering."

♠♠♠♠♠

It took another half hour to get to the hotel going through side streets. By then I was grumpy from not having eaten breakfast. I did my best to bite my lip and keep quiet. Now that I didn't have a dime on me, I couldn't afford a meal and didn't want to beg.

As soon as we were within sight of the hotel, Raven

lifted the center console and reached for my arm. He gripped it in his big hand tight enough to cut off the circulation for a moment, tugging me sideways. "Lay your head down," he said. "I don't want anyone seeing you."

I did as he said, but as my head landed by his hip, he put his hand on my hair. His fingers threaded through my hair and he massaged my scalp.

I slapped him on the wrist hard enough that my own hand tingled. "Stop," I said.

"What?"

"I'm not a puppy."

He grunted. "Will you just stay in the truck? I'll deal with you in a minute. Where's your note?"

I held it out to him, and dug out my room key card. "221B. And do me a favor and grab the gray book bag. I may as well get my clothes."

He waved me off, parked the truck and stepped out. He pointed a broad finger at me. "Stay." He slammed the door before I could remind him I wasn't a puppy.

I sighed, moving onto my back to stare up at the ceiling of the truck. So close. I wondered how Wil was doing. I told him in the note that I'd be gone at a new job that required me to be there overnight. I explained that was how I got the money for the hotel room. I told him we'd probably miss each other as I was only off while he was at school. I wondered if he could tell I was lying simply by writing. At least it would seem like I'd been there.

I missed him already and hoped Jack wasn't giving him too many problems. I hoped he wouldn't do anything stupid. I rolled over onto my side, tracing the grooves of the seat with my fingertips. Was I making the right choice to stick with the guys? Or was I giving in because I was curious about them?

A knock at the truck window made me think Raven was back. Maybe he forgot the room number. I sat up.

A man's gnarled face was pressed to the passenger side window. He squinted in at me. "You okay?" he asked.

One of the random residents. Was he walking by to get to one of the other trucks parked in the lot? I tried to hold back an eye roll. So much for not being seen. I nodded, waving him off and hoping he'd go away.

He made a motion to roll down the window. "Hey, let me talk to you for a second." There was a weary look in his eyes. I'd seen it before on these guys. Lonely and willing to risk a rape charge to get his dick in any hole he could find. Possibly mentally insane.

I mustered an angry glare and flashed my middle finger. "Go away."

He seemed oblivious to this. His hand slid down in front of his body, and from the angle, I could tell he was rubbing himself. "Open the door. I won't hurt you. Did you need a room?"

I started shaking my head when his hand shifted again. I thought he was going to pull down his pants, maybe step back and show me his wilted willy. Instead, he reached for the door handle.

I realized in horror that Raven hadn't locked the door. I lunged for it, but he already had the door handle open. I grabbed for the handle, yanking back hard, but he drew back his fingers before I had the chance to smash them in the door.

A booming shout erupted: "*Morgaly vikalyu, padla! Ebanatyi pidaraz*!"

I didn't know a lick of Russian, but I knew angry cursing when I heard it.

A fist smashed against the man's chin. There was a thick thud sound. The old man fell like a lump to the blacktop.

Raven positioned himself between the truck door and the guy on the ground. "Get up, motherfucker." He waved his fist at him. His shoulders appeared to have increased in size. The muscles in his bicep strained against the fabric of his T-shirt. The tribal and rose tattoos danced across his skin as he flexed.

In a moment of weakness, I thought about that morning with him shirtless and on top of me. And now he was defending me from bad guys. I felt the pull of visceral excitement as Raven defended my honor. The wild, crazed look in his eyes, the ruthless way he glared, the powerful stance like he was about to rip the guy in two, it was overwhelmingly erotic.

The old guy wriggled on his back, cowering, caging his arms over his head in defense. When it was clear he wasn't getting up, Raven spat at him and opened the passenger side door.

"Why'd you let him open the door?" he thundered at me.

He was going to blame this on me? Way to burst my fantasy bubble. "I didn't let him! You forgot to lock it."

He grunted, backed up and smashed the door back into place. He picked up two book bags off the ground. He jogged around, opening the driver's side door and shoved them in the back seat. He hauled himself in and we were back on the road in minutes.

I looked back. The man had rolled into sitting up, holding his head. At least he wasn't dead.

♠♠♠♠♠

Raven started taking city roads back into Charleston. I glared out the window, wondering if anyone had seen us or if someone was calling the cops because of the fight in the parking lot.

Once we were a good distance away, and there were no sirens, I sat back, glancing over at Raven. He flexed his right hand over and over on the steering wheel.

"Is your hand okay?" I asked, trying to sound softer. He did save me, after all.

His brows furrowed, he drove with his left hand, holding out his right. He flexed it in front of me. There were a few dry cuts and some redness but nothing looked out of place. "Nothing broken," he said in a low tone.

I stretched out, taking it between my palms. His arm muscles tensed. I wasn't sure if I was hurting him or if he thought I was going to hit him.

I pressed my lips to the back of his hand quietly and kissed at his knuckle. "Thank you," I said, hoping I sounded as sincere as I felt.

His brow lifted. "For what?"

"For helping me with Wil. And for beating up that jerk." I meant it. Despite me having given him such a rough time, he went out of his way to help me do what I needed to do. I wanted him to know I appreciated it. Not a lot of people would do that, not for someone like me.

He took his hand back, and for a moment I thought he was going to tell me off.

His fingers cupped my face, the thumb sliding across my cheekbone. Slowly. The edge of his thumbnail traced against my skin, causing a gentle shiver along my spine. He gazed at me, longer than he should have kept his eyes off the road. He didn't say anything, just stared.

I swallowed, uncomfortable. I tried to come up with something to break the tension. "Are we going back to the apartment?" I asked.

"Did you still want to talk to Axel?" he asked. He took his hand back and looked at the road again. "I should relieve him, anyway."

"Where is he?"

"At the gun range."

"Did he take all those guns and bullets you prepped yesterday?"

"Yeah. October is good weather for training. Not overly hot."

Part of me wanted to start hunting for a job and hurry along. I still didn't feel like I deserved time off. What else could I do? "Will you let me shoot a gun?"

He smirked, and the car sped up as his foot dropped on the gas pedal. "If there's any bullets left."

♠

INSIDE THE ACADEMY

*O*n our way to the range, I dug through the two book bags, thankful that Raven managed to grab the two that were mine. I guessed Jack wasn't there or was asleep. Leaving the note would have to do for now until I could think up some other way of letting Wil know I was okay.

I was kind of embarrassed about Raven seeing the place. Would he notice I had to sleep in the same bed as Wil? Since he didn't say anything, I tried not to let it bother me.

I dug out a pair of jean cutoff shorts, a better fitting T-shirt, and a pair of clean underwear and a bra. I'd been wearing the ones I had on a little too long. I shoved my hands through the sleeves of Marc's shirt and started undoing my bra underneath.

Raven slid glances at me. "What are you doing?"

"Changing. Keep your eyes on the road."

He turned his head, staring straight ahead. One of the cool things about being a girl is you learn early on how to change your clothes completely in public without revealing anything. I managed to weave the bra out from a sleeve without removing the shirt, and put another one on. I slipped off the old shorts, and the underwear, slipped new underwear and shorts on without revealing much other than my thighs. After that, I felt pretty covered so I just removed the shirt. I put the other one on and smoothed the T-shirt over my body. It had a slight V-neck to it and fit better around the waist. Boy shirts were cool, but mostly for lounging around the house.

Raven grumbled. "Why are you doing that here? There's

people watching."

"There's only you watching and no one else cares. And you should be paying attention to the road."

"This is why that guy back there was hanging on your door. You can't even sit in a truck without causing problems."

"You can drop me off back at the hotel. Seriously. Any time you want to get rid of me. Or drop me off here. I can walk."

He glared out the windshield. "Are you hungry?"

"Starving."

Raven paid for four Big Macs, two large fries, a Coke and a milkshake, of which I ate one and a half Big Macs, one of the large fries and some stolen from his box until he smacked my forearm to ward me off, and the milkshake. He ate the other half of the second hamburger before I got to it.

By the time my brain pulled itself together after eating, we were on a country road. Even for October, the envelope of greenery surrounded us, making it feel more like an alleyway inside a forest. It was a quiet back road, only one car passed us maybe every couple of miles.

"Where are we?" I asked.

"We're getting close."

Around the next turn, a white wood sign came into view. It had faded black lettering: SCPO Shooting Range, Closed to the Public Today.

"They're closed," I said.

"It's closed because there's training."

"What's the letters?" I asked, but after a moment when he didn't answer, I started guessing. "Is that South Carolina Police Officer or something like that? Is that what the initials stand for?"

"Yeah."

"So you do work for the police?"

"No."

"How are you using their gun range when it's closed to the public?"

"We're friendly with the police, but they don't know

who we are." He turned onto the gravel road. "I'd appreciate it if you don't tell them."

"Would you get in trouble?"

"I'd get in trouble and I'd take you down with me."

Oh boy.

Despite being with Raven, it made me nervous to be crossing into any territory that was considered police property. The gravel road continued for about a mile and then shifted to the left another quarter mile. He drove up to an open gate. Hanging wide open. Anyone could walk in if they'd found the road. I didn't see any security monitoring the entrance. I guessed they didn't figure they needed to really keep anyone out. No one would be stupid enough to invade a police shooting range.

The property was surrounded by barbed wire fence. The whole area might have been two acres, surrounded by trees. I supposed that's how they kept it safe, a great distance of trees made sure they wouldn't accidentally shoot anyone.

There was a blue building with a white roof planted in the middle of the property. Behind it was a brick wall, about head height. There was a gray shed nearby, and from the gravel parking lot, there was a row of short distance ranges, about twelve in a row, near the blue building. A long hill of dirt ran down the far side of the range, and this was covered in carpets against the slopes. An additional bullet barrier?

I jumped out the moment Raven parked. I was about to comment that it was quiet when a smattering of gunfire filled the air. I snapped my head around, spotting a row of guys each taking up a space at the short distance rage. I could only see their backs, but they had their arms up, aiming different pistols at targets hanging in front of the carpets on the back of the range. Targets were held up on wood poles. Each of the guys shooting wore blue ear protection. They focused, shooting the target, the bullets zinging through the paper and into the carpet pieces.

Raven marched forward, motioning for me to follow. We swayed to the left, toward the blue building. There was a covered concrete porch in the front, with picnic tables set up underneath the awning. The white doors to the building were closed, but there was a wide window to the right and there was a light on somewhere inside. From my angle, I couldn't see anything inside the window, just part of the corner from an inside wall. I didn't know if anyone was inside.

Raven sat down at one of the picnic benches that was closest to the boys, leaning back on his elbows so his chest puffed out. I dropped down next to him. We were still a short distance from the gun shooting, but I tensed at the sound of gunfire and wondered if I should worry about my ears.

Now that we were closer to the boys, I could see they were younger, maybe around fourteen.

I leaned into Raven's shoulder with my own. "Are these ... uh ... the people I'm not supposed to talk about? Are they your..."

"Yeah," he said. He leaned back into me, but stretched his arm around until he was resting on the table behind me and pointed with his other hand. "Today, they're getting a feel of different models of guns, from twenty two calibers up to forty five. After this, they'll have an idea of the difference. How they look. How they feel. The sound differences."

"They're young," I said. "Is this necessary?"

"Have to know what the bad guys know," he said. "Hopefully more."

We watched for a while. It took a minute for me to spot Axel, who was on the far side, standing and studying the boys vigilantly. He wore black jeans and boots and an olive short sleeve button up shirt. Part of his collarbone peeked out from the open buttons of the collar. A lock of his black hair framed the side of his face and teased his chin. He was wearing those dark-framed glasses again. With his high cheekbones, and intense stare, he was the quiet strength amid what otherwise felt like chaos to me.

He seemed to sense me staring and turned his attention to me. When magazines were emptied this round, he shouted. "Okay, boys, Raven's going to take over."

"That's my clue," Raven said. He stood up and stretched.

"You mean cue? That's your cue?"

"Clue, cue, cute. It's a word." He dropped a hand on my head, massaging my scalp. "Stay here, little thief."

I swatted his hand away. I was tempted to go hide somewhere when his back was turned just to tick him off.

Axel met him halfway, they exchanged a few words and then continued on, trading places. Raven took up position where Axel had been. He barked some order I didn't understand, and the kids started to open up their guns, checking to make sure they were empty, before passing off the gun, open, to the next person. There was a stack of ammunition in front of each of them. They selected the right one for that particular gun, reloaded, and waited. Raven found another ear protection headset and put it on.

I flinched again when they started firing. Axel directed himself at me. For a moment, my insides quaked as I realized he intended to talk to me. My heart raced and I wasn't sure why. Was I worried he'd pry into my past some more? Or was it his sense of calm composure when I felt anything but calm? Wasn't I supposed to yell at him? Isn't that what Raven brought me here for?

He turned his back on the teenagers and the gunfire as if to show me he was only paying attention to me right now. "So you're still here after all."

"You mean I surrendered to my kidnapping? Yeah, I guess I was a little tired this morning."

His eyes sparked with something that was almost humor but it disappeared quickly. He curled his fingers at me. "Come on," he said. "Raven said you wanted to shoot."

I jumped up, glancing back once at Raven but he was steady, paying attention to the boys.

Axel threaded an arm around my shoulders, drawing me away. "You probably shouldn't watch," he said.

"Why not?"

"You'll make them nervous," he said.

"Huh?"

"Distracted. They're not ready for that yet." He aimed me toward a red Jeep Cherokee parked in the lot.

"How many people are in the Academy?" I asked. "I

mean, how many spies do you have running around Charleston, poking their noses in other people's business?"

"Not as many as you think," he said. He released me and opened the back of the Cherokee. He pulled out a couple of long gun cases. "This is actually a training ground for our group."

"You mean this place? The gun range?"

"I mean Charleston in general." He passed off one of the cases to me so he could close the Jeep up.

"What do you mean by training ground?"

He started toward the large cinder block wall behind the blue building. He did it without directing me at all that I should join him, but I followed anyway. "Not all of us are from here," he said. "We recruit from all over the globe. Some grew up here, just because it is easier to recruit local to home base, but often enough, if you become an Academy recruit from somewhere else, you'll get transplanted to Charleston for training."

All of Charleston? My home? They used it like some crazy military base for an underground police force? I'd been here all my life and I'd never heard of such a thing. "Why here?"

"Because it isn't New York City, and it isn't Tiny-Town in the middle of nowhere. Charleston is relatively safe, but with its own problems. It gives us a home to work from. It's still big enough that we don't stand out, and we can blend in with everyone else and be that forgettable face in the crowd. We also have situations we can handle, that we can ask trainees to handle."

"You train them in a smaller town to be able to handle themselves outside of it later? Like what Marc was doing at the mall?"

"Unusual cases are one of the things we do."

"So you're in training?"

There was a flicker of amusement in his tone. "No. I graduated a while ago."

"But you stayed here in training camp?"

"We're here right now," he said. "Our team liked

179

Charleston, so we chose to make this home, but we could have moved anywhere. We help with training recruits, and help out in the local area where needed, usually on bigger assignments some of the kids can't handle. Sometimes we get sent out, and travel. It depends on what we feel like doing, but the guys like getting out of the country every now and again."

"How far does this go?" I asked. The idea that the Academy had a global stretch was intriguing. "I mean, okay say you go through training. You do your time and then you want to wander off on your own to Europe..."

He shook his head. "No, not that."

"No Europe?"

"I mean no going off on your own," he said. He turned the corner around the block wall. The other side contained two long rifle ranges. The ranges were really just marked off by the edge of the wall, and lines painted in white, like lines on a baseball field. A lopsided table was parked in the grass in front of the ranges. At the far end was another mound of dirt covered in carpets. There were wood poles set up for holding up targets. "You can't take assignments alone," he said. "You have to have a team."

"Why a team?"

"Working solo is not what we're about. It would defeat the purpose."

"What is the purpose?"

He planted the gun case on the table, hanging on to it as the table jiggled until he was sure it wouldn't slide off. He bent a little, opening the case to reveal a long rifle. His jet-black hair traced along his chin and fell in front of his face. It was startlingly exquisite. "Did you want to shoot or did you want to ask me questions?"

I planted the second case near his on the table. "Both."

"Then ask me questions about guns." He held up the one he had taken out of the case. "Have you done this before?"

"No." I really wanted to ask him more about the Academy, but he made it seem easy to talk about it, like I could ask him later. I was sure I would. Wasn't this supposed to be a secret? How was he able to talk about it so openly? Unless it really wasn't that secret. Just their jobs were confidential. It was confusing.

He rubbed the stock of the gun as if to show me it was harmless. "This is a 303 British." He opened it up, revealing an empty chamber. "It's a top loading rifle. You drop the cartridge in from up here." He demonstrated without a cartridge. "When you're ready to shoot, you have to flip this." He pointed to the safety. "And then pull here to load." He did the motion without actually pulling. "There's a scope on this one, too. You aim and fire. You have to reload a new bullet into the chamber every time you want to take a shot."

"So not an automatic?"

"No. Reload every time. This way if you fuck up, you've only hit someone with one and not the entire magazine." He passed the gun off to me.

"Wow, confidence booster there." I held it with both hands, holding the stock and the barrel, flipping it over in my hands to look at it. "You're not going to load it for me?"

"You fire it, you load it." He grabbed a couple of rounds of ammo and pointed to the grass range. "Let's try it over here."

My heart thundered against my ribs. Watching the guys was one thing. I wanted to shoot, but my nerves were getting to me about it. I guess I expected a longer lecture or for him to show me how before he let me hold one.

Axel stopped at the end of the range and motioned to the ground. "Come on," he said. "Get down."

"Huh?"

"I think it'll be easier if you drop to the ground and fire this. At least your first time." He took the gun from me, exchanged it for the cartridges of bullets, and sunk to the ground. He sprawled on his stomach, and then motioned for me to join him.

I sidled up next to him, laying on my stomach, feeling the grass on my legs. It kind of shocked me. When was the last time I sprawled out on the grass? I propped myself up on my elbows to watch.

He pushed the stock to his shoulder, and aimed downrange. "When you're like this, you won't get it so hard in the shoulder. You need to lock it into your shoulder, and this way you just naturally do it." He passed the gun back to me. I had to drop the cartridges to take it.

"How do I load?" I asked, unsure.

He showed me how to load the cartridge again, and walked me through positioning the gun. I held myself up on my elbows while aiming downrange.

Axel stayed shoulder to shoulder with me until he thought I was ready to start shooting. He went back to the gun cases, pulling out two pairs of ear protection. He passed one to me and then put some on his own head. Then he got on his knees to make some distance.

"What do I shoot at?" I asked.

"Try to hit those poles out there," he said.

I made a face. They were tiny targets. I guess he was saying it didn't matter, my first time shooting, he wasn't going to have me hit a target.

I lowered my head, using the scope, and sized up the pole. The scope was actually pretty neat. I'd have to depend on the accuracy.

I breathed out slow, lining up my sight again, and keeping the scope lined to what I thought was a good spot on the thin wood pole.

"Lock it into your shoulder," he said.

I jabbed it into my shoulder again, retargeting. I wasn't sure how tight I needed it to be. It felt good enough.

"Take your time." The tone indicated I was taking a while.

"I do have a loaded gun," I said, hoping my tone said shut up or I would aim at him.

"Never let intimidation hold you back," he said in that smoky voice.

I relocked the 303 to my shoulder. I yanked to load up a bullet, and aimed again using the scope, keeping an eye on the target.

I pulled back on the trigger. The gun fired.

The scope cracked against my forehead between my eyebrows. Pain radiated instantly. I put the gun aside, rubbing the spot. It was like banging your head into the corner of a cabinet.

"What's wrong?"

"The scope is stupid."

"You were scoped." He patted my thigh. "Leave the gun for a second."

I touched my forehead between my brows, wondering if I was bleeding. It didn't feel like it but I wasn't sure. I got up on my knees, feeling the heat running through me at messing up my first shooting experience. Thank goodness there was a wall and Raven didn't see.

Axel crouched next to me and held my chin in his fingers. He brushed aside my hair from my cheek. When I still didn't remove my hand, he curled his fingers around my wrist. "Let go."

I didn't want him to see, but he tugged and I relented. He scanned my forehead, his fingers touching the spot. When his fingers got too close, I yanked my head away. "Ow."

"Just a fender bender," he said. "You'll have a good bump for a while though."

"Oh great," I said. "Do I need ice?"

"Did you want to stop?"

I blushed; I didn't want to. If I stopped after one shot, I was worried the guys would call me a wimp. Plus, shooting wasn't that bad. It was actually kind of fun, since I wasn't shooting a person or at risk of getting shot at. I could see doing something like this on days off in the future. Without getting hit in the head. "It doesn't hurt too bad." It was partially true. It stung, but I could live with it. "Did I hit the pole?"

Axel looked out, squinting at the wood pole. He dropped down, picked up the rifle, and used the scope to check. "Fucking shit. You nailed it."

My heart leapt. I dropped down next to him. "I want to see." He passed the gun over, and I checked in the scope. Sure enough, there was a hole that split the wood, slightly to the left. "Was I not supposed to hit it?"

He clapped me on the back of the shoulder. "You're either a natural or you're damn lucky. Go ahead and empty the magazine."

This time I avoided the scope, and locked the gun into my shoulder better. I aimed at the back dirt pile, simply trying to hit a singular carpet. Dust clouds rose at every place I hit as bullets zipped into the carpets, and I managed to land them relatively close to each other.

After I fired every bullet, I felt a rush. Excitement surged through me to be holding something so powerful. It wasn't that I wanted to hurt anyone with it. I just liked the control and the risk.

"When you're finished, you pull the magazine out," he said, showing me. He also taught me how to make sure the barrel was empty, to check the cartridge.

He brought out another gun, a stage coach rifle, this one I only had to pull back once and after the first shot, it would reload and be ready for the next pull of the trigger. There wasn't a scope on this one, so I aimed with the barrel sight, trying to hit the pole again. I got it twice more. The pole tilted forward and to the left after so many hits and needed to be replaced.

Axel roughed his fingers through his black hair. "Even with a different gun, you're still hitting your targets."

"I kind of like it," I said.

"Maybe I shouldn't have shown you this. I don't want you shooting people."

I huffed and was about tell him I'd only shoot idiots, but stopped short when a cool black eyebrow lifted on his face. His look stilled me until there wasn't any fight left in me. It was fear of disappointing him if I even joked about this topic. Did I really worry that much about what he thought of me? I swallowed to shake off the feeling. "I won't shoot anyone," I said.

"Good." He got up on his knees. "Let me check that bump on your forehead."

I sighed, getting up. That was going to be a pain to

explain to the others.

He cupped my head in his hands again, his gaze focused on my brow. "It's puffy."

"Can I tell the guys you beat me up?"

"Did you want me to die today? You hate me that much?"

I must have had a temporary brain melt down or something. I forgot how Southern guys usually took hitting girls very seriously. Normally, if a guy hit a girl around here within sight of another guy, he could expect a beating. Once, I saw a guy kick a girl at school, and a swarm of guys swooped in on him. I don't recall seeing him at school ever again. Probably the only reason Raven got away with it with me in front of the others was because I fought back and you could tell he wasn't hitting as hard as he could. I was pretty much asking for it every time and it was fun. Probably because most *Southern gentlemen* wouldn't ever dream of it. "I don't want them knowing what really happened."

"Happens to everyone the first time. Suck it up." His palms warmed my cheeks and he pressed them until my lips made a fish face. "If you can't laugh at yourself, you've got no sense of humor."

"That doesn't make any sense," I said through my squished lips.

He released me with a slight shove that knocked me back a half step. "Help me clean up."

I helped by putting the 303 back into the case and collecting the empty magazines and the casings he could find. I worked beside him in silence for a while, trying to figure out if I would get a headache later from the welt on my forehead.

"So," he said. "You told Coaltar you were a biology researcher?"

I slowed in strapping the gun into place in the case. "Uh ... maybe?"

He had his head bowed, focusing on the gun. "Was any of that real interest, or were you just trying to talk to him?"

"Why do you ask?"

He shrugged, snapping the gun case shut. "It made me wonder why you talk about Wil going to college, but you never mention it for yourself."

I snorted. "Me? At college?"

"Why not?" He picked up the gun case, carrying it under his arm. He motioned to the wall, back toward the parking lot and started heading that direction. "You're pretty smart. You could take the SATs and probably start at a community college for basic classes."

I shrugged, carrying the gun case and walking beside him. "I don't know what I want."

"You seemed interested in the glowing fish."

"I'm interested in a lot of things. I just never really thought about what I wanted before. It was just always what I could get so I could scrape by."

We got to the Cherokee and he opened the back. We dropped the gun cases inside. He closed the back again and leaned against it. "If you had to pick something, what would you go for?"

I shifted from foot to foot. The truth was, a lot of things did interest me, like biology and other sciences, and now even shooting guns. It was impossible to pick. "Why do I have to pick one?"

His dark eyes sparkled with amusement. Was he pleased with this answer? "Pick two."

"I don't want to pick," I said. "I don't want to ..." I didn't know how to express it.

"Get locked down into one thing?"

I bit my lip to try to stop the heat on my cheeks. I didn't want to say yes, but couldn't deny that was how I felt. It was why I'd resisted the idea of college a long time ago and simply never tried at all in school. You had to pick just one type of study that ended up costing a lot of money in student loans and you had to stick with it. Why? I folded my arms over my stomach and leaned against the back of the Jeep. "How did you get into biology?"

"Kind of by accident," he said. "When I went into the Academy, they encourage you to explore and do what

186

interests you."

"I thought you were trying to say it was an espionage group. So it is like a school? Like a college?"

"It is more than you think," he said. "As far as your interests, they offer whatever they can so you can pursue your own talents. Their classes aren't exactly normal. For example, if you were interested in working with zoo animals, they'd find a place for you at the zoo with hands on training. If you want biology, they stick you in a biology lab."

"Wouldn't you have to take classes at the university? Get a degree first?"

"No."

My eyebrow lifted. "How can they just throw you in a lab?"

"You'll get any training you need, but you may get the short course. Your curiosity determines how much you study," he said. He pointed to the gray wall, indicating to the rifle range behind it. "You were interested in guns, right? I gave you a handful of instructions and you figured it out on your own without much push. Then suddenly you wanted to know how the next gun worked, and then next time you may ask me how to piece the thing together. You may go home and read up on it. Maybe you take your own class. I don't have to give you homework. I don't have to tell you there's a test. You'll learn if you're really interested. The Academy just has the resources to help put you where you want to be."

The underlying premise of the Academy seemed daunting. They'd teach you anything you wanted to know? "What if you don't know what you want to learn?"

He shrugged. "They'll pair you up with people who are driven by what they do, until you figure out what you want. Maybe you want to be a biologist. Maybe you want to fix cars and learn carpentry. Maybe you just like studying in general and want to learn everything. Whatever you want to know, they'll help you find the answers."

"How does this help them with the whole spy thing?"

He ran his fingers through his hair, pulling it away from his face and those glasses. A couple of locks fell back against his chin, defiant. "Your interests make you unique, and more of an expert than anyone else. When you're doing what you really want, you'll work harder to obtain it. With just the right push, the right support, you'll be unstoppable. It takes a very special type of person to fit in with the Academy. You're either naturally drawn to it, or you push back and resist and never know what you've missed."

"It sounds crazy."

"Crazy works sometimes."

I stared at him, wondering if he was just joking with me and didn't mean anything. "Why did you want to know if I wanted to go to college? It sounds like you've never been. Why did you ask me about biology?"

His eyes fixed on me as if quietly asking if I really wanted to know or if I was challenging him. He leaned an arm above me against the back of the Cherokee, and bent his head close to mine. "You're rather unique yourself. To be honest, I didn't see you as a college girl."

My heart started rattling in my chest. His demeanor made me feel like he shouldn't be this close to me. He was calmness. I was too wild. "You don't exactly look like the biologist type," I said.

"I don't?" he asked, though his tone made me feel like this wasn't a surprise to him. "It's the hair, isn't it?"

"More like the walking around the apartment naked thing."

He looked down at the ground without moving away. "Yeah, sorry about that. It was a late night the night before. I didn't know you were in the apartment yet. When I heard your voice, I thought you were that damn ex-girlfriend of Marc's. Thought I could scare her off."

"Did you sleep naked? Late night with a girlfriend?"

He shook his head, looking back up at me. "A late night watching over a shitty little hotel, for a girl that managed to slip by my team."

My mouth fell open. "What?"

"We knew where you were, and didn't want you to run off. So I watched for most of the night."

I kind of knew it before but it was a surprise to hear it from Axel. "You guys were stalking me?"

"You were stealing wallets."

I grunted.

He snatched my chin between his fingers and redirected my rolling eyes to focus on his face. "But you aren't going to do that anymore, because you promised, and I take promises very seriously."

Those dark eyes bore into me. My lips moved with whatever retort I wanted to tell him, but my words stalled and disappeared. His eyes told me to obey and I was afraid to think of the consequences if I ever betrayed him. I knew he'd come after me.

He released my chin, and ran the back of his knuckles over the crest of my cheek. My heart thundered at the touch. Was this his way of flirting or was he just trying to keep my attention? "And I want you to stop, because to me, you don't seem like the normal college or regular old job type. Outside of the stealing, you sound like an Academy girl."

My eyebrow rose. "Is that why you're telling me all this? Are you trying to recruit me?"

The corner of his mouth lifted. "Do you want to be recruited?"

Before I could answer him, there was the sound of footsteps on the gravel. He pulled away from me.

The squad of boys went to a couple of different cars, and started getting in. Some of the older looking ones got behind the wheels and started up engines. As they passed us, they waved at Axel, and followed up by waving at me. They didn't ask who I was. I guess maybe they assumed I was another Academy person if I was here talking to Axel. I wondered how much they knew that I didn't.

Axel motioned to where Raven was placing guns inside cases.

"How'd it go?" Raven asked without looking up. Before I could answer, his eyes settled on my brow. "You let her get scoped?" he asked, smirking. He knew exactly what happened and didn't have to be told.

189

I grumbled, irritated, and opted to join Axel for a silent ride back to downtown Charleston.

♠

A SUSPECT'S FRIEND
IS A LEAD

*B*ack at the Sergeant Jasper, I followed Axel inside. Raven caught up with us at the elevator.

In the hallway on the seventh floor, Axel stopped mid-step, picked out his phone and held it to his ear. I didn't hear it go off. Vibrate?

"Yeah?" he said, his tone suddenly serious. He frowned. "On our way." He punched the phone off and then pointed it at Raven. "We've got to go."

Raven mimicked Axel's dour expression and turned down the hall without question.

"Wait," I said. My heart was thundering at the sudden shift of their expressions and behavior. "What's going on? What happened?"

"Stay here," Raven barked at me.

They returned to the elevator. Both turned at the same time, facing me, shoulder to shoulder. Something was wrong. I could feel it. "Go find Corey," Axel said to me, more of a command than a request. "He should be in his apartment. Stay with him."

The elevator doors closed and they were gone.

The upheaval from a moment ago settled on me. What was that all about? Some type of emergency? Did it have to do with this Coaltar? Or something else?

I wasn't going to get answers standing in the hallway, so I tried to remember which door was Corey's and knocked.

Corey answered, his eyebrows lifting in surprise at seeing me. "Hi," he said. He was barefoot, and wearing a white ribbed tank shirt and a pair of long black shorts with a yellow Batman signal on the left knee. The tank shirt really showed off his broad shoulders and the lean muscle in his arms. It also clung to his stomach so I could count his abs.

"Oh man, those are awesome shorts," I said.

His lips quirked up, but his eyebrows were still cocked as if he expected me to tell him why I was there.

"Raven and Axel just ran out," I said. "They got a call."

"Oh," his eyes widened, and his hand darted to his back pocket. He pulled his phone out, turning it on and scanning the screen. "Uh ... okay. Sure. Yeah, come on in," he said. He backed up a step. "I mean, not that you can't come over when you want. I just ... sorry."

"I don't need a babysitter," I said. "If you want me to, I can just walk around downtown or..."

"No, you should stay," he said. He closed the door behind me and grabbed my hand. "When you were standing there, you looked worried, like I should come with you somewhere else. Come on."

I wanted to argue with him or even ask him more about this emergency and what he knew, but I let it go. Probably because his face was so lit up, like he was truly happy I showed up at his door.

He led the way to his room. I paused inside the doorway, glancing at the mathematical formulas written across the walls. Some had been erased and redone since the last time I'd been there. One wall was erased completely clean. "What was on this one?"

Corey glanced at it briefly just to see what I was pointing at. "A mistake," he said. "What were you doing today?" he asked, and I sensed he was trying to distract me from the board .

I shrugged. "I shot a gun today."

"Is that why there's a scope mark on your forehead?"

I reached up, touching the tender spot between my brows. "Is it bad?"

He grinned. "It's not bad, but it's a bit red. Does it hurt?"

"Only when I touch it."

He captured my wrist and drew it away. His eyes softened but still held an amused glint. "Then don't touch it."

I smiled, unable to help the sweeping warmth running through me from his look of amused concern and his friendly touch. Being with him felt amazingly comforting. I didn't feel as embarrassed as I did with Raven. Corey reminded me of my more memorable boyfriends back in high school.

Surprisingly similar. Did I like him?

His smile lit up his blue eyes. He squeezed my wrist gently. "What do you want to do now? Want to play a game?"

"I feel lazy," I said. "I haven't had a day off in forever."

"A day off from work or a day off from stealing wallets."

I grimaced. "Maybe both."

Corey guided me with a light hand at the small of my back toward the bed. The bed itself was pushed up against the corner, but above it were erased chalk marks against the chalkboard paint and I wondered if he woke up in the middle of the night to make notes. He eased me down until I was sitting on the bed. He relaxed on his side, his head propped in his hand as he looked up at me. The way he did it bulged his bicep. The view sent a warm shimmer through me, reminding me how completely sexy a nerdling he really was.

It felt weird to be sitting, so I wriggled down until I was on my side next to him. Suddenly, my heart was fluttering as I realized he managed to get me lying next to him in his bed. Near him, I felt tiny. His wide shoulders were overpowering. The way the white tank shirt clung to his skin revealed lines in his abs. Part of his skin peeked out between his shorts and his shirt at his hip and I was dying to move it a little to see more. How did he do that to me? One little smile, one sweet move to get me to be more relaxed, and suddenly I was way too comfortable, more than I probably should have been since I only met him yesterday.

"What's it like?" he asked quietly.

"What's what like?"

"Stealing wallets. What's it like to do that every day?"

"It sucks." I breathed out a huge sigh. "You're always

freaked out that you're going to get caught. You stress over every police siren like they're coming for you. You worry you're stealing someone's rent money."

"Is that why you only ever took a little bit? Not all of it?"

"Yeah," I said. "Which meant I had to take more wallets, which meant more time stalking people. I'd go look for a job for an hour and then need to go haunt different locations to get enough for rent."

Corey grinned, revealing those white teeth in a lopsided sideways smile. "I guess it probably feels weird not to have to worry about it anymore."

I squinted at him. "What do you mean not worry about it?"

"We'd said we'd help."

"Yeah, but I still need a job."

He shrugged. "Where do you want to work?"

"You guys keep asking me that. Axel was asking. But Marc said I can't get a job right now because of Coaltar."

"So take a few days off until we figure it out."

"Raven said it could take a month."

"You don't even know where you want to work Take a month off. Sounds like you could use it.." He reached out with his foot, knocking his ankle into mine.

He was flirting! I couldn't believe I was so excited about it; my heart was pounding. I wasn't usually the sort to stand back and let someone else flirt with me, playing the coy girl, but with him, I fell right where he wanted me. It was like having my first crush all over again. I grinned, knocking my ankle back into his, but his foot was bigger so I barely nudged it. "It's just all kind of crazy. I can't believe you guys caught me."

"You weren't that difficult to find, actually."

I sat up. "How did you? And why? Why not let the police handle it?"

Corey shrugged. "When we were told there was a pickpocket leaving wallets behind, we got curious. Most thieves don't. It was just kind of interesting."

"So you sent out Kevin with the jacket as a decoy?"

"We didn't start out with that," he said. "At first we had to figure out how you operated. We figured you'd look for easy targets in the beginning. We tried an old lady with an open purse but you never went for her."

My breath caught. Forget the flirting. This guy had been hunting for me for a while and I never knew? "That's how Dr. Roberts knew?"

He scratched lightly at his temple. "See, most criminals work in a similar pattern. Once they get used to a method of getting what they want, they fall into a routine going after easy targets or at least targets they are used to. Imagine our surprise when we figured out that a thief not only puts wallets back, but only takes wallets from grown guys who could defend themselves if they wanted." He tilted his head at me. "Probably would have caught you sooner if I'd known you were a girl. I could have worked that into the equation somehow."

I flipped over and looked at the wall where there were still slivers of lines, ghostly numbers and letters left on the board. More mathematical equations. "You used math to find me?"

"Yeah, but I was missing some data." He reached over top of me to a basket of chalk tacked to the corner. He picked up a piece and started writing letters and numbers in an equation. He wrote with his arm stretched over me, but focused on what he was doing.

I tried to follow, but his bicep passed so close to my face, the warmth of it radiating toward me. My fingers itched to feel the smoothness of his muscles.

"This," he said, finishing and then pointing at the formula, "is how they catch people like serial killers."

I scanned the wall, scratching a fingernail across my eyebrow. "I'm the same equation as a serial killer?"

Corey smiled, shaking his head. "No. Math can do a lot, predict the weather or calculate political movements. But getting math to compute the randomness of humans, that's usually very hard to piece together. Occasionally it can work. It's called geographic profiling." He patted the dust off his fingers, crossed his arms and leaned back against the bed. "You were an anomaly."

"But you caught me," I said.

"We may not have if it wasn't for Marc paying attention. We were looking for a guy, perhaps a kid that was showing off." His eyes studied me. "We found someone we weren't looking for. The math was right. The assumptions we drew from the data we had were wrong. I'd have to develop another formula to calculate better."

"So what's my formula?" I asked.

"Haven't figured it out yet."

I tried to smother my grin, but in truth, I was a little proud of that. "So why can't you use this on Coaltar?"

"He's a completely different problem," he said. "Right now, we don't know the crimes he's committing."

"Or if he's committed any at all."

Corey pursed his lips, staring at the wall.

"What?" I asked, sensing there was something more to this, something he didn't want to tell me. I planted a palm on his chest, trying to capture his attention. "If I'm going to be in hiding for a month, can't I at least know what's going on?"

He sighed and then refocused his eyes on me. His gaze darkened, and his tone dropped a few octaves. "Humans fall into patterns," he said. "We all do. It's natural. When you fall way out of a pattern like he did, something has changed so drastically that it forces you to alter your routine. You had a routine until we interrupted."

"Coaltar had one?"

"He was a social elite. He was interested in science, so he has a lot of connections with research facilities. He was mostly quiet and while he did travel, he pretty much stayed with his upper crust class and never strayed out. Now he's taking off in the middle of the night to talk with gang members. He is literally risking his life going out there like that and he still does it. Like he woke up one day and decided he was going to see who he could find that would kill him. I mean, that's how bad some of these gang members are."

"How did you know about this?" I asked. "I mean there's

millions of people in this town. Are you monitoring them all to look for inconsistencies?"

"We've got a few eyes and ears in different places," he said. "And it isn't like that. We're not snooping on everyone. Someone we've got networking in those areas saw him show up one day. One look at him and he knew he was completely out of place. When we traced back Coaltar's cell phone to see where he's been the last several weeks, we could see the severe change in his pattern."

I scoffed. "You can track him with a cell phone?"

"The phone companies do." He dug out his own cell phone, illuminating the front. "Every device you own that has a GPS unit in it can be traced if someone really wanted to. Cell phone companies keep records of you, your calls, your texts, everything. They keep records for as long as a year or two."

I'd heard rumors of something like this, but it all sounded like conspiracy theories to me before. Could it be true? "So you're able to check those records?"

His cheeks tinted and he turned his head to avoid my stare. "I may have access."

"Coaltar told me he was in Europe for the last few months."

"He lied," Corey said, his eyes softening like he didn't want to tell me this part. "I don't know why. I think he wanted to impress you. He did go to Italy for a function but it was a weekend trip. That part of his routine is normal, to skip off to Europe for a weekend or as long as a week. He doesn't really stay for months on end."

He lied to me? That jerk! But at the same time, I wondered if what Corey said was true. Was he lying to impress me? The fact that he thought he had to lie to impress me was somehow amusing. Wasn't it enough to be rich and handsome? "So you find out from a source that Mr. Coaltar is suddenly showing up in the wrong part of town. You take a look at his cell phone record and sure enough, he's broken his old pattern." I tapped my fingers against my thigh. "Your source who noticed him with gang members didn't listen in as to what he wanted?"

"He wasn't able to get in on that. He just thought we should know someone didn't fit there." He waved his hand through the air. "But we'll figure it out. He's just in a position to where if he wanted to do something really destructive, he could. He's got the financial power and some influence."

"But I'll be stuck here until you do."

"Do you feel stuck?"

"I guess I don't like the idea of hiding for a month."

"What would you rather do?"

I drummed my fingers. "Can't we just go spy on Coaltar and follow him when he goes to talk to these gangs? I mean why not just sneak around with him? Let's go do that."

"I'm not supposed to let you near Coaltar."

I huffed. "Can't we do something? I mean," I paused, trying to figure out the next move. "What about checking out that Fitzgerald guy?"

"Who?"

"That guy that cut us off. He looked like a bodyguard. At least I thought he was, but something was weird about him. He didn't act like a bodyguard. Maybe Coaltar's doing business with him."

He tapped his fingertip against his chin. "He mentioned that?"

"Not directly. He didn't want me getting closer to Coaltar. Isn't that a good reason to check him out?"

"Hm. Guess we could check him out. Next best thing to following a suspect is following the suspect's friends." He spun around, rubbing a palm over the top of his sun-kissed hair and sitting up. "If the others can keep Coaltar occupied, I suppose we could at least see who Mr. Fitzgerald is and why he might be interested in Coaltar."

"Can we look at Coaltar's phone records?" I asked.

He nodded. "Maybe Mr. Fitzgerald called him." He stood and hovered on the floor like he wasn't sure which direction to go first and then did a half jog to the bedroom door.

I followed him out into the living room. Brandon's bedroom door was closed. Music played from that direction, something deep and melancholy.

Corey sat at one of the workstations. I took the office chair next to him. He scanned a table of data and did a quick search for a name in one of his files. "There's a Fitzgerald that called three weeks ago. Mr. Coaltar called him back ten minutes later. Each call lasted less than a minute and neither has called the other ever since."

"Because they didn't want to talk over the phone?" I asked.

Corey shrugged heavily. "I can do some guesswork but what do I know? It could have been asking him to have coffee, or it could have been asking him for anything."

I tapped my fingers on the top of the workstation in front of me. "Has Mr. Fitzgerald ever called him before?"

Corey shook his head. "Not in the past year."

"When did Coaltar start going out on these wild goose chases to the shady parts of town."

Corey nodded slowly as he checked some notes. "Three weeks ago." He stood up, crossing the room at a jog and knocked on the closed bedroom door. "Brandon!"

"What?" Brandon called back, sounding muffled. Was he sleeping?

"We've got a new lead."

Footsteps sounded and the door opened. Brandon, wearing just a pair of boxers and a T-shirt, squinted his eyes out from his darkened room.

"Where?"

♠

SPIES LIKE US

*B*randon put on some jeans and a long sleeve T-shirt and Corey put on a hoodie. Corey traced Fitzgerald's phone number back to his residence: another one of the downtown homes. We hopped in Brandon's SUV and were off to find his house.

"We'll start there," Brandon said after we caught him up on the details. He turned the SUV out of the lot and headed downtown. "Check out his house for now, and try to figure out more about him."

Corey had his nose in his phone as he sat in the back seat. "There's not a lot on him on the internet. He's a supporter of local charities. He's got an adult kid that lives out of the house now. He divorced fifteen years ago and three years ago he married a girl half his age. His second wife adopted a little girl two years ago. The little girl is four now. They're rich, but not of interest to society journalists."

"He said he had a new wife at the party," I said.

"Sounds like he lied," Core said. "There's nothing about a third divorce and marriage so he had to be using it as a ruse."

I had thought so but this confirmed it. "Does he work?" I asked.

Corey shook his head. "I'd need to do some more research, but from what I'm reading, it's old money. Living on dividends."

Brandon found the street we wanted and made a circle around the block. Mr. Fitzgerald's house wasn't far from the Market Street tourist buildings. Brandon parked off the street near the outdoor market.

I climbed out, checking up and down the street at the handful of tourists and the occasional local walking around. It felt weird being back here after Dr. Roberts found me. Part of me wondered if more Academy members were walking around here and I just didn't know.

Corey dug out a black digital camera and hung it from his wrist.

"What's that for?" I asked.

"So we look like tourists," he said. "And if we find something interesting we need to check out later."

"I thought we didn't collect evidence."

Brandon's arm encircled my neck to redirect my attention. "Listen to you, saying all this we stuff. How cute." He tugged me toward the sidewalk. "Come on, smarty pants. Let's find your lead."

The crisp air I had felt the day before had changed into something warmer with the afternoon sun. October was a mix of weather in South Carolina, shifting every couple of days from summer heat to frostbite mornings. It also made for incredible allergies. I could already feel the ache of a headache right between my eyes.

Or maybe it was the throbbing scope mark.

We took our time as we cut across the street and headed west away from the tourist areas. We stopped occasionally to take photographs of old buildings. The closer we got to the house, the more they wanted us to look like tourists in case any of the Fitzgerald family drove by.

Brandon and Corey knew the area better than I did. I walked between them, feeling a lucky because they were good-looking and tall. I brushed arms with Corey a lot, sometimes by accident and sometimes on purpose. He'd push back with his arm and grin. When the back of his hand brushed mine and our pinkies met, I got the wiggles as bad as a girl with a boy band crush. When it got too intense with his incredible smile, I looked over, and there was Brandon, a mirror image. There was no escape. Brandon's sad eyes dropped me back a few notches as he looked quizzically at me like he couldn't figure out why I was smiling so much.

When we found the house downtown, Corey and Brandon turned at the corner, looking up and down the cross street.

I paused, standing in between them as if having a conversation, but my eyes went right for Mr. Fitzgerald's' front door. "There's not a car in the drive," I said.

"Will you stop staring?" Brandon asked.

"Someone's got to look," I said. I couldn't help it. We were here now and I was curious. "What are we here for?"

Brandon grabbed my elbow and spun me until I was facing both of them. "Look like you're talking to us."

"How are we supposed to spy on him if we can't even look at him?" I asked.

"Stop talking about spying, for one," Brandon said.

"No spy talk?"

"No spy talk. We're just here to take a few pictures of these pretty houses like all the other tourists."

Corey started up the black camera. He held it toward my face. "Smile, Kayli."

I made a face with my tongue sticking out.

He snapped a photo and then grinned at the result. "Beautiful. That's going on Facebook." He pointed toward the street. "Stand in front of that nice house over there."

Brandon snagged my arm to position me next to him. I stood on my toes so I could give Brandon bunny ears. To my surprise, when Brandon figured out what I was up to, he bent over slightly so I had an easier time. It was a funny move, since I considered him so much more serious than his brother. This was the type of Brandon I could tolerate, one who wasn't yelling at me and maybe actually enjoying himself.

"Do we need to know what his house looks like from the outside?" I asked. "Because it's green and there's not a car in the drive. And there's a bunch of bushes that are square shaped."

Brandon smiled for the picture Corey was taking and then talked through his teeth. "Will you stop talking about it and just go with the flow? You're the worst spy ever."

"You're not supposed to say the spy word," I said.

"Someone could be in this house we're standing in front of and hear us," he said.

"No one cares," I said. I looked up and down the street. We were a short distance from the main tourist section and since it was out of season, there wasn't much spill over. Every few minutes a couple of cars passed, but other than that, it was a quiet road. I wondered how the rich felt about being on roads that tourists often took over, photographing their front yards.

While Corey took photos, I kept my eyes on the house. It was pretty plain. In fact, something felt off about it. I didn't notice until I stopped looking at it and started looking at the other buildings.

"Are we sure he lives here?" I asked.

"That's what the records show," Corey said. He was looking at the camera and figuring out a better setting.

I squinted at the house next door and then at the Fitzgerald house and then I realized why it was different. I don't know why I didn't see it before. The boys were just too distracting. "Because he doesn't have curtains."

The boys blinked almost simultaneously and then turned together toward the house.

All the windows were bare glass. No blinds, no curtains. I didn't even see a garbage can. Most other houses had one either by the garage or somewhere visible. Other houses had signs of life, this one looked barren.

"He doesn't live here," I said.

Corey scratched his head. "That's weird."

Brandon shifted on his feet. He glanced up and down the road and then darted across the street.

"Brandon!" I hissed and chased after him.

"Stay there," he called back to me.

I followed him instead, right up to the low iron wrought fence that was about waist high and useless for keeping anyone out. He gripped the rail, hopped it and then darted through to the porch.

I started to hop over when I felt a pair of hands on my

hips. Corey was right behind me. He gave me a boost and then climbed over and landed next to me.

There wasn't a yard at all, just a tiny walkway and a lot of bushes. The house was really close to the road. The porch was empty and ran front to back along the side of the house, typical for sideways-built downtown Charleston homes.

"I told you guys to stay back," Brandon said.

I pointed a finger at Corey, planting blame. Corey pointed right back at me while trying to mask a grin.

Brandon rolled his eyes. He walked over to the window, cupping his hands around his face so he could look inside. "You're right, though. The place is empty."

I stood next to him. There was a barren front room, bookshelves built into the wall, a clean fireplace. Too clean. "Did they move recently? Are they selling this place?"

Corey checked his phone. "Not that I can tell. Looks like he owns the property. There's no recent real estate listing."

"But he may not live here," I said. "Maybe he's got another house."

"It's just odd," Corey said. "It's listed as his main residence."

"Let's check out the back," I said.

"We should leave," Brandon said.

I ignored him, and followed the porch around the side of the house, the long side. The windows we passed, and another door, all revealed more empty rooms.

"Kevin's right," Brandon said behind me, following close. "A girl's the worst thing to add to this team. She's not listening."

"She's not part of the team," Corey said, trailing behind him.

"Will you tell her to stop? I should have left her at the apartment with you."

"Hey," I said, stopping at the far corner of the house. I turned, facing off Brandon, who stopped short and tilted his head down to stare at me. It wasn't until then that I felt incredibly short compared to him. His broad shoulders and his height made him intimidating when he was angry. "You were the one heading in by yourself."

"I was just going to peek in the window."

"Well Axel said you're not allowed to run off and do things on your own. It's like an Academy rule or something."

Brandon sputtered and made hand signals like he wanted to say something but couldn't formulate what he wanted. "I know you're not spouting Academy rules at me."

Hypocrite! I poked a finger at his broad chest. "If you're going to break the rules, I don't have to listen to you."

He puffed out his chest at my poking as if to show he was immune. "It's a rule to not have a girl on the team!"

I ignored this, although I was a little perturbed by it. Axel was going to have me join, but I couldn't work with guys? That would have sucked. Girls are okay but are usually too prone to drama. I would have wanted a boy team. Maybe not theirs, but at least someone I could get along with. Maybe I could have Corey on my team.

Or maybe I didn't want to sign up at all.

The yard in the back was tiny. Other houses were built so close, cutting off the view of most of the sky. For rich people, they didn't have any yard space. I knew downtown homes were worth millions. Was it worth it for such little space?

I wound around to the back porch and checked out the windows, looking inside. The back room had a few pieces of furniture covered in white cloth. From what I could tell by the shapes, there were sofas, and upright chairs, and a useless corner table. Maybe that was why it was stored here. A million dollar storage unit?

Or a decoy? Like Mr. Coaltar's weird office that didn't have anything but empty filing cabinets?

I passed by the back door as I couldn't see through it. The second window was to the kitchen. The counters were clean, but something was different. It took me a minute. "The fridge is humming," I said.

"So?" Brandon shoved my arm in an effort to keep me walking and head back. "Now we've seen his fridge. Let's get out of here."

"No," I said. I pointed at the kitchen. "You don't leave

C. L. Stone

the fridge running if you've left the house. That's just weird. Let's go see what's inside."

"No!" Brandon grabbed my elbow and tried to drag me off the porch. "I've seen enough. Mr. Fitzgerald left his fridge running. We'll finally be able to make that prank call and actually mean it. Great. Let's get out of here before someone calls the cops on us."

Corey held up the camera, snapped a picture of the kitchen. "I'd say let's break in, but I mean, even if he keeps something in that fridge, there's no evidence anyone's been here. He probably keeps the electricity running to keep some kind of alarm system online."

"Let me see the camera?" I asked Corey.

"We're leaving," Brandon said.

I pulled myself out of his grip. Now that we were out of sight of the street, I felt a little better poking around. I don't know why, but this whole thing bothered me. The puzzle I couldn't figure out. "I just want to take a few pictures," I said.

Corey passed off the camera. I held it between my fingers, figuring out the right button to push as there were three on top. I held it up, testing by taking a picture of Corey with a lopsided grin. Another I took of Brandon, looking perturbed and arguing with me that we should leave.

I turned around, taking a snapshot of the interior of the kitchen. I leaned over, taking a picture of the abandoned back living room.

There was thudding next to me and I was pushed hard. The camera was ripped from my hands. I didn't see who was coming and I fell hard, crashing to the wood boards of the porch. I landed on my side. My hand and knee scraped against the grooves.

"Get off my porch," a voice boomed over us.

Terror swept over me as I looked up, staring into the harsh, cold eyes of Mr. Fitzgerald. He wore white shirt, his sleeves rolled up on his arms and his face was covered in thick stubble. He gripped the camera, and loomed over me like he wanted to throw it at my face.

His other hand held his .38 and he had it pointed at Brandon.

I didn't know much about South Carolina gun laws, but I was pretty sure he had every right to shoot us, and then tell the police he was protecting his property in self-defense. How did he sneak up on us? How did he know we were here?

Brandon raised his hands. "Sorry, sir," he said.

Mr. Fitzgerald's eyes widened slowly. Recognition must have settled in, and then got confused when he looked at Corey. "You ... you both." His eyes looked down at me and then again he seemed to put the pieces together as he remembered me from the party. His lips twisted into a snarl. "Get out," he said.

Brandon reached down, scooping me up and hauling me with his arms cradled under my back and knees. "We're leaving," he said. "Sorry. We were just ... we thought this house was for sale."

"It's not," Mr. Fitzgerald said in a near shout. He waved his gun at us, ushering us off.

My heart thundered in my chest, but I caught a strange vibe from Mr. Fitzgerald that now while Brandon held on to me, I couldn't place. It niggled at the back of my brain.

Brandon didn't let go. I felt myself clutching my arms around his shoulders as he marched off, putting himself between the gun and me. Corey stood by his brother, backing off slowly and apologizing nonstop.

When we were at the front fence, Brandon threw me over it. Corey jumped it and picked me back up. I was going to tell him to put me down, that I could run, but he held strong and Brandon marched next to him, squinting in anger, his mouth tight.

When we were a block away and heading back toward the market place, Corey released me and let me walk next to him, but he held my hand in a firm grip and was dragging me along as I had trouble keeping up. I half jogged as we made a beeline for the SUV. I jumped in between them in the front seat.

When we were on the road again, and I managed to

swallow back my heart in my throat, I broke the silence. "Mr. Fitzgerald is terrified," I said.

"What are you talking about?" Brandon asked. "We pissed him off for walking in his grass and his porch. He's a crazy old man."

"He's protecting something," I said. "He was ready to start shooting, and then he stopped when he realized it was us and we were defenseless. He's guarding an empty house with a gun loaded and ready to go."

Corey picked up my hand I was waving around as I talked and opened up my palm. "You're bleeding."

I pulled my hand away. It was just a few scratches. I just needed to wash it. I crammed it into my side to hide it. "I'm telling you guys, he's scared. Something's wrong."'

"We've got other problems right now," Brandon said as he turned the SUV down to head to Broad Street and headed south to the Sergeant Jasper. "We have to get that camera back."

"We do?" I asked. "Why?"

Brandon tapped his fingers against the steering wheel. "There's stuff on that camera. We need to get it back."

"What stuff?"

He turned to me. "It's the camera I used when I was tracking you," he said. "If he gives it to Coaltar, he'll know exactly who you are and where you live."

♠

BRANDON

*T*he full weight of what he was saying took forever to sink into my brain. I think maybe because looking at Mr. Fitzgerald and then thinking on it, I felt bad. We scared the guy by poking around his house. It was almost like getting caught pulling a wallet out of pocket. It was all those fears I'd had since forever coming to life. I hadn't meant to scare him and I felt horrible.

If what I said was true and Mr. Fitzgerald was terrified, was it true that maybe Mr. Coaltar was the one scaring him? Or if he did work for Coaltar, he'd easily give the camera over to him. Mr. Coaltar would recognize my face in the camera. He may want to know what I was up to. They could come after me at the hotel.

They'd find Wil. He'd be in the middle of this mess. And if Coaltar was as dangerous as we feared…

I tried to tell Brandon that we should go back, but he drove all the way back to the Sergeant Jasper.

"We need to get the camera," I said. "They can't know about me."

"I know," Brandon said.

"Then why are we driving away? Let's go knock on his door and ask for the camera. If we approach him slow and nicely, he may give it back."

"And get a second chance to get shot at?" Brandon asked. "I don't think so."

"But we can't—"

He reached out, grabbing my hand with his free one as he drove with the other. "Hey," he said. His eyes tried to hold mine as long as possible, occasionally glancing to the road.

"Look at me, sweetie." He squeezed my hand. "We're not going to let them keep it."

"What do we do?"

"We do nothing," he said.

He had to be insane! "We can't just assume he's not going to look at it."

"No, I mean, *we* can't do anything. If we go back there, we're looking at a gun in our faces, or even the police chasing after us. Our team can't get any closer right now."

The way he said our team was troubling. "You have another? That teenage squad I saw at the gun range? You're going to send them after it?"

"Or another group," Corey said from the back seat. He had his face in his phone and he was pushing buttons in a mad wave of texting. "We need to call in a few favors."

"Do it," Brandon said.

"What favor?" I asked. "What's this? Like in those mafia movies? Someone owes you a favor and you call it in?"

Brandon released my hand to drive. "Not really."

"Then what is it? How can you just send someone else after it?"

"We ask nicely," Corey said. "Don't ask any more. We can't tell you anything."

I pressed my fists to my eyes to block out the light. This whole Academy thing was complicated and infuriating. It was crazy! We should be the ones to go and get it. I didn't trust anyone else to understand why we needed to go back and do this now. Why would they risk their necks? They didn't know who I was.

When we got back to the Sergeant Jasper, I followed the twins back up to their room. I trailed Corey to his bedroom as Brandon took over the computer desks and put in a phone call. I washed up my cut palm and my knee. They weren't bleeding anymore, though they did sting a little.

Corey crashed onto his back on the bed. "Well that's a dead end for us."

"What do you mean?" I asked. I sat on the corner of his bed, unsure what else to do and feeling like I should be doing something. "He held a gun at us to get off his property. Something's going on."

"That doesn't prove anything," Corey said. He nudged my side with a foot. "We've proved he's a grumpy old man who doesn't like people on his porch."

"He's called Coaltar, who may be doing crimes, from a phone registered to an abandoned house that he guards during the day. He didn't park in his drive or out front. He wanted it to look abandoned but then guards it anyway?"

Corey breathed in deeply and then let the air out slowly. He stared up at the ceiling. "Odd."

I flopped back on the bed next to him. He made room by scooting closer to the wall. "Did we screw up?" I asked.

"Yeah," he said. "We screwed up."

"Is Axel going to yell at us?"

"Axel doesn't yell. Marc, however…"

I knocked my ankle into his. "Do we blame it on Brandon?"

He rolled his foot against mine in a playful kick back. "We'll still get yelled at."

"Yeah, but it just feels better if it's at Brandon."

"Brandon's not so bad," he said. He nudged an elbow into my ribs.

I grunted as I didn't want to answer him. So far every time I ever talked to Brandon, we ended up in a fight. And now he was going to blame me for this mess. Still, there were moments, like when he held my hand in the car and promised things would be okay, or the hug at the party, where it left me in a weird position with how I felt about him. Maybe Corey was right and he wasn't so bad and we just totally misunderstood each other from go. I gave Brandon a pretty hard time, and I didn't listen to him, so could I blame him for being angry?

I avoided thinking about it by stabbing my elbow back into Corey. Corey was fun; I liked him.

"Ow," he said, in a flat tone while still staring at the ceiling. He aimed his elbow at me, but knocked it into mine as I tried to block.

That did it. I tucked my knees up, and then pushed at his side, trying to do the same thing I did earlier to Raven and slide Corey right off the bed. Except I was on the outside so he only ended up getting squished into the wall. I didn't do it hard. Just playfully.

"Oof," he cried out. He spun around with a grin. He caught both my ankles and twisted.

I had to flip around to relieve the pressure and the next thing I knew, I was dangling precariously off the edge of the mattress. I had to do a weird, twisty sit up to avoid falling on my head. I squealed loud and patted at his arms as he kept me trapped there. A laugh rippled from him, deep and mischievous. He was a nerdling, but he was strong and he knew how to defend himself.

"No fair!" I yelped at him.

"Say mercy," he said.

I knew how to win fights like this. Feign that you're giving up and then when they let their guard down, go in for the attack. "Mercy!" I cried out.

"Say uncle."

"I just said mercy!"

Brandon materialized in the bedroom doorway. He spotted his brother first, and opened his mouth to say something, but stopped when he caught me on the bed. "Kayli?"

"Hi!" I squealed, a little louder than necessary. I patted Corey's arm. "Let me up."

Corey laughed, getting off of me, but hanging on so I didn't just fall on my head. I wriggled onto my back but ended up spilling onto the floor and tumbling until I was sitting up. I swept back the hair from my eyes, laughing.

Corey hovered on his hands and knees, looking over the edge of the bed. "You okay?"

"Fine."

Brandon's eyebrows scrunched together. "What are you two doing?"

"Nothing," I said. "Just playing."

Corey stabbed a finger at my head. "She started it."

"I did not!"

Brandon sliced his hand through the air. "Okay, don't care that much." He jerked his chin toward Corey. "Axel wants you to do ... Academy things. There's something on his computer."

"He didn't call?" Corey asked. He pulled his phone out, checking it. "There's no message.

"I was just on the phone with him," Brandon said. "He was checking in but asked..." He glanced at me. I got the unspoken signal that there was some business I wasn't allowed to know about.

I grunted, picking myself up. "What do you want me to do? Lock myself in the bathroom?"

"Just go sit in my room for a minute," he said.

I sighed, crossing the room, sending Corey a small wave and a playful pout. Play time was over.

Corey waved back, a smile caught on his lips.

I crossed the apartment, and found Brandon's bedroom door. I hesitated going in, wondering why I couldn't just sit on the couch. It felt awkward going into his bedroom without him there.

I twisted the handle, opening the door.

If I wanted to say Corey and Brandon had polar opposite bedrooms, I wouldn't be stretching the opposites far enough apart.

Brandon's bed was in the middle of the room. Against the far wall was a surfboard, leaning into the corner. There was a single short dresser near the foot of the bed, and a flat screen television hanging on the wall. That was it, Spartan.

I moved to the bed that had a deep green comforter. I sat on it, eyeballing the rest of his bedroom. His closet was dark. Music was playing on the stereo system built around the television, playing a sad Mayday Parade song.

I was about to start poking around his closet when Brandon materialized in the doorway. He looked in on me sitting on the bed and then quietly entered the bedroom, closing the door behind himself.

My eyebrows shifted up on my forehead, as I felt

suddenly claustrophobic. "What's going on?"

"I wanted to talk to you," he said. He leaned against his door, folding his arms over his chest. "What were you doing with Corey?"

"Huh?"

"I mean the cutesy wrestling on the bed and all that. What were you doing?"

I blinked rapidly at him. "I don't know what you're talking about. We were just ... I don't know. Horsing around."

"You were flirting."

I didn't care if it was true, I didn't like the way his tone was accusing me of it like I had done something wrong. I climbed off the bed to stand on the carpet. "Did you want to ask me what I was doing, or are you going to tell me? And why is it any of your business?"

"Kayli."

"Corey and I were just hanging out," I said. I felt the heat rising inside me. I couldn't date Coaltar. I couldn't flirt with his brother. Was I not good enough? Did he still see me as the mall rat stealing wallets? "I'm doing what I'm supposed to, staying here when I could be out working and earning enough for rent next month. I'm stuck here, because Marc gave the order I had to be. Now what? I'm not allowed to have any fun? I have to sit there and do nothing?"

"Corey's gay."

I had my mouth open with whatever else I was going to say and then choked. "Huh?"

Brandon planted a palm against the back of his neck, rubbing. "I didn't want to say anything while you were in there. My brother's gay."

I blinked after him. I didn't get that vibe from Corey, but then, I hadn't known him that long. Still, in my head it didn't make sense. He held my hand. He was the one that started half of the times we were fooling around. "He didn't say anything."

"He doesn't really tell anyone. I'm not even sure if he's admitted it to anyone else yet. He's never told me directly."

"Then how do you know?"

"Because I know," he said. He moved to the bed, sinking, folding his arms in his lap and bent forward to stare at his feet. "When we were kids, our parents had us always on sport teams. They thought it was cute to pair us up like that. He'd walk around the locker room trying to look normal, but he'd get a hard-on when the team had to shower." He rubbed his palm against his cheek, his faint stubble making a scratching noise. "I mean, I guess that's not the only thing. There's the way he looks at guys sometimes, staring at their bodies. When the guys started talking about him, I'd kick their asses just to get them to shut up. There's other reasons I know, too, but I figured it out and went through a lot to make sure no one messed with him about it back then. Guys can be shitheads in high school."

"What's the big deal now?" I asked. I sank back onto the bed next to him. "He's a big boy. He can take care of himself. And who cares if he's gay?"

He smirked. "Well, it is the South. I try not to just tell everyone."

"You haven't asked him?"

"I wanted him to tell me when he was comfortable."

"He's good looking and fun," I said. "But I still don't know him that well. Maybe I was flirting, but I ... I mean I was just playing. I wasn't really thinking..."

He nodded slowly, his cheeks tinted. "I wanted to warn you before maybe you went too far and he wasn't ... you know. If he didn't respond back."

I waved my hand through the air. "No, actually, this is perfect."

A blond eyebrow shifted up in curiosity. Now that was very similar to Corey. "What's perfect?"

"Gay guys are awesome," I said. "You can do all kinds of cool things together and it never goes into a weird zone."

Brandon huffed. "You've got strange ideas."

"Unless you're telling me Corey and I can't hang out together."

"No, no," he said. "That's fine. Hang out with who you

want. I just didn't want to see you disappointed later."

I stilled on the bed, watching him for a moment. "Are ... uh ... are you?"

He smirked, shaking his head. "No. I thought maybe I was when I was younger. Probably because he is and I thought maybe it was genetic or something. But I'm not interested in guys."

Just to be clear, I had to ask. "Are you interested in girls?"

He scoffed. "Yeah."

"Sorry. I... yeah, Corey and you said you'd had girlfriends before. Forgot." I combed my fingers through my hair, pulling it back away from my face.

An uncomfortable silence started between us. I stared at his blank wall. I realized that again I had jumped the gun on assuming what he was talking about and he had not only been looking out for his brother, but also looking out for me. I felt stupid.

Brandon looked at his feet. The music played on his stereo, now a slow Breaking Benjamin song.

"So ..." he said.

"Is Corey going to be busy for a while?"

He shrugged. "He's probably going to be working late in the other apartment."

I nodded. "What do we do? It seems like everyone's working but us."

"I'd be working," he said, "except I'm supposed to not be."

"Is it because of Coaltar?"

"Yes."

"And me?"

"Yes."

I twisted my lips and sighed heavily. "I messed up."

He let out a breath, reaching to plant a hand between my shoulder blades and started rubbing. "I think we both did. I let Coaltar see he was getting to me. There was a rumor that he's been known to tick off a few husbands, cause divorces, and ditch the wife after a week."

I blinked, shaking my head. "Is that true?"

"I don't know. Maybe. I was reading about it in the gossip columns."

I huffed. "You read those? Aren't those about old lady rose-society types, and old farts pretending the war is still going on?"

"I was doing research on Coaltar," he said. "I needed an in, so I found one by studying where he went. I showed up at some local country club he was hanging out at."

I sighed. I leaned back to sprawl out on the bed. "Is he really that bad?"

"We don't know," he said. He leaned on his side on the bed, his head held up by his hand, looking down at me. "That's the problem. There's rumors about people on his staff disappearing and never being heard from again. There was one about some gun program he was involved in offshore."

"He said he did forensic testing on bullets a few years ago."

Brandon nodded. "He's weird. Eccentric. And I've got a bad feeling."

I sighed, staring up at the ceiling. "What do we do?"

"We wait until we're sure," he said. He drifted a hand out, slipping his fingers across my brow to draw back a lock of hair stuck on my cheek. "Think we can get along until then?"

I smirked. "Maybe I should stay here with you. I end up getting bruised over in the other apartment."

"If you want Raven to back off, come talk to me."

"I can handle him," I said.

"He's not from here," he said. "He hits you back. You know that doesn't usually fly around here. One day he'll do it to you in front of someone else and he's going to get his ass kicked. I may not stop it when it happens."

I turned my head to look at him. "Isn't he your friend?"

He nodded slowly. "He is. I don't always agree with him, but the only reason why I let him touch you is because I know if you really said stop, he'd stop. Or I'd make him stop."

"We were just having fun. I'll tell him to stop if I need to." I paused, gazing at the depth of those blue eyes. "You act like an older brother, you know."

The depth of Brandon's blue eyes softened. "Yup. Born a couple minutes before Corey. Maybe it doesn't really count, but I guess I was always the one looking out for him."

"I'm the older sister," I said. "Sucks, doesn't it?"

He laughed a little. "He used to get on my nerves a lot worse. I think it's because of the comic books and video games. He was always wanting me to play with him, and I didn't really like those."

"What do you like?"

He shrugged. "Normal things, I guess. Movies. Surfing."

I leaned my head back, looking at the surfboard against the wall. "So you do use that thing?"

"I wouldn't have it if I didn't use it."

"Where do you surf? I didn't think the waves at the beaches were high enough here."

"Usually, I'm out at the North Shore. I get a chance every now and again," he said. "And when we travel, I like to go to the beach when I can."

"How often do you guys travel?"

"Seems like a lot," he said. "Along the coast, to Europe, or Africa. Depends on a few things."

I propped myself up again, looking at him. He was on his back now, looking up at the ceiling. "I've never been outside of Charleston," I said.

He turned his head toward me. "Do you want to leave?"

I bit my lip, not wanting to admit it. "I used to love it here. Now, I don't know why," I said. "Ever since... I guess a few years ago when..." It was hard to talk about. It was something I didn't talk about with Wil as much. Like if I didn't say it, it was easier to deal with.

He propped himself up again on his hand. "What?"

I swallowed. "I guess after my mom died, I just never felt the same. I wanted to run off a hundred times just to get away and couldn't."

His face softened. "I'm sorry," he said quietly.

I felt the pang in my heart at his words, felt the sympathy he was trying to share. Accepting it, however, hurt. I tried to hide my desire to scoff at it, because I knew he was trying to be nice. Instead, I fell back on the bed, staring up at the ceiling.

"Want to watch a movie?" he asked after a few minutes.

"Yes," I said, eager for a distraction to get me out of this conversation.

He picked a movie he liked, a western. I followed it for a while, sitting on one side of his bed, propped up by pillows. He sat on the other side of his bed. After a while, I was sinking lower on the bed.

Before the movie was over, I was dozing. It wasn't boring, it was just a really long day.

Brandon leaned over, hovering over me. "Kayli," he said, touching my arm gently. "Just get under the blanket."

I did, thinking he was going to continue to watch the movie and let me sleep. Instead he hit the power on the television, casting the room into mostly darkness. He crossed the room, opening the door and checked the rest of the apartment. I saw lights being turned off. It reminded me of my old routine of checking the house and making sure everything was locked up before going to bed.

He returned, closing the door. The room stilled, and the sliver of light from the window gave me something to focus on. There was movement toward the closet. I think he changed from his jeans and T-shirt into pajama pants. Brandon slipped into the bed beside me, rocking it as he flipped over once, and then stilled.

For a while, I couldn't sleep. I stared at Brandon's frame, at the way his shoulder sloped and how the blanket draped across his body. The cotton sheets were soft on my skin, a different feel from the crisp starched-to-death hotel sheets. The bed was more comfortable and didn't smell like bleach. I supposed the night before I'd been too tired to think about things like that.

Now that I was a little more comfortable with the guys,

my head was filled with a mix of feelings, and trying to figure out how I ended up here. I wondered where Raven and Axel were. I wondered if Marc was with them. I wondered why they left. I might have even missed them.

I didn't want to admit it, but they were growing on me. I had friends in high school, but when I'd had to leave abruptly after my mother died, I lost contact with a lot of them. Not to say that I was that close with a lot of people. Even when I was younger, I wasn't shy, but found it hard to trust. Too many early days with bullies and jerks. Too many friends who betrayed me. Even when I was friendly with people, they never really knew me.

These guys were different. I felt it. I was in a bed next to one of them now, and I wasn't weirded out. It had only been a couple of days, and I was trying to figure out my life by including them in it, no matter what happened with Mr. Coaltar, one way or another. I kept thinking about introducing Wil to the guys. It was hard not to dream about getting an apartment inside the Sergeant Jasper. Corey had brought up the idea. Brandon hadn't argued with him on it. It was like they wanted me to.

I thought about what Axel told me earlier, about being recruited to the Academy. Did I want that? I didn't know what it was, some sort of private surveillance group. Something more than that, maybe. It was a tempting offer.

But who was I now? Two days ago, I was the girl who hid in the shadows, trying to go unnoticed and survive until Wil could have a better life. I was still doing that, but who was I going to be when this was over, and Wil was in college? Maybe Axel was right about me not being a regular job girl or college girl, but did that mean I had to join the Academy? I didn't even know anything about it. Where does a thief belong? What about when she makes a promise not to do steal anymore?

What good was I to anyone?

I tried to brush the thoughts away because I didn't have the answers and I wasn't sure I'd ever find them. Eventually, the thoughts mingled into dreams.

♠♠♠♠♠

Sometime in the night, sirens screamed, cutting through the silence and drawing me out of a dark dream. My heart thundered and I sat up quickly, trembling.

I was sure those sirens were for me.

"Kayli?" Brandon's voice drifted to me, soft and deep.

I wanted to answer him, but images flashed through my mind of the dream I'd been ripped from, of being chased by a blackness that knew my faults and wanted to keep me forever. I tried to swallow back the emotion, telling myself that those sirens were going away.

But my heart refused to believe it. In my panic, I choked instead of telling him I was fine.

Brandon stirred and sat up. My heart leapt into my throat, and I started to fling off the covers to jump from the bed. I needed to run from the room, run from him. I needed to be alone. I'd run to the bathroom and cry to get some relief and feel better. I was weak and disoriented after being in such a deep sleep. Kayli doesn't cry. I'm not that type of girl. I couldn't let him see me like this.

Before I could put my feet down on the carpet, an arm encircled my waist. I clutched at it, my mouth opened to tell him to let go.

He turned me toward him. Brandon's bare, strong chest met mine, and my head instinctively found the crook of his neck. I gripped at his shoulders, because I had nothing else to hold on to.

His palm met with the small of my back and he drew me into him. His other hand dove into my hair, his fingers twining into the strands as he pressed me against his chest. "Kayli," he soothed. "They aren't coming for you, sweetie."

It was the thing I needed to hear and the relief was too overwhelming to bear. It was admitting at how much wrong I'd done. I was scared. No matter what I did, no matter how much I wanted to make up for what I'd done, there was nothing I could do to get away from the nightmare that one day, policemen would find me and I'd be in jail forever.

Because I deserved it.

I swallowed back sobs, but it didn't stop my tears from reaching his skin. His sympathy broke me. The tears were the ones I'd always hidden from Wil, usually running to the bathroom to wipe away in private. Doing this in front of Brandon was worse, but now that I'd started, I couldn't stop.

Brandon shifted, not letting go, but moving until he was sitting cross-legged on the bed with me in his lap. The hand in my hair drifted until his palm was on my cheek, wiping away the wetness. "You're fine," he whispered. "You're safe. Kayli; they're not coming for you. I promise. If you stay here ... if you stay with me, I swear." He dipped his head, and his lips met my skin. He kissed a spot near the corner of my eye. "I swear, you'll never have to do it again."

I sniffed heavily, my fingers gripping and regripping at his chest. I realized I was probably digging into his skin, so I slid my hands around his neck, hanging on to him. "I'm so stupid," I mumbled, surprised to be talking about it, but I couldn't stop. "I could have done something else. I tried."

His arm tightened around my body, pressing me to him until my breasts were squished against his chest. "You did what you had to," he said. "You did what any older sibling does."

"I messed up."

"You're done messing up." His palm lifted my cheek until I was facing him. Through the blur of tears, and the dim light from the window, I only caught the outline of his face looming over me. His thumb traced over, rubbing a tear into my skin. "We all make mistakes." He sighed, and dropped his head, pressing his lips to my cheek below my eye again, kissing away the tears. He whispered against my skin, his lips tracing. "I'm sorry I yelled at you at the party. And I'm sorry I accused you of going after Coaltar for his money. I was wrong about you."

I started to shake my head. "Brandon..."

"Shh," he breathed. "Kayli." He kissed my cheek, trailing across to my ear. I let him, because I couldn't find the willpower to push him away. Part of me didn't want to. I hadn't had a boyfriend to kiss in a couple of years. I hadn't realized how much I'd missed the feeling of being held. Maybe that was why it felt strange to suddenly be in a group of guys like this. It reminded me of what I'd been pushing away for years.

My fingers rubbed at the nape of his neck, and up through the short strands of his hair. He was comforting me, and I wanted to feel this. I wanted his touch and those kisses to eclipse the panic in my heart. I wanted to hide away in his arms.

"Maybe when this is over we'll get you an apartment in this building. Or stay with us. I don't care. Maybe Corey and I will get a three bedroom and..." he paused. His hand at my back drifted up, until both his palms cupped my cheeks. "Or maybe if you don't hate me too much, you can stay with me."

"Brandon?"

"I can't stand to think of you crying alone in your bedroom when a police car goes by. You may as well stay here. You'll save me the walk."

My heart stilled. He was talking crazy and I wanted to tell him so. Too close!

I didn't have the strength. I didn't really want to. My usual resistance had faded somewhere amid his promises. "You wouldn't want me," I said as my only defense. No one did.

He turned slightly, the light from the window catching in his eyes as he zeroed in on my face. He dipped his head, and for a moment I thought he was going to kiss my cheek again.

His lips brushed against mine, sending the lightest of fluttering butterflies to sweep down into my chest. He was testing to see if I was willing.

I sucked in a breath, parting my lips to do so. This caused me to glide my lips back against his. Maybe I was teasing him, testing. Are you sure?

His mouth crushed down on mine like he'd been waiting for forever. His lips parted and he kissed me deeply.

I responded weakly at first, but the more he kissed me,

the more of him I needed. My hands opened up behind his head, holding him against my face.

He released my cheeks, slipping his hands around my waist. His fingers rubbed against my sides and then massaged my back, holding me to him until my stomach pressed to his.

I tilted my head, opening my mouth more. Letting him in.

His jaw loosened as he deepened the kiss. He dove in, and my lower lips glided in between his teeth. He grazed at it, suckled gently. He slowed, deliberate, giving of himself with every movement of his lips.

His hands tightened at my hips, and he lifted me. His kiss softened and he moved me slowly until I was on my side next to him. He lifted an arm, pillowing my head, tucking his elbow around the back, drawing me in again. He kissed my nose, my cheeks, my eyelids. When his lips found mine again, he tasted like the salt of the last of my tears.

My hands slid to his chest, finding it easier now to press my palms against it. My fingers traced his collarbone, and felt the toned muscles in his strong chest. I'd admired it before, and now touching it made the butterflies in my chest start flipping around.

His other hand held onto my hip, collecting the material of the shirt I wore into his fist. He loosened his grip and then tightened again.

Slowly, as if making sure I was okay with it, his fingers moved up, under the shirt. He kept his fingertips against my skin, tracing until he was at my ribs. He followed my ribcage, rubbing his fingers until he met my spine. His palm settled at my mid-back and drew me closer.

In that moment I understood him. Whatever pain he'd experienced, he used it to fuel the passion he expressed in those eyes. Passion from pain.

I broke the kiss, breathless, stunned, and a confused mess. There were things I wanted to say, questions I wanted to ask him. My mouth couldn't form words.

What did this mean? What were we doing?

He looked back at me in the darkness. He didn't have the

answered.

His fingers massaged in small circles against my spine. His lips traced along my forehead. He nestled into me.

I fell asleep with the questions on my lips, and my cheek pressed to his chest.

♠♠♠♠♠

I woke up with Brandon's arms still wrapped around me. My back was pressed into his chest as he spooned me. Sunlight was peeking around the closed blinds. I studied the light, the surfboard against the wall, the bareness of his bedroom.

What in the world was I doing? How different my world had become in a few short days. Part of me was nervous. Would Brandon have second thoughts about what happened last night? I didn't know what to do with this. Brandon was attractive, and he'd been sweet last night, but I still hardly knew him. He made promises, but were those just to make me feel better? I couldn't ask to stay with him, even though I was here now.

With Brandon pressed to my back, with a hand up my shirt and his palm against my stomach and his other arm under my head, my senses were overwhelmed. Doubt crept in with the light from the window. If he was going to disappoint me, I didn't want to know. I didn't want to give him a chance.

I started to get up, to pull away.

The hand at my stomach tightened, pulling me in until I was pressed against his chest.

"Ugh," I said.

A muffled reply came from behind me, and he dipped his nose into my neck. "Don't go yet."

The tug of a heartstring resounded inside my chest. I couldn't resist.

I turned over, facing him. His arm went around my neck, catching my shoulder, pulling me in closer. He kissed my forehead, his lips lingering as his other palm rested on my exposed side.

I couldn't take much more of this. If he held on, I'd start to fall, and my heart couldn't bear it. Not now. I was too much of a mess for anyone to love. "Brandon."

"Hm?"

"I need to talk to Marc." If I had to stay with the guys, I needed to figure out for how long, or push them into figuring this out faster. Get this problem with Coaltar out of the way. I couldn't move on with my life without it.

"Why?"

"If I need to stay here, I need to talk to him."

He sighed. "I'll take you to him."

♠

UGLY ANGER

I wanted to take a shower, but Brandon was up and dressed quickly, with such a determined look on his face that I didn't dare take any more time than necessary.

My book bags were sitting on the couch. Raven must have come in during the night sometime, or Axel, or someone else. Maybe Corey brought them over.

At that thought, I checked his bedroom, but his light was off and the room was still.

"Where'd he go?" I asked Brandon.

Brandon fished out his keys and found his wallet sitting on the coffee table. "He's probably at the job site."

"Job site?"

"Where we're going now."

I hurried to the bathroom to put on a pair of shorts and a black T-shirt from my bag. I swiped on deodorant and brushed my hair. When I looked in the mirror, I cringed, and dug out some of the makeup samples I had. I dabbed on some concealer to mask the deep shadows under my eyes. I didn't want to look like a complete mess. I added some mascara quickly. When I looked like I was at least among the living, I ran back out again.

Brandon waited by the door. We got into his SUV.

I dazed out a bit when we got onto the Interstate. My thoughts were muddled with what I was going to talk to Marc about and trying to not think about Brandon.

Brandon granted me the grace of being quiet the whole way. By the time I was paying attention to where we were going, he'd pulled off of I-26 and I had no clue where we were, but the chemical smell in the air and the craters in the road made me think we were in North Charleston.

Brandon pulled onto a narrow street. The homes in this neighborhood were cookie cutter, with broken wire fences, and tiny lawns, where the only differences between them were the angles of the leaning porches and the paint colors in various shades of faded.

There were a couple of trucks parked outside one of the houses at the end of a cul-de-sac. There was a large construction Dumpster on the front lawn, and this home's fence had been pulled back to allow room for it. Ladders leaned against the exterior to allowed access to the roof.

Kevin was on the front lawn, studying a clipboard, a pencil behind his ear. Brandon pulled up against the curb. Kevin took one look at me and frowned.

I climbed out, but he focused on Brandon. "What's she doing here?"

"She's got to stay with us," Brandon said.

"So you brought her here?"

"Yeah. Why?"

Kevin frowned. "Take her back to the apartment if you want to play. This is a work zone."

"She's here to work. Marc mentioned she could work here with us."

"What? When did he say that?" Kevin asked.

"The other night while you were out. Again."

Kevin brushed his palm against his forehead. "I knew it. He's going to start fucking up. She's going to figure out everything."

"She already knows half of it."

"Come on," Brandon said. "I'll fill you in."

I sighed, guessing this was something they needed to keep secret for the Academy, and I wasn't allowed to know. I wondered how much Kevin really worked for their team, because he wasn't around all that often. It seemed at every moment he could, he ran home to his girlfriend. Did she really need him that much? They didn't seem perturbed at her like they did Marc's ex-girlfriend, and she seemed like a clinger.

Nail guns cracked noisily up on the roof. I made my way to the ladder, not wanting to stay on the ground with Kevin if they were going to come back. I started up.

I found Axel and Raven on the roof on their knees. They both had nail guns and were starting at opposite ends, nailing the roof tile down. Both had on jeans. Raven wore a black tank shirt, soaked through with sweat and Axel was bare chested, the darker complexion along his body glistening in the sunlight. Raven's shoulders were wider, but their biceps and their bodies were exquisite. Raven was a powerhouse, a tank, and Axel's muscles seemed more precise, a little leaner.

I crouched on the roof, which had a soft slope. I sat on it, watching the guys work. I wondered if Brandon was going to ever talk about last night with me. I told myself I wouldn't start. It was too soon to act like we were a couple of anything like that. He'd said he wanted me to move in. I'd been a mess and terrified, and he comforted me until I could sleep again.

Now that it was morning, I knew better than to hold him to those same promises made in the night. You can't cry in front of guys, and make them promise things, and then force them to stick to it after. I wasn't that manipulative, and I didn't need to be taken care of in that way.

Maybe it was best to pretend it never happened.

I was a thief. I worked alone. Alone was best for me, for someone who didn't fit in anywhere. It never hurt. It never made promises it didn't mean. Alone was who I was.

I had no idea what he saw in me. It was too terrifying to think that last night had been merely a moment of weakness and he didn't have any intention of making whatever was between us a relationship. I wouldn't want to make things awkward. If he really wanted me, he'd tell me in broad daylight when our emotions weren't so stirred up.

Raven was the first to notice me. He jerked his head back, shooting the last nail into the roof without looking. When it was done, he lifted the nail gun and hit the switch to power it off. "Where have you been?" he asked.

"Where have you been?" I responded without really expecting an answer. "You didn't tell me you did construction."

"Little thief, I do everything."

Axel stopped his nail gun and turned, looking at me. "What are you doing up here?"

"Brandon brought me."

"You're here to work?"

"I'm here to talk to Marc, but if you want me to work…"

Axel waggled a finger at me. "If you start a fight with Marc, I don't want to be on this roof when it happens." He shuffled on his knees, putting his nail gun down carefully on the roof. He wiped his brow with the back of his arm. Beads of sweat zigzagged down his chest, following the lines of his body. "So Brandon's here?"

"Yeah, he's down talking with Kevin."

He stood up and bent at the knees to start easing his way over to the ladder. "I need to talk to him. Stay up here with Raven."

"Want me to nail things?"

"Sure. Have Raven show you how." He moved to the ladder and disappeared.

Raven curled his fingers at me. "Come on."

I started to crawl over until the rough tile below my knees started to bite into the cuts from the day before. Raven held his nail gun in his hands and fiddled with the plastic casing.

I waved a hand at him. "Don't shoot me."

"I'm more worried you'll shoot me." He showed me the gun. "This isn't bullets, but it's just as bad."

He showed me his nail gun, which was mostly gray with a black handle. There was a holder for the nails sticking out of it that looked a lot like a smaller version of the magazine I'd used on the 303 rifle.

"Shiny," I said.

"It's got a safety." He flipped the button that powered it up. He aimed it at the roof but left an inch of space between it and the gun. He pulled the trigger but it locked up short and a nail never spit out. "You can't fuck up. You have to push the nose down into the tile." He rammed the end of the nail gun at the tile and shoved it until the frame around it pulled back. He pulled the trigger and the nail shot out.

"So you can't shoot unless you push down?" I asked. Seemed easy enough.

He lifted the nail gun up. He used two fingers to pull back on the safety, showing me how it worked. He held the safety back and aimed the gun at the roof like that and let it spit a nail into the tile. "You could hold it back on your own like this, and it'll shoot. Hurts like a bitch on your fingers after a while though." He held the nail gun out to me.

I took it from him, aimed it at the tile and fired a quick shot right next to one of his nails. My arm jerked a bit at the force and my nail went in crooked

"You've got to lock your arm, like shooting a gun," he said. "Didn't you learn anything yesterday?"

"I didn't get to shoot a pistol," I said. "Just the rifles."

"Remind me to show you a pistol. Shoot it again."

I shot two more nails into the tile and when he was satisfied that I wasn't going to shoot myself in the eye, he took his nail gun back. He planted another tile on the roof and lined it up.

"How come you didn't tell me you did construction?" I asked. I sat on my butt next to him, watching him work. "I thought you just did spy stuff."

"I do whatever job is on the table," he said. "This week, we rebuild a roof. Next week, we're in Europe chasing down someone's long lost brother. I do whatever Axel tells me to do."

With his Russian accent, the way he pronounced "r" rolled off his tongue in a way that made me want to get him to talk more just to hear it. "What if you do have to go to Europe next week?"

"Are you worried I'm going to leave you behind?" He snapped seven nails in quick order into the tile. "You think I'm going to leave you here to let you reign chaos over my city while I'm gone? No. You'll go to Europe with me."

He was so full of it. Still, I enjoyed the idea. "I don't have a passport."

"I'll get you a passport." He planted another tile into place, and aligned it.

"I don't have money for a plane ticket."

"I'll buy you a plane ticket."

I smirked. "What if I don't want to go to Europe?"

He started firing. "Then we'll go to Russia," he shouted over the noise of his nail gun going off. "Or China. Or Africa. Whatever the fuck. I don't care." He finished the nails and then started lining up another tile. "Get out of here. You're distracting."

I figured I'd pushed his buttons enough, and he did have a loaded gun. I backed away and claimed Axel's nail gun that he'd left behind. His was yellow, and older, but it had pretty much the same design. I started lining up the tiles and nailing them in.

I worked beside Raven for two rows of tiles until my arms started to ache and I was sweating. I powered off my nail gun and set it aside. I laid against the tile and planted a bent elbow over my eyes to block out the sun. There was a small bite to the wind that felt good, but the sun was trying to roast me on the dark tile roof. I hated that it felt like I was wimping out but my sore arm needed a break.

"Little thief," Raven called to me over his shooting gun. A moment later I heard it powering down. "What's wrong with you? Did you eat this morning?"

"No."

He grunted. "Remind me to kick Brandon's ass. I can't trust him to even feed you."

"I need a Big Mac," I said without moving my arm. "I need tacos. And a steak. And maybe spaghetti."

"Just stay there," he said. "I'll go find something."

"No problem." That sounded like an awesome plan. Food being brought to me was always the best sort of food.

I heard him make his way to the ladder and then it clanged as he made his way down.

A few minutes after he was gone, I sat up, letting the blood flow down slowly. I picked up the nail gun. I wanted to finish his row of tiles and at least get that done before he got back. It was my way to thank him for reading my mind.

A shout erupted from the ground somewhere above the noise of the nail gun going off in my hand. I thought for a moment it was Raven maybe asking me what I really wanted to eat since I gave him a big list to choose from.

I took my nail gun with me and eased myself closer to the ladder where I could see the front lawn.

Marc stood there, his hands on his hips. He wore a pair of jeans and a blue T-shirt. From the way he stared up at me, with his angled chin pointed upward, I caught the scruff of his unshaven face. "Hey," he shouted. "Are you up there by yourself?"

"There you are," I called down to him. I suddenly hated that I was on the roof now. Made it harder to yell at him. I had to shout louder. "Where have you been?"

He squinted up at me. His brown hair swept across his eyes against the breeze. He planted his boot on the lowest rung of the ladder, grabbing the end as if he was going to hold it in place. "What?" he asked, shouting up at me.

"Are we done chasing Coaltar yet?"

"No."

I grunted. "Then what are we doing here? Shouldn't we be chasing him or something? I can't stay here forever. Wil--"

"He's fine," Marc said. "You aren't. Coaltar is looking for you."

"But--"

"Do you want to lead him back to your hotel room? Do you want him to know who you really are? You already fucked up yesterday and we need to get the camera back."

"Did you get the camera?"

"Tonight," he shouted. "We had to track it down first and someone's going to be risking his neck an awful lot to retrieve it. Coaltar may already know who you are if they looked at it. You have to stay with us probably forever now." He smirked at that, like he really didn't disapprove of the idea. Like he found it funny that my whole life got turned upside down.

"He knows Brandon! Brandon's out here doing things. What's the difference? I don't need a babysitter."

"Brandon sticks with us. There is no difference."

I groaned. He was impossible. I aimed the end of the nail gun down at him. "Why are you being a jerk? Just let me call Wil so he's not freaking out."

"No contact," he said. "You probably shouldn't even be here. You need to go off the radar for a while."

"What am I supposed to do?"

"Stop pointing the nail gun at me for one."

I lifted the gun up, pointing at the air above me. "Tell me why I shouldn't pop a nail down at you right now."

"What?"

"You told me one job," I said. "One pickpocketing thing. Now you're saying I'm stuck with you all until you figure out Coaltar? But you're not even doing that now. You're building a roof."

Marc shrugged. "He's not doing anything right now. We're waiting him out. We're trying to make sure he forgets about you."

"How am I supposed to get a job if I'm supposed to go under the radar?"

"You can stay with us until we figure this out. Stop yelling at me." He took a step back. "You shouldn't be up there by yourself. Why didn't they give you a hardhat?"

"Don't come up here. I might shoot you with this thing."

"Try it."

I don't know what came over me. Maybe his attitude and the fact that I was worried about not hearing from Wil. Overnight was one thing. Now that I was hearing it from Marc's lips that I may be here for a month or even longer, I was terrified for my brother. How would I even know he was okay if I couldn't hear from him? What if Coaltar had him now?

Wil would start looking for me if I didn't contact him soon. He'd think something happened to me. He'd be alone to deal with Jack every night. I'd let them talk me into staying away this long, lured by their promises.

I aimed the gun down, toward the grass at Marc's feet. I pulled back on the safety. I just wanted to scare him. And shooting nails felt good.

"Bambi!" he called in a warning tone. "Don't you dare."

I pulled the trigger. The moment I did it, I regretted it. I knew it was wrong, even just to scare him.

I lost track of where the nail went. Once it popped out of the gun, the wind caught against my eyes and blurred my vision a bit.

Marc stepped back and then fell on his butt into the grass. He reached forward, putting his hand around his knee in a protective move. "Shit! Bambi!"

And then I saw the blood.

My heart stopped. I released the nail gun safety slowly. What did I just do?

♠

DESOLATE

*A*n hour later, I was sitting in a hospital waiting room. Axel drove, and the guys left the nail in the leg after calling a doctor to ask what to do. They didn't want us to just pull it out, in case it was holding an important artery together or something.

I'd climbed down from the roof, feeling out of place and unsure of what to do. The guilt was heavy on my lungs and made it hard to breathe, hard to focus.

Marc didn't say a word to me on the drive over. No one did. I replayed the event in my mind, of how they swarmed on him, and collectively worked together to carry him into the car. Raven, Kevin and Brandon stayed behind to finish what they could, mostly at Marc's insistence since he said it wasn't that bad.

And Marc had lied to them. He said he did it to himself. Accident. He shot himself in the leg and then rushed down the ladder so they didn't have to carry him down.

He lied to protect me. And all I did was stare at him in silence. He didn't even look at me. I wasn't sure if I should contradict him and confess the truth. I worried the boys would hate me after. And then I felt horrible because Marc lied to his friends, which made the guilt of shooting him in the leg so much worse.

Axel was the one who addressed the emergency room nurses and handled nearly everything. Corey was there and helped, but soon Axel told him to take the car and go back to the work site. Neither of them said anything about me, and I wasn't sure where they wanted me to go, but Corey left without inviting me along, maybe assuming I wanted to stay.

I wasn't sure if I should, if Marc would want me to stay and then I felt horrible again for wanting to bail when it was my fault he was here in the first place.

I sat alone. Axel was with Marc somewhere deeper inside the hospital. I think Axel had told me to go with him, but I ignored him. If Marc didn't invite me, I didn't feel comfortable going. I didn't think he wanted me to. Not after what I'd done.

I sat in a sofa, facing a wide window that looked out across the parking lot and at the buildings across the way in downtown Charleston. There was a television on the wall nearby tuned to CNN. Nurses and visitors walked by occasionally. I ignored it all. I leaned forward, my head in my hands, staring at the floor.

I told myself I should go. I should get up and walk out. Wouldn't it be a relief to them if I just disappeared? The hotel room was paid for. I could get a job in another town and wire money to Wil somehow. I had been wrong to think when this Coaltar thing passed, that the boys and I could possibly work together. I wasn't the sort to work with anyone. I didn't play well with others.

Why did I have to be so angry all the time? Was that how I was going to live for the rest of my life? Jumping in head first without thinking? Shooting nail guns at people in a stroke of fury? Axel was right. He shouldn't have taught me about guns because now I wanted to fire off a bunch of them just to let this burning energy out of my body. And the only thing I wanted to shoot at was myself for being so stupid.

Walking away seemed easier. They'd done enough for me, and I knew what I was like. Look at the trouble I'd caused already. Brandon was a potential target for Coaltar now, and perhaps Corey, too, since he was with us yesterday. It was obvious now that they were brothers, when that detail may have slipped by them before. I shot Marc in the leg. Would Raven be next? Or Axel?

Every time I told myself to stand up and walk out, I couldn't move. I was terrified of who I'd run into next and end up hurting in some way.

I sensed someone sitting beside me and without even needing to look, knew it was Axel. Even as his boot and jean-clad ankle came into view, I couldn't get myself to sit up. Staring off at the floor numbed out my feelings.

"Don't look so strung out," Axel said, his voice as deep and calm as when he'd been talking about his Sea Sparkle. "They'll pull out the nail and patch him up. He'll be walking out of here."

"I shouldn't be here," I said. "I should go home."

"Why do you keep insisting that you should go back there? You didn't want to be there when you lived there. Is it just for Wil? Why do you need to see him? Where is he right now?"

"He should be at school."

"So he's probably safe. He's a hell of a lot safer than you are. So why do you keep saying that you need to go home?"

I sighed, covering my eyes with my palms. "I can't do this."

A hand spread over my back, rubbing between my shoulder blades. "Can't do what?"

"I don't know any more. I don't know what I'm doing."

"You were doing fine," Axel said. "You were perfect at the party."

"Except when I got too close," I said.

"That was an accident," he said. "You didn't know. That was probably our fault. You seemed to have a good time yesterday at the shooting range. And you were doing well today putting in roofing at the house."

"I put the nail in his leg," I said flatly. "We were arguing and I shot him. I did it because I was angry at him. I wasn't really aiming at him, just at the ground near his feet. I wanted to scare him. I missed." I rubbed my palms deeper against my eyes, causing a wash of colors behind them as if trying to dig out the memory. "And he lied to everyone and said it was an accident."

Axel was quiet for a long moment, but his hand never left my back. "Kayli," he said, his smoky voice deepening, softening. He shouldn't have. I didn't deserve his sympathy.

238

"I'm going to end up in jail," I said. "I'm going to end up going home and pickpocketing until I get caught. Or one day I'll shoot someone because I'm just mad. I'm no better than Coaltar. Probably worse because we don't even know if he's a bad guy."

Axel's hand lifted and he laid his palm on my head, gently drawing it over. He sat back against the sofa, and folded me into him, until my head was resting against his shoulder. He kept his arm around my neck, and pressed his cheek to my hair. "Stop talking like this."

"Tell me to go home," I said.

"You're not going home right now," he said, the strength returning, rising with every sentence he spoke. "You're going to wait here with me until Marc is on his feet again. And you're not going back to pickpocketing. You're too smart for that. You're going to come back to work for us. Or if you want, we'll get you a job somewhere else. But you aren't going to retreat back into your little hotel room and push everyone else out."

"Why would you guys even do this?" I asked. "Why won't you give up on me?"

"You're not giving up on us," he said, "or you would have gone home already. If you're waiting for us to push you out the door, you're going to be disappointed. That's not what we do."

"I just put a nail through your friend's leg. You want me to stick around?"

"I want you to stop talking like you've lost your spark. So you've found out you've got some anger issues and you're not as perfect as you thought you were. Welcome to life, Kayli. It's hard and it sucks, but when you've found something good, you don't walk away from it."

"Uh, hello. That's what I'm saying. Why aren't you telling me to get lost?"

"Same reason," he said. His arm lowered, until his hand was on my shoulder and he rubbed there. His voice softened considerably as he continued. "You're no worse than Marc when I found him."

"What?"

He sighed. "When I met him, Marc was thirteen years old, and living in a single room in a trailer his uncle owned. For three years, he fought coming with me; he would rather have stayed in the gutter."

"Why?" I asked. "Why keep trying when he didn't want you to?"

"Because he saved my life," he said. "That's another long story, but basically when it came down to it, when it became a choice of totally going over the edge, or stepping up and doing the right thing, he did do the right thing. He isn't perfect. He makes mistakes. We all do. If you're willing to learn from and make up for those mistakes, and try to do better next time, doesn't that deserve a chance?"

I rolled my palm against my eye. "I don't understand you guys at all. No one does this."

"Maybe if more people did, we wouldn't be so surprising." His fingers traced over my shoulder, making circles against my skin. "But do me a favor. Can you stay with us at least long enough to figure out how to keep our promise to you, and to make sure you aren't at risk of endangering yourself or your brother? I'll invite you to stick around longer if you want, but stay until at least then. You risked a lot, diving in head first with Coaltar at our request. It's our fault for putting you in this mess. Let us make it up to you."

I breathed slowly in and out, feeling the cushion of his shoulder under my cheek. It surprised me how easy it had been to sink into him, like a longtime friend. What was it about this group that I simply felt comfortable among them even when my brain told me I shouldn't be?

I'd been fighting for so long, keeping people away to protect myself. Here was this group that knew me and was trying to protect me, without me asking. Coaltar could have been anyone I'd tried to pickpocket at the mall, or downtown, or anywhere. What if he had been the one I'd targeted downtown instead of Dr. Roberts? Would I be in this same dangerous situation and not know it? I didn't even know for sure if I was in any danger or not.

Yet still, I didn't have an answer for Axel. I didn't trust myself to say anything when he was asking me to stay for so long. I couldn't promise something I wasn't sure I could do.

His cheek slowed against my head, until his lips pressed down. "You could learn a lot from us, you know," he whispered against my hair. "I think it's been good for some of the guys. And you don't seem to mind how rough the guys can be. It might do you some good to hang around them. Learn a few new tricks."

"What about you?"

"You don't want to hang out with me. I'm boring. I work too much."

"Because of the Academy?"

"Shhh," he said. He lifted his head and the moment he did, I missed that closeness. I wanted it back but I was too terrified to ask. "That's supposed to be a secret, you know."

"No one's listening."

"You never know who is listening. That's something you should learn. Watch what you say all the time. Talk like the world is listening in. Usually because someone is."

I twisted my lips, gluing them together. I didn't want to talk any more.

♠♠♠♠♠

Later, Axel left me alone so he could go look in on Marc. When I got up, I just wanted to walk around the interior of the hospital. I needed to expel the energy I was feeling, because sitting still was too much. The frog in my throat, the thickness I felt in my eyes from forcing a brave face had solidified until I could barely stand it.

When walking the halls of the hospital wasn't enough, I walked out into the sun to circle the building.

I told myself I was taking a walk. I wouldn't admit I was running away. I didn't really want to. I just wanted to think, and I couldn't think with the boys around. They muddled my brain. I needed to calculate my own next move, and not have

C. L. Stone

them pressuring me one way or another. I wouldn't go see Wil, but the further I got away from the guys, I felt my head clearing of all the sudden feelings and the lure of promises I wasn't ready to believe in.

And every step away, I felt like I swallowed another rock in my gut. It killed me. Disappointed faces followed me wherever I went.

Once I tasted the air outside, I couldn't go back. Not now. Not until I knew the answers.

I got my bearings and started across the parking lot. A silver BMW pulled around just as I was crossing, and stopped short almost at my knees. The glare off the windshield kept me from seeing whoever it was. I kept walking. The person blared on the horn before driving on behind me, stopping to pick up some blond teenage girl waiting for him back at the hospital entrance.

I repeated that this was the right thing to do over and over in my head. Despite what Axel was telling me, it was all too hard to believe. People don't just walk up to you and become friends, ready to do all those things for you. Maybe what he said was true, and they saw something of themselves in me and wanted to help. I appreciated what they had done for me, but I needed to find my own path and not depend on anyone else. If they could take care of Wil's future, that's all I wanted.

I didn't know what I wanted for myself. Maybe nothing. What kind of future did a thief deserve? The Academy guys had no idea. They were college boys. They were some secret protection police. What did they know about the darkness that followed your soul when you've done horrible things? Redemption doesn't get handed to you like a get out of jail free card. The only way I was going to redeem myself was going to be doing the right thing for other people. No credit. No help from anyone. Not for someone like me.

I stood on the corner, debating on hitching a ride somewhere, or wandering downtown. Eventually I found Marion Square and started heading east. Six blocks later, I was facing those old brick buildings on Market Street.

There was no real reason to go there. Maybe I needed a place that reminded me of a mall, where people wandered aimlessly, because that's what I needed to do. I needed to lose myself a little to figure out where I wanted to be.

I ignored the pang of hunger in my stomach. With not a penny on me, it was hard not to revert back and lift a wallet, even just for a five dollar bill for some food. Maybe the boys were right. It had become too easy for me. I resorted to it because, in my mind, it was simply the fastest way to pick up what I needed.

But was it? There was more to it, too. I felt the itch inside of me now, walking along the streets. In a twisted way, I felt that edge of risk slipping under my skin pulling me back to the challenge. Like a drug, it was tempting me. Reasons whispered into my brain. That guy would only waste it on his girlfriend. He would never miss a twenty.

Maybe it wasn't about the hunger, money or even needing to save Wil. What I felt, that edge of insanity right before each pull, that underlying feeling that I was doing something clever and risky was what kept me going.

The more I thought about it, the more I convinced myself that was why the boys excited me. If I had really wanted to, I'd have walked out of their apartment the first time, knowing my rent was paid and have taken a job. A month of work would have been enough to save up for even a better place.

Instead, I stayed for the party, and even after, when I could have let them deal with the aftermath, I let them talk me into staying. Lifting Coaltar's wallet had been one of the riskiest pulls I had ever done. The memory swept a wave of thrills through me that left me shaking with pleasure. The lure the boys promised me, especially Axel since he mentioned I could join the Academy, was the possibility of doing things like that as my job. Like Raven with his punching me back, or feeling the pull of the trigger and learning about guns, I was hanging onto the excitement, and one that possibly came without too much chance of getting caught. Relieving the guilt, I was freer to be a little more reckless.

But what happened when Coaltar was proven to be either a good guy or a bad guy? What happened when they no longer felt they needed to protect me? Wouldn't they want to move on? Axel made offers, but was he even serious or just trying to make me feel better because he felt sorry for me?

Brandon's kiss from last night reentered my mind along with the promises he'd made: that I could stay with him and he'd care of me.

But that wasn't who I was. I didn't want to fall into that role. I didn't want him to develop feelings for me under that illusion. The protector and the protected. No, I wouldn't deny that I felt the flirt of something inside me when I was near him. I couldn't stop thinking of his lips now, of his soothing touch. I felt a strange twinge with Raven, too. I thought I felt similar about Corey, but could easily pin that as an early bud of a friendship. While it was tempting to spend a month exploring their world by hiding amongst them, it also wouldn't be fair to them. They felt forced to look out for me. I didn't want to be forced on anyone.

No. I needed my own space. I needed to take care of me. Doing it alone would be the only way I knew for sure if any of them cared. If I did it on my own, and they still wanted to be friends, or more, that was my answer.

I needed to get rid of Coaltar, one way or another. That was the only way I'd know.

♠

CAT AND MOUSE

I took off along King Street, heading east toward White Point and the edge of the peninsula. I didn't have a plan, but I had an approximate idea of where Coaltar's house was, and that's where I was headed.

It didn't take long to come across the house in the South of Broad area. The neighborhood itself made me too uncomfortable to linger for very long on his sidewalk. The homes here were even more of a spectacle as they surrounded White Point Garden, a popular tourist spot. Not to mention the locals used it to walk the dog, exercise, and do whatever normal people who didn't have to steal wallets for a living did with their time. I found a bench on a corner of White Point that still allowed me to see the house. I parked myself there, catching my breath after the brisk walk.

It was dusk. The house was still. Neighbors' homes were still. An occasional car passed. I wasn't sure what I was going to do. If I were to sit and stare at his house too long, it probably would become obvious that I was scoping it out. At night, however...

I couldn't be sure if he was even home. I was starting from ground zero now. What in the world did I know about spying on anyone? I just had to wait for him to do something. I settled into the bench, pretending to be more interested in the park and watching the sun set.

After a while, I ended up on my back, staring up at the trees and propped up my head where I got a good view of Coaltar's front door.

♠♠♠♠♠

Spying was starting to be really boring. Staring at an unmoving house was worse than watching grass grow.

Lights turned on after the shadows of twilight fell over the city. The house illuminated, with no other signs of life. People walking by with their dogs or jogging or driving were distractions, but temporary ones.

It took another hour of waiting on the bench, and my back killing me from the hard seat, before anything interesting happened. Movement caught my bored eyes. I stilled, wanting to sit up to see better but not wanting to draw attention.

The front gate at Coaltar's house opened. A shadowed figure passed through. Black ball cap, jeans, and a baggy T-shirt wasn't enough to mask that it was Coaltar. Despite trying to look casual, the shirt and jeans looked expensive and the hat appeared brand new.

Perfect.

I followed him back to King Street. He started west, and kept at a decent pace, enough that I had to do almost a jog at times. I had to wait to let him cross the street. Luckily at this time of night, the streets were nearly empty. It wasn't too hard to keep an eye on him from a reasonable distance.

The boys had been right. He left the house at night, plain clothed. My mind jumped to conclusions of my own though. A secret lover? Or maybe he simply couldn't sleep and he wandered around to think. Maybe he wasn't a snob and could pull off talking to a few thugs along the way. Was it too far of a stretch?

I kept waiting for him to turn off King Street, maybe circle the block, but when he passed by Market Street, which was a decent stretch from his neighborhood, it became clear that perhaps this wasn't some night stroll. There was some business he needed to get to.

Slowly, the neighborhood began to change from big houses to fancy shops, to less-than-attractive brick buildings. Charleston peninsula was constantly being renovated, but there were still places closer toward I-26 that were left in the shadows. Old factory buildings crumbled with time and every hurricane that barreled through. Ghosts of old fancy homes stood gutted, either from a storm, or from lack of funds to fix them up. While Charleston's city council slowly pushed the lower class out further into North Charleston, they couldn't get rid of the gritty underbelly completely.

Coaltar finally diverted from King, taking a right onto Woolfe. I bristled at the change of some of the more shabbier homes into this run-down industrial area. Old factories surrounded us. The brick walls used to have painted advertisements of what they made inside, but the paint had peeled away after years of Charleston weather, and weed-filled gravel parking lots told me no decent person had been near here in a while.

Mr. Coaltar passed by two of these buildings, and then made a left onto a side street. I slowed, not wanting to catch him around the corner if he stopped.

But when I got to the corner and checked, there was no sign of him.

I cursed to myself, and stilled. I didn't think he caught on that someone was following him, but I couldn't be sure. My fingertips brushed at my thighs. I wished I'd had worn jeans. With the sun down, the temperature had dropped. The walk had kept me warm up to a point, but the night breeze was starting to ice me over.

I was tempted to go back, maybe find my way back to that bench and wait again. I suddenly felt exhausted. Only pride kept me from returning to the Sergeant Jasper now. I'd been arrogant to assume maybe I could find out quickly what Mr. Coaltar had been up to. Wasn't this what the boys had been doing? What made me think I could figure this out by following him?

I stuffed my hands into my pockets and waited, checking the streets in front and behind me. I started up between the two buildings where I last spotted Coaltar. If I bumped into him or he rerouted, I may be out of luck. I'd have to go back. Maybe I could break into his house while he was gone. Or at least peek through his windows.

I was about to give up when I heard the scratch of sneakers along pavement. I checked behind me. A person crossed the street and then followed the sidewalk behind me at a distance, but getting closer.

Either Mr. Coaltar had turned around, or this was someone new. I debated my options.

I turned left, cutting through a ragged parking lot. There were two industrial buildings close to each other, but on the other side was King Street again, and it wouldn't take long to get to a more crowded spot. I hurried through the lot, planning to make a dash between the buildings. My imagination went wild with thoughts of who this was and what he wanted. Whoever it was, I suddenly felt like I was being hunted, so I wanted to lose him quickly.

The path between the two industrial buildings was darker than I'd thought once I dipped into the deeper shadows. The footsteps behind me slowed. I could have been wrong and this person wasn't that interested in me, but I didn't want to take that chance.

I marched faster and darted between the two brick walls of the buildings.

My heart stopped in my chest when a cluster of teenagers stood at the end of the alley. I couldn't have seen them in the dark with their black clothes. Hanging out together in a sketchy part of town, they were certainly not Boy Scouts.

Before I could decide to turn around, they'd noticed me, straightening. Their dark faces curious.

I turned back; I could take on one guy, not a dozen. I squared my shoulders to face off my pursuer.

The guy had black hair, dark eyes, dark skin. Not Coaltar.

I made to walk around him, and his hands shot out. "Hey," the guy said. A strong waft of alcohol floated to me.

The familiar feeling that he wanted something from me that I wasn't willing to give settled in. I wasn't going to stick around to find out what he wanted.

"Rape!" I screamed. Why not? It worked before.

Instead of backing up, he pounced. I tried to dart away,

but in the darkness, my ankle caught on his sneakered foot. I stumbled, but he caught me by the waist in a harsh grip.

"What are you? Crazy? High?" His voice was irritating, a squeaky pitch.

I kicked. I fought. I bit, but his arms, as wiry as they were, crushed me. His legs evaded my attempts to knee him in the shin.

"Who's that?" one of the guys from the group behind me called out. "That you Dale?"

"Yeah. Who let the crazy girl out tonight? These hoes are getting feisty."

Crap. They knew each other.

Since he wasn't letting go, I dropped like a dead weight. Dale was too slow, and I landed on the ground.

I kicked up at his groin. My leg made contact.

Dale yelped but it suddenly died off as he choked. He grabbed at his crotch, and knelt, holding his junk.

I scrambled up, trying to fly off. An arm caught my shirt, tearing it. Another hand grasped my arm.

I made a fist with my free hand, turning, striking someone in the face.

Another hand wrapped around my throat.

I struggled, but soon I had to stop clawing and scratching, and wedge my fingers against the hand that strangled me. I hung on to it, trying to pull it away, but it squeezed. Breath left me, but never came back in. I wanted to cough, but couldn't.

My eyes were open, but the light around me changed, becoming hazy.

Loud shouts started going on around me. A thick thud. A scream -- male and full of pain.

The hand around my throat released and I dropped to the ground. I choked, grasping at the ground and sucking in air. I coughed hard, enough that my body tilted and I was on my back on the ground.

The last thing I remember is being lifted.

♠

COALTAR

*T*he sound of a car driving somewhere below me, on the street, had me feeling like I was back at the hotel. My throat felt itchy. I worried about getting Wil sick with a cold when he had tests coming up.

When I woke enough to realize the bed felt different, I suddenly remembered Marc. Was I supposed to be in his bed? Or with Corey? Or...

I flipped over, willing my body to move when it felt stiff and sore, especially at my throat. I blinked hazily at the ceiling, disoriented.

The ceiling struck me funny. Did one of the boys have carved woodwork edging?

Didn't I shoot someone in the knee? With a .303 rifle?

I sat up with a jolt, looking around. The bed was plush, with crisp white sheets and blanket, and a rich black wood headboard. There was a thick black rug under the bed, and the floors beyond it were a dark cherry wood.

As the details of the room sunk in, and a memory didn't surface that told me why I was here, I panicked. Where the hell was I?

The spot next to me was unmade. I reached over to feel the coolness of the pillow, and the indention in it. Someone else had been here.

I was wearing the same black shirt and shorts I'd had on the night before. The sleeve had been torn, reminding me of the struggle in the alley. My heart thundered at the memory, but I needed to focus.

Beside the bed was an overstuffed chair, appearing to have been moved close so I'd notice. There was a black tank top and pair of shorts similar to what I was wearing splayed out. Different, though. The label at the neck of the shirt said International Concepts. Definitely not a Wal-Mart brand, which was about the extent of my knowledge about clothing labels.

I held my breath, listening. I couldn't hear anything. The fact that someone had been here beside me made me want to pinpoint whoever it was within the building.

I jumped from the bed, going to the window. I studied the street, trying to figure out where I was.

I spotted a familiar bench within eyesight down the road and White Point Gardens behind it. I calculated the distance.

Shit.

Maybe I could get out of here without Coaltar noticing. The guys thought I was too close before? I was neck deep now.

I looked around for shoes, but there weren't any available. My boots were gone. I grunted. I really liked those boots. I hated the thought of leaving them. But I wasn't going to start looking around.

I padded to the door. It was open and all I had to do was nudge it a couple of inches to give myself enough room to step out.

The hallway was narrow, and there were a lot of doors. I spotted the start of the stairwell at the end of the hall. I stilled, listening. Silence.

I stepped forward and the floorboards creaked below my weight. This is why I never broke into houses. Wasn't my style to sneak around like that.

More creaking sounded behind me, like someone moving in a room further down the hall. It was all I needed to know.

I zoomed down the hall, not caring about being heard, as long as I had a head start and he couldn't get in my way. I thundered down the stairs, found a second level, zoomed down to the first.

I was at the back door, where the party had been. I took a turn, finding the hallway I remembered going through toward the front door. The coast was clear. I dashed down the hall.

251

My heart slammed against my rib cage. I was going to make it!

A form launched from a side door as I started to pass. I was caught in a pair of strong arms, and I had been running so hard that we both tilted. He gripped my waist protectively, holding me up and catching us both with one hand hard on the floor before his elbow crumbled and we crashed.

I knocked my head into his shoulder, getting a jolt of pain between my eyes as the bump there resounded. I cried out, and started clawing away in a panic. I closed a fist, punching him hard in the temple. He grabbed my wrist.

My body was twisted, and he pressed his full weight on me. His knees bit down tight against my thighs. He pinned my wrists to the ground. I was uneven on my side, unable to move under his weight.

"Kate!" Coaltar shouted. "Calm down."

"Let go!" I choked, and then coughed hard. I was forced to stop fighting. I twisted my face away from him, a hacking cough taking over.

His knees moved. He kept both of my wrists in one hand, grabbing my body with his other arm. In a near flip, his arm encircled my shoulders in a headlock, with my arms pinned behind me. He lifted me with him and sat up, with my back pressed into his chest. His lips found the back of my ear.

"Breathe," he said, his voice raspy. "Kate, calm down and breathe."

I wanted to tell him off but my throat wasn't going to let me. I coughed once more, and started sucking down air. Him sitting me up had helped for the moment. The air stung my throat but it was what I needed.

"I'm going to let you go," Coaltar said.

I shifted, squirming, resisting against his grip.

His arms hardened around me, tightening enough to threaten to cut off my air again. "Nu uh. I'll let go when you promise not to run off. And you tell me what you were doing following me, and trying to take on a team of gang members singlehanded."

"You're going to let me go," I wheezed out. "And I'm

going to walk out that door and..."

His arms tightened a little more, cutting off my air briefly. "Don't go getting your feathers all ruffled. You're going to get yourself killed walking in neighborhoods like that."

I wedged an arm out from his hold and swatted at his in response, unable to do much but try to breathe slowly and not cough. When panic mode subsided, I was simply angry. Probably more hurt that I was caught, but then if he hadn't come for me back in that alleyway, I would have ended up dead in the gutter.

"I'm not going to hurt you," he said, the syrup thickening in his Southern accent. "I wouldn't normally wrestle a girl in my house. At least not like this."

I tried to twist, but with his arm around me and his strong body at my back, it was difficult, and I'd lost what energy I had.

"I'm going to let go," he said. "But if you try to run, I'll run after you. And not to be arrogant, but I think I'm faster."

He slowly eased his arm from around my chest. I sucked in air. When he let go enough that I could move, I launched myself to get away from him, scooting across the floor on my butt and backing up. I planted a hand at my throat, feeling the tender spots.

He knelt in front of me, holding his hands out. "Don't run," he said. "Do you need help? Do you need a doctor?"

I stilled, unsure. All I had to go on about him was what the boys tried to warn me about. Still, he could have left me back in the alley. He could have called the cops on me. Instead he brought me back. He didn't remove my clothes when he could have, considering I was unconscious. If he was a bad guy, he really sucked at it.

I shook my head. I didn't need a doctor.

He inched closer. I backed up a foot until I was pressed against the far wall

He stopped. "Easy," he said, still holding his hands out toward me. "Easy, sugar." He wiped his fingers across his mouth. His brow furrowed, as if trying to figure out a puzzle.

"Okay, listen." He pointed down the hall. "There's a kitchen that way. Now I'm not a cook, but I make a pretty decent cup of coffee. Or would you want water?"

At the thought of water, I stiffened. I desperately needed it and was reluctant to say so. I didn't want to accept anything from him.

"Just come talk to me," he said. He lifted one of his knees and planted a foot on the floor and inched forward again. He held his arms out as if to offer me help up. "Come on, Kate."

I tried not to flinch at the name. I moved my feet until I was steady enough to rise, using the wall as a balance. He got up in the same slow movement. His arm stretched out, not touching. He just hovered over my arm, the other hand motioning the way.

I allowed him to guide me down the hallway, toward the rear stairs. He edged me through an archway. He encouraged me through a dining room and onward until we got to a set of swinging double doors. He moved ahead of me, pressing his back to one of the doors and pushing it open.

The kitchen was as big as the boys' apartments, probably both of them together. There was another smaller table near a wall by the window. The counters were a smooth blue marble and the walls were white and blue tile. The fridge, and duo stoves were black, new, huge. How many people lived here? Was all this for him?

He backed his way to the fridge, opening it, there was a collection of bottles of water inside among a variety of other foods stacked in tidy rows. He picked up a water bottle, opening it and held it out to me. "Here," he said.

I reached for it. His fingers brushed against mine as he passed it to me. I locked eyes with him. The gold flecks glinted. I took a quick sip. When the water splashed against my throat, it seemed to absorb it in seconds. I swallowed half the bottle before I took a breath.

His lips cocked into a sly smile. "There's more," he said.

I took another drink, swallowing thickly, forcing myself to calm down. If he was going to hurt me, he would have already.

He stilled, seeming to relax his shoulders. He wore a dark gray collared shirt with two buttons undone, the sleeves rolled up to almost his elbows, and the bottom hem was wrinkled and skewed, probably from when we were fighting. The jeans he wore were a darker gray and he was barefoot. His blond hair was mussed on the side.

The handsome sight sent my heart racing again. A guilt weighed on me about it, but I forced it back into a small crevice of my brain. He was supposed to be the bad guy I needed to stay away from, but I could enjoy the view while I was here, right? At any rate, he didn't give off the bad guy vibe like I'd expected, although there was something off about him.

He seemed to understand that I wasn't going to run like I'd intended to before. He waved me on toward the door again. "Come on," he said. "Let's sit and talk about this."

He showed me to a back room, where a collection of plush white couches surrounded a television and a stereo system. There was a wide open window that let in light. There wasn't a coaster or a magazine left on the wood and glass coffee table. The spectacularly large television screen was clear of streaks and was angled perfectly to not get a glare from the wide window. I didn't have to look, but could imagine the underside of the couch didn't have a single dust bunny. Untouchable. I wanted to lick my hand and pat the coffee table to make a smudge.

He gestured to the couch. I sat in the middle, with my feet flat on the floor at first. It was an awkward pose and I lifted my feet, forgetting propriety and drew my knees to my chest to be more comfortable. It was also a good way to be ready to launch myself up and running in case this didn't go well.

Coaltar lowered himself beside me, easing to sit against the cushion. His arm stretched across the cushion behind my back. The open part of his shirt curled back a bit, revealing more of the collarbone and threatened to distract me. It almost worked until his eyes demanded my attention. "Okay,

Kate. Tell me why you were following me."

I swallowed hard again, pressing the water bottle to my throat, letting the cool condensation soothe. "It seemed like a good idea at the time."

His lips curled up. "That's not an answer."

"Why do you walk in shady parts of town in the middle of the night?"

His head cocked, but he kept his eyes on me. "Why did you?"

"I was curious," I said.

"Maybe I was, too," he said. "Maybe I wanted to see how far you were willing to follow me."

Touché. I stared at him and he stared back. We weren't getting anywhere with each other bluffing.

"There's a rumor going around about you," I said.

His eyebrow lifted. "There's all sorts of rumors about me. Why don't you fill me in on which one you've been hearing about."

I was this far. May as well go for broke. "Someone said you're talking to gang members in the city. There's people who are worried you're into drugs, or guns, or doing something weird."

His lips parted and he stared intently at me a moment. Those golden flecks glinted with amusement. "That's a new one. So you go off half-cocked and thought following me all the way down to that run-down neighborhood was a good idea?"

"I just wanted to see if it was true."

He sat back, his eyes darting between mine as if trying to decide if I was serious. "Why?"

"What?"

"You didn't have a camera," he said. "You didn't have anything on you. Nothing to collect evidence, no weapon to protect yourself. You're not police. You're a little too young to be a detective. What drove you?"

"Curiosity."

His smile strengthened. "Don't tell me we're playing this game again."

"No, really," I said. "There's a..." Only I couldn't say it. I didn't know anything about the Academy. I couldn't betray the guys after what they'd done for me and Wil. "Word got around to some of my friends, who happen to be ... informants for the FBI."

"Do go on," he said, though his amused look didn't fade. "So they sent you?"

"They'd been following you. I just thought..."

"You were trying to get one up on them," he said. There was a slyness to the way his gaze settled on me then. His eyes pinched at the corners and his lips tightened at the edges. "I ticked off that boyfriend enough that you got into an argument, and you wanted to show him up by being the first to witness me doing something I shouldn't be."

I realized I made a mistake being too honest. I pinned Brandon as an informant. It was bad enough I was at risk of getting myself killed if he was a drug dealer. It was another to involve the boys. "He's not part of it. I just borrowed him for the night. I actually met him that day."

"He was pretty jealous for someone on a first date."

"I think he's the jealous type."

He smiled, lifting his hand to run through his dirty blond locks a couple of times before sliding his thumb across his lower lip once. "You've got to be the worst little spy I've ever come across."

"You run into them often?"

He rolled his eyes and shook his head. "Now, now, don't go thinking that. Anyone with more than a barrel of money around here gets followed in one way or another, by crooks or cops who think *you're* a crook."

"Actually," I said, "it doesn't matter either way to me."

"Oh?"

I shrugged. Maybe I should play good cop. "If you aren't, makes my job easier, I think. I clear your name, they become disinterested and move on to someone else."

"Ah." He shook a finger at me. "See? For now you'd be satisfied. But the next time I go to some no-name place around the globe and come back in the night, or talk to someone even remotely shady, someone else is going to be wondering what I'm up to. It's a never-ending cycle. They want you to walk naked in the street to make sure you aren't up to something, and then they want to arrest you for public indecency."

"Life for the rich must be crazy tough," I said, unable to curb my tongue.

He leaned in, his hand lowering until it was almost hovering over my shoulder, close enough that I could feel the warmth of his fingers. I sensed he was testing me to see how close he could get. "See, why does it have to be like that? You act like I'm the bad guy, but you're the one that walked into my home, crashed my party, and stalked me like a teenager following a boy band. Do you get people breaking into your home and wanting to know all your dirty little secrets?"

Yes. "Maybe."

He laughed, the sound rich and genuine. "Maybe you do. Most people don't. Maybe it's just you and I are the lucky ones."

I removed the bottle from my neck to take another sip of water. His smile faltered, and his gaze lowered from my face.

"Sweetie," he said. He reached for my neck.

I let him. I don't know why, but like Raven and the others, I sensed that he wouldn't really hurt me.

His fingertips traced along my skin. There was a coolness to his touch at first, but it warmed quickly. He smoothed over the corner of my neck. I winced as he got to a sore spot. "You're bruised," he said. His fingers slid down, following to my collarbone. I bit back a shiver and turned my head away. He hooked a finger at the material, pulling it back to expose my shoulder. "Baby doll, you've got bruises all over."

"Huh," I said in a tone suggesting that I wasn't surprised.

His eyes narrowed. "And these are older. Who's doing this to you?"

"No one."

"Kate," he said, stronger and determined for an answer.

I flinched, and smacked his hand away. Between Raven and the other boys, and then my own father, I had all kinds of bruises, but I wasn't going to tell him that. He wouldn't understand. "I'm not here to talk about me. I'm here to do you a favor."

He smirked. "Some favor. Next time I'll let you carry me home and then I'll wrestle you on my way out the door."

My eyes flared. "You—"

"Wait." He dropped a finger across my lips, cutting me off. "Hang on, sugar. Let's not start this again. I'm sorry. Okay? Let's try to get along for a minute here."

I glared at him, but stilled, trying to control my breathing. I was flying off the handle. Probably because I was hungry. And my throat hurt. This was the same problem I had with Marc and the others. I needed to stop before I got myself killed. Or worse, got the cops called on me.

He released my lips and his palm cupped my jaw. His fingers rubbed at a tender spot behind my earlobe. It was a slick move, but his fingers were incredibly skillful, picking just the right delicate area to stroke. It relaxed me incredibly. "All right, I'll let you in on what I'm up to. But you have to promise not to tell them exactly what I'm doing. What I do is my business, but you can tell them I'm not up to anything evil. Would that work to satisfy their curiosity?"

I wasn't sure. Would they trust me? I'd already left them behind. They wouldn't trust me when Axel told them what really happened with Marc's leg. "They may want to know."

His fingers smoothed back and forth along my jawline. "Kate, I need you to promise you'll try to convince them. I think when you see, though, you'll agree. It needs to stay a secret."

I hesitated, considering. It would require the Academy boys to trust me, and they had no reason to. I'd abandoned them. My curiosity was getting to me. He didn't seem like the monster they told me about. His warm fingers and those eyes, the golden flecks sparking, made me silent promises, and I surrendered. "I promise."

♠♠♠♠♠♠

He showed me back to the bedroom, where I could get the clothes he'd purchased for me. I used his bathroom to shower. I shaved by borrowing one of his razors and got dressed. I tried not to focus on the fact that his bathroom was bigger than the hotel room. I allowed myself to be jealous of him for having plush towels that felt soft against my clean skin. I wanted to wear one all day and even toyed with the idea of stealing it.

When I was dressed, I opened the bathroom door. He was sitting on the bed, studying something on his cell phone. I approached, and his head lifted. Those hazel eyes lit up, sending a wave of sparks through me that I didn't want to think about. He turned his phone off, tossing it back onto the comforter. He leaned back on his hands. "See, I didn't think you were a pink dress type of girl when I first saw you."

I twisted my lips. "I hated that thing."

"I could tell." He curled his fingers in a *come hither* motion.

I hesitated a moment before I approached slowly. He snagged my hands, and pressed our palms together, intertwining our fingers. "Well, before I show you my devilish side, let's go out."

"Huh?" I tried not to be distracted with his open flirting. I didn't encourage him, but I didn't stop him, either. It was tempting to see how far he went. Part of me was flattered, this handsome, rich guy who could have had anyone was at least curious and playing with me. I tried not to forget that he probably had girls in his bedroom all the time. I didn't want to be another notch on the post.

"We've got a few of hours to wait," he said. "Until then, what do you want to do?"

"Why do we have to wait so long?"

"Who we want to see won't be available until later."

"Who are we going to go see?"

His smile broadened and he brought one of my hands to his mouth and kissed the knuckles. "So you can knock me over with a vase and run out on me? No thanks."

My heart was tripping over itself.

This was becoming difficult to control.

"I may not use a vase."

He laughed, pushing me away and standing up. He grabbed his phone, putting it in his pocket. "When's the last time you went sailing?"

♠

SAILBOATS

*I*t wasn't like I had much of a choice. He was going to go sailing with or without me. Now that he knew people were on to him, he could skip town if I left him alone. Not that I was any sort of law enforcement, but I didn't want to leave him alone if he decided he wanted to run.

And it wasn't like I could just lose him now. I was going to find out what he was up to. Wouldn't Marc, if he had any sense in him, have done the same thing?

He had a Mercedes in the garage. It was black, with tinted windows. At first look, I recoiled as it seemed so gaudy a car to have. He opened the passenger side door for me. The interior was heady with the smell of new leather. Is that what new cars smelled like? I'd never been in one before.

I'd gotten my boots back, and I retied them to distract myself as he got in. Guilt weighed on me a bit as I thought my shoes were too dirty to put inside his nice new car. He didn't say anything so I forced myself to forget about it.

After he started the car and pulled out of the garage, he headed south toward City Marina.

To get to it, he passed right by the Sergeant Jasper. At the sight of the boys' apartment tower, I pulled back in the seat, trying to be small. At the same time, I scanned the parking lot, looking for their cars. The guilt was heavy, even though I felt I shouldn't be. I was still a stranger to them. If I disappeared forever, they would forget about me in a couple days. They were probably at that house from yesterday, on the roof finishing the work I had caused a delay in. Everyone except for Marc, who was probably recovering. He was probably happy I was out of his hair.

"Something wrong?" Mr. Coaltar asked.

"No," I said. I turned my head and purposefully avoided looking at the apartment tower any more. "What's your name, anyway?"

He grinned. "You forgot? Like you forgot your boyfriend's name?"

"I know your last name is Coaltar," I said. "I mean your first name."

He tilted his head around as he looked at me. "Are you sure you're an FBI informant?"

"The rumors I heard were only about what you were up to. There weren't too many details."

"Like my name?"

I rolled my eyes. "I can call you Bob if you'd like."

"Close. Try Blake."

I twisted my lips. "Blake?"

"Something wrong with it?"

"I don't know yet. I don't know if you're a Blake."

He laughed. "Is there anything you do like about me?"

I stilled, unsure how to answer him. The truth was, I didn't know how to behave around him. Blake Coaltar sent new thrills through me, tempting me to play whatever game he was up to. I think I was tempted because he felt different. Most guys were predictable. He was a lot like the Academy guys, unpredictable, impulsive. I liked that. "Your car is okay," I said.

His smirk broadened and he stepped on the gas.

It was a short stretch before he turned into the marina. He squeezed the Mercedes into a parking space. He shut off the engine and hopped out quickly, opening the door on my side. I joined him in walking toward the docks.

The chill of the night before still lingered, even with the sun beating down on us. The light made the water sparkle and it dazzled my eyes. The air was fresh, salty.

He hung an arm around my shoulders. "Come on, Kate. Tell me you've got a pair of sea legs."

"Might have paddled around in a canoe once or twice."

Lie. I'd never been anywhere but to the beach. I hadn't ever been on a boat.

We ambled our way toward a length of dock and passed a handful of people as we went. I scanned the various sized boats rocking on the water. I didn't spot anyone that could be identified as security. There appeared to be so many boats parked close to each other. A number of them were huge, including a few three-story yachts that were parallel parked along the broadest side of the dock. We walked right past the dock house, and no one stopped us or bothered to ask why we were there. What if we were here to steal one of these things? Would they even notice?

"You do this often?" I asked.

"I'm not home too often. And when I am, I usually don't have time for sailing," he said. He stopped along the edge of the dock, facing into the wind. His blond locks swept into his eyes and he brushed them away from his face. He pointed to one of the smaller sailboats at the far edge. "There she is."

I squinted. The boat's sails were down, and compared to some of the other boats around it, it seemed so small. "All that money and you've got that thing?"

He grunted. "You just don't know anything about boats. That, my dear, is the biggest boat a single person can sail on his own. Unless you're going to tell me you know a thing or two about sailing."

"And if I did?"

He grinned. "Then I'd buy a bigger boat."

"I thought you said you had a yacht."

"Do you want to go sailing, or do you want to go to Europe?"

"What?"

"I only take the yacht for long distance trips. I'll show you my yacht when you're ready for that." He nudged me toward the sailboat.

He climbed on first and then held out a hand to me to help me get onboard. He pointed to where he wanted me to sit on the front deck. I wanted to do something besides watch him, but he insisted on doing it himself. He tugged this rope, and he pulled that lever. Soon he had the sailboat pulling away from the docks and out beyond the edge of Charleston.

And he did it in exquisite precision, with that broad smile on his face, the tan clashing against his white, perfect teeth. His hazel eyes were wide, excited. His hair blew around in the breeze, the tips teasing his cheeks, and he had to release the helm on occasion to brush hair away from his eyes.

I stared at the water to relieve the butterflies doing whirligigs in my core.

When the boat went past the stretch of peninsula and out into the harbor, he opened the sails fully and the boat sped up. I wanted to compare it to driving with the top down on a car, but it was much better than that for some reason. The air felt cleaner. The water splashed as the boat lunged forward. We were getting away from people instead of diving into traffic. Freer. Fuller.

He didn't go far, just out into Charleston Harbor. The city sat behind us, with Mount Pleasant to the north and John's Island to the south. When we were near the middle of the harbor, he slowed, dragging in the sails until we were almost dead still.

"Okay," I said. "I may like your boat."

He released a rich laugh, running a hand through his hair. "At least I have something going for me." He sat down on the deck next to me, sitting cross-legged and leaning back on his hands. "Girls are usually into the good looks and tat pocketbook."

"Meh," I said.

He smirked. "Well shut my mouth. Miss Kate doesn't like handsome faces."

I rolled my eyes and looked out toward Mount Pleasant. Sailing really wasn't all that bad.

But if I had felt uncomfortable wasting time with Corey the day before, I felt worse now. Again I felt the guilt that I should be working instead of masquerading like this. I had to think about Wil. It seemed deeply unfair.

Suddenly, it hit me how Wil was out there somewhere, at school, maybe even worried about me because I'd been gone for so long. Was he mowing lawns still on his way home when he should be studying? Was he distracted because he hadn't seen me in a couple of days? He'd probably get a kick out of sailing.

"Sugar," Blake captured my chin, drawing me from my sad thoughts to look at his hazel eyes. "Hey, what's wrong?"

I shook my head, pursing my lips. I couldn't tell him about Wil. Despite everything, I still needed to prove what he was up to. I couldn't have him chasing down Wil in case this was all an illusion.

When it was clear I wasn't going to answer his question, his fingers released my chin, and he planted a palm against my cheek. "I'm not the bad guy, Kate. I wish you could trust me."

"I'm not allowed to go on just your word," I said.

His eyes narrowed. "Who really sent you?"

My lips pursed. The truth was, no one did. I came on my own, but the whole mess started because the Academy guys had a curious itch. And I'd already promised not to tell anyone about it.

Blake's palm soothed over my cheek. "You're full of secrets," he said. "And you come to me demanding mine? Seems a little unfair."

"If it were a good thing, it wouldn't need to be a secret." I didn't hide the distrusting edge in my tone. I regretted saying it after.

His frown deepened. "What's happening to you, Kate? Maybe I don't know you, but you can't even tell me exactly why you're following me. Or who you're working with."

"I don't want any recourse just in case you're really out here to tie my legs to a rock and throw me overboard."

He huffed and backed his head up. "Are you serious? Listen to yourself. Is this what you think of everyone you don't know? All you had was a rumor to go on. I let you into my home, onto my boat, and you want to still pretend I'm some crazy person?"

I didn't have a good answer for him. I didn't know him at all a few days ago. If I had passed him on the street like any other person, I may have paused at his good looks but I wouldn't have thought anything more. However, I still couldn't forget how Raven had looked warning me about him, or how serious Marc had been about protecting me from him. Now that I was here with Blake, it felt all muddled. He felt like just a normal person. He didn't feel like a drug dealer. Or was I just hoping?

Blake released me, sitting back on his hands. "Sweetie, I don't know what to tell you. I'm not a perfect guy, but I don't do drugs. I'm not interested in them." He paused. "But telling you this isn't helping."

I shrugged. "Doesn't hurt."

His gaze didn't move from me. "What about you? Who is this Kate that showed up at my door out of the blue?"

"What about me?"

"Let's start with something easy. Where are you from?"

"Here. Charleston."

"A local," he smiled. "Ever been out of the state?"

I shook my head.

"Not much of a traveler?"

"Never had the chance."

He nodded slowly, his hazel eyes tracing over my face. "Was Brandon really someone you just met that day?"

My heart fluttered at the thought of Brandon. The kiss we'd shared I could still taste on my lips. I kept telling myself I was doing this for him, as much as for the others. He wouldn't feel obligated to protect me any more after this. I swallowed back my feelings. "Yes. Well, I bumped into him the day before, but that day of your party was the first time we'd said more than a few words to each other."

"What did you argue about? That night at the party?"

Heat drifted across my cheeks. My fingers wandered, tracing the smoothness of the wood of the boat as I thought of a lie. "Sports," I said. "Apparently he's a Yankees fan."

Blake leaned into my shoulder. "And who are you for?"

"… The Steelers?"

Blake grinned. "So you prefer football to baseball?"

Damn. "Yeah?"

C. L. Stone

He shook his head. "Nice try. If you're going to lie, you need to at least get the teams right." He stood up, and dusted off his jeans. He opened his hand to me. "Come on."

"What are we doing?" I planted my hand in his.

"I'll show you how to drive this thing."

"Me?"

Blake taught me how to hold the helm and direct the boat this way and that. He kept control of the sails and had me just focus on turning the rudder via the wheel. We made circles around the bay. It was a good distraction, keeping me busy with something so I didn't have to think about the boys and why I was there.

It only lasted a couple of hours before my stomach started growling louder than the boat splashing against the water.

Blake beamed at me. "Someone keeps a tiger in her shirt." He drew in the sails again until the boat was turned around, heading back toward the harbor. He nudged me out of the way. "My turn to take over."

"You won't let me drive back to shore?" I asked.

"It's best if I do it," he said. "Until you get more practice in."

"It can't be that hard to aim the boat at the dock and go," I said. Not that I had much confidence in my sailing skills, but it had been fun while it lasted, and what was the likelihood I'd ever get another chance?

"Don't pout those sweet lips at me and pretend you're the sudden expert sailor," he said. "There's things out here you need to look out for and you don't even know."

'Like what?" I asked.

He lifted his head, gazing around and spotted something in the water. He pointed out to it. "That."

I followed his line of sight to a buoy out in the middle of the water. It was white, with red markings and numbers that I didn't understand. "So I shouldn't run into those?"

"You shouldn't pass that invisible line. Well, we could there, possibly, because this little boat would float right over the sand bank it's trying to warn you about. It'd probably stop the yacht." He scanned, pointing to another buoy close by. "But see that one? The depth of that rock or sand bank or whatever is just below the surface, that's one we don't want to get close to. We'd crash, and my boat would sink."

I scanned the water now, looking for the markers. Now that I'd noticed them, they were everywhere. Little red or white buoys that were really discreet warnings about what was below the murky depths. "You have to stay between the buoy lines?"

"Sometimes. You have to know when you need to change course. You have to know the rules to know how you can bend them."

"Is that your philosophy?" I asked.

He grinned, steering the boat toward the harbor. "Seems to be yours, too."

♠

THIEF VS. THIEF

*B*y the time we got back to City Marina, it was just after noon. He parked the boat and tied it off. When everything was put away, he jumped off onto the dock, holding a hand out for me.

I waved him off but he insisted, grabbing my hips and planting me beside him. I wobbled on my feet, but he held me steady until I stopped swaying.

"Whoa," I said, embarrassed. Why did solid ground feel so unstable?

"You've never been on a boat before," he said, the sly smile playing on his lips at catching me out. He released my hips, but snatched up my hand, holding it palm to palm on our way back to the parking lot.

He unlocked his Mercedes and held open the door.

"Where do you want to go to lunch?" he asked.

I shrugged, wanting to say the closest hamburger stand. The truth was, I'd eat his car, I was so hungry.

He gunned the engine, looking up and down the street and taking his time, before making a right. "I've got an idea. I don't know if it's open yet. It might be just a dinner place, but we'll see."

"I hope it's not one of those places that serves rabbit food."

"Do I look like a rabbit? I'm hungry, too."

He made his way into downtown, winding between streets I didn't recognize. Blake pulled into a back lot between two close buildings on Broad Street. I hopped out before he could run around to open my door just to irritate him. Southern men hate it when you open your own door.

"How does a hamburger strike you?" he asked, he caught my door before I could close it and did it for me.

"Perfect," I said. I glanced around, feeling closed in as we were behind four different buildings, the only way in or out was so narrow, only one car could pass at a time. There was a high fence between the buildings, as high as my head. There was a collection of trash containers, and closed doors to the surrounding buildings. It felt more like a private parking lot, with only two other cars parked there. I wondered how he knew about it. We had to go through that same entryway to get back to the street. It was nerve-wracking as a car could need to get in, and we'd have to squeeze to possibly get out of the way.

He planted a palm at the small of my back, guiding me to the sidewalk. When we were beside each other, he shifted until he caught my hand.

He'd done it once already, but now I was irritated by hunger and it felt a little too close. I tugged at my hand and he didn't let go. I lifted an eyebrow. "Really?"

"Darling," he said. "I know you're in denial right now, but I am trying to win over your cool little heart."

"Why?"

He grinned. "I think you're smarter than that." He stopped, and then patted his pockets. "But I'm not."

"What?"

"Forgot my wallet in the car." He released my hand and turned. "Stay here, I'll get it."

Did he really leave his wallet in the car? Maybe he's not as smart as I assumed he was. Who leaves their cash and credit cards in the car?

I counted off a few minutes, enough time to grab a wallet and run back. When time passed and he didn't return, I bristled. Maybe it was instinct, but I wondered what was wrong. Did he ditch me?

I turned, heading back.

I came around the brick corner of the building when I spotted Blake at his car. I paused when the scene caught me off-guard. The passenger door was open, but he was standing there with his hands up.

A guy wearing a dark hoodie had an arm out. The gun in his hand looked like a .22.

The gun alone was what set me off. Over the years, it always irritated me to work as hard as I could to pick up a wallet and walk away. I took some pride knowing no one got hurt. It took skill and a lot more risk. Using a gun was too much and always felt like a cheat, in a way. It took absolutely no brains.

I glanced around, finding the trash bins. I stopped, considering when I saw a stack of old newspapers next to the bin. I eased back out of sight, and collected two, and started folding them into a couple of little squares, putting them behind my back. I had half a plan, which was good enough.

I eased back to the corner again, breathing out slowly. Waiting.

Blake had his wallet out, showing the man with the gun that he was willing to fork it over. The guy motioned with his free hand. Blake tossed it, the man caught it, and slid it into the front pocket of his hoodie.

I caught the outline of his own wallet on the back pocket of his dingy camouflage pants.

I hoped my promise to Axel didn't include stealing from another thief.

"You've got it," Blake said, keeping his hands out. "Now walk away," he said.

"Shut up," the guy in the hoodie said. He waved the gun at Blake's face. "Now hand over the keys."

Greedy bastard! I'd had enough. I stepped forward, slowly, which was hard to do in the gravel. Here's hoping his heart was thundering as loud as mine was and wouldn't hear.

Blake spotted me, and kept his face cool, but the corner of his mouth dipped in disapproval. "You don't want the car," he said. "It's an old model. Two years. There's problems with the engine."

"Just shut up and give them to me," the man said, pointing the gun closer to Blake.

"But you've already got the wallet. What are you going

to do with the car? I really like this car."

I got the impression Blake wasn't just stalling, he was covering my footsteps. Fantastic. I tried to silently tell him I was going in for a distraction. He should run and get to safety. I'd switch wallets and take off, too. A little twenty two, wouldn't do much damage if we were running and he tried to shoot us, maybe hurt our feelings. It was a really wimpy gun for a holdup.

I aimed myself, readying with two folded newspapers. This was going to be one of the most difficult pulls, never done two at once before.

Not with someone holding a gun, either.

"Give me the keys," the guy said.

"Well, if you keep yelling at me, that makes me nervous." Blake fished into his front pocket for his car keys. He rattled them between his fingers loud. "These things? Can't I just take off the car key?"

"Give me those," The guy said, growling and wiggling his gun.

"But how am I supposed to get into my house without them?"

I was close enough now, only a foot away. I could smell the stench of the cigarettes he'd been smoking rolling off of his clothes in a stale waft.

I breathed out slowly.

Took a step forward.

Lifted from the hoodie pocket at the same time as dropping a newspaper. The easiest pocket is always a jacket. I managed to get Blake's wallet into the spot between the back of my shorts and my underwear, pulling out the second newspaper.

The man turned, gun lifted in the air, letting out a shout of surprise.

Blake dashed forward, catching the guy's wrist and twisting.

I lifted the second wallet, replacing with another newspaper and backed up.

Blake kicked smoothly, catching the hooded guy in the

stomach. He had the guy's arm twisted around. The guy dropped the gun, having to move his body to relieve the pressure without snapping his bones.

The man cried out in pain. Blake punched the side of his throat and took a step back, swooping to pick up the gun.

The man tried to lunge for it. Blake had it turned on him, pointing at his face. He snapped the safety off, and cocked to load a bullet into the chamber.

The hooded man lifted his hands, backing up. "Hang on. Don't get crazy."

"Kate," Blake barked. "Get behind me."

I'd been so in awe of Blake doing his karate thing, that I froze to the spot. I dashed around, holding the guy's wallet behind my back. I stood behind Blake, peeking over his shoulder.

The man held his hands out. "Hang on."

"Give me my wallet back," Blake said.

"Uh, don't do that," I said.

"Hang on," he said, wriggling the gun at the man.

The man started backing off, heading toward the exit. "Man, let's just part ways here."

Blake grunted, still holding the gun. "I'd like my wallet back."

"Hey," the man said. "Okay." He reached into his back pocket. I guessed if he had a choice, he'd try to pass off his own wallet for Blake's and walk away with the most money.

Uh oh.

The man lifted his hand, and appeared stunned to be holding a folded newspaper. "What the..." His gaze lifted until he met mine. "You! You stole my wallet."

Blake lowered his gun, looking back at me. "You..."

I tried not to grin. "Can we just get out of here please?"

"She stole my wallet!" The guy cried out. "They're stealing my wallet! Help!"

"We should go," I said.

Blake grunted. I dove for the passenger side door and he ran around, getting in and starting the engine.

A couple of other guys came around the corner, trying to

figure out the commotion. The hooded man waved his hands in the air, shouting. "They stole my wallet!"

Blake gunned the engine, pulling out of the lot. The two men tried to stand in the way, the only exit, but when it became clear Blake wasn't going to stop, they dove, landing in the heap of trash bags.

The Mercedes pulled out into the street and we took off.

♠

TRUTH AND HOT POCKETS

We were silent in the car. I was waiting for police sirens. I had no idea what Blake was thinking, but I had a wild guess.

He twisted his hands at the wheel, checking the rearview mirror repeatedly. He took several side streets, wound around until we were back into South of Broad territory. His eyes were dark. His jaw was firm. When he pulled into his driveway, I hesitated, because I knew there would be questions and accusations.

My stomach growled.

Blake's head jerked back, as if realizing again that I was there. He studied me with side glances. "Still hungry, huh?"

I bit back a snappy retort. I really wasn't in the position to be a smart ass. "Yes."

This seemed to relax him somehow. At least for the moment, we were on a different sort of mission. We were both hungry.

Blake hopped out and opened my door before I got my seatbelt off.

It was tempting to use the opportunity to run away, but I found myself following him back inside his house and into the kitchen. If I left now, I'd have to find my own food, or grovel back to the boys. I wasn't ready for that yet.

"Have a seat." He motioned to the kitchen island, where there were stools by the bar. I ignored him, poking around in the cabinets just to see what was behind them.

Blake opened up the fridge door. "There's champagne."

"No," I said.

He chuckled. I saddled up beside him, looking over his

shoulder. The fridge had only one bottle of champagne, and the rest were sodas, bottles of water, and a couple varieties of beer. There was a collection of ketchup, and mayo, and other common condiments in the door. He opened the freezer part, and there were boxes of frozen foods stacked neatly. "Do we want pizza or..."

"I'm not going to wait on a pizza," I said. I pointed to the individually wrapped hamburgers. "Is there a microwave in here?"

"Of course I've got a microwave. Do I look like a complete savage?" He pulled out one. "How many do you want?"

"Three."

His lips twisted up into a smile. "You better eat them all."

"Better make four."

He laughed, putting the sandwiches together on a plate and stuffed them in the microwave. I leaned against the counter with my arms across my chest. I didn't want to go too far from the food. I felt better simply being in sight so I could stare down the timer.

He leaned against the counter next to me, crossing his arms similarly.

"So," I said, wanting to avoid the topic of what had happened earlier. I wasn't ready to explain myself. "I thought rich people had, like, personal chefs and things like that."

He shrugged. "A little impractical to carry one of those around all the time. I'm on the road a lot. I suppose I could if I wanted. Some people cart them along as they travel."

"You have Hot Pockets and Eggo waffles."

"So?"

"Isn't there like rich people frozen dinners?"

His arm nudged into mine. "You're talking like there's a secret barrier between rich and poor."

"Isn't there?"

He blew out a sigh. "So I don't have to buy Hot Pockets only when they're on sale. That makes me a bad guy? Look, there's a few things I can buy that maybe some people can't afford."

"Like everything."

"Like things other people make. For example," he opened a cabinet and pulled out a bag of Pop Chips. "Okay, this one might be more expensive than a bag of Lay's, or generic store brands, but there's people in these factories, too, you know? My buying these keeps people in business."

I huffed. I didn't really have a response to that. Luckily the timer beeped on the microwave. He moved to open, and I hovered at his back. He chuckled, putting the plate down on the counter.

He plated a couple for me, and I took one more from his plate and turned away to go sit in the living room. I put my plate on the coffee table.

He flipped on the television, but I completely ignored it, inhaling three sandwiches and half of the bag of Pop Chips, which I hated to admit, but really liked.

He sat back after finishing his one sandwich. His arm went up around the back of the couch. "Well, you have a healthy appetite."

I shrugged, and sat back, stretching my legs out and planting my palms on my stomach. "I told you I was hungry."

"I didn't realize you carried a black hole in your stomach. You weigh about as much as a pillow." He prodded a finger at my stomach. "Where do you stuff all that?"

I smacked him on the wrist, and then my heart stopped, realizing I'd just hit him like I did Raven. Somehow it felt awkward now because he was rich. And good looking. Proper people didn't smack.

He only chuckled and shook his head. "Vicious. I like it."

"You don't know anything about me."

"I'm learning," he said. He wiped his fingers on one of the napkins. "By the way, can I have my wallet back?"

I felt my cheeks heating, and I slowly pulled out a wallet.

He glanced at the one in my hand. "That one isn't mine."

I may as well have lit my face on fire. I plopped that one

on the table next to our empty plates and produced the other one."

He took it, opening it up and checking the contents.

"I didn't take anything."

"You did, pumpkin," he said. He pointed to the other wallet. "You took that."

"I just thought it would be fair."

He squinted his eyes at me. "You just pickpocketed an armed robber, Miss Kate. Tell me how you learned to do that."

I pursed my lips, not wanting to answer his question.

"You don't work for the FBI, do you?"

"I'm not exactly on their payroll."

He grunted in frustration, stuffing his wallet into his back pocket again. "Who the hell am I fighting these crazy accusations from then? What kind of agency sends a girl like you after me? Tell me who you're working with."

"I can't?"

"Darling," he barked at me. He leaned toward the coffee table. He pinched the corner of the wallet between his fingers like he didn't want to get too much of his fingerprints on it. "This isn't just some hobby you pick up, like whistling. Why are you really here?"

I bit my lip. I didn't want to reveal the truth and at the same time, we weren't getting anywhere. I still hesitated. Like the boys, I supposed I needed more convincing. "I don't want to sound mean, but I don't want to reveal who or why. I'm here on my own because I don't want any repercussions on anyone else."

His blond eyebrow arched. "What repercussions? From me? What kind of person do you think I am?"

I stared at him. I didn't know and didn't have an answer for him. Not until I could figure out what he was doing, and why Raven, and Marc, and Axel, and everyone else had pleaded so vehemently with me to stay away from him.

He shoved a palm at his face. "Fine. I can't win." He checked his watch. "Are we ready?"

"For what?"

"For you to discover my bad side."

♠

A FINE LINE BETWEEN SNOOPING AND SPYING

Blake drove out of downtown Charleston, taking I-26 out past the Mark Clark Expressway and pulled off into Hanahan. It'd been a while since I'd been that far out. Hanahan was a sprawl of middle class. To me, that was the high life.

He took a couple of roads until there was nothing around us but green trees.

"Where are we going exactly?"

"I've got to go see someone."

"Who?"

He smiled, and swung his head around to look at me. "Someone with information."

"Who?"

"Someone with important information."

"Who?"

"You sound like an owl," he said. "Relax, sugar. You'll see in a minute."

I crossed my arms over my chest, hoping this wasn't the part where I was taken into the middle of the woods and shot. If it was, I would have been ticked my last meal was frozen hamburgers.

Blake finally turned off the road onto a dirt driveway that led to a two-story old farmhouse at the top of a hill. Down the slope were a couple of crumbling, weathered wooden barns, and a smaller shed in the same disrepair, leaning precariously.

What surprised me was the amount of antennae and

C. L. Stone

satellite dishes surrounding the house, and littering the front lawn. You could almost feel the radio waves getting sucked into the space, drawn in by the electronics. Cancer central.

Blake opened my door before I could finish staring. "Where are we?" I asked.

"I think we're still on Earth," Blake said, grinning. He snagged my hand and tugged me forward. "Come on, spy girl. You're the one that wanted to be nosey."

The smell of cigarette smoke was thick, even as Blake led the way up the steps and to the wrap-around front porch. He let go of me to knock sharply once at the screen door and opened it. The front door was already hanging open, revealing a barren living room, with a single faded couch against the wall and nothing else.

"No one's home," I said in a low voice, feeling really creeped out.

"Oh he's home," Blake said. He walked in, stretching his neck out and looking right. "Doyle!"

"Aye!" a voice shouted from the back, beyond an archway on the far side of the room.

I tiptoed behind Blake as he crossed the living room. To the right was an open archway with a kitchen, the counters littered with pizza boxes and empty bottles of soda, and more than one ashtray overflowing with cigarette butts.

Beyond the living room was a hallway with a set of stairs to the second floor, and a parlor ahead, with glass doors that were open.

The parlor was clustered with a variety of desks of different sizes, and computers, AC radios and mechanical things I didn't know the use of. It was all stuffed together on top of old tables and some coffee tables and couches. It was like all the furniture had been shoved into this one room just to hold up equipment.

In the middle of the fray was a guy, maybe twenty-five, with an unruly mop of brown hair, a dimpled chin, and heavy, tired brown eyes. He had a corded phone stuck to his ear, propped up by his hunched shoulder as he tapped at a keyboard. His eyes were fixed on the dual monitors each projecting moving texts and screens that changed so fast that I couldn't tell what he was doing.

"Doyle?"

The man ignored Blake, staring intently at his computer screen. Doyle had a lean figure under his thin T-shirt and was narrow at the hips. His jeans were a little short at the ankles and the material was a bit faded.

Blake inched closer, stuffing his hands into his pocket and leaning over the desk that separated them. "Doyle!"

Doyle let out an exasperated breath, snatched up a yellow sticky note pad, and a Sharpie. He sketched out something on the paper, lifted the paper and stuck it to his cheek within our view.

On phone.

Blake grunted. I fidgeted behind him, feeling odd in this particular rabbit hole. I was also trying not to breathe. The thickness of smoke hovered like a fog in this room, tickling at my already dry throat.

Doyle started scratching additional notes on a pad of paper. When he finally dropped the phone onto the cradle without another word, Blake planted his palms on the desk and leaned over it. "Doyle," he said. "I need the last one."

Doyle lifted his eyes from his paper and locked on me. "Who's she?"

"That's Kate," Blake said. "She's working with me now."

"Is she?" Doyle tilted his head as his gaze dropped to my feet and back up to my head. "Blake Coaltar never works with anyone." His accent was thick, and decidedly Irish.

Blake sidestepped to block off my view and his. "I need a name, Doyle."

"Everyone needs a name," he said. "They need a name, and an address, and a phone number, and a bank account, and a new ID, and cold medicine, and an elephant, and Elvis Presley." He shoved his chair back, standing up, nearly matching Blake's height. "You, sir, are too nosey for your own good."

"What do you want?" Blake said.

C. L. Stone

"I need a new maid. The old one left."

Blake's eyebrow rose. "Left? Old Mrs. Jennings? She said she needed the money."

Doyle zipped his hand back and forth in the air as if to cut off the conversation. "Left. Died. Whatever. Same thing. This place is disgusting."

"Fine," Blake said. "I'll send someone over."

"A good proper Irish woman," Doyle said. "None of those local mammies they've got around here." He pointed a finger at me. "Or that one. I could deal with one of those. Does she come in a maid outfit? One of those short miniskirt ones?"

I was about to open my mouth and probably throw in a middle finger, but Blake cut me off. "Stop talking about her like that. She's not a maid. Real or prostitute."

"Yeah. You're probably right. She's not my type anyway. What with the hair, and the legs, and the face and all."

"Doyle," he said in a sharp tone. "Her name is Kate. She is with me." His eyes darkened and his face stiffened like he was holding his last bit of patience. "Can you please stop?"

Normally, I would have stopped him there. I didn't need anyone's help in defending myself. This, however, struck me. Blake seemed to have no problem teasing me. It was kind of cute he had a problem with his friend doing it.

"Oh, it's *please*, huh?" Doyle nodded in my direction. "Did you hear that, Kit? Three years and he's never said please for anything."

"Her name is Kate."

"Kid. Kate. Bubba. I don't care."

"Just give us the last location, or I may slip a little tip to the FCC about some Irishman infiltrating phone calls."

"See, now that's just mean." Doyle returned to his desk, and sorted through a collection of notes. "You make me sound like some sort of perverted phone hacker. I can do more than intercept phone signals, you know." He selected one of the pieces of paper and read from it. "The last batch is in an abandoned house in Moncks Corner. A few bits have already been sold off, but they are having problems selling

284

the rest. They've only had one buyer return for more."

"Surprised anyone wanted more."

"Yeah, well it's a low ranking cell that caters to the high school kids. Kids are stupid."

I coughed once. "What's going on? What kids? What high school?"

Blake started shaking his head but Doyle turned on him. "What's this? I thought you said she was working with you now. She doesn't even know why she's here?"

"Still showing her the ropes," Blake said. He reached out for the piece of paper with the information he wanted.

Doyle jerked his hand back to hang on to it. "Wait a second. Who is she? When did you meet her?"

"It's a long story."

"Shorten it."

"I don't have time. She's fine."

Doyle frowned. He slowly relinquished the paper to Blake. He picked up a packet of cigarettes by the keyboard and selected one out of the box. He fished a lighter out of his pocket, lit the cigarette and inhaled deep. He blew out the smoke in my direction. "If I end up in a jail cell, or deported, I'm not going alone."

♠♠♠♠♠♠

When Blake and I were back outside, I coughed hard, trying to replace the thickness of smoke in my lungs with clean air. I felt like I had breathed in a sponge.

Blake popped me on the back in an effort to help. "Don't die," he said.

"When were you going to tell me you are buying drugs?" I asked in as cool of a voice as I could muster given that my throat was in dire need of some water. I'd been holding back the question while we were inside.

Blake made a face. "Who said anything about drugs, pretty bug? No one's said any such thing."

"The fact that neither of you said it made it obvious. And the fact that there is a batch being distributed to school kids

285

C. L. Stone

in Moncks Corner. Is it pot or crack?"

"Kate..." He strolled to the passenger side of the car and opened the door for me. He pointed to the seat. "Come on."

I stalled, and tucked my hands into my pockets. "Oh, no. You lied to me. And I've seen enough. I get it. If you get me involved in your little crime antics, you'll hold it over my head and threaten to take me to jail with you if I rat you out."

"That's not..." He made a face, shoving a palm over his eyes and rubbing. "I know what it looks like, but you have to trust me. And we don't have time to wait."

"Why?"

"Because the longer we stand here, the higher the chance this stuff gets put out on the street and we don't want that."

I squinted at him. His face was stern and the golden flecks in his eyes darkened. He wasn't joking with me now. "What's wrong with the drugs?" I asked. "And why are you so concerned?"

"Get in," he said. "I swear, Kate, I'm the good guy. Just get in. You can come help me. We won't get into trouble. You'll be able to tell whoever you're working for that I'm not dealing drugs. It's just the opposite."

"I don't understand."

"Just get in," he said. He pressed his palms together in a pleading gesture. "Sweetie, just this once. After everything we've been through today, haven't I proven myself? You're the one who has all the secrets, now. I don't know anything about you other than your first name, that you can pickpocket, and you've got a black hole stomach."

I masked my urge to frown. One of those three wasn't even correct. Maybe he was right. Maybe the guys were making the same mistake, jumping the gun on assumptions about this guy. Maybe he's just like them. He's on to something that he's trying to fix.

"And you're beautiful as hell when you sleep," he said in a quieter tone, the same serious note in his voice. "And in those moments when you're not worried about whatever it is you're keeping to yourself."

I snorted. "So I'm ugly otherwise?"

"No," he said. And those gold flecks started to shine. "Otherwise you're ... no, angel's not the right word."

"Enough," I said, disbelieving.

I waved my hand through the air to cut him off but he captured it. He brought my hand to his mouth and kissed at the knuckles. "Honey doll, I'd love to play with you right now, but either you come with me, or you're staying out here with Doyle. I don't have the time."

That part I hadn't thought through. It was several miles to the next house, and miles beyond that to the nearest town. I'd be stuck here with the odd smoking Irishman. And there didn't look to be any food in the house except old pizza. "Okay," I said, unwilling to admit it was more than just my irritation at being left behind. I didn't want to think of it, but Blake, and not for the first time, was pulling on heart strings I didn't know I had as recently as a few days ago.

He urged me into the car, shutting the door for me and running around to his side to get in. He turned over the engine and started down the road.

♠

THE WORST
DRUG DEALER EVER

*B*lake found a local road that led straight to Moncks Corner. It was a quiet side road that occasionally met with bits of neighborhood that required slowing from 70 miles an hour to 45. He shifted gears, speeding down the road and barely slowed for the 45 miles an hour stretches.

"What are we after?" I asked. "What are we doing?"

He glanced over at me, as if having second thoughts about telling me. He pursed his lips for a moment. "A few weeks ago, a new brand of synthetic weed rolled into Charleston called JH-14."

"Synthetic?" I asked. "Why make a chemical based one when the real thing is out there? Why not just grow and distribute that?" It seemed impossible. Creating a new drug similar to one that already existed would require a lab, and the brains to use it. Drug dealers did this?

"Synthetics go under the radar. They're undetectable on drug tests. It attracts middle class buyers, interested because they can use it and not get fired from their jobs when they get selected for random drug screening. Kids tend to like it, too, because they can hide if from their parents and school easier. It's also not illegal yet. This makes it very popular."

"But why not call the police? I mean if it's a drug deal. Shouldn't the DEA or someone be taking care of this?"

"The DEA and the police can't do anything about it," he said. "Not until there's a ruling by a judge to make it illegal. First they have to find a sample, and then test the product, find the chemical sequence and at the end of it, they have to go through court proceedings and bureaucracy. By the time any judge gets things together to make it illegal, this batch will have been distributed and they move on to the next formula. A new synthetic drug that they have to start all over again. It's an endless cycle."

"I don't understand why you're interested."

"Because this particular batch is bad," he said. "Normal side effects of synthetics are extreme cases of paranoia and aggression. This batch is much worse, and can create permanent damage. Not to mention the physical side effects vary from person to person. It's the worst I've seen."

"Could it kill people?"

"I believe it already has," he said. "There's been an increase in the local suicide attempt reports and we've made the connection that they were using these drugs. There's people going into the hospital with flu symptoms and dying but they've not made the connection yet to this. Some people react differently to it and don't get sick, but I think it depends on how much is injected or smoked or whatever the hell they're doing with it. While instances seem to have been contained, I'm hoping to stop anything more from happening."

"So we're going to go find the individuals that bought it and warn them?"

"No. It's possibly too late for that and we have no chance of tracing all those distributions. It gets to the point to where we're chasing ants. We're looking for the ant hill."

"The last batch?"

He nodded. He brushed his palms against the steering wheel. "We may not stop everything, but we can stop any more from being distributed."

"How?"

He smirked, and looked over at me. "Sweetheart, you may not have noticed, but I've got a few extra dollars in my pocket."

"You're buying?"

"I'm buying it all," he said. "I walk in, pretend to be

interested in catering to the super wealthy and in dire need of a synthetic."

I placed a fingertip along my eyebrow, smoothing the fine hairs over. "Let me see if I understand. You found out there's this batch of synthetic weed that's really bad. So you're buying it all so no one can have it?"

"That's the gist."

"What are you doing with the stuff once you've got it?"

"Don't worry. I've got that taken care of. The important part is, I'm getting it out of the city."

Could this be true? It sounded crazy. But then, was it any crazier than a group of guys snooping around the city and looking for trouble in order to make it better? Was I going to judge him for doing what it sounded like the boys would have done? They probably would have helped him if they knew. "But what about the next time? What happens when the next box of synthetics arrives in town? Are you going to have to keep buying it up?"

"We're working on that," he said. "Doyle and I. We're finding the source. In the meantime, I just have to hope the next batch isn't deadly."

I tapped my knee. I wasn't sure if I was going to tack on any of my own information, but I needed to ask. "Does Mr. Fitzgerald work for you?"

His hands clutched tighter at the wheel. "How do you know about him?"

"He was at the party and then ... I don't know how to explain it."

"Kate," he said. "Look at me sweetie. I need to know. What do you know about him? Is this informant group you're with investigating him, too?"

"They were interested in you," I said. "They wanted to know who you were connected with."

His eyes darkened. "He's an innocent player who got mixed up in it. You'll have to tell your buddies that. Leave him alone. I can't explain it, but what we really need to focus on is getting this last batch and then finding the source."

"What happens when you find the source?"

The sly smile slid across his face. "Maybe we'll leave a friendly note with our own lovely neighborhood FBI informant."

I rolled my eyes and then looked out the window at the trees and homes as we passed by. Slowly, the countryside turned back into residential sprawl. We were getting closer to Moncks Corner. "You couldn't have told me this before?"

"I needed to know who you were, Kate. I needed to know you weren't going to get crazy and run to the local police with what I was up to."

"Could they have done anything?"

"They could slow me down. Make things difficult for me. I've got a rather tidy criminal record, meaning to say, there's nothing there. I'm not usually on their radar. I'd like to keep it that way." He smiled and looked at me. "Not that I mind beautiful FBI informants crashing my party, but you have to admit, not all of them are as lovely and interesting."

I hid an eye roll and the glint of a smile at the corner of my mouth. He did it so smoothly. I didn't believe him for a moment, but you had to admire a guy when he was trying. "What do we do?"

"Well," he said, leaning over the wheel and checking a street sign. "If you're not put off by this plan, I say we go in as a couple planning an expensive party."

"How can we just walk in?"

"They know this is a bad batch. I don't think they know exactly how bad yet. Word on the street is people aren't coming back, buyers aren't buying, now they're looking to get rid of it. It's probably why it's out in Moncks Corner. They couldn't get the middle class to buy again after samples were spread out. They're just trying to pawn it off on kids. The ones I've had to deal with so far have been more than happy to relinquish it for a lot of cash."

"They didn't worry about you being the FBI or DEA?"

"It's not illegal to buy," he said. "They only work in this underground system because when smoke shops started selling this stuff, the cops would seize merchandise in raids. Cops wait until a batch was made illegal, and raid the shop looking for old merchandise. They'd use the opportunity to get a hold of new merchandise and test for new synthetics to make illegal. Handling it through the underground drug rings made it easier. Made it harder for cops because it takes them longer to make these illegal. Now smoke shops just give you an address. This last batch was hard to track, because it was the last one, and it's a big one, because no one wanted it and they all funneled it out to Moncks Corner. I was about to get it last night before it got that far."

"But..."

He smiled. "Turns out I got distracted and had to rescue a damsel in distress."

If everything he was saying was true, Blake Coaltar wasn't doing anything illegal at all. He was buying what was currently legal synthetic weed and he was getting rid of it in a way that he had every right to. "If you buy this, doesn't it just encourage drug dealers to continue making bad batches?"

"Not when we're done with this," he said. "Drug dealers generally don't want to kill off their market. Doyle is helping spread the word about this particular batch, but word of mouth is slow in an underground world where they have to filter out rumors. When they hear this stuff killed people, they'll want to get rid of it. There will probably be a lot of change higher up this particular drug ring. But this will be a process. For the moment, we're getting this really bad batch off the street before anyone else gets too hurt. One thing at a time."

I sat back. "What do you want me to do?"

He slid a glance at me and then back out front, where rain drops had started to splatter against the windshield. "Let's just get through this part. If you don't believe me after this, I don't know what else to tell you."

He rolled into the location, which really wasn't an abandoned house, but a pit in the ground where there may have once been a house, and a warehouse planted nearby as if watching over the pit.

He stopped the car a short distance down the road, but we were still within sight and probably pretty obvious to anyone paying attention.

"Okay," I said. I'd been quiet for a while, trying to absorb all of the information. It all seemed surreal. He seemed surreal. I felt a million miles away from home, and completely out of my element, drawn to Blake Coaltar and his cause, and to him in a strange way. Part of me was excited that I was finally getting an answer. I was starting to feel that the boys had been completely wrong. That my brother was safe. That after this was over, those Academy guys didn't have anything to worry about and I ... I wasn't sure what would happen to me, but whatever it was, it had to be better than what it had been.

"I understand what you're doing," I told Blake. "I still don't understand why. I mean, you've got a big house, and a yacht, and a fancy car, and a tiny boat."

"Hey, now. Don't you start talking about my sailboat."

"I mean, you didn't wake up one day and decide to start buying synthetic drugs and save a bunch of strung out teenagers from themselves."

"Shows how little you know me, sweetie." The sly grin spread to bunch up his cheeks. "Maybe I do have a few secrets left."

"What makes a wealthy playboy want to take the risk?"

"What makes a girl crash a party of a man she doesn't know, just to try to sniff out all his dirty little secrets? Why not just get a job in a retail store and behave like everyone else?" He swung his head around as he tapped his fingers against the steering wheel. "It's the same reason you're in this car now. You're not begging me to take you home. I see that look in your eye. You're curious."

"Are we playing that game again? We're doing things because we're curious?"

"It's been the same since the beginning, we just didn't know the details that made up what we were curious about." He reached out, taking a hold of my elbow. He slid his grasp down until he could capture my wrist. He clutched it between his fingers and brought it to his lips. "Kind of sad, though."

"What is?"

"I was kind of hoping during any part of this, when you figured out what I was up to, I thought you'd finally admit the truth."

I raised an eyebrow, my fingers twitching in his grasp. "What truth?"

"That you were curious about me," he said, the gold flecks glinting. He kissed the knuckles of my hand. "You like me."

I tried to pull my hand from his but he held on too tightly. "I don't know anything about you."

"But what you do know, you like. You're intrigued."

"Can we just get this over with?"

He laughed, releasing my hand and started opening his door. I opened my own door, closing it loudly.

"Now listen," he said. "I don't want to make a fuss about this, but I think it's best if I do the talking."

"Go ahead," I said. "You're the expert drug dealer."

He smirked and led the way to the warehouse.

Despite the light smattering of rain, we took our time to get to the door. The small warehouse was big enough to be packed with criminals and my mind was thinking something along the lines of a mob movie I'd seen once. Wouldn't they have loads of guns and take out anyone they didn't know? I didn't know who we were up against, but I wanted to duck behind Blake if someone started shooting at us.

Blake stepped onto a small concrete porch and knocked twice at a door and we waited.

The door opened, and a head poked out. He wore a thick hoodie that shadowed his already dark face. He was young, maybe my age. His shoes were worn, Wal-Mart brand. His tight curly dark hair was cut short enough at the sides of his head that you could see the skin. He took one look at Blake, one look at me and then looked at Blake again.

"This is private property," the guy said.

"Yeah," Blake said. "I'm looking for Ronald."

"He's not here." He started to shut the door.

Blake leapt, jabbing his foot into the opening to prevent it from closing. "I'm buying the new stuff," he said. "The JH-

14."

"Who are you?" The guy asked.

"Look, I've got a party happening tonight, and I need something. The girls, you know, they like their shit." He swung his head, jerking his chin in my direction as if he was talking specifically about me. "Got to get them to loosen up, you know? I heard you had some of the new stuff."

The guy was shaking his head. "Back off."

Blake wasn't going to get anywhere this way. I didn't know how he was dealing with other drug dealers, but this was a street kid. They didn't trust anyone other than their own. The poor and equally run down. It didn't matter if the stuff they were selling was illegal or not. They avoided business with people they didn't know or trust.

I crossed my arms, trying to pretend to look irritated. "He don't know nothing," I said, faking a hick accent. "He's just a kid."

Blake's eyes met mine, as if trying to silently call me insane. "Pumpkin," he said.

"Look at him," I pointed to the hooded kid. "We'll go down to Tucker's. He's probably got a new batch of the real stuff anyway."

The man inside the door opened up wider. "Who's Tucker?"

I shrugged. "He's got some real weed growing out back on an island in one of those mini-lakes out in Goose Creek," I said, going with an old rumor I heard in high school. "They don't get many batches, but I heard he got some of the real stuff."

"Sweetheart," Blake said, starting to make a bit of a whine. This was better. He thickened his Southern accent, moving from his refinement to something I could consider middle class. "They don't want the real thing. They want the fake shit."

"God knows why," I said. "If you want to waste your money on them." I turned to the man in the door. "Do you have anything that will shut him up? I don't even care if it's good."

The guy made a face, pouting his lips. "We already have another buyer."

Who was buying this? I recalled Blake had said someone else had returned to buy more. Probably some crazy stupid kid? Or maybe this stuff didn't give whoever was buying the same side effects.

I slid a look across at the street, as if checking to make sure no one was around. I leaned into the door. The man inside willingly inclined forward to hear me out.

"We'll take it off your hands right now. Whatever it is, he'll probably pay double the price you were going to sell it for. They're a bunch of rich snobs from the peninsula. In my opinion, it'd serve them right to get the fake stuff."

He glanced once at Blake and then at me. "You don't tell them where you got it?"

"I'll tell them it's a smoke shop blend," I said. "Bath salts or whatever they're calling it now."

He laughed and opened the door wider. "That shit will kill you." He side stepped away from the door. Blake followed behind me. Smart. He was willing to let me take the lead.

The inside of the warehouse was a barren space. There were two chop shop cars sitting around with the hoods up. The tops of the cars were dusty, though, and I suspected it was the front used in case cops did come poking around.

The man walked up to one of the cars, inserted a key into the trunk, and opened it up. "They even prepackaged them," he said. He lifted out a tiny bottle that looked like it was supposed to hold eye drops but without the label. Inside was a half a teaspoon of crystal-like grains, like clumpy sand. "These kids only buy twenty to a hundred dollars at a time. It's all they can come up with."

"Must be slow business," I said, sidling up beside him and glancing into the trunk. There were cartons full of these little bottles, and all stacked neatly together, and the trunk was packed. "Oh wow, there is a lot."

He shook the bottle in his hands again and then passed it to me. "Do you need to test?"

"Never touch the synthetic stuff," I said. I held the bottle between my fingers and became temporarily dazzled by how the light reflected off of the tiny crystal particles. Deadly and beautiful. "I don't really get the big deal."

"Me neither," the guy said. "But I'm just a distributor. We don't get to touch the merchandise."

I nodded. "Is this it? Is this everything?"

"The other trunk is full, too," he said.

I turned to Blake. "Do we need that much?"

Blake grimaced, planting a palm on the back of his head and rubbing at his hair, looking sheepish. "Might as well. I won't have to make another purchase later. It was hard enough to find."

I rolled my eyes, angling toward the drug dealer guy conspiratorially; he leaned in to hear me out. "He's still new to this."

"I can tell." He straightened. "If you really want the whole set, you're looking at $25,000."

I bit my tongue to hide my shock and steadied a stare at Blake.

Blake shrugged. "That's a lot for a bunch of cartons."

"You wanted to double the price," I said.

He nodded and then turned to the man in the hoodie. His face changed into something more professional, businesslike. "I'll tack on an extra five grand if I can get someone to deliver."

"Where to?" the man asked.

"There's a yacht at the City Marina," he said. He reached into his front pocket, pulling out a business card. "Pack these bottles into food boxes, but closed and use packaging tape to seal them. If someone stops you, give them this card. There's a dozen deliveries made to those yachts every day. You won't be noticed."

"A yacht?" The man sucked saliva through his teeth, making a clicking noise. He turned to me. "Is this joker serious?"

I waved my hand in the air. "That's what I said."

He shrugged, rubbing his fingers over the back of his

head. "Alright. You're lucky this shit isn't illegal yet."

Blake nodded. He reached into his back pocket, pulling out a wallet. "I've got five thousand now."

"Five thousand? Bitch, you said thirty."

"Five thousand on hand," he said. "What do I look like? A walking bank? When you deliver, the rest will be in cash on the yacht. It'll be in the fridge. Place the cartons on board, take out the cash and walk away with it."

"Make sure that shit is in twenty dollar bills."

Blake rolled his eyes. "You guys need PayPal."

"*You guys* will get into shit if you leave electronic trails. Paper's the only way to go." He took the cash from Blake and tucked it into his back pocket. "When do you want it?"

"Deliver it tonight if you can. There won't be much in the way of security at the marina. Just a girl stationed in the boathouse. Look like you belong there, and she won't give you any problems."

"How come this sounds like more trouble than it's worth?" he asked. He looked at me. "Maybe you should go with Tucker."

I smiled and shrugged. "I keep telling him..."

♠

THE REAL KATE

Within less than an hour, we managed to get back to South of Broad and back to his house. Rain followed us the entire way. It fell in sheets by the time he was parked in his drive as close to the front door as he could get. Blake ran over to open the door to his house first, before he came back to open my door. It was pointless. By the time we were inside, we were both drenched, anyway.

My heart was still pounding in disbelief. I couldn't believe this whole time the boys had been worried about Blake, and Blake was really actually helping out. He might not be doing it exactly perfect. If it were up to me, I'd probably have worked out a deal another way. But Blake was probably right. This way, this dangerous drug gets off the street quicker. It sounded crazy, I didn't think the drug pushers would stop. They'd get a new batch of bad stuff at some point. Then what?

"What do you do now?" I asked him as I stood in the foyer of his house, dripping. I shivered at the cold water making my shirt and shorts stick to my skin.

"Right now, we get a towel and change our clothes." He motioned to the stairs and started toward them.

I followed, stepping up the stairs behind him and trying to keep up. I tugged my shirt away from my body but it fell back heavily against me and clung. "I mean where are you taking the drugs?"

"I'm about to make another trip. I'll dump it all in the ocean somewhere along the way. It'll be gone, and no one will know." At the third floor, he turned down the hall, opened a door, and I recognized the bedroom I had been in earlier. He went to the closet, turning on the light. It was huge, with racks of clothes hanging up on either side, more than I thought he could ever wear in years.

I stepped onto the black rug, only feeling mildly guilty about dripping on it. "Will you go to Europe?" I asked, trying to ignore the size of his closet.

He shrugged and grinned opened mouthed at me. "I don't know. Why? Want to go?"

I blinked at him. Was he serious? Now that the charade was over and I knew what he was up to, reality had settled in for me. I was a creepy girl who had invaded his party, his life, to find out he was actually a good guy. "Blake..."

He started unbuttoning his shirt, letting it slide off his body and onto the floor. Underneath was a white-ribbed tank shirt. He caught the hem at his neck and pulled upward, revealing fit abs and then his tight muscled chest. His tan was perfection along his skin, all the way down to where his jeans hung low on his hips. He crumpled the tank shirt. "Kate, are you telling me you still think of me as the bad guy? After everything I've just showed you? After everything you've helped me do tonight?"

I couldn't answer him. I didn't feel like he was the bad guy. We had possibly stopped kids from dying. And my brother was safe. I didn't have to hide anymore. This was what I wanted.

Wasn't it?

The only problem was, what was I supposed to do now? I was eager to go back to the guys. I wanted to go back to my brother and let him know I was okay. I wanted all the promises the boys made about getting Wil into college and maybe, finally, for once, having a normal life. I wanted to apologize to Marc. I wanted to go back to Corey and Brandon. I even wanted to play with Raven and Axel.

I also wanted to stay with Blake. I was afraid to go back. I was afraid once this job was done, the boys would send me back to my hotel room, or even if they kept their promises and helped me get an apartment, maybe with a job at the pretzel stand or elsewhere, I wasn't sure if they would want me hanging around. And Blake wanted me, but I wasn't sure *what* he wanted from me, either. I'd still just met him.

The confusion was overwhelming. I didn't have a plan after this. I wasn't Kate. I didn't even feel like Kayli anymore.

My non-answer took too long. He winced, dropping his tank shirt and letting it fall to the floor in a wet clump. He marched forward, a wicked spark striking into those golden flecks.

"Blake," I said, taking a step back. My eyes went wide, caught off-guard by his aggressive approach. "I didn't mean…"

His smile turned sly. "I've shown you my secrets, Kate," he said. He reached out and caught me by the waist.

I tried to take a step back again, but he was faster. He drew me in until I was pressed up against his chest and he lowered his head.

"I want yours," he whispered against my mouth. His head dipped and he kissed me.

His lips melted against mine. His palms claimed my face, fingertips brushing away wet strands of hair against my cheek until he could hold me. His grasp was unrelenting as his kiss deepened, claiming me by opening his mouth and loosening his jaw. He breathed out a half moan.

I tried to retreat, overwhelmed. He took a step into me, and then another, forcing me back. I felt the bed at the back of my knees. His hands lowered, finding my hips and he lifted me off the ground. It forced me to find his shoulders to hang on to.

He paused and put me on my feet again. He slid his hands up, catching the hem of the tank top, still soaked to the touch. He lifted slowly, exposing my skin to the air. I trembled from the coolness in the air against my wet flesh, but didn't stop him.

When he lifted the shirt up over my breasts, my arms rose out of instinct, and he broke the kiss only a moment to pull the shirt away. The moment it was off my face, he claimed me again with his lips. He wasn't going to give me a moment to reconsider.

When his hands went to my waist and he tugged at the shorts, that's when I pushed his hand away. I had enough sense not to go further. The bra and shorts needed to stay. I wasn't ready to be completely naked in front of him. Not tonight.

He seemed to understand me. He clutched my hips again, and with a jerk, I was up in the air for a moment. I crashed down on the bed, on top of the comforter. Blake followed, hovering over me. He planted a knee on either side of my hips. His bare, rippled stomach lowered over mine. His chest brushed against my breasts.

His lips crushed against mine.

The heat between us I couldn't define. I hated that this kiss, his touch, I'd been craving since the moment we met. During the time we'd spent together, especially today, he wasn't just handsome. He had a regal charm, but none of the snobbery I expected. He was smart, concerned, exciting, willing to risk everything to help people he didn't even know.

He kept things slow, but his lips demanded a lot. His mouth parted, deepening and I responded. When he lifted his lips, he suckled my lower lip once quickly before sinking again into me for another kiss.

His tongue darted between his lips, tasting at my teeth, willing me to open up more. I did, and his tongue darted in, searching out mine, tasting every corner. His head twisted so he could deepen. His stomach leaned against mine, brushing against my skin.

My heart was flurrying. My mind couldn't keep up. Part of me was simply overwhelmed. I'd felt like I'd spent so much time with him. I wanted this to be real. I wanted it so much it hurt. It felt like he knew me and wanted me to be his. Like I belonged to him.

After a few moments though, the truth finally settled in. It'd only been a day. Maybe I felt like I knew him, but there was little he knew about me. And if that was true, how could he care about me enough to kiss me? Most of what he thought he knew was a lie.

I started pushing at his chest.

He stopped the kiss, his eyes wide, wild. "Kate," he breathed against my face.

I swallowed, trying to get my body to stop shaking from the chill and excitement and the fear. This was just like every other boyfriend I'd ever lied to. Suddenly, I was ashamed. If he only knew the real me. If he knew I lived in a hotel with a drunk father, and stole money from people to feed and house my brother and I, he probably wouldn't like that. After all the nonsense I put him through to get to the answers I needed, he'd see me as a hypocrite. I was also in danger. If I got my hopes too high with him, and he left because of my lies ... I didn't want that pain.

No. The truth was, he was melting through the wall I kept around myself. I'd do anything to stop it. Avoiding heartbreak by never giving out my heart was the best solution.

"I can't stay," I breathed. I needed to run. I needed to get away from this place. If I disappeared into the night, knowing he'd never be able to find me, I wouldn't have to tell him the truth. "I should go."

"Kate," he said. "No..."

"I can't," I said. I pushed at his bare chest, trying to ignore the pounding heart inside me, and feeling his own under my fingertips. I felt the fine smoothness of his skin, and every desire inside of me screaming that I enjoy and give in, but my brain wouldn't shut up. I couldn't enjoy it knowing it was all a lie. "I need to go."

At first, he looked indecisive. His face lowered.

Suddenly, the gold flecks glinted in the light and something appeared there that I'd not seen before. A driving force. A low growl emerged from his throat. His fingers clutched at my hips. He pushed me down against the bed and his lips fell hard against mine. Stronger this time. His mouth sought out to devour every corner. His tongue split between his teeth, seeking mine and slid along it.

He broke his hold only to clutch at my chin, tilting my head to the side. His lips claimed my jaw and then the skin just below my ear.

"Not tonight," he said, his tone octaves deeper than before, and that hint of a growl rumbling through every word. His hands roughly massaged my chin. "Kate, you're not leaving tonight. If you're going to leave me, if you're going to walk out on me, fine. Do it in the morning. I may even chase you down if you tried. Tonight, though, you're staying right here with me."

"Blake..." I said, pushing lightly at his chest but unable to find the strength like before, or I didn't really have the heart. "I'm not going to have sex with you," I said, trying to make it clear.

He nipped at my ear. He didn't challenge my request. He sunk down, until he could claim a bit of my neck between his lips. He suckled at the skin and released it from his mouth with a pop.

"What do you want?" I asked.

"The real Kate," he said. He backed his head up, gazing down at me. "I want to know what makes those eyes look so lost whenever you're not angry, which is almost all the time. I want to know how you learned to pickpocket. I want to know why those bruises are on your body. I want to know how a beautiful, maddening girl ended up crashing into my life and why I can't stop myself when nothing good could possibly come of this." He dipped his head, kissed my lips briefly and then backed up again, but only a little, to whisper against my mouth. "And if you think you're going to try to fight me on this and run away, I'll kiss the shit out of you until you give up and stay with me."

Why did he have to be so perfect? Even when I tried to fight him, he stepped up to the challenge. A worthy opponent in every sense. The devil inside me made me push back against his chest, with a coy, eyebrow lift and a playful smirk, feigning resistance. "I shouldn't," I whispered, with no real energy to my words. I didn't want to tell him the truth, but I didn't want to leave, either. I'd let him kiss me. I'd even kiss him back. I thought that was a pretty good compromise.

But in the next moment, my body jerked with an uncontrollable shiver. I was exhausted and cold, despite his warmth. The wetness of the shorts and the underwear and then the coolness of his bedroom racked me until I was trembling.

Blake didn't miss a beat. He jumped off of me for a moment, diving into his closet. He pulled out a soft cotton button up shirt with long sleeves. He tossed it at me and pointed to the bathroom. "I'm going to walk in there and put on some shorts to sleep in," he said. "If you're not here when I get back out again, I swear..." He wagged a finger at me and his eyes locked on mine, a curious look on his face.

My eyebrows popped up. "What?"

"You're not going anywhere." He turned with a satisfied smirk and snatched a pair of boxers out of his closet, marched to the bathroom and closed the door.

By the time he got out of the bedroom, I'd put on the shirt he gave me and kept my underwear. My underwear was wet but I opted to get into bed and stay there instead. I thought I could stand them as long as I got warm. The long sleeved shirt covered my butt for the most part.

I was underneath the blanket, by the time he got out. He ripped the comforter and sheet aside, planting himself beside me. I didn't want to talk. My eyelids drooped. The warmth of the bed had me ready to sink into oblivion.

I think it was affecting him, too. When he was beside me, he reached for me, finding my waist and pulling me close. He stuffed an arm under my neck, and another around until he could warm the small of my back with his palm. He held on to me close, warming the coolness of his exposed stomach and chest against me. His leg hooked over one of my thighs, locking into place.

He traced kisses along my face, along my forehead, by my ear. He kissed, soft and slow, until I passed out.

♠

THE REAL BLAKE

Sometime in the middle of the night, I felt him shift and move away. Half asleep and disoriented, my heart broke over his leaving me. Then I realized he'd probably just gone to the bathroom and turned over on the bed, wrapping all the covers around me so when he got back, he wouldn't have any.

Voices drifted to me. I turned over. It took my brain a while to realize that the bathroom door was open and the light was on, shining into the room. Blake wasn't in the bathroom. Where did he go?

I rose, checking the time on a clock. It was about two in the morning. I went to his closet, found another pair of boxer shorts and stepped into them. I didn't want to walk around the house half naked. At least my panties had moderately dried.

I padded out into the hallway, following the length of carpet runner. The voices were louder now. I don't know why it bothered me, but it did. I willed my heart to stop pounding, trying to give myself some sort of explanation for what was going on. It didn't sound like a television. I hadn't seen a maid or servant here, but the house was spotless and the bed was made when we'd returned. I assumed someone did that. Was he talking to one of them now? Since I never saw anyone but him in the house, it was hard to conceive someone else might be here. I imagined invisible servants wandering around, doing his bidding. If you're rich enough, you can afford invisibility.

I eased my way to the front stairs, following the sounds.

On the first floor, I paused as the words became easier to make out.

"You've risked my entire business," a young male voice said.

"You shouldn't have been in business in the first place," Blake responded.

Talking business at two in the morning? I inched down the hallway to listen in.

"You don't understand," the young man said. "No one will do business with me anymore. I'm marked now."

"And with good reason," Blake said. "You were the one stupid enough to get poor quality merchandise from a competitor to this territory. Did you think you were smarter than they were? That they wouldn't figure it out?"

"The man said they'd buy it for three times what I paid. He promised—"

"Well, what do you expect?" Blake said, his voice stern, with a confidence I recognized from his business transaction earlier, once he had gotten serious. "He's the one who knew exactly what he was doing. You're a spoiled kid whose trust fund ran out and he was trying to put one over on you."

"He's going to come after me."

"The cartels would have, too, once they found out someone was distributing stuff that almost killed off their market. Do you know who they would have pointed the finger at? You. And they'd come after your family, which is why they had to go into hiding in the first place. I can't believe you're standing here arguing about your business when that little sister of yours—"

"That's not my sister," he spat out.

I got to a door that was cracked open and peeked inside. Blake was in an office, with a big mahogany desk dead center in the room. He had on a dark gray bathrobe in a shiny silk material, though the chest hung open as if he'd thrown it on in a hurry.

In front of him was a young man, and at first I didn't recognize him since his back was turned to me. I eased the door open a little more.

And then I recognized him. It was the guy from the party, the one that was acting odd. I'd only saw him that night, but I was sure. What was he doing here?

"I want you to give me the drugs back," he said.

"I can't do that. Your dad hired me to get the stuff and get rid of it."

I sucked in a breath. This kid was who brought it into town? What did it mean that his father had hired Blake?

"You don't understand. He expected that stuff to go out on the street."

"He expected it to kill a bunch of people and shake up the market. He wanted to create distrust in the system."

The guy jerked his head back and gave a small snort. "Who cares what the drug-heads do? But this guy will come after me and kill me if he thinks I didn't complete the deal. He's on my ass."

"You shouldn't have been doing deals. This isn't the movies. Whatever he promised you is a lie. You need to go home. Lay low for a while."

"I'm not staying home," the guy said.

"Jason," Blake said sharply. He squared off with him. "Listen to me. You've got one shot to live right now. Keep your head down. Stay at home. I know you've been prowling around, but the house I got for you and your family is a secure place. If you're running around, you're putting more than just your life at risk. The cartels know you got into the middle of this. You're lucky they're not after you."

"What about this guy? He's going to kill me. You may have had my dad move from the downtown house, but it won't take long for him to figure it out."

"If things go according to plan, you won't have to worry about it."

My breath stopped. He'd said Doyle was checking for the source. Wouldn't this guy know the source if he's the one Blake was protecting?

"What plan?" Jason asked, the same question I had in my mind.

Blake drew his shoulders back, breathing in deep and

letting a puff of air out slowly. "They wanted me to make sure this distributor never tries something like this again."

"You're going to shoot him? Is that it?"

"No." Blake made a face. "Who do you think I am? We'll just give him a taste of his own medicine. There's a well in that village. We'll get rid of this batch there. Once the locals start fighting amongst themselves, sick with the same poison, that'll send the message."

Jason marched forward, nearly toppling the chair he was standing in front of. "Then he'll really come after me! He'll kill me!"

"He'll come after the cartel. They've been in contact. They want their mark left behind."

"Is that who you work for?"

"It's who's interested in what's going on here. They control the territory. They're sending a clear message. Stay out. We're taking this war out of the city." He pointed a finger at Jason's face. "The war you started. You're lucky we caught this in time. If this got out wider than it had, if the police caught on and exposed everything, it would have been the cartels after your ass."

I backed up, terrified by what I was hearing. My heart was going crazy. Blake Coaltar worked for a Mexican drug cartel? He helped this bratty guy and was going to poison a well in a village? What war?

All the fears I'd thought I'd gotten rid of swept into me with a ruthless drop across my eyes and weighed heavily along my chest and shoulders. If he had been a simple drug dealer for the wealthy people in his circles, it would have been better. This ... this was so much worse. He was helping the cartels! That was horrible, wasn't it? And he had me help him?

I had to run. I had to get out of there. I was getting mixed up in things I didn't understand, couldn't figure out in the moment.

"Kate?" Blake said, and I jumped, driven out of my wild thoughts.

I bolted, not wanting to hear another word. I made a dash

for the front door.

"Kate! Stop!" Blake called after me.

To my surprise, the door was open, probably because Jason had visited and Blake left it unlocked. I shoved it open until it crashed into the wall and dashed out.

The rain hadn't let up. I jumped down the front porch steps in my bare feet, and raced through the open iron gate.

I ran across the street, to the park. I changed course, running barefoot through the grass, through the maze of trees, hoping to lose him if he was chasing me.

♠

DELIVERANCE

I emerged on the far side of the park, and dashed down a side road between two houses. I kept cutting through streets to make sure I wasn't being followed.

I probably looked like a mad woman running like I was, but I didn't stop. I couldn't stop. Blake was bad. The boys were right. I should have never done this alone. Now I knew everything. I had to get back. I had to get help. He could find me. He could find Wil.

I'd heard things about the cartels from Mexico, the reports about how they distributed the most drugs in the United States. How they had legions of military-trained assassins from the Mexican army and they controlled most of Mexico, and how that war was spilling out of the country and going global. All the ghost stories I'd heard in high school about not messing with drug dealers or distributors or you'd get into the line of fire, it all came to me. If you didn't want to get involved, you got out of their way. Live in ignorant bliss. It was the way you survived. Someone else, the police, the DEA, those were the ones fighting that war.

And even then, that didn't include the underground war. I remembered that from some Internet articles I'd read. The claim of territories. The control of distribution. Creation. Civil services to instill trust in buyers. Factions sought to take out others and become more powerful. It was a battle that never made the news if they could help it. The war normal people never saw.

I'd ignored it, like everyone else who didn't live among it, and then suddenly I was in the middle of everything I'd willingly blinded myself from.

It wasn't until I was several blocks away that I slowed. My feet ached from running barefoot on the pavement, uneven bricks and the occasional gravel. The rain pelted against me, and rivulets of water ran from my hair down my forehead, dripping into my eyes. I wrapped my arms around my body, pushing the shirt against my skin, trying to keep in whatever warmth my body could produce.

I had to find a street sign to get my bearings and start heading south. If I could make it to the river...

But I was lost. The dim street lights and the houses that all seemed to look the same confused me. My panicked state wasn't helping, but I couldn't slow down. I needed help. It was so late and there wasn't anyone driving by.

I was about to try heading east again but after another house, I saw a familiar-looking lake. I ran for it and by the time I got to the corner of the park, I could see the lights of a single high rise apartment building. The Sergeant Jasper.

My heart lifted. And at the same time, I walked slowly toward it. Nerves caught up with me. The boys would be angry with me. I'd have to hide forever. Marc might still be mad I shot him in the leg with the nail gun. Maybe they wouldn't even believe me. After what I'd done, I wasn't sure I could explain.

But I had nowhere else to go, especially if Wil was in danger already.

I continued to wipe at my face, taking the long way around the lake. The area was barren now, but a few lights reflected on the surface in shimmers and it rippled with the rain. It broke up that better world I had imagined earlier, becoming a nightmare of strange shadows and colors.

I entered the building from the back door. The shirt stuck to my skin, and dripped to the tile floor. It didn't at all mask my nakedness underneath. The black boxers were jacked up high on my hips and stuck in places I didn't want to think about. I must have looked like a royal mess. I wondered if security would even let me upstairs.

To my surprise and relief, the security guard wasn't at the podium. Either temporarily in the bathroom or checking out another problem elsewhere. Either way, I dashed to the elevator, hopping inside, and pressed at the button for the seventh floor.

I stood outside of apartment 737, shaking. In my head, I was trying to come up with excuses. I ran through scenarios. I was trying to come up with lies and my frantic brain wasn't able to piece together a good enough story. I thought if they wouldn't let me in, if they sent me away, I'd at least beg for clothes or a ride back to the hotel. I'd ask for my things back. I'd go back to the hotel. I'd find Wil. If I had to, I'd make him go with me to another hotel or something. Whatever I had to do.

I stared down the door, willing it to tell me the mood of anyone inside. It wasn't answering, so I knocked. My rattling bones shook, leaving me unable to knock too strongly. I wasn't sure anyone would hear. I wrapped my arms around my body as if to hold myself together against my shivering.

I was about to knock again when the door opened. Brandon materialized. He wore a blue T-shirt and black boxer shorts. Part of the T-shirt got hung up on his side, revealing part of the golden tanned abs near the waistband. His eyes were slits, as if I'd woken him. His hair was mussed, the short, sun-kissed strands pressed against his head.

I thought Brandon would be the last one who would want to see me. I supposed that's why I went to Marc's apartment first, to avoid him. If I had any warmth in me, I was sure my cheeks would have heated up, embarrassed about running away and forced to return.

But Brandon took one look at me, and his eyes adjusted from sleepy to recognition. "Kayli?" he whispered, his voice choked with surprise.

My heart thundered. This was it. He'd slam the door. He'd curse me out for daring to come back.

I was about to say never mind and leave but he jumped out.

His arms threaded around me, taking me in. Without questions of *where have you been,* or *why did you leave.*

Instead, his arms strengthened as he pulled me in, drawing me to his body. He locked me into him, as if not daring to let go or I'd disappear again. His head bowed until his cheek pressed against my wet hair.

If I had never known what it was like to be truly missed, this would have told me.

That did it. I broke. I buried my face into his shoulder and clung to him like I was going to die without him, not caring that I was soaking wet. My fingers gripped at the material of his T-shirt, bunching it into my fists. I tried to say something, but my voice came out in a choking sob and I cut it off quickly.

He never released me. He picked me up by the waist until he could cart me inside, and then he kicked the door shut. "Are you okay?" he asked. He buried his face into my hair. "Did you walk here? Are you hurt?"

I wanted to answer, but a shiver took over.

"Who is it?" Raven mumbled. I caught sight of him over Brandon's shoulder. He wore only a pair of gray sweatpants. The tattoos covering his chest and stomach. It attracted my attention for a moment, distracting me from all the lies and questions in my brain. Even as I stared, I couldn't really make out the pictures. My eyes were too blurry and burned with tears and exhaustion. But it didn't matter; it was Raven. Raven. My heart dared to be happy that he was there. It was sinking into my brain that I was back and the guys may not kick me back out into the street after all.

"It's Kayli," Brandon said. He carried me over to the sofa, where there was a blanket and a pillow splayed out like he'd been sleeping there. He picked the blanket up, wrapping it around my shoulders. "Kayli," he said to me, tucking the blanket tighter around my body as he kept me near. "Where were you?"

"I..." I said.

Raven started talking, and at first I tried to jerk my head around because I thought he was talking to me.

"We found her," Raven said. When I turned, I realized he was talking into a cell phone. "No, she's here. She's like half naked and soaked. She walked here. No, I don't think she needs a doctor." He pulled the phone away from his ear. "Do you need a doctor?"

I shook my head.

"She doesn't need a doctor," Raven said. "Just get over here." He hung up.

Brandon captured my chin, drawing my attention back to the depths of those cerulean eyes. "Are you okay?"

"I'm fine," I said, my teeth starting to chatter. "I'm just cold."

"No shit," Raven said. "You were walking in the rain naked."

"Get her some clothes," Brandon said.

Raven left for his room and returned a moment later with a T-shirt. He went into Marc's room and returned from there with a pair of pajama bottoms. "Marc's on his way."

"Where are they?" I asked.

"Out looking for you," Brandon said. "We took shifts."

My head jerked back in surprise. "Looking for me?"

"Axel figured you'd come back," Brandon said. "But when a night passed and you never showed up, Marc had us looking for you. He had Axel watching Wil and the hotel in case you showed up there. Raven and I had been at the malls all day. Then he started checking out ... all over, I guess."

"Let her put some clothes on," Raven said. He marched forward and collected my elbow in a firm grasp. "Take that blanket from her."

Brandon removed the blanket from me. He started folding it up carefully since it was wet.

Raven tucked an arm around my waist and nearly carried me to the bathroom door. He planted the new clothes on the counter and pushed me inside the bathroom. "Hurry," he barked at me.

I didn't know what I was in a hurry for, but I guessed that he meant the sooner I changed, the sooner I could come back out and warm up again. I thought about a hot shower, but didn't want to wait for warm water. I just wanted to get under a blanket and fall into bed.

My body trembled as I removed all my clothes this time. It was slow agony to even move now. My muscles were solid with chill. Even with the wet clothes removed, I was shaking too hard. I had to press a hand against the counter to steady myself. I gasped, trying to draw up the strength to shift my bones. They hurt at every small movement I made.

"Where were you?" Raven asked through the door.

There was a thump on the other side. "Leave her alone," Brandon said. "Wait until she gets dressed."

"She can talk and put clothes on at the same time. I've seen girls do it."

My mind flew into all of the things to tell them without knowing where to start. After a moment, trying to put my legs into the pants without falling over from a shiver, I remembered something they'd said. I flung myself at the door, pressing to it to steady myself, but also because I needed him to hear me. "Raven!" I called to him. "Call ... someone. Whoever is closest. Axel was at the hotel?"

"Yeah," he said.

"Call Axel. Have him stay there. Get Marc to go there, too."

"Why? What's going on?"

"It's Blake."

"Who?"

"Coaltar." I backed up from the door a step. "Call him. Make sure he stays with Wil. Make sure Coaltar doesn't show up."

The handle shook on the bathroom door. I leapt backward, shoving the pants up and then turned around to face the shower as I tried to find the opening of the shirt to put it on.

The door opened behind me before I managed to even thread the arms through the T-shirt. I leapt again, drawing the shirt toward my body to cover my bare breasts.

"What the hell are you talking about?" Raven asked. His eyes were shooting lightning at me. His shoulders seemed to swell and his massive body appeared to take up the entire opening of the door. "What's wrong with Wil? Is someone after him?"

"Raven!" Brandon barked, though his voice wavered. He looked in from behind Raven's shoulder. When he saw I wasn't fully dressed, he turned on Raven. "You can't barge in on her."

"I couldn't hear what she was saying," Raven said. He turned to me, unflinching, as if the sight of a half-naked girl was as ordinary as the sight of the bar of soap on the sink. He was way too focused to think anything of it.

"Coaltar," I said, uncaring about this right now. Raven was listening to me, and seemed to understand this was more important. I had the shirt shoved up against my chest so it didn't really matter. "He may be looking for me. You need to call Axel and tell him to stay there. I don't think he knows I live there, but just in case."

Raven fished his phone out and started pushing buttons. He shoved the phone to his shoulder, holding it with his ear pressed against it, his neck scrunched up. He shuffled the bathroom door half closed so he could access the closet door that was behind it.

At the same time, Brandon angled himself inside the bathroom. He yanked my shirt from my arms, and readjusted it. "Don't just stand there. Put your shirt on," he said, using an older brother tone I imagined he used on Corey a hundred times a day. He swooped the shirt down over my body, covering me. I shoved my arms through the sleeves. Brandon wrapped his arms around my body rubbing along my back to warm me up.

"Axel," Raven said into the phone. He selected a towel from inside the bathroom closet and passed it to Brandon. Brandon collected it without a word, and wrapped my hair in it, massaging my scalp to dry. I slipped my arms through the sleeves of Raven's shirt again to cover them up and shove them against my body to warm up. Raven took the phone from his hunched shoulder and talked into it. "No, go back. Stay with Wil. Coaltar might be looking for her after all. She wants someone to keep an eye out for him."

"Why is he after you?" Brandon asked.

I shivered, but his warming hands drying my hair was helping. "I know," I said. "I know what he's hiding. He ... the drugs. The kid..."

"Kayli!" Marc's voice called from the living room.

"She's in here!" Raven called back.

Marc materialized in the door. Corey was behind him. Corey took one look at me and then settled back with a relieved smile, as if he didn't believe I'd come back until just now.

Marc, however, clenched his fists, his eyes narrowing on me. "I've been looking all over for you. Where the hell have you been?"

I grunted. Now that I'd warmed a little, I found a little bit of strength. "Coaltar's been buying a new synthetic drug called JH-14 from all of the local dealers."

"What are you talking about?"

"Mr. Fitzgerald's kid, Jason. He brought it into the city. Only the drugs are defective. They kill people. Coaltar made a deal with Fitzgerald to get the drugs back so the local Mexican hired guns wouldn't go after his son and their family for killing off their market, and drawing unwanted attention to their operation. From what I understand, it's another drug gang from somewhere else, who wanted in on the territory, so they were sending defective drugs to shake up the market. Only they swindled this kid to do it."

Marc's jaw fell open, the two-toned eyes glided back and forth as if calculating. "Coaltar's been paid to cover up for someone else."

"Yeah. Only he's not planning to just get rid of the drugs. He's looking for the source. He may have found it. He wants to dump the drugs into the local well in the village — wherever it is. He wants to poison the locals there to let them know they know. There's a cartel that contacted him that wants him to do it."

"How do you know all this?"

I swallowed, tugging my head away from Brandon's soothing hands. My eyes lingered on the wall, avoiding everyone's eyes. I felt they weren't going to like this. "I've been hanging out with Coaltar for the past couple of days, since I left."

The silence was so heavy after that, and I felt the weight of it as if it could sink me into the floor, dragging me under. I clenched my jaw, waiting. I had run to the only person they had told me to stay away from. It was probably why they never found me if they were searching. They presumed I would stay away.

"That's impossible," Corey said. "How?"

"What?" I asked.

"We've been watching him while you were gone. We've been monitoring phone calls and…" He checked with Marc and the others, waiting for permission to reveal whatever he wanted to say.

"You weren't on the video feeds," Brandon said.

"What video feeds?" I asked. Did they not believe me? "You have his house under video surveillance?"

Marc held his hands up and toward me. "How can you say you've been there? We checked there. I thought you might show up there, but he's been at home for two days. He even called Mr. Fitzgerald saying he was going to lay low."

"He left home two nights ago to go downtown, and talk to those drug dealers," I said. "And we've been walking in and out of his place all day yesterday. If you were watching, you'd have seen me."

Raven's fists clenched hard. In a flash, he swiped at the counter, knocking soap and other bathroom items to the floor. He punched at the counter top and then pointed at Marc. "I told you."

"We were watching!" Marc barked at him. His eyes widened and they squared their shoulders off at each other. "He must have cut the feeds. I didn't want to waste time there if she wasn't—"

"He got tipped off because we broke into his office," Raven said. "The motherfucker's had her? What kind of shit…"

"We don't need this right now," Marc said.

Raven took a swing at Marc. Marc ducked. "Don't tell

me what I need! I told you we should have looked there first. I knew she was there." Raven bellowed.

"Guys!" Brandon said, stepping between them. Corey swept around me, cutting in front of Raven, and putting a hand on his chest, pushing Raven to step back. Raven kept his eyes on Marc, his mouth tight and his jaw firm. His gaze slowly slid down to Corey.

"This isn't the time," Corey said. "Coaltar must have known for a while. He's been biding his time, letting us watch him when he wants. He probably just looped old video."

Raven grunted.

I had backed up against the wall, my hand pushed up against my heart. "He's got a guy," I said. Everyone turned to me. "Doyle. Some guy out in Hanahan. He's got a farmhouse and a front lawn filled with satellite dishes and a big computer mess inside. A hacker of some kind. He's able to listen in on phone calls and…"

Axel's voice coming from the phone spooked me, until I realized that Raven had put the phone on speaker. "Marc," he barked from the phone, "I need you to call Kevin. Have him replace me here. Get everyone on new lines."

"We need to get her out of here." Marc said.

"His first move is going to be to try to cover up what he's doing. Does he have the last of this synthetic?"

Everyone looked at me expectantly, waiting.

"He's supposed to get the last of it tonight," I said. I was wondering if Doyle was listening to this now. If he was, could I stop him? How could I tell the guys without him knowing? He could have the walls bugged as they'd done to Coaltar. "He's getting it delivered to his yacht at City Marina. I don't know what time. He didn't seem to need to be there for it to get delivered and when I left him, he was still at his house."

"Raven," Axel said through the phone. "Find a trainee who isn't busy to go with you to the docks. I want twenty-four-seven monitoring. Try Silas Korba. He knows a few things about boats. He should be able to help."

"What if he's already there?" I asked. "What if he's already gone?"

"He's not leaving tonight," Axel said. "He could try, but the yacht he owns takes more than one person to run. He'd have to get his crew together quickly. And if he's waiting on this last shipment, he's not going to leave without it. But we do have to be careful. He may suspect Kayli's watching, so he's probably going to be trickier. He may even divert where this shipment is going. We'll need someone to intercept it if possible."

"He's not doing the delivery himself," I said.

"Right," Axel said. "We still need someone to watch him. Brandon, go down and start. Corey, I need you to start listening. Phone calls, emails, anything he might be using. Set up a monitoring team and figure out how the hell he's been able to cut our feeds without us knowing."

"What about Kayli?" Marc asked.

"What about me?" I sliced my hand through the air. "Don't worry about me. Just make sure Wil is okay. Actually, you probably need to get him. I should probably go with Raven to the docks. I know what the guy making the delivery looks like. I know where Coaltar's at now but if he's already on his way..."

"Does he know your name?" Axel asked. "Does Coaltar know who you are?"

"He still knows me as Kate. He doesn't know anything about me."

"We don't want to take any chances. Marc, stay with Kayli. Kayli, stay in the apartment."

"What?" I cried. "I can't stay."

"Kayli," Axel barked from the phone. "I'll be forever grateful that you took the initiative. You found out more in a day than what took us a couple of weeks of surveillance. You've done a wonderful job, but let us take it from here. Go to sleep. You need to recover."

"But—"

"If you want to help, you need to stay put. If he's looking for you, if he thinks you'll be watching, you won't be able to go anywhere near City Marina without him being aware of it. He'll have people looking for you. He won't be expecting Raven. You need to stay away from Wil, and you especially need to stay away from Coaltar. We should probably even get you out of town for a while."

"I can do that," Marc said.

"Right now, stay put," Axel said. "We may need her for information and to make any identifications. But if you see any sign of trouble, get her on the first plane out of here. And stay with her. Call up the Academy for a couple of favors if you have to."

I grunted, shoving my fists at my eyes. I realized then why I was so frustrated with this group. I wasn't used to letting anyone else tell me what to do. It was annoying when I wanted to go back and kick Blake's ass for being a lying bastard. Had he known they were on to him? How much did he know? I wanted to go get Wil myself and warn him. I didn't want to sit and do nothing.

The worst part was that they were probably right. They had been right from the very beginning. I was too stubborn and too angry. Like shooting Marc in the leg. Like getting jumped by a bunch of thugs in a back street alley. I bit my tongue now, hard, simply to stop myself from protesting. Even Blake saw it in me. I was going to get myself killed jumping the gun and not listening.

I sighed, with a lot of emphasis, just to show how much I really didn't like it. "Fine," I said.

"Everyone move," Axel said, and he hung up.

With that, everyone started moving at once. Corey, who had been standing by, patted me once on the shoulder, looking like he wanted to say a whole lot of things to me, but couldn't at the moment. He dashed out of the apartment to, I imagine, his own place where he could use the computers and do what he did best.

Raven ran for his room, stuffing his feet into boots and shoved on a shirt. Brandon did the same, borrowing some clothes from Marc's room.

"Emergency phones, guys," Marc said. He walked out to

the computer desks in the dining room. He opened a drawer, pulling out what looked like brand-new flip phones. He curled his fingers at the other guys, and passed the phones off to them. He collected their old cell phones, too, leaving them on the desk.

"I need another ID," Raven said. "I need to borrow a boat."

Marc disappeared into his bedroom, and came back with an ID card, and a wad of cash. "There's a hotel by the marina, plus there's a little restaurant. See if you can set up surveillance from the hotel room. Get Silas to make friends with whoever is in the dock house. When it opens, go to the restaurant that has a good view of the docks. Call Silas from a pay phone. Make sure he brings an emergency phone and leaves his own behind. He needs a non-GPS car, too."

"I'll take the bike," Brandon said.

"You need another car," Marc said. "See if anyone has a spare. The bike will work for now, but it's too loud and obvious. Have them replace your bike. Use the park to hide in for now. And you need some protection since Blake knows your face. I should probably be doing your job."

"I could make it obvious," Brandon said. "I could tail him and make sure he knows. He'll be reluctant to make a move then."

"He may figure out a way to divert you, instead. If he is with one of the cartels, that makes him more dangerous. We don't want to take that risk right now. Just watch, but from a distance."

Brandon nodded. "Have Corey send someone to find me. I'll stay in the park if I can. If I need to, I'll circle the block."

I had my arms crossed around my stomach, and hovered in the hallway. I was in awe simply hearing them talking like this, the way they worked together. They talked about their plans. They came up with a solution. Marc made the final decision and they went with it. The fluidity of how they worked dazzled me. Raven, the least likely I suspected to take orders or advice from anyone, accepted what Marc had to say and simply absorbed it. It was like their fight from before had been forgotten completely.

I felt out of place where I stood, but inside I desired this. I didn't understand it so well, and while I worked alone, being with the guys was like being more confident in my choices. With more than one person making the decision, it felt like more of the right thing to do. I didn't feel like I was messing up any more.

I'd messed up enough. Now they were doing all this to fix my mistakes. Maybe Coaltar didn't know about the cameras and the rest until I tipped him off. And I'd pointed him right at the boys by mentioning Brandon and their suspicions.

Marc walked over to the door to open it for the others as they left. As he moved, it was the first time I noticed the limp. Panic settled in. If the guys left, I'd be alone with him. He'd curse me out for shooting him. He'd tell me how stupid I was for getting caught up in this. I couldn't run now. I'd already promised I'd stay.

Before Marc shut the door, I approached him. "Maybe we should go hang out with Corey," I said. "Maybe we can help him." I thought a third person being around would ease the tension.

"Corey works best when he's alone so he can listen and think," Marc said. He closed the door and turned the lock. "If he needs us down there, he'll call. Besides, he may not stay here. He may need to work from somewhere else. We don't want to slow him down."

I tapped my fingers across my upper thighs, and started the awkward gazing around the apartment. Silence settled in. The crazy moments of before still coursed through me but I had nowhere to expend the energy.

Not much had changed since I left. The place still smelled like special blends of coffee. I curled my toes against the fibers of the standard beige carpet. Blake's carpets had been softer. I cringed at the bitter thoughts of him, at thinking of how he had tricked me.

"What's wrong?" Marc asked, his voice softer than I expected.

I flinched and looked up. He stood by the door still, leaning against it with his shoulder. His mismatched eyes focused on me.

"Nothing," I said quickly.

"Liar," he said quietly.

That stung. "Stop saying that," I said. "Don't call me that."

"You were lying."

"If I'm lying, there's probably a reason."

"Like what?"

"Like I don't want to tell you."

He blew out a perplexed sigh. "Bambi..."

"And stop calling me Bambi!"

"What the hell are you so mad at me for?" he barked back. He pointed his hand at his chest. "I've been looking for you for two days, and you come back in trouble and you're mad at me?"

My breath became hard to manage. "I ... I don't ..." I couldn't think of the words to use, at the same time trying to stuff my anger back before I did anything else stupid. Why *was* I angry with him? Why couldn't I stop?

Or maybe I wasn't mad at all, but terrified. I simply didn't know how to express it, too proud to admit it. Blake Coaltar was more trouble than I imagined.

And besides that, I worried that if and when this was over, the world Marc had dragged me into would suddenly disappear.

Being back, having the boys touch me, scrambling now to help me, when I'd been the one to bring them this trouble, it moved me in ways I couldn't express.

Every moment I spent with them, it lured me further in. The guys were amazing and I wanted to spend more time with them. I wanted to learn what they knew. I wanted to go with Axel and Raven back to the shooting range. I wanted to play video games with Corey. I wanted to learn how to surf with Brandon. I wanted to know why their apartment smelled like a coffee house. I wanted Marc not to hate me. I didn't feel so out of place here. I didn't feel like I had to hide who I was.

I was scared of the truth. Because the truth was, I didn't want to be alone. The more time I spent with them, the more I craved to be part of this. Perhaps that's what drew me to Blake. He brought me in without question, too. He tried his best to involve me. Maybe he wasn't what I thought it was, but he seemed to be genuine at the time.

I pushed back thoughts of Blake and simply stared at Marc. There were shadows under his eyes. The cord that hung from his neck, the silver sand dollar, dangled on top of his blue-collared shirt. The dark blue jeans and black boots, the whole ensemble with his sculpted chest and arms was exquisite. What didn't match his otherwise striking face was the terrified expression he held.

He took a step forward. "Are you spacing out on me? What's wrong now?"

"I don't know what to do right now," I said, trying to push back all the lies that were teasing my tongue, since he seemed to know when I lied anyway. This was the best I could do to answer, and it was true. I had no idea.

His shoulders relaxed. He held his arms out and open and he slowly stepped forward. "Kayli, come here for a second."

I closed the distance between us, with my hands up in front of me, unsure what he wanted.

The moment I was close enough, he captured my wrists and drew me in. His arms weaved around my shoulders and he held on tight in an embrace.

The hug was awkward to me at first. I felt I didn't deserve it, least of all from him. I'd shot him in the leg. I left when he said not to. I ran to the only person he'd warned me to stay away from. Even after all of that, he came looking for me. He didn't give up on me, even now. It took the last of my strength to close off my emotions so I wouldn't cry.

His cheek met the side of my head, and he whispered. "I promised you," he said. "I promised I'd never let you see Jack or that hotel again if that's what you wanted. I promised I'd make sure Wil would be okay. What I forgot to mention was that I would make sure you were okay, too."

"I'm fine," I said, though I choked. I stuffed my face against his shoulder. "I don't need anything."

"You do," he said. "I know you do. I was like you, once, and I needed the same thing."

"You don't know anything about me," I said.

"You're Kayli Winchester," he said. "You've had a hard life, but you're intelligent, and brave, and reckless. You push others away because you don't want to be hurt. If people get too close to the real Kayli, you start lying or run away if the lies don't work."

I grunted and tried to push at his chest. "I don't—"

He held strong, his arms tightening around my body. His head tilted until his lips met my ear. "But the real Kayli is amazing. She's selfless. She'd risk her own life and freedom for anyone she cares about. She's tender and a die-hard loyal person who demands only the best of loyalty in return. She'll test you at every possible moment just to make sure you stick around. God help anyone who could win your heart and your trust, because he wouldn't realize what would be unleashed in you."

I swallowed, and tried to bury my head further into his shoulder, as if that was the way to get all the feelings inside of me to disappear. I wanted him to stop. The truth was, I didn't want to look at myself as closely as he seemed to see me. "Marc," I said, my voice smaller than I'd ever heard it before.

He sniffed hard and as he continued to hug me, he stepped forward, until my back met with the bathroom doorframe. He stopped there and pulled his head back. He lowered it until his forehead touched mine. "Don't run any more, Kayli. If you're worried I'll see something I won't like, trust me, I've got plenty of ghosts in my own closet for you to pick through."

"What?"

"I wasn't always like this," he said. "I wasn't even like you. You have Wil. You had a lot of excuses, reasons for what you've done. And even when you stole money, you were always thinking of other people. I wasn't like that. I was horrible. I was mean. I was..." He shook his head against mine. "I did a lot of shit. Stuff I'm not proud of. Axel and the other guys, they got me out of it. They saw things in me I didn't know about, things I hid from everyone by trying to be tough and put on a fake face. When I was young, I did it to survive. Then suddenly I just became that bad guy and just didn't care. Until Axel showed up."

"Axel said you saved his life," I whispered.

He moved his arms from around me, until his palms cupped my cheeks. He kept his body close. I couldn't move my hands from his chest, and I didn't want to. Heat drifted from him and I wanted to absorb it. It was more than that, too. His closeness was something I wanted as well.

"I was in a bad spot," he said. "I'd gotten mixed up in this street gang that did nothing but steal money for the drugs we wanted. We took over an abandoned section of houses down in North Charleston. Axel was part of an Academy team sent to stop us and clean up the area, only he infiltrated our group, trying to figure out if anyone was worth saving. He mixed in too far and the gang was going to kill him."

"They killed people?"

"It was all about the drugs for them and he was a threat. They were being assholes. They stole a couple of guns and were going to drive by his house and shoot. Classic drive-by. Chicken-shit stuff. They wanted to stop anyone from taking over, which they thought Axel was doing. They thought he was part of another gang. Only I found out and I warned him. From that point on, he wouldn't leave me alone. Every chance he got, he was inviting me to come to the shooting range with him, to go surfing with him. Anything and everything. Like a lost puppy that you feed once and you try to shoo off and he never listens."

"Why did you change? Why did you finally listen?"

His thumb traced over my cheekbone, slowly, like the breath from his lips that trailed over every little inch of my face. The gentle touch sent waves of warm shivers through me. His eyes burrowed into mine. "He never gave up. The times I would come around, he never hesitated. He'd feed me, invite me to stay. He had me working with him on his research. I'd run off when I thought it was too much, but when I came back, it was like I never left. He took me back every time. Eventually I just stopped leaving."

Something Axel had told me before about the Academy clicked inside. "And did he make you join this Academy? Was that why he wanted you?"

"That's something else." He smoothed his palm down, tracing over my jaw. "But the Academy trusted him when he said I was a good person, and they supported him. So when I did finally decide I wanted in, he supported me fully, every step, and the Academy did as well."

"Sounds nice," I said, with no real conviction. I didn't know anything about the Academy other than the bits I'd been able to piece together. It wasn't the current puzzle I'd been trying to work on, because of Coaltar. I was curious, but I'd work it out later.

"Kayli," he said. "My point is it took me a long time to figure out I didn't have to run off any more. I'm trying to help you. It's easier if you just give in."

"What are you saying?" I asked. "I already agreed to stay here because Coaltar."

"I'm talking about you not running away all the time."

"What do you want from me? I just said I'd stay," I barked at him.

"For now," he said. His fingertip trailed back up along my jaw until he was rubbing the soft spot just below my ear. "But I see it every time anyone looks at you too long. I was trying to talk to you at the mall, and you didn't even know me, and you lied about your name and tried to run away. We had to corner you, and threaten you to get you to come with us. It feels like we've got to threaten you to stick around. I'm trying to tell you that it doesn't have to be that way. Not with us."

I tried to tilt my head away from his fingers. They were making it hard to keep the wall over my heart up. I closed my eyes. I couldn't take this. I couldn't surrender to his promises. Like Brandon, I couldn't believe for a moment he

329

really wanted to, but that he just felt obligated.

Marc seized my chin, shoving it back until my face was close to his. His fingers roughed over my jaw. "Kayli, stop shutting me out," he commanded.

"I don't know what you want me to do," I said, but my voice was nearly gone, thick with the fear that he was way too close and seemed to think he knew what I wanted. I didn't want him to know he was right. I don't know why. My pride was too strong. I'd been this way for so long, I didn't know how to give in. I didn't know how to trust.

He opened his mouth, like he wanted to say something else but stopped, and his eyes drifted down to my mouth and held. My breath caught in my throat.

Before I could think to even push him off, his mouth claimed me. He kissed me hard enough that my head pressed back into the wall. His hands slid back to cup around my jawline to keep me from pulling away. His lips pressed down, mouth parted.

I kissed him back. I don't know what came over me, but I wanted to feel those promises. I wanted to believe, for the moment, that maybe I could just let go, like he said, and trust that I could be accepted for who I was. Was I just like him? Could I be like that? Could I find a place just for me among these guys and waltz in and be with them? Corey had accepted me without much of a fight, it seemed. The others were a little harder. Brandon had been the most difficult, but once I understood what he was about, it seemed like he never hesitated, either, he just wanted to be sure I knew what I was getting involved in.

I opened my mouth, inviting Marc in, just a little.

Like opening the gates, his mouth claimed me again. In every possible place I could think to hide, he found me. My mind blanked out. I didn't have room for anything else other than Marc and his kiss that told me everything would be all right. His kiss sank into me over and over again. Lips pressed against mine, tugging at my skin, at heart strings, at my core.

When he finally released my mouth so I could breathe, his lips trailed over my face, across my eyes and my brows.

"Why did it have to be you?" He breathed out as he whispered against my face. "I was hunting a thief, and I found a beautiful wreck. I wasn't ready for this."

"Ready?" I murmured.

His head dipped down, and he kissed me once, closed mouthed, against my lips slowly. He released me again but kept his head a breath width away and his lips nearly grazed mine as he whispered. "You feel it, don't you?" He took my hand and shoved it toward his stomach, pressing my palm against his abdomen. "Those goddamn wriggly sparks."

I didn't have a response to that. I wasn't sure how I felt. I thought maybe I did, but my mind didn't want to let go of some nagging feeling. I'd felt it with Coaltar, too, the same strong desires. I felt it with Brandon, when he kissed me before, or so I thought. There were other tugs against my heart strings, with the other boys, with Raven, and Axel, and even Corey. For that reason, I wanted to close it all off. I blamed it on the lack of being really close to anyone for such a long time. I was Kayli, the unwanted thief, for years. Now I was tempted by so many emotions that I hadn't felt for so long. Suddenly there was a group, and they were welcoming, but all too overwhelming.

My hand clutched at his abdomen, as if I could pull those feelings from him and find the surety he seemed to be feeling. As if I could find the courage to tell him the truth; that I felt it, too, it was just much more complicated. "Marc," I said, unable to think of anything else to say.

He growled, low and guttural, like an ache he was fighting. His arms encircled me once again, drawing me from the wall. He picked me up, hefting me over his shoulder.

"Marc!" I cried out. I punched him in the hip and butt. "Put me down."

He ignored this, and instead limped to his bedroom. He kicked the door shut behind us and angled for the bed. He plopped me down onto the mattress. Before my sense of what was right-side-up came back, he flicked off the light and crawled into the bed next to me.

"Scoot over," he said, lifting the covers on the bed.

"Shouldn't we stay up?" I asked. "Should we pay attention? What about Wil? What about Coaltar?"

"If there's one thing you're going to have to learn," Marc said. He picked up the second pillow on his bed, fluffing it and placing it near my head for me to rest on. "You're going to have to trust that if they need us, they'll call. Until then, it's a good idea to get some sleep. Besides, we may need to take a little trip soon, if it looks like Coaltar is coming after you."

"I can't leave."

"I'd go with you," he said. He sat up, ripping off the blue shirt, revealing his bare chest. He unbuttoned and slid off his jeans, kicking off his boots and socks, until he was just in boxer briefs. As my eyes adjusted, I caught the shapes of his hips, the muscles along his stomach. He wedged himself between the covers and then leaned over, collecting me in his arms until I was next to him. The best I could do, the most comfortable position, was actually pressing my hands to his chest.

"I mean I can't just take off," I said. My fingers traced along his warm bare skin. "There's Wil. He's probably really worried about me now."

"We may take him along, too. But if we start taking him, involving him, he'll be in the same mess, he'll have to hide just like you. Coaltar might connect him to you and he'll use him to get to you." He kissed my nose. "Sleep."

"Marc," I said, wanting to be honest. I didn't know how to explain it. "I don't think I'm ... I'm not really ready for this."

"Like I am?" He nestled up against me. "Just sleep for now. Don't leave. We'll figure it out later."

I didn't want that. I wanted to stay up and figure out what I wanted. I wanted all the answers to what I was feeling, and the confused guilt over that just a few hours ago, I'd been kissing Coaltar with nearly the same desires I suddenly felt for Marc. Marc was incredibly handsome, like Blake. He wasn't rich but he worked hard and he did the right thing. Didn't he?

And what about Brandon?

None of my relationships had ever been perfect, and this felt like incredibly bad timing, bad circumstances, bad everything. Still, I couldn't help the feelings. In the dark, beside Marc in his bed, with the other boys out there working to solve the problems that I'd created and dropped upon them, this had to be the worst moment.

I wanted to know the future. Marc made it sound like they'd invite me to stay with them, just like they did with him. His kiss told me he wanted something more from me. A deeper relationship, perhaps. Again, I felt trapped, like he wanted to take care of me, and I was helpless with nothing to offer in return. No job, no future, nothing. I wasn't even wearing my own clothes, but his and Raven's.

I wanted to know if Marc was thinking beyond Coaltar, too. If his kiss meant he wanted me or if he was just trying to make me feel better. An old boyfriend once told me I couldn't analyze the future by a first date, or a first kiss with a guy. Girls, he'd said, would go out with a guy for a day, and then want to work out exactly if he would keep her forever before they went out on a next date, when it simply didn't work like that. It took me a long time to realize a kiss, or a date didn't mean he was thinking about forever, or even a month from now. It's just too soon.

It was simply hard to accept, because I was lost and didn't see a future me at all, so seeing one with Marc, or anyone else, simply didn't work. Maybe he did feel those sparks he was talking about. Maybe I felt them, too. Maybe we were both lonely and needed someone right now to hold onto until things looked better. Like Brandon, who had made me stay beside him until morning, until he was sure I hadn't fallen to pieces and could move again. Like Blake not wanting me to run off into the dark, alone in the middle of the night. Maybe he just wanted to keep tabs on me, but why did I feel there was something more? Or had I just been hoping?

And why was I thinking about Blake now? God help me, but I was. As horrible as the truth was when I found out, I discovered a tiny part telling me that I still didn't understand the whole thing. He'd had so many opportunities to do me in. He could have left me to those gang members. He could have done so many things to me and he didn't. Why? I didn't understand him at all and that was what drove me insane. I needed an answer.

I swiped away the thoughts for now. I willed sleep to take me, to help me to forget and to help me build that wall around my heart again until I could figure it out. How could I even think of a relationship, of liking anyone, and least of all love someone, when I wasn't even sure who I was anymore?

As I fell asleep, I still clutched to Marc, because my secret hope was that when I did, someone, maybe Marc, maybe anyone, would see the real me. Maybe then, I wouldn't need the wall around my heart.

It felt impossible, but in the weakness of the moment, I wanted that. More than anything.

♠

MARC

I slept deeply. I couldn't figure out the time, but I sensed it was before dawn when Marc got up and left the room. I drifted to his side of the bed, feeling the warmth of him in the sheets, and the spot his head made in the pillow, smelling where he'd lain. Even when I wasn't really sleeping, I gazed at the wall of his room, simply staring off. I was too numb, too empty of thought and I luxuriated in that. It was the brief escape from the mess inside of me.

The scent of fresh coffee drifted to me, stronger than the usual lingering fragrance the apartment seemed to have. I stared off at the door, brain dead. I eyeballed the shelf with books and knickknacks. The corner of the floor piled with shirts and other clothes. The half-open drawers with boxer shorts hanging out. The closet that stood open from when Brandon had borrowed some of his clothes the night before.

Marc materialized in the bedroom doorway and came to me, and stood by the bed. He held out a coffee mug.

"Bambi," he cooed.

I stretched a leg out, nudging him in the good thigh with my foot in a faux kick. He caught it, eased it back over on the bed to place it gently down. He lowered until he sat next to me on the bed.

"I've got something for you," he said.

"It's coffee," I said, in an unsurprised tone.

"It's mocha. I think you'll like it."

I grunted, sitting up. My hair fell against my face, and I had to rake back the strands several times to get it out of the way. My hair was too long and needed to be cut.

He waited until I was on the edge of the bed beside him

and then passed me the large black mug.

The warmth drew me in first, followed by the rich aroma of coffee infused with mocha and a spritz of hazelnut. There were other things, too, but I couldn't pick them out by smell. I put the mug to my lips, sipping to check the temperature. The liquid filled my mouth, rolling down my throat. The caffeine splash forced my eyes open. The taste was smooth, better than I expected. I usually hated the bitter taste of coffee and masked it with plenty of milk and sugar. His didn't have the acidic bitterness, which surprised me. Was this really coffee?

Marc's eyebrows rose on his face and a smile touched his lips. "Not bad?"

"You talk like you grew the beans yourself."

"I made the flavor blend," he said. "Do you like it?"

Coffee came in flavors? I didn't drink it much, but my extent of coffee knowledge was the cheap brands and usually it was a luxury we couldn't often afford. "I like hazelnut."

He smirked. "I have a knack with hazelnuts."

I rubbed the last of sleep out of my eyes and took another sip. "Where's everyone else?"

"Still out. It's just you and me." He stood up, and held out his hand, palm up. "Come on. Breakfast is ready."

"Breakfast?"

"Upstairs."

I blinked at him, confused. His eyes sparked with something mischievous. He was holding a secret back and was waiting for me to follow to find it.

I stood up slowly, unsure about surprises. He captured my wrist, taking the coffee mug and escorted me out the bedroom door.

I followed him out into the apartment and he headed toward the front door.

"How is breakfast upstairs?" I asked. They didn't have an upstairs.

"You'll see." He passed back my coffee mug and then opened the front door. He snagged a cell phone off the desk and then nudged me out into the hallway.

I padded barefoot out with him to the elevator, careful not to trip on the long legs of the pajama pants I was wearing. I felt out of place next to him since he was already dressed, in jeans and a black button-up short sleeved shirt, opened to reveal the black tank shirt underneath. The T-shirt and pajama pants I wore were way too big on me and I felt like a shapeless mass.

We boarded the elevator. He smacked the button and we started heading up. I kept the mug close to my face, sipping coffee and keeping warm.

When the elevator doors opened, a breeze swept in, chilling me. I flinched, pulling away, from the bright sunlight barreling in, cutting through thick clouds that still lingered from last night's rain. My heart skipped a moment when I realized the elevator reached the roof. Were we supposed to be up here?

Marc tugged my wrist and drew me outside. I blinked several times, adjusting to the change in light and to the continued breeze. Once I got used to it, the wind felt glorious on my skin, and pushed the material of the clothes into my body in a silky motion. The roof was concrete, and while it chilled my toes, it wasn't too bad.

Marc drew me further out until I spotted the ironwork table and chairs set up near the edge of the roof. The view overlooked the West Ashley River that emptied into Charleston Bay. From our vantage point, we could even see the start of the City Marina. Down below, cars were driving by on their way into the city, or out toward John's Island. The Ashely River Bridge was gleaming under the sunlight. Everywhere my eyes turned, there was something new to look at. I'd seen it before, but not from up here.

"I used to come up here a lot when we first moved in," he said. He tugged me toward the chairs. He held one out for me so I could sit in it. "Personally, I think it's the best view in town. Not even the rich cats over in the South of Broad have this."

I imagined they didn't. I sat, and realized that when you did, it cut off the street closest to the building and the parking lot right below from view, but left the river, the bridge, the bay, and beyond it, to the homes facing the river on John's Island. Picturesque perfect.

Marc gripped the edge of the iron table and angled it closer slowly as to not spill anything on it. On top was another coffee mug, along with an old fashioned metal coffee pot, with sugar and cream canisters beside it. There were two covered black bowls on top of server plates. He took the cover off of the one in front of me to reveal a generous helping of hash browns, eggs, sausage, green peppers and gravy with a biscuit on the side.

"You cook?" I asked.

"Someone has to," he said.

If he had told me that the first moment I met him, I probably would have fallen head over heels for him then. I didn't have room to think about it now, and my stomach started growling so loud, louder than the breeze that picked up around us. I claimed my bowl, and for a good ten minutes or so, I was simply lost in one of the best breakfasts I'd ever had in my entire life. I didn't even realize what I was eating, I was just shoveling, as if worried if I didn't, it would all disappear.

I only slowed when I was almost to the bottom of my bowl and wanted to savor the last bit. I looked up, gazing out at the sky, and the homes nestled among greenery looking out into the water of the bay. There were a couple of small boats making circles in the water.

I stared off, with my tongue glued to the top of my mouth. Marc had parked himself on the chair next to me, and had eaten his, although he took his time.

Now that this silence had dropped between us while eating, I couldn't think of anything to say. I swallowed, hating the awkwardness. "It's good," I said.

He laughed. "I hoped it was if you ate most of it already." He reached an arm out, resting a palm at the nape of my neck. It was such a casual and cozy move, and my stomach's wiggly sparks started coming alive.

"You didn't have to do this," I said.

"Nope. I don't have to do anything." His hand clutched at my neck gently, massaging with intention. "I did it because I wanted to. I asked you to join me because I wanted you with me."

Why did he have to be so incredible? And it didn't even feel fake. He was making an effort. I still wasn't ready to explore what this was between us. I was afraid to ask, because I was afraid he'd say he was trying to comfort a friend, and the kiss last night was just a weak moment. I was afraid he'd say he liked me a lot and wanted a relationship. I was afraid he'd tell me he was teasing me and he'd drop me off at the street now and wave goodbye. Every possibility was scary.

So I ignored it. "How's the whole Coaltar thing?" I asked. "And Wil?"

Marc sucked in a breath, and raked his fingers through the longer locks of his brown hair at the crown of his head, pulling it back away from his eyes. "From what I understand, when Axel started watching last night, he hadn't seen Wil, but when he asked around, neighbors were pretty sure they'd seen him enter earlier. The only one to leave was Jack, and he returned early in the morning. There wasn't a ruckus or a complaint, so Wil is probably okay. Kevin traded places with Axel and has been watching the hotel since. He said he hasn't seen Jack or Wil leave the room at all this morning."

He wasn't going to school? I tried counting off the days. "Is it the weekend? Already?"

He smiled. "Time flies."

At least I didn't have to worry about if he'd get kidnapped on the way to school. I waved it off. I would have felt better if one of them had actually seen him but if the neighbors said he was inside ... although I didn't know if the neighbors actually paid attention to us. I couldn't even tell you who our neighbors were. I barely knew the manager. "Did someone see him get to school?"

"Corey checked the computer records. They said he was there for his classes on Friday. He signed in."

I nodded. "Where's Coaltar now?"

"I don't know," he said. "I just got updated on Wil and what was going on there. I haven't heard about Coaltar."

"They haven't told you?"

"They only tell me what I need to know, and they'll call if they need me, or you. Right now, if it's quiet, there's a reason."

"What if he's on his yacht? What if he's leaving?"

"They'll do what they're supposed to."

I frowned. The sight of the water left me unsettled. There was something I was missing, something not right.

If I were like Coaltar, and I had to get drugs out of the city, and I knew someone was watching my house and waiting for me to leave, what would I do?

First, there was the delivery. I'd have to divert that so maybe if anyone was watching, they wouldn't see the drugs being brought onto the yacht.

And if I knew people were watching City Marina, I'd probably want to steer clear of it completely.

"What if he stops the delivery to City Marina?" I asked.

Marc sighed, shrugging. "He might. He may have the guy hold on to the shipment. He may cancel the deal altogether."

"It didn't seem like he wanted to."

"There's really little we can do," he said. "The police can't stop the purchase. The product isn't illegal. At least not yet. Even then, they'd have to get search warrants and by then, this distributer could get rid of everything on his own if Coaltar asked him. That batch was just the last one, but not the only one. He could have told them to dump it into the river, he just didn't want it distributed."

"Can't we get to the batches he has?"

"They're probably all on his boat."

I tapped my fingers against the wrought iron arm. "So he could get away with this?"

"He could," he said, though his eyes diverted from me, glaring at the rooftop.

"What is it?" I asked. "What aren't you telling me?"

He traced a fingertip on the table, grinding tiny dust

340

particles into the top. "The truth is, there's nothing we can do."

"What do you mean?" I sat up sharply. "You're ... the Academy. You do things."

He blew out a heavy breath. "That's just it. We're not the police. We're not the FBI. We monitor the city. We fix what problems we can ourselves. When someone breaks the law in a way we can't manage, we inform the proper people and let them handle it. Even if we see him taking drugs to the boat, even if we know what they are and he's taking them out of the city, there's really nothing we can do but monitor. If we tried to stop him directly, it's exposing ourselves in ways we don't want and risking the lives of everyone involved. The best we can do is warn the town he might be going to. That might be up to Corey to figure it out. We'd have to find them. We may not have any Academy folks there." He dusted off his fingers and wiped them along his jeans. "He's not really doing anything against the law, at least not yet. And the only crime he could be committing would be in a completely different country. Different laws. Out of our hands. And telling the police this stuff might poison people, well, there's a hundred different batches of these synthetics they're trying to deal with. They're not going to take the time to stop someone taking a non-illegal substance out of the country."

I stood up, clutching the table and leaning on it as I focused on him. "How can we just sit here and let him poison an entire village? There's probably innocent people there. They shouldn't have to suffer. Coaltar shouldn't get away with this."

"We might be able to detain him under suspicious motives, but intent is hard to prove. We'd have to expose ourselves to do it. And you're our only witness."

"So?"

"So if you think he's chasing you now, he'll really hunt you down if he thinks you could be someone who could put him in jail. Last I checked, thugs don't really like it when you rat them out."

I made fists and pressed them to my eyes. "We can't just

sit here."

"Sometimes we have to," he said quietly. It was his stillness that captured my attention. The command was gone from his voice, stripped until all that was left was Marc, who once was a thug himself, and now was something completely different. "I hate it, too, sometimes. We protect our families. That's how the Academy works. We protect ourselves and where we can, we help those around us. We start with home and work outward. If we tried to solve every problem out there, we'd wear ourselves out. We can't do it all. There's a point where we have to draw the line and take ourselves out, for our own safety."

"So we just sit here and do nothing?"

"The threat is trying to leave," he said. "If he's more interested in getting out of town with these drugs, and lost interest in you, then I think we've won." He stood, the chair sliding across the grit of the roof behind him. "If we can warn the town in time, they can avoid drinking from the well. They could probably stop him before he tried, protect it somehow. We just have to trust that we can do the best we can and hope he'll make a mistake somewhere else and someone will stop him." He shook his head. "As far as the Academy is concerned, we're just making sure the drugs leave our town. Our goal now is to stop this cycle. The drug war is DEA territory, but maybe we can find a way to stop these synthetic productions. It may take some time. Getting the dangerous one out of circulation is most important. We've got our hands tied now."

My eyes narrowed on him and then suddenly I was distracted by the water of the bay. Sunlight sparked up the surface. With the clouds starting to part, it was really a beautiful sight. It reminded me of the day I spent with Coaltar on the water, and how he would let the boat drift with the wind, gliding around in circles. I remembered driving the boat, and how I'd felt free.

And then I was angry. I'd trusted him and he flat out lied to my face to tell me he was a good guy. I let him kiss me, when all along he was planning to poison an entire village. I couldn't stop my heart from tightening like a ball in my chest. This wasn't right.

"You might have your hands tied," I said. I turned zeroing in on the door to the elevator. "But I don't."

"Wait," Marc snatched my arm with a firm grip. "You're staying here."

"No, I'm not," I said. I punched at his arm but he didn't release me.

"You're not going out there with him looking for you."

"What is he going to do?" I asked, squinting against the rising wind and stared him down. "Is he going to kill me? Set me on fire? Break me?"

"Maybe," he said. "He's already in with criminals and he's very good at hiding what he's doing. I really don't want to find out how far he's willing to go."

"Well, it isn't your choice, is it?"

He pulled me around, nearly shaking me. "What the hell do you think you're doing, Kayli?"

"I'm going to go see Coaltar," I said, as plainly as I could.

"You're crazy."

"I'm going to go talk to him," I said. "So maybe there's nothing we can do. Maybe there's nothing anyone can do to get him to back off. Or maybe there is. Maybe I'll just talk to him. Maybe he'll change his mind. And I don't think he'll kill me. He's ... I mean he's interested in keeping himself out of jail, right? Or else I don't think he'd touch this."

Marc's mouth set. He stared at me, as if trying to figure this out.

"Let me go talk to him," I said. "Have Kevin stay with Wil. I'll go talk to Coaltar and see if I can't at least talk him into doing something else. Maybe he didn't think it through."

"And what if you can't?" he asked. "What if he's just waiting for you to come back so he can do whatever he wants? He could get rid of you if he wanted."

"Then you'll have a good reason to bust in with the cops and take him down." I don't know what drew me to want to take such a risk. I didn't know the people in whatever village he was after. All I knew was, someone could die. One kid could drink from that well if no one stopped him, and if I didn't even try, it would be my fault. I couldn't live knowing I might have been able to do something.

Marc shook his head. "You can't do this."

"You can't stop me. Last I checked, it wasn't illegal to go talk to someone."

"We can't."

I turned on him, planting a palm on his chest and shoving. "You can't," I barked at him. I pushed again and he released me, looking angry and gritting his teeth but simply stared at me. That set me off worse than ever. "You can't do a thing because you're tied to some mysterious weirdo group that won't let you think for yourself."

"You don't understand," he said.

I shoved again. Each shove did absolutely nothing as he stood firm and didn't shift but I felt better doing it. "I don't care. All I know is that every moment I stay here, he's one step closer to doing this horrible thing and if I've got the opportunity to stop him, I will." I turned, heading for the door. My heart was pounding. My brain wouldn't stop working out my plan. I'd tell Coaltar I was scared he'd kill kids. That ought to work, right? If he was reasonable? Maybe there was another way. I could convince him...

My train of thought stopped as I stared out into the water. One of the biggest yachts I'd ever seen was making the trek out from the marina on the Ashley River out into the bay. There were three decks, and the second deck was painted blue. The whole thing screamed opulence.

My brain flew into orbit. That was him. I knew it. I don't know how I knew, but I could tell. Coaltar was leaving. I'd run out of time.

Or had I? A plan formulated, a crazy one.

"We have to go." I turned, running for the elevator.

"Kayli!"

I didn't stop, I was running full speed. When I got to the elevator, I had to wait for it to get to the top and for the doors to open.

"Wait," Marc said.

"That's him. That's his boat."

"Then Raven is probably on to him. We need to step back."

"You step back. I'm going to stop him."

Marc reached for me. "Don't."

I smacked his hand away. "I'm going," I said. "You can stay behind if you want. I don't care. I'm not going to wait."

He groaned, shifted on his feet, looking out into the water.

"Marc," I barked at him. I pointed out at the river. "I know that's him. He's getting away. We have to hurry." The doors opened, and I lunged inside.

Marc hesitated only a moment, gazing in after me. He waited until the doors almost closed on him before he wedged himself through and we descended.

"You're not going to stop me," I said. "If you try, I'll scream bloody murder until..."

He grunted. He turned, facing the mirrored doors and stared them down. "I may not be able to stop him. I'm not allowed," he said. "But there's nothing to stop me from watching over a crazy girl while she does one of the stupidest stunts ever."

It took all the strength inside me not to beam with happiness. I'd convinced him. I blinked hard not to let the threat of happy tears ruin this moment.

The wriggly sparks invaded every part of my body.

He shifted on his feet as he stared at the elevator doors, rubbing at the back of his head. "What are we doing, anyway?"

I was piecing it together as we moved. "Ever been sailing?" I asked.

♠

PIRATES

We took the black truck to City Marina. I sat on the edge of the seat, clutching the middle console and the suicide handle, as if I could will the car to go faster. I bit my tongue to stop myself from barking at the windshield when someone in front of us dared to go only *ten* miles over the speed limit and slowed us down. Coaltar was already well ahead of us, and I was scared to death of losing him, losing our chance.

Marc drove with the phone attached to his ear. He called Raven first to warn him we were coming, and then Kevin to make sure he stayed with Wil.

The moment he stopped the car, I jumped out and slammed the door. I ran ahead of Marc past the boating house.

Raven and Axel stood shoulder to shoulder on the dock. They waited with their arms crossed. Axel's face was grim.

Raven's was completely unreadable.

"Where's Silas?" Marc asked.

"Had to get home," Axel said. "Family emergency."

I started forward. I wasn't going to wait. I knew what I wanted.

Axel held out a hand to stop me as I approached. "This isn't a good idea," he said.

"Tell me about it," Marc said. "You try to stop her."

"Kayli," Axel said, turning to me. He used that quiet power of his eyes on me. Every syllable he spoke was severe, threatening to bend me at the knees to do what he ordered. "We need to stop and think. You don't know what you're doing."

"What I know," I said in a cool voice, drawing up every ounce of strength I had left to fight him off, "is that, that boat," I pointed out to the water and the last place I spotted the yacht, "has lots of drugs on it that could kill people. He is intentionally going to dump them in into a well somewhere, where who knows how many people, maybe kids, could die. Do you really want to stand in front of me right now?"

Axel flinched. He grunted, looking troubled. Slowly, he lowered his hand, turning his head and staring out at the water, as if trying to figure out his next move.

I took the chance and I side-stepped around him. They could all stay. I'd do it all myself. I'd driven Blake's boat. I could figure it out and get myself out there.

Raven angled himself to stand in my way, arms crossed, shoulders pulled back. I imagined the fierce bear on his back was snarling. He glared down at me with that stony expression.

"Don't," I told him. I drew my hand back, ready to strike. Not that I thought I could knock him out, but I'd at least distract him while I kicked him in the groin. That would at least give me a running start.

He shook his head as if reading my mind and silently telling me that wouldn't work on him. "Which boat is his?" he asked.

I squared off my shoulders at him.

"Don't waste time, little thief. Which one? I need to know."

I pointed to the sailboat. He followed my finger, picking out the one.

"Not that one," he said.

"Why not?" I asked, slowly realizing he wasn't trying to stop me.

"It's too slow. You'll never make it." He looked around, pointing to a motorized speed boat at the very end of one of the docks. "Let's take that one."

"We can't steal a boat," Axel said.

"Who's we?" I asked. I headed toward the motorboat. "I'll do it."

347

Axel grunted.

"We'll bring it back," Raven said, starting off beside me, matching my pace. Axel and Marc followed behind us. "We take it now and we'll bring it back when we're done. Fill it with gas. Leave them nice flowers. Pay off their docking fees. They'll thank us after. It'll be the best boat theft they've ever experienced."

I glowered at Raven, but he ignored my gaze. I wanted to tell him I'd do it all myself, but I stopped before I let pride ruin this. Raven was willing to break a few rules to make sure the right thing was done. Maybe he understood.

He rushed with me toward the boat, hopping into the back, taking over steering. He glanced over the controls, and then tapped at the ignition switch. I had a moment of panic, realizing the engine wouldn't start without a key.

I was about to suggest we should go back to the sailboat when Raven reached into his pocket and pulled out a bump key and a pocket knife. He jammed it into the ignition, and then slammed it with the broad side of the pocket knife, at the same time, turning, starting up the engine. I was thoroughly impressed.

Axel and Marc climbed aboard. My heart pounded in my chest, buzzing to life every fiber of nerves inside of me. It was the craziest thing we were doing, but I'd never felt more alive, never so sure.

"What's your brilliant plan?" Axel asked me as Marc and Raven figured out how to untie the boat from the dock. Axel eased himself until he was standing next to me, looking out at the water. "Are you going to shout at him from this little dingy? That's a two-ton yacht we're chasing."

I gazed out, hoping, crossing my fingers the motorboat had some gas and we weren't going to be sitting ducks. "I'm going to get on that two-ton thing and I'm going to talk him out of this."

"And what if he doesn't listen?"

I stared at him, and then glanced at Raven, asking him if he'd help me. He caught my gaze. He seemed to understand. He nodded and I returned to Axel with more confidence. "I'll distract him while Raven gets the drugs and dumps it all overboard."

"And then he calls the Coast Guard," Axel said. "We'll all be arrested."

"Stay behind if you're going to complain," Raven said.

I caught Raven's glance this time, and we shared a secret grin.

Marc rolled his eyes. "We're all crazy." He dropped the tie-off rope into the boat and nudged Raven toward the helm. "Let's get this over with."

Raven rolled the boat right out of the dock. No one stopped us. We had to pass the Coast Guard station at the end of the peninsula before we headed out to the open bay, but even then, no one seemed to care. My heart was in my throat, worried we'd see helicopters chasing us, but no one stopped us.

I wanted to do something, but there was nothing to do but wait until we caught up to Coaltar's yacht. Raven drove and I stared off at the distance, willing for us to catch up. I shifted from foot to foot, bracing myself for what I was going to say to Coaltar when I saw him again.

Before, I wanted to stop Coaltar, and maybe I didn't have a prayer of doing it, but I didn't want to back down, no matter how impossible it seemed. Now, with the boys beside me, I felt like we stood a slim chance. I hoped it was enough.

Axel sat down next to me and then tugged my arm to get me to sit with him. He gazed out into the water. The motor was pretty loud. For a long time, we sat in silence next to each other. Our last little talk hadn't gone so well. I don't know what he was thinking, but I still felt the guilt over running off when he'd asked me to stay.

His mouth twitched after a while. "What if we don't catch him?" he asked.

"We should."

"We still might not. He wasn't headed out very quickly, but he pretty much knew there was nothing we could do about him. He could have sped up by now. I don't really know if this little boat could outrun him if he put his motor to full haul ass."

"We'll do our best."

"What if it doesn't work?" he asked. He turned, his face a blank slate. "What happens then? Are we going to chase him forever?"

I didn't have an answer for him. This could be a mad chase for nothing. "I don't know."

"I need you to think very carefully how far you're willing to take this, Kayli. You're not just putting yourself at risk any more. Marc and Raven are bull headed enough to follow you wherever you want to lead them on this crazy campaign of yours. But how far will you chase the white whale?"

"How far would you?" I asked quietly. I met his eyes, and while I wasn't certain how he felt, I hoped I showed I was somewhat confident in my answer. "How far would you go to save a life?"

"What would be the price?" he asked.

I shrugged. "Right now, it's a few hours of our time, a borrowed boat, and the risk of getting caught and hoping the owners won't feel too bad if we try to explain why we borrowed it."

Axel exhaled. "How in the world do you do it?"

"Do what?"

The corner of his mouth lifted, softening his face into something that looked almost like pride. "Less than a week and you've got those boys breaking protocol to satisfy your own need to do whatever it takes to do the right thing."

"I thought you didn't like this plan."

"I like the plan. I just don't want you to go crazy." He reached behind his body, at his hip holster that I hadn't noticed before, and pulled out a .38. He knocked back the hammer and turned it over.

"What are you doing?" I asked, a little wary of the gun.

"Making sure this Coaltar doesn't go crazy," he said. He stuffed the gun back into the holster and turned to me. "Now listen to me. I hope Coaltar might be reasonable. Maybe he'll change his mind if you talk to him. Maybe he'll listen. He seems like a sensible person trying to right a wrong. He helped the Fitzgerald family when they could have suffered. He hid them in a new house, and tried to stop a gang war. I have to admire him for that."

I choked, but bit back a retort. I didn't want to think of Coaltar as doing the right thing.

Axel picked up my hand that was against my thigh. He squeezed it. "But more important, I want you to know we're here for you. If there's any hint that this could be deadly, if he has a gun and starts shooting at us for trying to invade his boat, he'll have every right to do so. I don't want you hurt. I don't want Raven and Marc hurt. I'll go on this little chase, but I won't let anyone risk their lives for this, including you." He leaned in, until our heads almost knocked together. "Am I clear? I don't want you fighting me if I'm trying to save your ass."

I twisted my lips. "I guess," I said. I didn't want to die, either. I couldn't help anyone if I was dead.

He nodded.

"That might be it," Marc called to us. I looked back at him, and he pointed out across the water.

The yacht was still in the water a good distance from us but we were closing in. A ferry boat was crossing in front of it. It had two levels and from where I was sitting, I could tell there were people standing on both levels. Lights flashed from cameras.

"Did he almost hit that other ship?" I asked.

"It's the Fort Sumter ferry," Axel said. "He had some bad timing. He's having to wait until they clear."

"That'll give us an advantage," Marc said. "And a distraction."

Raven turned the boat toward the yacht, and sped up the engine. "Where do we want to park this thing? Or do you want me to just ram into it?"

"Check the back end of the boat," Marc said, pointing to the rear of the yacht. "There's a lower deck and a ladder off to the left. Get near that."

"They may see us coming," Axel said.

"They may not," Marc said. "They've got to watch out for that ferry. But they may hear us. We'll have to be careful."

Raven pressed onward. Maybe luck was on our side, but that ferry seemed to slow down. I didn't realize why. Maybe they were gawking at the big yacht. I probably would. At any rate, anyone aboard the yacht was probably paying attention to what was going on in the front.

Our boat neared the yacht. Raven slowed as we got close. Marc took to the front of the boat, waiting until we were close and then grabbing a hold of the low hanging ladder that was on the left side. He gripped it and weighted himself against the boat to keep the motor boat from drifting too far away.

Raven killed the engine. "Someone has to stay here," he said. "Make sure the yacht doesn't just fly off and we have no way to get out."

"I'll stay," Axel said. He grabbed the rope and tied the boat off to the end of the ladder. "You three go."

"Marc should stay," I said. "He's got a limp."

"I'll show you a limp," he said. He grabbed the rail of the silver ladder and started to climb up.

I sighed. My heart was pounding. This was insane. How in the world did I talk myself into this? And what was I going to say to Blake when I found him? *Hi. So, maybe I ran out on you, but could you dump your drugs into the water in the ocean instead of in this well? Pretty please?*

I followed Marc up the silver ladder.

Raven followed me. On occasion, he nudged my calf, as if encouraging me. Or worried I'd fall into the water if he didn't keep a hand on me.

Marc moved up until he could haul himself over a balcony that protruded out over the water on the first deck. He reached back, finding my arms and heaved me up and over until I was standing beside him. The balcony had a few lounge chairs and side tables. I nudged into one to get out of the way as Raven climbed aboard.

Marc waited until Raven was next to us. Then he pointed

at me. "Okay, you and I are going to locate Coaltar." He pointed to Raven. "Go find the drugs."

"They could be in food cartons," I said. "And in other things that look like supplies. He wanted to hide them so no one would have a problem with people bringing them aboard."

"Oh, so you're saying they could be anywhere," he said. "Sure, make it easy for me."

Marc waved a hand to get my attention. "If we get separated, head back here and grab Axel." He dipped into his pocket and he pulled out what looked like an ear piece. He caught my hand and planted it in my palm. "Here," he said. "Put this in."

"What is it?"

"Contact," he said. "You always have to stay in touch."

I sighed and shifted the ear bud in my fingers, trying to figure out how it was supposed to go. Raven pulled it from my hands and straightened it. He gripped my shoulder, aimed the thing at the side of my head and wriggled it into place.

"Brandon," Marc said. "Say something so she can hear you."

"You're in deep shit, Kayli," Brandon said.

"Can he hear me?" I asked Marc.

"I can hear you," Brandon said in my ear, a little fuzzy, like he was standing in another room with the door closed, but I could make out what he was saying. "Just wait until I get a hold of you."

"Raven," I pretended to plea. "Brandon said he was going to hurt me."

"I'll kill him," he said. He jammed his own ear plug into his noggin. "Corey? Yeah. Hit your brother once for me. No, in the dick. No, he won't hit you back. I promise."

"Cut it out, you guys," Marc said.

"How come I can't hear Corey?" I asked.

"I get Corey," Raven said. "You get Brandon."

"I want to switch."

"I said stop," Marc barked at us. "Okay, everyone go quiet." He pointed a finger to Raven and then to the sliding glass doors in front of us that lead to the rest of the boat. When we were out of the glare of the sun, I could see through to an empty bedroom. Raven went to the doors, tried the handle and they slid open instantly.

"Not much for security," Raven said.

"He's probably not expecting company after he's taken off from the dock," Marc said.

The bedroom was as wide as the back of the yacht. There was a king sized bed on top of the immaculate cream carpet. The wide windows extended to three sides of the room, giving an almost overwhelming sense of being outside with the water surrounding. The headboard was done out in delicate gold with an overlaid painting of cherry blossom trees done in beige. Perfect. Decadent.

"Oh my god," I said, staring at the large television off to the corner, the pillows that appeared to be without a single wrinkle or blemish, or the inlay of the woodwork against the ceiling. "I hate this boat." It felt so opulent, too much.

"Don't be jealous, little thief," Raven said.

"Why?"

"His bed is empty," he said.

"Enough," Marc waved him off. "Go find what you're looking for.

"You hearing me okay, Kayli?" Brandon asked, now dropping the threatening tone and getting to business.

"Yeah," I said.

"This schematic of the ship says the helm is two decks above you."

"How did you get a schematic?"

"Did you think we were sitting on our asses here? Just trust me. You probably want to start at the helm."

"Does he drive his own boat?" I asked. "I was thinking he'd probably be ... I don't know. Where do rich people sit on their boats?"

"There's probably more than just Coaltar on this ship," Marc said. "Someone's driving."

"Get out of the bedroom," Brandon said. "Head left."

Marc started out. I felt a little better with them taking the lead. It wasn't my first instinct to try the helm, but what else was I going to do? Lurk around until I found him?

Brandon gave us directions as we went. Beyond the bedroom, there were hallways and then the floor plan opened up. Raven disappeared down a small staircase, where I assumed there was a deck below this one, possibly with storage. The floor we were on hosted a living space, with another wide screen TV mounted on the wall. There were plush couches. The area felt a little stiff, unused. Like the bedroom, no one had been there in a while.

"Up the stairs," Brandon said in my ear. "On the next floor, there's a small hallway."

I found the staircase and went for it, but Marc cut me off.

"I'll go first," he said. He turned from me. It's when I noticed the gun holster hanging from his belt. I sighed. I guessed I missed the part where Axel handed his gun over. That made me nervous for Axel being left alone behind us. I hoped he would okay.

The next floor up had a dining room. The table was empty, and there was seating for twelve. I didn't know enough people to fit twelve chairs.

The quiet of the area had me spooked. I felt we were on a ghost ship of some kind. Like his house, I expected employees somewhere but never spotted them. Was it even possible to run this boat with a single person driving?

"There should be a door to the observation deck," Brandon said. "But if you pass—"

Silence.

"Brandon?" I whispered.

Marc paused in the hallway we stood in. He tapped at his ear. "Brandon," he said a little louder.

Nothing.

"Did we lose him?" I asked.

"We might be mixing signals with some equipment on this boat," he said. "Keep it in just in case he can reach us again."

Marc directed me through until we found a hallway with a closed door marked off as the observation deck. We passed it and he found one for the bridge. We planted our backs on either side of the door. My nerves radiated to life. We may have slipped in this far, but there had to be someone on the bridge.

Marc glanced at me. "Last chance," he said. "Do you want to head back?"

I swallowed hard but shook my head.

Marc eased the door handle and pushed the door open. I turned toward it, my fist clenched and I hid it behind my back, for no other reason than I didn't want him to know I was nervous.

The bridge had wide windows looking out over the observation deck and out to the rest of the boat and the water beyond it. There were mechanical and electrical panels all over the place, some with flashing lights and buttons. Some had display touch screens.

Blake Coaltar stood at the helm, gazing out at the water in front of him. The ferry had moved on, but he didn't seem to be interested in going faster. He was staring out at Fort Sumter. The ferry had docked. People were getting off the ferry and standing on the dock. Some were continuing toward the fort for the tour, but a few still lingered, looking back at the yacht. Some were pointing at the different features. A few took pictures.

I rolled my eyes. He was showing off.

Blake tucked his head down, studying the controls. He selected one, and then pushed the throttle. There was a gentle roll forward. He'd started the engines.

"Blake?" I said quietly. I thought I'd try coy first. That seemed like a good plan.

His body rotated slowly. The light captured his figure. He wore a crisp gray shirt, the sleeves rolled up to his elbows. His dark blue jeans looked brand new. He was barefoot. It was an odd look not to be wearing any shoes but I supposed he felt at home on his own boat. The clothes fit perfectly against his fine figure. I found it difficult to not recall the night before and the tanned body underneath. His jawline had that fine overnight growth, but it only matured his face a little into an exquisite, gruff look.

I pulled my thoughts from that place, closing off the still lingering feeling of his kiss, his touch. I buried it as far as I could.

"Kate?" he said, his hazel eyes widening. "How in the world..."

"You're boat's really big," I said, trying to be funny. "I don't understand how it's just you in this big space. Did you see that table? There's seating for twelve."

The corner of his mouth lifted. "There's only one bedroom. And that's made for two."

My heart thundered. I hoped Brandon and Marc weren't hearing this. There were some things I didn't want mentioned. "I was hoping I could talk you out of going to ... this village. Wherever it is."

"Kate," he said, stepping forward. His hands went up, showing me his palms as if to show he was harmless, unarmed. "I know what you heard last night. I know it's probably confusing, but you have to trust me."

"I did trust you," I said, and unfortunately couldn't stop the coldness from seeping in. It had hurt. I couldn't hide it. "You told me you were dumping this into the ocean."

"I wasn't sure you could understand," he said.

"You lied to me. You'll hurt a lot of people."

"They'll be sick for a while but they'll get over it."

"Someone could die. That's why you were getting rid of this stuff. What if someone dies?"

"I won't let anyone die." He stepped forward, but stopped, and then returned to the helm. "Just hang on. I have to drive this thing."

"There's no autopilot?"

He laughed darkly. "Sweetheart, did you come along to tell me how to drive my yacht? I just have to keep her heading out to sea while the captain is busy down below. Then you and I can talk as much as you want."

I hoped Brandon and Marc heard this. I wouldn't want Raven or Marc to get caught snooping around with other people on board. "Will you let me talk you out of this?" I asked. "Isn't there anything I can say?"

"Come here," he said. He patted the spot next to him at the helm. "Just stand here a moment."

I shuffled up beside him, gazing at all the equipment. He may as well have been flying an airplane, I didn't recognize anything in front of me beyond the steering wheel thing.

"Now listen," he said. He glanced at me sideways while he drove. "I love that you came back and that you're aboard. I don't know how you got here, but you're the type of stowaway I may just not throw overboard."

There was a *thunk*, and a slew of cursing. My hand caught at my chest, over my heart, and I put my back to the panel of dials, and faced the door.

Through the open doorway came Marc with his arm twisted behind his back. He grunted and cursed, tripping forward as a very large man shoved him through. The man clenched down on Marc's arm, pulling it back tight until Marc was forced to kneel. The man kicked hard at Marc's leg, his favored one, and Marc was down on the floor, clutching at his thigh.

"But your friends," Coaltar said, "are not welcome here."

WHATEVER SIDE YOU'RE ON, YOU'RE RIGHT

I made a dash toward Marc, but Coaltar cut me off by catching me around my waist. He pulled me back into him.

"Hang on there, sugar," he said. He planted me down beside the helm again. "And stay right here. Let me drive so we don't crash and all die."

"Let me go!" I cried out. I raked my nails against his arm and tried pounding at his shoulder.

The ogre towering over Marc was nearly double his size. Marc lashed out at the towering man with a wild kick, but it was uneven since he was on the floor. The big man raised a boot and crunched down on Marc in the chest. While Marc clutched at his own ribs and tried to breathe, the monster pulled Marc's gun from his holster and yanked back on the hammer, shoving it at Marc's forehead. Marc held his hands up, surrendering.

I wrestled with Coaltar but he held strong. "Let him go," I screamed at him. What had I done?

"Darling," he barked back at me. "If you two would stop fighting, I wouldn't have to do this. You snuck on to my boat with a gun. What exactly are you planning to do? Shoot me?"

"Maybe," I said, pushing at his arm.

"I thought you were better than that," he said. He shoved me up against the helm. He planted a leg up between mine, grinding me back against the wheel. He placed a hand on either side of me, holding me up against it. "If you can't stand still next to me, you have to stay here a minute."

The way he had me pinned, I couldn't see where he was driving and I couldn't see Marc any more. He was too strong to fight and with that big guy, I didn't stand a chance. "Let us go," I said. "Let him go."

"So you can shoot me?" he asked. He watched what buttons he was pushing. "So you can go hide again and then the next time I throw a party or decide to go somewhere, you can shove a gun in my face and tell me I'm the bad guy?" He shook his head. "You're all crazy."

"You shouldn't do this," I said. "You can't kill people."

"I'm not killing anyone," Blake barked at me. "You're not even listening."

"You lied to me!"

"You lied to me, too! You came to my house with a fake boyfriend, telling me you were some researcher. Next thing I know you're telling me you're a stooge for the FBI. And then the next time, you're pickpocketing someone like you're a pro."

"You told me you were going to dump the drugs into the water."

"I am," he said. "I just didn't tell you which bit of water. One little thing and you're going to hold it over my head."

I grunted and then rocked myself, trying to break free.

"Stop it, sweetie," he said, pressing his body against mine. "I'm not letting go until you stop fighting me."

I glared at him, at the way his gold flecks glinted. His grin was set firm. He thought he'd won!

"Well," I said. "Now you're kidnapping me."

"You're the pirate boarding my boat," he said. "If I call for the Coast Guard, they'll haul you two to jail."

I huffed and then started to relax. Talking him out of this was the only thing I had left. "Don't," I said, and suddenly my voice was ten times softer, and with an edge like I was going to crack. I'd worked this hard, come this far. Was it all for nothing?

Blake had his gaze out on the water and then on the dash as he drove the yacht. When his eyes caught my face, he focused on me and his once proud grin softened into something much more reasonable. "Listen, darling," he cooed. "Sweetheart, please. Just this once."

"You're going to kill people," I said, exasperated. "If

you dump it in that well—"

"No one is going to die," he said calmly. "That well is hundreds of feet deep and I've got maybe only a few hundred pounds of this stuff. The water will dilute it a lot. By the time anyone drinks it, it'll be so much weaker. They may all get a bit sick, but they'll be fine."

Was that true? Or was it another lie so I'd let him go on with his plan? "Why do you have to do it like this?"

"Because if I don't," he said, "the cartel *will* come here. They *will* hunt down the Fitzgerald family. Then they'll go after that same village and they *will* kill them all. They're trained assassins protecting their livelihood, their territory."

I breathed in deeply, trying to catch his eyes. He met my gaze. I wasn't sure. I had a hard time reading people for the truth. I was the liar. I was the thief. What did I know about honesty? "Won't this village come after you, if you do this? Won't they retaliate?" I was trying to find a flaw in his plan. Somehow this still felt wrong.

"This is a message, sweetheart," he said. "I'm to leave the mark of the cartel behind. The people in this village were looking to start a war. I'm trying to stop it."

"Couldn't you have told me?"

He pursed his lips. "I looked you square in the eyes and told you this wasn't what it looked like. You had a hard time believing me that I was buying drugs just to dump it. I told you as much as I could and you still resisted and thought I was the bad guy." He leaned in, until he was nose to nose with me, and his eyes fell on my mouth. He talked softly. "But I swear, Kate, I would have told you. If you had stayed, if you had come with me, I would have told you everything."

My heart raged against my ribs. I cowered at his intense eyes begging for me to understand and I had no idea what to do.

"Let us go," I said quietly. "Let Marc go."

"Kate…"

"If you want me to trust you," I said, "let him go. I'll send him back."

He raised an eyebrow. "Just him?"

I couldn't look around him to see Marc if this was a good idea. I had a feeling he would tell me no so I thought it was best I couldn't see him. "I want to see for myself," I said. "I want to know for sure you aren't killing anyone."

"It'll still be dangerous," Blake said. He pressed himself against me, against the helm, but lifted a hand, brushing those golden locks away from his cheek and out of his eyes. The unadulterated view caused my breath to catch. "But I swear, Kate. I swear on all your cute little toes. All this will stop more people from dying. If you really want to do people some good, you've got to trust me."

I hesitated, gritting my teeth. I swallowed hard. "Let me get Marc off the boat," I said quietly. "Let me take him back. I'll stay and make sure…"

Blake nodded slowly. An inch at a time, he eased his body off of me. "I'm going to stand here," he said, nodding toward the helm. "I'm going to still drive this thing." He turned his attention to the man behind us.

Marc was on his butt, holding his leg tenderly. The man lorded over him, holding the gun in Marc's face.

"Give him the gun back," Blake said. He turned to Marc. "Sorry, man. You've got to understand, though. I thought you guys were here to kill me. But just so you know, if you try to shoot me now, you won't make it off this ship."

Marc's jaw clenched. The man standing over him held the gun out to him. Marc didn't take it and just stared at Coaltar. The man dropped the gun next to Marc and backed out of the door, disappearing.

I crossed the room, dipping down to help Marc as he tried to stand.

"What are you doing?" he seethed through his teeth.

"Getting you out of here."

"You can't stay with him."

I leaned over and picked up the gun, shoving it back into his holster. I grabbed his arm, crossing it over my shoulders and tried to boost him to standing. "I'm going to make sure this stuff doesn't kill anyone," I said. What else could we do?

"Look at me, Kayli," he said, his two-colored eyes

locked with mine. "He's lying to you."

I squinted at him. "How do you know?"

"I can tell."

"You couldn't even see him."

"Trust me," he gasped as he stood on one foot. "For once in your life, please. Trust me."

My heart fought against my ribs, threatening to explode where I stood. I tried to tell myself that maybe Marc was mistaken. Maybe he was hurt because it felt like I was choosing Blake over him. I wasn't, or at least I didn't think I was. I didn't know if I could trust Blake completely until I saw no one was hurt because of this.

But Marc's eyes, those awful, unrelenting eyes, told me something else. Every time I'd lied to him, he called me out on it, so I knew he could tell for me. Maybe it was also the kiss I'd felt last night, and the breakfast from this morning. Maybe it was the way Raven and Axel, everyone, had helped me. If they had thought it was a good thing, if they thought dumping these drugs in the well wasn't going to hurt anyone, they would have told me so before and avoided this mess.

If it would have been good for everyone, they would have told me that, from the start. They wouldn't have needed me.

But how much was the lie and how much was Marc telling me whatever he could so I'd run off the boat with him instead? How much was jealousy talking through those pleading eyes?

I turned on Coaltar, ready to ask him a few more questions to figure it out. Hoping to give Marc a chance to run off if he wanted.

A lean figure cut through the side door. His face was grainy with overgrowth and his hair was cut short. There was something about him that was familiar and I couldn't place it. He headed straight for Coaltar like he was very familiar with him.

Coaltar's eyes went wide when he spotted him. "I told you to stay below." He jabbed a finger in the air at him. "Go..."

"There's someone down there," the man said. "Knocked out the kitchen boy." He turned, looking at me full on. His eyes widened. "Her? What's she doing here?"

I flinched. His voice set my mind reeling, back to a narrow alleyway, with a gun pointed at Blake.

"You?" I pointed a finger at him. "What are you doing here?"

But I didn't really want an answer. Suddenly this whole thing was chaos. He was cleaned up, but I was sure. This was the guy who held us up in the street. But his clothes, the confident way he stood beside Blake, made it clear. The man worked for Coaltar.

Blake held his hands out toward me, palms up in self-defense. "Now, wait a second..."

"You!" I cried at him. I stabbed the air with my finger, pointing at him. My eyes flared. If I could have breathed fire, he'd be incinerated. "That was all a set up!"

"Don't ... you've got the wrong idea," Blake said in a warning tone, as if he could stop my brain from putting together the pieces.

"You tricked me?" I asked, incredulous. "You staged that whole thing?"

"I didn't—"

"How much else was staged?" I asked. "And you made me feel bad for taking his wallet? And you lied to me again!"

Blake grunted. "I just needed to make sure. You didn't tell me anything about you. You clam up whenever I ask you anything personal."

"Tell me about it," Marc said, favoring his leg but stepping back a bit, out of the line of fire.

"So you faked a hold up?" I yelled at Blake. "What was that about? You knew I'd come back looking for you. What did you expect me to do? Cry bloody murder? Call the police? Did you want me to think you were some sort of hero when you kicked him and got the gun?"

Blake took a step forward, edging in. "Now, now, don't go jumping to conclusions."

I threw my hands up in the air. "You lied this whole

time? I can't believe..."

"Kayli," he barked at me. He inched closer. "Just hang on a second. Let me explain."

It was as if the boat had stopped dead still, as well as the earth and the universe around us. I played what he said over in my mind again. "What did you call me?" I wailed at him, unable to contain the fury in my voice.

"Kate," he said, and then took a small inch back as if he realized he'd made a mistake. "Baby doll, listen to me."

"No, you just called me Kayli," I said. I pointed a finger at him. "How long have you known?"

He huffed, and straightened. "Like I'd let you walk into my house without knowing your name."

"You knew all this time?" I smashed a fist at the air toward him. "You lying jerk!"

"You lied to me!" he cried out. "You're not with the FBI. You're not even on their radar. You gave me a false name. You couldn't even tell me your name when you've fallen for me."

"You're crazy."

He smirked in a smug way. "Admit it. You're head over heels. It's all over your face."

"Oh my god!" I didn't want to hear it. And I certainly didn't want to talk any more. I lunged sideways, finding the holster behind Marc's back and I yanked out the gun, swinging the barrel around at Blake.

"Whoa, whoa," Blake said, as did the man next to him. They both stepped back, with their hands up in front protectively.

Marc coughed once. "Easy, Bambi."

"Yeah, take it easy." Blake flinched. "Wait, did you just call her Bambi?"

"Stop calling me that," I said.

"It's her nickname," Marc said, a satisfied grin washing over his pained face. "She loves it."

"Ugh!" I howled out.

I did have the gun pointed at Coaltar, and then suddenly he lunged for me. I scrambled to back up, but he was quick.

He captured me around the waist and then shoved the gun down to aim at the floor. His startling move shocked me. I squeezed the gun in my hand to hang on to it so he wouldn't take it.

The gun fired.

I stood stock still, as if terrified I'd shot myself somehow and hadn't felt it yet.

Blake released me, slumping to the ground and then clutched at his bleeding thigh. "Shit! Kayli! You shot me in the leg."

My heart was wild in my ears. Maybe I could have gotten away with everything else, but I just shot a billionaire in the leg. I was headed to prison now.

"Kayli," Marc said, reaching for me. "Sweetie, the boat."

I nodded. For once, he had the right idea. I looked around, but the fake mugger had vanished, possibly off to warn the Coast Guard that a lunatic was onboard shooting everyone.

I ran for the helm, and then gazed out the window. We were out in open water now. I scanned the horizon, unsure what to do.

"Darling," Blake said. He gasped, holding his knee. He rolled onto his side and tried to sit up. "Sweetie. Don't do anything stupid."

I ignored him. I looked out at the water and then I spotted it, the red buoy. A sand bank or a rock just under the surface. I spotted more behind it, and realized we were at the river and little inlet between Folly Beach and Kiawah Island. There were rocks all over. If I could just angle the boat.

I turned the helm, making the boat head west back toward land. I may not have known any controls, but I could turn a steering wheel.

When the boat was aiming for the tiny island sitting in the middle of the river outlet, I straightened so the boat would head right for it.

"Kayli!" Coaltar called after me. "Damn it. Don't wreck my yacht."

I leapt over Coaltar on the floor and went for Marc.

Marc gave a half laugh. "Wasn't really what I meant, but I'll go with your plan," Marc said.

I huffed and grabbed at his shoulder, easing myself under his arm so I could assist him out.

"Doll face," Coaltar cooed after me. He sucked air through his teeth in a pained breath and clutched at his thigh. "Sweetie. What do you want from me? You can't leave me like this."

"Maybe if you had changed your mind," I said coolly, closing off my heart, unwilling to look back at him. "Maybe if you hadn't planned on killing a bunch of people. Maybe if you had been different and could just dump the drugs into the ocean and didn't even think to hurt anyone else in some petty revenge. You'll still make them sick. Someone could die. This war goes on whether or not you want it to. They'll come back here. This has to stop. You can't hurt people like this. If you hadn't lied to me, maybe we could have found another way."

"Come on, Kayli," he said. "You have to understand. Every dog has a few fleas."

Marc glanced over my shoulder, smirking at him. "You've got a few big ones. May want to get a collar, or a spray, or something for it." He grimaced and I could tell he was biting back some of the pain from his own leg.

"Let's get out of here," I said.

He nodded, and used me like a crutch to hobble.

"Kayli!" Coaltar called once more, and then flattened onto his back.

And he laughed.

It was a laugh that would haunt my dreams. Satisfaction, amused, not a hint of anger that I'd hurt him or for his boat that was about to crash. He relaxed against the floor and looked to be waiting. He was giving me what he thought I wanted.

His was a laugh that, on the surface I cringed and tried to show Marc I thought was crazy.

Secretly, inside, I luxuriated in it. I found my heart pounding in a way that I was proud. Despite all his dirty

tricks, in the end, I'd won.
This time.

♠

PROFESSIONALS

I fled with Marc, helping him as best as I could. "We should hurry," I said. "We should get off this boat before it crashes."

"I agree."

We made it back to the stairs, but he slid onto his butt so he could butt hop down each of the steps, and I helped him to stand once we got to the bottom.

I was about to help him down the second set of stairs when a looming figure charged at us from a side door. I started to cover Marc, but he shoved me to the floor, taking the full brunt of the man.

Marc went down, but in a flash, he was up again. While he still favored his leg, he punched the ogre man in the gut.

The monster took the hit, but with his mass, he wasn't going down. He took a small step back and then ducked low, aiming to head butt Marc against the wall.

"Marc!" I cried out, and clamored up, ready to kick the guy, or claw his eyes out, whichever worked better. Probably both.

Before I could ready a kick, a body dropped down from the stairs. A leg shot out, catching the brute in the back of the knee. The monster went down hard.

Axel stood over him. He readied a fist and it landed straight into the guy's throat. The man reeled back. Axel punched him again in the nose, and then again in the same spot.

Marc stepped back, getting out of the way. The man went down. Axel hovered over him, fists tight. He was ready.

But the monster didn't get back up.

"Axel," I called.

Axel looked up, his eyes a wild mess. He tapped his ear quickly. "Corey is telling me there's another one at the balcony. He's releasing the boat. I'll go get him. Go ahead and get Marc to that balcony. I'll get the boat."

I nodded. I went back for Marc, becoming the crutch again. Axel disappeared. I couldn't believe what I just saw. Axel seemed like a rock, steady and waiting. Suddenly he became the hurricane force. The calm that hid a storm.

Moving Marc was slow progress. He hopped a few steps and then needed to stop to catch his breath. "Just go," he said. "This boat is going to crash."

"Raven!" I called when we were on the living room deck.

Raven materialized from the bedroom section. He took one look at Marc and leapt forward to take the other side under his arm. "Holy shit, you shot him again."

"No," Marc said. "Didn't shoot *me*."

Raven's eyebrows went up and he glanced at me for answers. "Who *did* she shoot?"

"Too much to explain," I said. "We have to go. Now."

Raven started walking beside Marc, and then gave up, heaving Marc up over his shoulder.

"Christ!" Marc shouted. "Put me down."

Raven ignored this and ran for the bedroom. I followed.

Out on the balcony, we looked down. Axel and the boat weren't there.

"Where is he?" I asked.

"The yacht's going at top speed," Raven said. He gazed out across the water and pointed. "He's way back there."

Axel was standing at the helm, soaked like he took a swim to catch the boat. He was trying to hurry and catch us.

"We can't wait," I said.

Raven crossed the balcony, putting Marc down on the floor. "You can swim, can't you?"

"With this leg?" Marc asked. "I can try."

"I was asking her." He turned. "You up for it?"

My heart thundered. "Sure."

"Don't sound so confident." Raven assisted Marc to standing. Marc gazed down over the edge of the balcony.

"It's a jump," Marc said. He pulled himself up with a groan, swinging one leg over. "Help me with my other leg."

Raven stooped over, picking up his foot. Marc growled and yelped the whole time, cursing. Raven released his leg once he had it over the balcony edge.

I got beside Raven, pushing myself up to sit next to him on the edge. I gazed down at the water. "It's kind of high up," I said.

"We need to jump now," Raven said. He hauled himself up and over. "On three."

"Three," Marc called, his hand landing on my shoulder blades and he pushed.

I cried out, probably a slur of curses all jumbled together, including Marc's name into the mix. I had a flash of an idea, like in the cartoons where I had a split second of air and falling and I thought perhaps I would stop just before the water.

I splashed down hard, in the most sprawled out belly flop ever performed. I sunk deep, and felt the push of a current. I was going under.

Hands went around my body, and then clutched at me. I turned, finding Marc. His face was grim, and he was looking up at the surface. His hand flew out, above his head, and he swam, with me in his other arm. He clutched me toward his body.

I did my best to help, kicking my legs, trying not to kick him in the effort.

We surfaced, and I sputtered, feeling the slice of chill as the wind picked up around us, stronger than before, and completely icing my body. The water was cold, but it wasn't so bad with the surprise of it. Now that we were on the surface, and the breeze swept around us, it was killer.

I floated next to Marc, glancing around. "Where's Raven?"

Raven popped up a few feet from us. He jerked his head back and wiped water from his eyes. He growled. "It's like

Russian bath water."

"Russians are fucked up," Marc said.

I pointed to Axel coming around in the boat. Marc pulled me up in the water. Raven got beside me. When Axel pulled alongside us, he killed the motor and leaned out.

"Kayli," Axel said, reaching for my arm.

Before I could protest, Marc and Raven pushed me at Axel. I was hauled up and tossed into the floor of the boat. I sprung up, reaching down for Marc's arm, as Raven assisted by pushing him, and Axel yanked him from under his armpits, leaning back with everything he had and sitting on the bottom of the boat to haul him in.

We were starting to haul up Raven when a thundering rumble nearly startled me into falling back into the water. We finished hauling in Raven and turned together.

The yacht had collided with the bank. It seemed to have turned slightly, as if someone had tried to redirect the boat, but it was too late. With the motor turned on and running, the yacht continued to shove itself onto the bank until the front crunched. It stopped and the engine suddenly died.

I was about to make a comment when an explosion blasted out of one of the lower decks. Debris soared out. Some crashed into the water and other pieces soared up for a while before landing. A large hole was left, smoking and revealing an open fire.

"What was that?" I cried out.

Raven grunted. "You told me to get rid of the damn drugs," he said.

I flared at him. "You blew it up?"

Raven picked himself up off the floor of the boat. "Well, that was just a bonus."

I gaped at him a moment. With all the chaos, with wanting to get Marc off the boat and trying to get away before Coaltar came to his senses and called the police, I had completely forgotten about the drugs. Raven remembered. He kept his promise.

When the shock wore off, I lunged at him. I wrapped my arms around his neck, beaming and hugged tight. "You're the best."

"What can I say?" His arms encircled me and he pressed his body close. "I'm a professional Russian."

Marc dropped himself until he was flat on his back on the boat. He grunted and clutched at his leg. "I think we're done here. Can we go now, Kayli? I think I need to go back and see the doctor."

♠

GONE

*W*e returned the boat to the Marina. First, Raven and Axel assisted Marc to the car. This time, the girl in the boat house came out and asked if we were okay. Axel waved her off. He told her Marc just twisted his ankle. He'd be fine.

He lied pretty smoothly. He drove off with Marc, heading to the hospital.

True to his word, Raven left a soggy wad of cash with her, pointing her to the boat, and telling her to fill it with gas and pay the docking fee. He even added an extra couple of twenties and asked her to pick a nice bouquet of flowers to place inside. "I just want it to look nice when he comes back for it," Raven had said, making it sound like it was Marc's boat. We left before the girl could figure out the truth.

Back at the apartment, I took a long hot shower and changed into a shirt that belonged to Marc and found shorts from my own bags. I took over one side of the couch. Raven, dried, and in a tank and sweatpants, claimed the other side. I was dead asleep for a few hours. After a swimming in the cold water and all the stress, I could have slept for a week. Still, it felt like a job well done.

When I did wake a couple hours later, I didn't want to move. My legs were intertwined with Raven's. I stared off at the silent entertainment center. It was strangely cozy and quiet, the first moment I felt relaxed in days.

Was it really over? Now that we had escaped, my mind flew to all the possible results. Blake may call the police. He would sue me for damages at best. What about the drug dealers? Would he rat me out to them and have some goons hunt me down?

Sirens started up deep in the city. I turned onto my back at first. When the police cars got closer, I sat up sharply and held my breath, a palm pressing against my thundering heart.

"Little thief," Raven called to me, in a deep voice raspy with sleep. His brown eyes locked on my face. He untucked himself from under the blanket and opened his arms up to me. "Come."

I untangled my legs from his and crawled over. His arms drew me in until he could fold me into the small space between himself and the back of the couch. With my back against the couch, he pressed himself into me.

His face nestled into my shoulder. "They aren't after us," he said quietly.

"They might come," I said. "Eventually."

"If they ever come for you, they better bring an army. I wouldn't let you go that easily."

I smiled at his arrogant boast. "Is that how a criminal thinks?"

"It's how I think." His arms wriggled around me until he hugged me close as we snuggled on the couch together. "You and your crazy plans, and fucked up boat crashing." He released me for a moment to curl fingers under the collar of the large T-shirt I wore. He slid the material down, exposing my bare skin. His head lowered and for a moment, his lips only brushed along my flesh, sending warmth. His lips puckered and he kissed me at the corner of my neck, close to the shoulder. His lips parted slightly, and he suckled gently for a moment before releasing me. "Beautiful."

My spine rippled with the spark his lips ignited inside me. At the same time, I tensed. The cuddling had been felt friendly up to that point. I was already in a mess with Marc and possibly Brandon. I wasn't ready for Raven to mix in with it.

"Raven," I said, in a voice that was more delicate. I didn't want to hurt him. I didn't want him to stop, but I didn't think my heart could take any more.

His lips grazed my neck, lighting up every nerve along

my spine. The warmth spilled right into my heart. "Do me a favor," he murmured against my skin. "Don't tell Marc or the others."

My breathing hastened. My mind whirled for his meaning. I was ready for some reasonable request. Like when he helped me get a note to Wil. Or maybe when he beat up that guy in the parking lot. Was he warning me not to tell them that? Could he get into trouble? "Tell them what?"

His lips met with the back of my earlobe. He breathed against me. His hand shifted down to hold me around the waist, pulling me closer. His voice came to me, guttural and low in my ear. "I'm pretty sure Marc has a little crush on you. I think if he knew about us, it may break his heart."

I eased myself up to sit. He pulled back, putting an arm up to pillow his head with a sleepy smile on his face. I didn't get it. I mean, I guessed at was he was implying, but I couldn't tell if he was serious. Was he teasing me?

"Us?" I asked.

He smirked. He opened his mouth and started to say something but a rattling of keys in the door stole his attention. He twisted himself to look back at the door.

Marc appeared first, followed by Axel. Brandon and Corey tailed behind them. Kevin followed and he closed the door behind himself.

I sat up further, pulling myself away from Raven. Raven shared a small smirk with me, like I was doing exactly the thing he wanted me to do. I didn't know how to tell him I was just confused and didn't know where to put myself.

Brandon worked his way around the group of guys, his arms open and his face full of concerned lines. "Kayli, what the hell were you thinking?"

For a flash of time, I thought he was talking about sitting on top of Raven. "Huh?"

He came around, pulling me up by the arm. He hugged me to his body. He pushed his face against my ear. "You shot him in the leg! And the boat?"

"Sorry?" I wasn't sure if that's what I should say. He didn't sound peeved as much as it was like, *oops, you spilled the milk.*

He sighed heavily and whispered quieter so only I could hear. "How am I supposed to protect you when you're running off half-cocked like that? Next time, give me a chance to keep up, okay?"

I grinned into his shoulder. I couldn't help it.

A body slammed in behind me, nearly knocking us over. Corey's face loomed near mine, the grin was broad. "Marc told us about the boat crash. That was awesome. I wish I'd seen it."

I struggled to breathe between the two, and then started wriggling. "Guys, you're such dorks."

"Hey," Axel barked at me, but in an amused tone. "What did I tell you about the name calling?"

The twins released me, and I stood on the carpet with my hands up in defense, as if waiting for one of them to strike.

Axel gestured to the couch. "Okay, sit. We need to figure out what happens next."

Raven pulled himself up on the couch, and he slid over, making room for the others. Corey sat next to him. Raven gave him the *I wasn't making room for you* look but Corey was oblivious to it and grinned happily at him. Raven smirked, shook his head and sat back.

I sat next to Corey and Brandon took up the space my other side. Between them, it was like two mirrored bodyguards, equally exquisite.

Axel and Marc sat on the coffee table. I guessed they really did need the coffee table. They used it for these meetings. Kevin sat on the floor.

"Okay," Axel said. "From what I'm hearing, Coaltar's crew called for a tow boat, saying there was a small accident. Coaltar was toted out, and has a private doctor looking at his leg."

"How do you know all this?" I asked.

Corey coughed lightly and grinned.

I smirked at him and poked him in the arm. "You sneaky devil."

"Yeah, well," Corey said, rubbing his hand across the

back of his head. "I figured I'd tap in and at least figure out if they were coming after us."

"He's going to be in surgery soon," Axel said. "And from what I hear, he's already planning a recovery retreat down in Palm Beach, Florida. He's telling people he'll be there for at least three weeks. For now, he may just be out of our hair."

"What about the cartel?" I asked. "Did I mess up? Are they coming after us?"

"Actually," Axel said, sitting up a little straighter. "From what I understand, the man that attacked Marc on the boat *was* a member of the cartel. He's heading back to his gang, but Coaltar's made a deal with him not to talk about you. This gang member wasn't happy, but apparently Coaltar's already gone above and beyond what they expected and they appreciate his intervening early." Axel raked his fingers through his jet-black hair and yanked the strands away from his eyes. "No one wanted a turf war in this area. The JH-14 drugs were from an offshoot of their own gang looking to start an uprising. They're going to infiltrate and pick out the key personnel and take care of it their own way."

I gasped, my hand reaching for Corey's leg for stability. "They can't—"

Axel waved his hand in the air. "They're drug gang members," he said. "Every one of them. The village is safe, but the persons responsible will be hunted. When Coaltar told you that part about the drugs not hurting anyone if they drank it from the well, he was telling you the truth, or at least he believed. Maybe he even believed part of what he was saying when he thought he could save lives, but the truth was, the cartel would have never let these guys get away with this. The drugs may have actually warned the village the cartel was coming, but it wouldn't have stopped this assassination."

Corey gently wrapped his hand around my wrist and tugged it until he could clutch my hand. "Kayli," he said quietly, drawing my attention. "These aren't good guys. These are murderers and drug dealers fighting their own war. But now they're going back home and out of Charleston. The battle is over there now. The DEA and other government agenices need to take care of this. This is beyond what we can do. We can't take on the world."

I had to agree. Outside of stopping Coaltar, I had no idea what else to do about this. Maybe Axel was right. Corey was right. They all were. How far do you go to help people?

And with that thought, I sighed heavily. "It's over," I said softly. It was true. They didn't need me anymore and I wasn't in danger. There was nothing to hold me here. I was a stranger they met a few days ago, and despite so much that had happened, this all had to end.

The others nodded grimly.

Kevin looked confused. He brushed his palm against his dark curly hair. "Why the hell do you guys look like that? I say it's about time this was over. Now we can get back to it being almost quiet around here."

Raven smirked. "When is it ever quiet?"

"It certainly isn't usually this bad," Kevin said. "Apparently I missed most of it."

"Consider yourself lucky," Axel said.

I started to say something, and then realized Corey was still holding on to my hand. He'd intertwined our fingers. I grinned at him, as it was so cute. He didn't strike me as gay like his brother said. Still, Corey's smile was again melting that wall inside me. It made it hard for me to say what I had to.

"Guess you guys don't need me anymore," I said. "It's time I went home."

There was a collection of grunts and coughs. They looked at each other.

Axel shrugged. "If Coaltar's out of the way, and there's no sign of him looking for you, there's no reason to hold you here."

Marc frowned. "Kayli," he said. He jerked his head and motioned to the door. "Can I talk to you? Outside?"

I glanced at the others, wondering, but no one questioned this. I stood, worried that if I didn't go with him, he'd come after me and carry me out like last time.

I stood, releasing Corey. I waved shortly at Brandon and then at the others and followed Marc out into the hall.

When the door closed behind us, I hovered on the carpet. The hall was empty, and I was nervous, wondering what trouble I was in now.

Marc still favored his leg. I was surprised to see him up and going and not strung out on pain killers. "How's your, um…" I said. I didn't know how to bring it up.

His eyebrows shifted above his mismatched eyes. "My leg?"

"Yeah," I said.

He smirked. "At least I didn't get shot this time."

I rolled my eyes and took a step back. He could joke about this?

"It's fine." Marc faced me and waved off his hand like he didn't want to talk about his leg any more. "I promised you," he said.

I wasn't sure which promise he was referring to me. "Huh?"

"I told you that you'd never have to see that hotel again," he said. "And I didn't want to tell the others yet." He leaned on one leg and hobbled closer. "You can stay here, you know? I mean, if you're uncomfortable in the bedroom right now, there's at least a couch. And Wil could come with you. We'll make room."

My mouth dropped open and my heart thundered. "Marc…"

"He's cool," he said. "I would have done it sooner, but it got kind of crazy. It's no big deal. A few months and he'll be in college. And even before then, we'll get you an apartment. Or you can just move in. I don't care. Whatever you want."

I squared off my shoulders at Marc. I knew he wouldn't like my answer, but it needed to be done. "I have to go," I said.

"Not this shit again."

I made a fist, aiming a loose punch at his chest. "I mean I have to go home."

His eyebrows hunched together. "Bambi, I promised you

that you wouldn't have to go back."

"I know," I said. "I appreciate it, but..." I stumbled for words. It's not what I wanted. In my heart, I'd already grown really fond of everyone.

At the same time, I was afraid. I wanted to retreat to a place where my head could clear. I wanted to be sure. I wanted them to be sure. They'd felt obligated before.

He sighed. He captured my wrists, drawing them together and holding tightly. He pursed his lips and his eyes closed. "I know," he said, his voice deep.

That broke my heart and I didn't know how to repair it. It made me want to take everything back to not hear those words. It confirmed everything I'd been feeling, split between two worlds. And in his voice, I sensed he did know exactly what I was doing. I could have called Wil and told him to come meet me and explain everything. There were a thousand different scenarios. What I needed was more than just a talk with my brother. I needed to escape.

Doing this in front of him made it much harder to leave. And we weren't really together. Not really. And this wasn't even goodbye. I just needed to get away. I needed to know for myself I could leave and come back if I wanted to and this wasn't some desperate attempt from them to take care of me, because they felt they had to. Because they felt I couldn't make it on my own otherwise.

I needed to know I was wanted for who I was. And I didn't know who I was outside of Kayli the thief.

I stood with him clutching my hands. Neither one of us knowing when, or if I'd be back, or if I'd be too scared to ever return to this. Because when you run away from something, a return is too hard to imagine. There was too much focus on the leaving to even think about what was next. The frown on his face, though, was too much to bear.

So I kissed him.

I was up on my toes to do it, and he must have sensed me zeroing in because he tilted his face toward mine. I first meant to just peck his lips, but the peck turned into a lengthened, closed-mouth kiss.

When he parted his lips, and turned his head, I parted mine. His tongue felt for my lips, and mine darted out to meet him. I was his echo. In more than a few ways.

It was the kiss that drove my heart to dare think about the future. Every thought of doubt I had before, it suddenly buried into the back of my mind, and was replaced by a will, a desire of what I really wanted.

It was then I knew. I wanted to come back. On my own terms, later. I wanted him, wanted Brandon, wanted Raven, wanted the rest. It was for that reason that I had to go, and that reason why I knew I'd return and want to figure out. This feeling that crept into my heart at his kiss, I wanted it to come back.

He was telling me with his lips that I could come back. That the door would be open. That he'd be waiting.

I tried to tell him without saying a word that I would. Eventually.

And as much as I wanted the kiss to last so long that I never left at all, I broke away from him and backed up. I still had a few things I needed to do.

When I was back on my feet, I couldn't look at him. I was too embarrassed that I had opened myself like that. I hadn't meant to.

"You felt it, too," he said in a low and guttural voice.

"Hm?" I glanced up at him, unsure.

His hand darted out, clutching my gut. "The goddamn wriggly sparks."

My lips twitched to answer him, but the truth buried itself into my tongue. It was too painful to tell him. Yes, I felt them. Except I'd also felt them with Raven moments before. And with Corey. With Brandon. It was part of the reason I had to go now. Before this went too far. This was a friendship of guys that I didn't want to cause chaos in. I needed to break away, let everyone cool off, and when I returned, I'd either make sure we were all friends, or select one. The choice was impossible right now. They were all good and tugged my heart in different directions.

He sighed, pulling his hand away and then lightly pushed

me off. "Go," he said.

He was right. I had to go or I would never leave, and that simply wouldn't be right. "There's a bus that stops in front of the building, isn't there?"

He nodded. He fished into his pocket, pulling out one of those emergency phones. He also plucked out his wallet and selected a wad of bills. He put both in my hands, and then closed my fingers. He ducked his head down until his forehead touched mine. "Call me any time. I mean it. I'll come get you."

I wanted to push away what he'd given me. Charity wasn't me. But in the moment, I couldn't refuse. I didn't have a dime to get back to the hotel. And I really needed the phone. Suddenly it was a lifeline. I realized it now. This was my way back to him and the others. I could call and hear his voice when I needed it. I knew I would need it.

I took it all, shoving it into my pocket. I pulled away from him before I could choke on a sob and swallowed back my emotions, steeling over my heart.

Marc disappeared for a moment into the apartment, and then came back with my two book bags. He planted boots in front of me and I realized these were his. They were too big but they would do for now.

I collected my bags, trying to do it quickly to hide my shaking fingers. I stuffed my feet into the boots and didn't bother to tie them.

I turned to the elevator. He lurched forward, holding down the button on the elevator until the doors opened. Southern in every sense.

"Thank you," I said, hoping he understood that I meant more than just for him opening a door for me.

He leaned in, kissing my temple. His lips seared my skin, like he had branded me. "I'll be waiting."

I wanted to tell him I'd hurry, but I couldn't make that promise. I was taking my things back with me, after all.

I lumbered further into the elevator with a heavy heart, gazing at the floor. I couldn't even face him when the doors closed, and then when they had, I'd wished I'd stopped myself. I'd wished he'd have come after me.

But I had to do this.

The elevator slid down to the sixth floor. A couple of guys got on. I recomposed myself, trying to look normal.

One of them turned to me. His face sparked up with interest. "Hi," he said cheerfully.

I smiled brokenly at him. "I'm taken," I said.

♠

CAN NEVER
GO HOME AGAIN

T he bus ride felt like the longest one I'd ever taken. I had to get on a different bus somewhere in North Charleston, in a not-so-friendly part of town. By then, I'd collected myself to at least glare hatefully at anyone that looked like he wanted to approach me. Daggers could have flown from my eyeballs at the way everyone swerved in a wide circle to avoid me. I really wasn't in the mood.

Even this short distance from the boys felt like hundreds of miles. The world I was returning to shadowed my brain. What would I do when I got back? What would I tell Wil? How could I explain the last couple of days?

When the bus drove past the mall, I gazed at the building. There was a strange love and hate feeling toward it now. It had brought me the boys, but it also brought with it a lot of pain. I honestly never wanted to see it again.

The bus rolled down the main road through West Ashley and I got off at the closest bus stop to the hotel. I stood at the platform, willing my feet to work. There was a terrible clash inside me. As much as I thought I needed to return, I really didn't want to go home, either. It didn't feel like home any more. I wasn't sure I even had one. Wil, of course, I needed to return to but what would happen when I told him that maybe Corey could get him into college early? That they were willing to help him, even let him move in.

Somehow I knew Wil's answer already. He said it every night. He hated the hotel. He'd do anything to get out of it.

He'd jump at the opportunity. And then he'd be gone.

I needed a little more time. I didn't know what I wanted for myself. A job? A new place?

I didn't want to deal with Jack. As much as I hated him, he was my father. Broken because his wife died and stuck with two kids and no job, he'd sunk into himself until he didn't resemble the man I'd grown up with. Maybe my time away from him had allowed me to grow a little sympathy for him. Without me, he'd eventually become a hobo, or dead, I'd wager. The month would eventually end and he'd be out in the street. I'd work to pay the rent, but when I finally left for good, what then?

I started off toward the hotel, with my bags slung over my shoulders. I needed to get this over with. I'd settle into a routine. I needed to find all the answers so I could truly be myself. When I figured it out, I'd call the guys and see what they were up to. Wouldn't they be proud of me if I got my own job? Wouldn't they freak out when they saw me get my own apartment? For the moment, I thought I would work really hard and surprise them all.

Could I ever go back to the old Kayli though? Even without picking pockets, I tried to imagine myself working the counter of some store, or in some office. The picture didn't really fit.

The hotel looked gloomier to me. The clouds rolled over my head. It wasn't going to rain, just hover and block out the sun. I stood in the parking lot for a bit, staring up at the second floor, at the door of 221B. It was shadowed by the overhang. Cold. Quiet.

Lies whirled through my head, and I was trying to come up with the best one. I don't know why I bothered. Wil would spot them in a heartbeat.

I started up the stairs when I felt eyeballs looking out at me from different hotel rooms. I didn't want to run into the limp willy freak without Raven there to back me up.

I clutched the phone in my front pocket. Somehow the act of holding it made me feel better about doing what had to be done.

I climbed the steps two at a time and when I got to the door, I realized I didn't have my room key so I knocked and waited.

I had to knock again.

The locks clicked and the door opened a sliver. From behind it, feminine eyes, unfamiliar, peered out at me sideways. "Hi honey," the lady said. "Did you have the wrong room?"

I blinked after her, and then rechecked the door number again. For a moment, I was lost. "Jack..." I said, unsure where to start. Did he move rooms while I was gone?

Her eyes widened and she opened the door wider. She was covered in a towel, her unnaturally red hair was wet and dripped to the carpet. "Oh. You're here to see Jackie? He's asleep."

Discomfort swept over me as I realized he'd dragged home another woman. "Sorry," I said. "I'm his daughter."

Her eyes brightened. "He never told me he had a little girl! That's so sweet." She shifted the towel around her body. "Sorry about this."

I waved it off. "Don't worry about it." I stepped into the space so she could close the door behind me. That's when I caught the two pieces of paper on the floor behind her, folded notes that had been kicked aside. I stared at them absently. Notices from the maids? Maybe a warning if there had been a fight? I shook it off. "I was actually looking for my brother, Wil."

"Wil?" she asked. "He has a son, too?"

I nodded. I lowered my bags to the floor. "If Jack came home with you last night," I said, unsure how to be delicate, but tried to use a pleasant voice. At least she didn't appear to be a *crazy* hooker. Just one of the nice ones. "I mean, he may have called Wil ahead of time to scatter. So he's probably downstairs somewhere."

She planted her palms on her hips. "Well, that's just rude. He shouldn't kick his own kids out."

"You get used to it," I said. I scanned the room, spotting Jack in the bed. His bare ass hung out from the blankets, and he snored like a chainsaw.

A sense of something being wrong thundered through my head. My eyes settled on a faux Coach handbag I didn't recognize sitting on top of the bed Wil and I had shared. The bed was made up but the top was ruffled as if she'd been sitting on it.

"Still," she said. She shrugged and pointed to the bathroom. "Let me get dressed."

I nodded, feeling the awkwardness between us. Neither of us expected the other, and neither of us had a reason to be upset the other was there. She didn't know she was invading anyone else's space. I wasn't going to throw her out naked.

I marched forward, hovering over Jack. I stared down at him, at his temporarily peaceful face. I wanted to smack his head for being an idiot and making Wil hang out by himself while I was gone and so far into the afternoon.

"Jack," I called to him.

"Mergh," he replied.

I stepped closer, weary. He could roll over and pop me a good one. "Jack!"

"What?" he called, not opening his eyes.

"Where's Wil?"

He waved his hand in the air. "I don't know. Go away."

"Where's Wil?" I asked louder.

"How the hell should I know? He ran off with Kayli again."

I rolled my eyes. His disoriented state wasn't helping. I turned, looking over the mess. There were beer cans on the table, a couple on the floor. Again, I had a strange sensation that something was off.

The woman emerged from the bathroom in a miniskirt and a low hanging top. Her hair brushed back, and she wore a thick layer of lipstick. She smiled pleasantly. "Want to look for your brother? I'd like to meet him."

"Yeah," I said. I headed for the door. "I'll be back. Could you wait a second and open the door?"

I dashed downstairs to the main lobby and stood there for a moment, contemplating where Wil could be. I checked the workout room, the laundry room, and then searched the office with the computer. All were empty.

I circled back to the front desk. No one was there, so I knocked my hand against the bell, trying to get someone's attention.

"Hang on. I'll be right there," Cody's voice trailed to me from somewhere down the hallway.

I side stepped until I faced the office down the corridor. "Cody!"

"Is that you Kayli?" he emerged from the office, standing just outside the door, his arm half stuffed in a sports jacket but he stopped when he saw me. "Just you?"

"Yeah. Have you seen Wil?"

He shook his head and shrugged off the jacket again. "Hey, I was going to tell you. One of the business suites opened up. For a few hundred dollars more, we could put you guys in there. It'll give you more room for the three of you."

I shook my head. "Not now," I said, not wanting the sales pitch. "I just need to find Wil."

"Haven't seen him in a few days," he said. "Not since I last saw you."

That struck me. "Did you tell him about the rent being paid?"

"I left a note under the door."

My body stiffened. Realization cut through me like a cold knife against my bones. I started off back toward the lobby.

"Kayli?" he called.

I didn't stop. I marched through the glass doors and let it slam back behind me. I jogged toward the stairs. I thought I heard a cat call but I didn't stop even to flip a middle finger. My mind whirled, in a panic.

I came back to 221B and had to stop, knocking again, this time short and with fury.

The woman answered again, blinking at me. "Find him?"

"No," I said, unable to hide the note of fear in my voice. I nudged her aside and then caught the two pieces of paper behind the door again. I stopped, picking them up. One was from Cody, a note to Wil, just like he'd said. It was still folded, like no one had read it.

The other was mine. My eyes looked over the words I had written. There was a small note at the bottom in another handwriting. For a moment, my heart raced, thinking it was Wil leaving a note back for me.

She's with her boyfriend. She's fine. - R

I rolled my eyes. Raven. I didn't have time to comprehend his reasoning now.

I looked up, and then scanned the room again, putting the pieces together. Did Wil miss the notes? Was he out looking for me?

I scanned the room, looking for any sign of him. Some of his textbooks sat on the floor in a neat stack beside the bed. A couple of pieces of clothing were by the entertainment unit, old socks and a pair of shorts. I checked the drawer where he normally kept his clean clothes and other items.

It was empty.

I checked the others, ripping them open. In a mad search, I sought out any sign of him. He had to have come back. He had to.

I spun.

"Is there a phone number?" the woman asked, hovering back as if sensing my panic. "What can I do?"

"I don't know," I said. Did he see I wasn't here and then go to stay with a friend? I had no way to reach him if he did.

And then my eyes dipped toward the kitchen. A doughnut sat on the counter, on a napkin. It was the same place I'd seen it last. It was the last time I saw him.

And then I knew. My heart stopped. My breathing slowed to a crawl, even though I desperately needed air right then. I knew, and I don't know how I knew, but I was sure. If he had come home that night, the first night I was gone, he would have gotten there before I normally would have returned from work. He would have eaten that doughnut. He would have known I left it for him.

No. I felt it. It was why Axel and Kevin never saw him. It was why I felt uncomfortable when they said the neighbors claimed they'd seen him around but weren't sure where he was exactly. They didn't know. They had no clue.

Wil was missing.

And I was the last one to see him.

♠

~*A*~

*M*arc stood in the middle of his apartment, looking
down at the coffee table. His arms crossed over
his chest. His friends were sitting on the couch,
their eyes glued to Axel.

Despite standing in his own apartment, Marc was a
million miles away. His fingers traced over his phone. The
ringer was on at the loudest setting and it was on vibrate. He
had Corey switch the number on the phone Kayli had to a
straight up emergency signal. There was no way he'd miss a
call from her. It had made him all too nervous to be sending
her back to Jack. He wanted to follow her, but Axel, once he
learned she'd left, had told him to stay. She'd be back. If he
chased after her every time, she'd stay away longer.

Marc knew that. He'd been the same way with Axel. It
was just hard for him to accept this. Once he had changed his
mind for good, and settled into just staying with his new
friends, everything had changed. The weight on his shoulders
disappeared. He'd found a second family with his Academy
team.

Before he had found him, years ago, Marc had thought
he would forever be trapped inside his old gang. The gang
had taken him in when he was young, and brought him up,
but they'd fed him drugs and laughed when Marc did stupid
things under the influence. They forced him to be the
underdog, and when he worked his way up in the ranks, he
grew to hate himself and the things they did, until he couldn't
feel anything anymore.

It wasn't until Marc worked beside Axel and the others

that he realized the truth. Axel and this Academy family were completely different. The gang he'd been involved in controlled him through threats on his life. Axel and the Academy weren't like that.

Axel sat on the coffee table now. His face was stern. Marc recognized this look. Whenever one of his team members was out on some dangerous assignment, he wore this expression. Since all of the team members were here and accounted for, he knew that face was now for Kayli.

Axel coughed to get their attention. "The Academy is unhappy with what we've done. First the camera was stolen, which we were able to get back, but there's no telling how much information Mr. Fitzgerald got out of it and possibly could have shared with Coaltar. And now we've shown ourselves to not only Coaltar and his crew, but also to a member of the cartel. We've exposed ourselves."

"Did you explain we weren't in the lead? We were just following her?" Raven asked.

"It doesn't seem to matter," Axel said. "We still broke protocol. They understand and they sympathize, but they can't allow members to be persuaded by an outside source to break the rules. We got lucky this time. They only docked us a few favors."

"Should we appeal?" Brandon asked, frowning and sitting back.

"I don't think we should fight this," Axel said. "I think we're getting off pretty lightly." A small smile crept onto his face. "But when were we ever the type of group to follow the rules?"

The boys laughed at this. Marc did, too.

"We shouldn't have done this at all," Kevin said, his deep voice grumbling. His fingers ruffled through the tight curls on his dark head. "I can't believe you let her steal a boat. You helped her crash a multimillion dollar yacht, and she shot someone."

Marc shrugged. "She was upset."

"What happens next time she's upset?" Kevin asked. "What's wrong with you guys? You're giving her excuses for firing a gun at someone?"

"It was an accident," Raven said.

"You're all insane," Kevin asked. "If it were any one of you guys..."

"We've all done it," Axel said. "Yourself included."

"I've never shot someone!"

"But we've all made mistakes," Axel said in a sharp tone. "You were no different than her when you first started."

"Why are you talking like she's coming back?" Kevin sat back and shook his head, frowning. "The job's done. We can ask the Academy to send a scout team to monitor for trouble. We've tagged Coaltar and we'll keep an eye on him, too. The Academy will help Kayli get the job we promised. We don't have to be involved anymore."

"I promised her I'd help her brother get into college," Corey said.

Kevin shrugged. "That's nice of you, but you should have made him do it himself. He shouldn't be handed anything."

"Like we weren't handed things?" Brandon asked as he stared at the leg of the coffee table.

Kevin rolled his eyes. "That's different. We work for what we're given."

"Which doesn't mean he won't," Corey said. "I've seen his transcripts. He's good."

"Well transcripts don't tell us anything about him. He could be a shithead."

"Enough," Marc barked at them. He turned on Kevin. "What's with you? We agreed to help her. We can't just go back on that."

"I just don't want another accident involving us," Kevin said. "I'm trying to protect us. We worked too hard to be making these kinds of mistakes."

Marc frowned. He wanted to argue the point with him. Maybe it was a mistake, but Kayli didn't know any better.

Personally, he doubted if even the Academy could have held her back. He saw that determination in her eyes. She was going to hunt Coaltar down to the ends of the earth if it meant she could spare someone's life. She didn't even know the village Coaltar was headed to was abandoned except for the very worst of outlaws that had taken over, determined to overthrow one of the major cartels in Mexico. But he was glad they did it. There was no telling if an innocent woman or child may have drunk that water from the well, and poisoned themselves. Even if they'd just gotten sick, something like the JH-14 could have killed a little kid. Marc may have never known for sure. Schrödinger's cat.

But now, he didn't have to wonder. Kayli found a way to stop it. Despite her tough outer shell, she was all heart.

Axel shook his head. "We need to come to terms with this, guys. She's seen a lot of what we do. She's a lot like us."

"I don't know," Kevin said. "Why not send one of the girl teams to make friends?"

"You know how picky they are," Axel said. "And we're her first contact."

"Are we looking to bring her into the Academy?" Brandon asked.

"I don't know," Axel said. "She expressed interest. She has some potential."

"But we don't know if she'll fit in," Kevin said. "Right now, she'd never pass registration, let alone the extensive testing. She's too wild and angry."

"Right," Axel said. "And there's a chance she's simply not interested. But at the same time, she's a useful tool."

"Is that what we'll think of her as?" Corey asked. "Something useful to use?"

"Aren't we?" Axel replied. "We work together because we offer different talents. Maybe some of you don't want to hear it, but she jumped in and worked with us pretty well. I haven't seen someone blend in with our group as quickly since Marc."

"You can't be serious," Kevin said. "You're talking like you want her to join with us. I mean our group."

"I wouldn't have a problem with it," Marc said.

Kevin slapped a palm against his forehead. "That's

ridiculous. We can't have a girl on the team."

"Why not?"

"Because it's against Academy rules."

"Not it isn't," Corey said. Marc had to hide his smile at Corey knowing policy. The Academy had very few actual rules to follow. Everything else was just strong suggestion.

"Okay, it isn't a rule," Kevin said. He held out his hand. "But they don't want us to work like that. I mean, let's assume she's a good match and she joins our team. What am I going to tell Mindy when one day she spots me out with her on a job? How am I supposed to explain that?"

"We'll work it out," Marc said.

"No." Kevin stabbed his finger at his thigh as if trying to make a point. "This is exactly why a single bird doesn't join a team like this. I'll admit, she has talent. I don't mind adopting her for her own protection. I'd even let Corey help get her brother into college, but I have to draw the line somewhere."

Axel sat back on his hands, and sighed. "You're probably right."

Corey perked up. "Well, if she joins a girl team, she'll still be around, right?"

Marc shrugged. "How often do you see girls on other teams? I don't think I've worked with one in the past year. They're so short in supply, so they get asked on assignments all the time."

"Which is why the Academy would be interested when they find out she's as talented as we know she is," Axel said.

"But we'd be her contact," Brandon said. "We'd be her initial adopted team."

"And we've fucked with her a lot," Raven said, grumbling. He tightened his arms around his chest, sitting back and glaring at the floor. "Once she met up with the other teams, she'd probably find a bird team she liked better."

The team grew quiet. It was true. Now that the initial threat around her was gone, she was free to pursue whatever road she wished. If she did express interest in the Academy, if the Academy investigated closer and decided they want to put her into a test team, more than likely she'd pick one of the girl teams. Wouldn't she? The Academy would encourage it, and she'd be so busy that they'd never see her. With everything the Academy provided and did, it would probably win her over and she'd do anything for them. Just like they'd do anything for the Academy.

"Then again," Axel said. "She may not care to do it at all. She might go for college, or a normal job."

"Do you really believe she'd go for any type of normal job?" Marc asked, eyeballing him.

Axel shrugged. "She could surprise us. I don't think she would, but she'd be the one to do it just to throw me for a loop."

Raven huffed. "I don't think she's the normal type. More like crazy with a side order of insane."

"She is a lot of fun, though," Corey said.

Marc grinned. He had to agree with that. "We'll have to find her work where she'll be happy. Maybe that'll be the answer. Something crazy on her level. She'll stay in town. Maybe we'll work together outside the Academy. Who knows?"

Kevin nodded. "I could live with that. Look guys, I don't want to cut you off from a new friend. She's certainly got the spark. She's got a whole lot of talent. I just don't want you all setting your heart on her joining the team when it's likely not possible, or is never going to happen."

Marc sighed and then sank down beside Axel. "Too many what ifs," he said.

Axel rocked his head back. "But she will come back."

"We should adopt her," Corey said. He perked up with that goofy smile that made Marc chuckle every time. "Her and Wil. Let's adopt her and then we'll get her a cool job. Like a bounty hunter. Or private investigator. She'd like that."

Kevin shrugged. "Sure. We can do that."

"Make it a closed adoption," Raven said.

"That may cost us a few favors," Axel said.

"We found her first," Raven said. "We'd be team lead.

C. L. Stone

We could monitor if anyone is interested and warn them about her craziness. They may back off."

"You don't want to hurt her potential Academy career," Kevin warned.

"Let's take it one step at a time," Axel said. "Let's adopt her, and go for the closed adoption. We can spare a few favors for her. I'd like to monitor her progress anyway. Chances are, we'll urge her into a challenging career and we can still work with her if we want. I think private investigation may be right up her alley. Or forensic science."

"Once she learns to follow the law," Kevin said.

Axel shrugged. "Or bend it once in a while."

The boys continued their discussion for a bit, and Marc fell quiet. He didn't have a problem guiding Kayli into what sounded like a great career. Although he wondered if Kayli could settle into anything like that. Even as a private investigator or bounty hunter, and with the full support of an Academy backing, she was a pretty wild girl. Marc thought if she ever discovered the true and full meaning of the Academy, she'd probably want in.

But even that was uncertain. And at the thought of Kayli entering the Academy, he wasn't so sure he'd want her working for a girl team so he wouldn't see her. Other Academy guys would show interest in her, too. Some who may have the opportunity to treat her better than they'd been able to. Kidnapping her and practically holding her captive hadn't been the best sort of introduction.

But his lips burned with the memory of her kiss from before she'd left. It had the underlying promise that she'd be back, and when she did, she'd be coming back for him. At least that's what he hoped. He'd never felt so out of himself before with a girl. Before he'd met Kayli, he'd wanted to take a break from dating, especially with the recent disaster with the crazy girl who hurt herself for attention. He didn't want to deal with another crazy girl like that.

But Kayli was a different kind of crazy. Those emerald green eyes. That dark hair that contrasted with her fair skin and made her eyes nearly glow in sunlight.

He felt a zap at his butt and the buzz of vibration before the ringing started.

It was an emergency signal. Kayli.

He launched himself up off the coffee table, and started heading away to answer it down the hall.

Ideas floated through his mind. She walked into that hotel room and changed her mind. Maybe she took one look at that drunk father and realized quickly she didn't have anything to stay for. Maybe she told Wil to pack a bag. Maybe she was calling to let him know they were going to another hotel room together. He'd tell them to come back. They'd keep them here until they could figure out another solution. And he knew he'd do whatever possible, cook her a hundred different breakfasts, and even put on his best manners. He'd do what Axel taught him. He'd try to convince her to stay this time.

But even as he thought all this, something nagged the back of his mind. This was Kayli. If she was anything like him, she wouldn't have called so soon. Something was wrong.

He sensed the others quieting as he answered. They'd known him too long. They knew something was up.

"Kayli?" he asked into the phone.

"He's gone," her voice quivered on the line like she was trying to hold herself together.

"Who's gone? What are you talking about?"

"Wil. He's gone. He left the morning I did. The day that old man caught me and you ... I mean since that day. He hasn't been back."

"What do you mean?" Marc asked, his brain flew to find an answer for her, to help her. He had to be around. He must be with a friend or maybe stepped out at the wrong time. She was just on edge because of the past couple of days. "He had to have been there. Axel asked around."

"He's not been back," she said. "There's... I don't know how to explain it but I know. He's missing."

"Could he be with a friend? Could he have..."

"I don't think so. I don't ... I..." Her voice broke, and he was sure he heard her sob. "I don't..."

His spine stiffened. "Where are you now?"

"I'm at the hotel."

"Stay there," he said. "Just stay where you are. You hear me? Hang on a second." He glanced at his friends and then he went back to say to her, "I'm going to pass the phone to Corey. I'm on the way but he's going to get some information from you about Wil. We're on it, okay? Just hang on until we get there."

At this, everyone stood up at once. Corey turned to Marc expectantly, his hands out. Marc tossed the phone to him and Corey took over, heading out the door, talking to Kayli and asking pertinent questions.

"What's going on?" Brandon asked. His fists clenched and knocking impatiently against his thighs. Raven mimicked him, the same determined look.

"Wil's missing," Marc said. He dashed for his bedroom, grabbing a pair of boots, and then tossed them aside for a pair of sandals since those would be quicker. He grabbed for his keys and another phone. "We need to go. Brandon, come with me. Raven, you should..."

"I'll head toward the school district," Axel said. "If he's checked in there, I'll see if I can't find any of his classmates that might know where he's at. Brandon, come with me and we'll scope out the neighborhood and ask around. Raven, you should go with Marc and help Kayli. She may try to panic and run all over the place. Keep her calm. Bring her back here if you have to."

Kevin looked like he was going to say something and stopped. He plucked out his own phone from his pocket and answered it. "Hi, baby," he said. "Hang on, it's not a good... What? Oh. Yeah, uh..." He grimaced. "Hang on." He covered the phone with his hand. "Guys, it's Mindy."

"We're a bit busy," Axel said.

"She's ... look, I have to go."

Marc reeled back a step. "Kevin, her brother is missing."

"Yeah, I know, but," he said, looking conflicted. "She needs me right now."

Marc wanted to punch him but he didn't have the time. He knew it was panic talking and he tried to calm himself. This wasn't Kevin's fault and it wasn't Mindy's. The Academy had warned them that as they grew older and got girlfriends, sometimes they needed to plan accordingly. Family first, and Mindy was part of Kevin's family now. He had to respect that. "Okay."

"If you need me," Kevin said, looking pained by this. "Really, I mean I'll come if you need me. I don't know how else I could help you guys."

"No," Axel said. "We've got it covered." He clapped a hand on Kevin's shoulder and held it firmly. "You've been away for a while. Go to Mindy. We've got this."

Kevin didn't look too happy about the decision. "Call me with updates?"

Marc nodded, but didn't say anything.

"We'll call you," Axel said, confirming.

Kevin sighed. Marc turned from him, heading out the door, with Raven, Brandon and Axel in tow. Kevin lingered back in the apartment, talking to Mindy and assuring her he'd be there soon.

Marc waited until the elevator doors were closed and he was alone with Raven, Brandon and Axel. "I can't believe he'd do this now.

"Let's not think like that," Axel said. "After all, we didn't even ask what was wrong with Mindy, or ask if there was something we could do to help."

Marc frowned. He was right.

"Probably nothing we could do," Brandon said. "She's getting more clingy. She's asking more questions."

"They're in love," Axel said. "She's naturally curious about where he spends all his time. And when he's gone overnight on assignment, it's going to keep getting harder. We don't have parents, or school work, for the Academy to hide behind any more. Now that he's telling her he's working at the Academy full time, she's going to look for some consistency. We all knew it would happen someday. Kevin wanted her in the dark as much as possible so she wouldn't worry, and this is the price you pay for it. We can't all date Academy girls. We're lucky if we get a girl that can know about the Academy at all."

"Kayli knows," Marc said quietly, staring at the corner of the elevator. It was moving too slow for his liking. Every moment was a stall until he could get to her.

The others didn't respond. They didn't have to. Suddenly Marc sensed it from them. They liked her too. Kevin was wrong. She fit with them. Marc's guts told him that. He'd tried to deny it for years when he first ran into the group, but he never got rid of that feeling of how easily he fit in with his friends now, and the bond they now shared thanks to the Academy. Kayli had slipped into their group and fell in so naturally, it was like himself all over again.

No, Kevin was wrong.

Kayli belonged with them.

Thank you for purchasing this book. Keep in touch with the author to find out about special releases and upcoming events, including spoilers, author chats and swag.

Website: http://www.clstonebooks.com/ - Sign up for the newsletter - It's the best way to stay up to date with the latest from C. L. Stone.

Twitter: http://twitter.com/CLStoneX

Facebook: http://www.facebook.com/clstonex

BONUS:

Turn the page for exclusive sneak peeks at the next books in

The Scarab Beetle Series

&

The Ghost Bird Series

The Academy

The Scarab Beetle Series

Liar

Book Two

Written by C. L. Stone

Published by

Arcato Publishing

♠

MISSING

Wil was missing.

The hotel room was silent. I sat on one of the beds, glaring down at my father, Jack, who was passed out on the opposite one.

The prostitute he had brought home had left after awkward apologies and a good luck wish at finding my brother.

"Kayli," Corey said to me through the cell phone I held to my ear. I could imagine him at the computer in the apartment, typing away. Hovering over the keyboard, his sun-kissed hair messed up in the same way I'd seen it earlier that day. "Are you sure he's not with a friend?"

I hesitated. A few days ago, I got mixed up in a group of Academy boys who needed my help. In return, I was promised a lot of things, including assistance in helping Wil with getting into a college in a hurry and getting out of the godforsaken dump of a hotel we currently lived in. When I got back, Wil's clothes, school books, most of his things were gone. I'd been so worried about getting back to him and letting him know where I was while I was temporarily missing, and the whole time he hadn't been home. I wanted to believe Corey and think maybe he was at a friend's house.

But I knew that wasn't true. I could feel it. Like a piece of me was missing that couldn't be replaced until I found him. He was gone. Someone may as well have chopped off my hand. "I know," I said as coolly as I could, remembering this wasn't Corey's fault. "I'm telling you, he's been missing for," I counted off on my fingers, "what is it? Three days?

Four? Ever since Marc first picked me up."

"The school record shows he's been to class all last week."

I sucked in a heavy breath and held it, sitting up on the bed. I stared hard at the silent television, as if that held answers that my brain wasn't able to put together in my panicked state. "He has?"

"Yeah," he said. "He's been going every day. He's probably spending the night at a friend's house."

I stood up, and stumbled forward a step as I wasn't sure what direction to start pacing first, and Marc's clunky boots on my feet were hard to navigate. I glanced at the two notes sitting unfolded on top of the kitchenette counter next to an uneaten doughnut. All had been left for Wil and none had been picked up, so I knew he hadn't been by. He'd never spent the night at someone else's house before. "I should ... I don't know. What am I doing standing here?" I asked, even though I already knew the answer. I was waiting because I didn't know what to do next. I didn't have a car so I couldn't run off to find Wil, even if I wanted to. I didn't know where to start now. I needed another pair of eyes. I needed Academy boys.

There was a hard pounding knock at the door; I felt the vibrations resonating through the floor. "Kayli!" Raven shouted.

I ran for the door. "Raven's here," I told Corey.

"Let me hang up on you and check in with Axel. He was heading out to the school district so he could check out any classmates who might have seen Wil. Don't worry. We'll find him." He said goodbye and hung up.

I unlocked the door and got shoved back as it was pushed open from the other side. Raven towered in the doorway. He wore the same black T-shirt and sweatpants I'd seen him wearing a few hours earlier. He hadn't bothered to change. Somehow that made me feel better. He took this as seriously as I felt.

His shoulders rolled back. His arms seemed to swell, making the tribal and rose tattoos on his forearms shift. His eyes darkened when he saw me and realized what a mess I was. "Tell me," he said, the Russian accent thickening. "What happened?"

I stepped back from the door to let him in. "Where's Marc?" I asked.

"He's downstairs asking questions." He lumbered forward, his eyes going all over the place, from the tiny hotel kitchenette, to where my father was with his bare ass hanging out, still passed out from whatever drunken stupor he'd been in from the night before. He nodded at Jack's direction. "Did you ask him?"

"I can't get a coherent sentence out of him," I said, avoiding looking at Jack. The more I did, the angrier I got. I wanted to feel sorry for him, but it was getting harder and harder to drum up any sympathy. He lost his wife, my mother, years ago. Since then he fell apart and drank his way through life. After all the crap he gave me during the times I tried to drag Wil with me to get away from him and his abuse, he chose now to not give a damn.

Raven went to the bed and leaned over, checking my father's pulse at his neck. He split Jack's eyelids open and checked his pupils. He released him, and wiped his fingers across his shirt as if to clean them. "We need to wake him. Make some coffee."

"He won't drink coffee."

"Make some water," he said. He bent over, grabbing Jack's arm. He shoved it over his own shoulders and started to haul him up. "Open the bathroom door."

I ran to the bathroom, opening it up and then dove in to push aside the shower curtain. Raven dragged him into the stall and dropped him on his butt onto the tile. I averted my eyes; I could see with my peripheral vision enough of what was going on, but avoided looking at Jack naked.

Raven leaned in and turned the cold water faucet on full blast.

It took a moment, but Jack started sputtering and opening his eyes, crying out. He rolled back and forth against the wall, trying to use it to haul himself back out of the unrelenting spray. His grimy face streaked as the water washed some of him clean. "Turn it off!" he howled.

"Get up," Raven said. He positioned himself in front of Jack, for which I was grateful. I'd seen enough. Raven crossed his arms over his chest, standing out of striking distance if Jack decided to attack him, but still looming. "Where's Wil?"

Jack coughed, long and hard and thickly enough that I thought he was trying to vomit. He reached up, turning off the water. He managed to twist the faucet until it was only dribbling and then scooted himself out of range. He rotated and peered up at Raven. "Who are you?"

"Kayli's looking for Wil," Raven said. "When's the last time saw him?"

"Hell if I know." He cringed and then looked around Raven and spotted me behind him. "Who is this, Kayli?"

I clenched my hands into fists. He wasn't listening at all. "Jack, Wil's missing. I can't find him."

"Well, shit, tell me about it," he said. He wiped water away from his face. "Get me a pair of pants, will you?"

I picked up a dirty pair of cotton pants he'd left in a corner of the bathroom and tossed them at him. I turned, looking at the wall. "You haven't seen him at all?"

"I haven't seen you, either. Not in a few days." There were sounds behind me like he was stumbling into his pants and then a thud like he fell against the wall. "I thought he was with you."

"I called you and told you to tell him I was at a job."

"How am I supposed to keep up with either of you?" he bellowed.

"So you haven't seen him at all?" Raven asked.

"Who the hell are you anyway?"

"I'm her boyfriend," he said.

"What? How come I've never heard of you?"

I turned around. Jack stood, his short hair wet and stuck against his head, his face dripping. His bare belly hung over the hem of the pants. Raven and Jack had squared off and were glowering at each other. I stared hard at Raven for a

4

moment, trying to figure out if he was saying 'boyfriend' to keep things simple, and for some reason I took it like that. Seemed like the easiest thing to rattle off rather than just saying friend or, the real truth: that I'd just met him a few days ago and still barely knew him.

"He's not helping," I told Raven. "He doesn't know."

"Kayli?" Marc called. Footsteps sounded by the still-open door of the apartment. Marc nudged it further open as I stepped out to meet him. He spotted me and limped toward me, favoring one of his legs. His soft brown hair hung over in front of his mismatched eyes: one blue, one green. He gripped me by the elbows. "You okay? I..."

"Who is *this*?" Jack bellowed. He padded out into the main hotel room. "Why do you have all these boyfriends coming out of the woodwork? What kind of job were you at?"

Marc's jaw hardened, making his high cheekbones stand out a little more. The black and brown plastic bands on his left wrist seemed to tighten against his arm as he made fists. He positioned himself in front of me, warding off Jack from getting any closer. "We're here for her. We're taking her with us."

"What is this shit?" Jack said. He tried to look over at me from over Marc's shoulder. "Kayli--"

Raven bumped into him on his way out of the bathroom almost knocking him over. He scanned the kitchenette again, and then the beds and the dresser. He spotted my two book bags on the floor by the beds. He picked them both up, slinging them over his shoulder. He turned to me. "Do you have anything else here? We'll take it with us."

"Hang on a second," Jack said. He marched over to Raven, his finger pointed at him. "What the hell are you doing?"

"Someone should stay here," I said, ignoring Jack. "I mean, maybe I should. If Wil comes back--"

"He's not here and he hasn't been back," Marc said. "I checked the computer logs downstairs in the business center and I've asked the manager. He said he hasn't seen him, only

Jack." He looked over where I'd opened up the drawers, finding them empty. "If he's taken his things, he's not planning on coming back. Not for a while."

"But..."

"You don't take all your things and plan on coming back," he said. He grabbed my hand, tugging me to the door. "Come on."

"Wait a second, you're not dragging her out of here." Jack stomped over. "Let go of her."

Marc moved over again, blocking access. "She's coming with us."

"Kayli doesn't get dragged anywhere." Jack looked at me, his eyes wide and wild. "You can't just leave here."

"You mean you can't find beer money without me?" I asked.

"Don't give me that shit."

"No," I said. I yanked my arm out of Marc's grasp and stepped toward Jack, getting in his face. I didn't want to do it this way but I had no choice. He was my father, but I'd had enough and I was wound up too tight to stop now. "I was gone for four days and you didn't give a damn. Wil's gone and you're not out looking for him. You don't even care. You just want me here to pay for this hotel room and to give you money. I'm nothing to you but an income source. The only reason I was doing it at all was for Wil. He's gone. So I'm gone, too."

Jack clenched his hands and shoved one toward me. "You selfish little ... after everything I've done..."

Raven clamped down on Jack's wrist and twisted. Jack bent over backward to relieve the pressure. He howled and clawed at Raven's grasp. Raven pushed back until Jack was on his knees and then shoved.

"Don't touch her," Raven said in a cold, deep voice.

Jack held his arms up in defense, easing himself up. "Fine. Take her." He focused on me, pointing a finger. "You think I need you? You don't know anything about nothing."

I ground my teeth together to stop myself from arguing. Over the years, I dreamed of the day I would walk out on him and let him rot in his own mess. Now that it was here and I was doing it, all the words I'd wanted to spit at him didn't want to appear. And did it matter? Nothing I could say would make any of this right.

But why was there that still persistent nag at my heart? Maybe it was because I still had a picture of him in my mind of what he used to be. Before my mother died, he'd kept a job, even if it wasn't a good one and didn't pay very well. He wasn't always the friendliest, but he'd worked hard and kept us kids in line. It was what you'd want in a dad, at the least.

How could he dare ask me to stay, and beg me with those eyes that look struck and horrified? After all the fights? After becoming a bum and forcing us to cart him around while we barely survived? He'd given up on us.

"You have about a month," I said as coolly as I could muster. I could leave him that at least. It relieved some of the guilt over abandoning him like a helpless animal. "The hotel room has been paid until then. If you don't cause too much trouble, and they don't have a reason to kick you out."

Jack's lips twisted and his head jerked back. "You shrewd girl. You've been holding back money? Paid a month? For this place?"

"Come on, Kayli," Marc urged. He reached out for my wrist and tugged. "We should go."

"You're an idiot," Jack called after me. "The rent is outrageous here. I was going to move us somewhere else. After the next check came in, I was going to..."

I turned from Marc, looking back at Jack. What was he babbling about? "What check?"

Jack shook his head. "You think you're going to get a dime from me? You've got to be kidding. After all I've done to teach you to fend for yourself."

"Teach me?" I asked. My shoulders drew back and I pointed a finger at him. "You mean drinking all our money and getting into fights at night until we were nearly out in the street? You couldn't afford a cardboard box."

"Stop, Kayli," Marc said, tugging again, gentler this time. "He's just egging you on."

7

"What check?" I asked Jack again.

"You think I need you?" Jack shoved a finger back at my face. "It doesn't matter if Wil is here as long as he's going to school and the cops don't catch him living somewhere. And if you're both off on your own, then the state may reduce it, but I can still live on..."

It was like ice water striking at my very heart. "You..." I couldn't believe what I was hearing. "You get checks from the state?"

"You think I do nothing around here?" he bellowed. "You think I can't support myself? You think your little contribution makes you tough shit?"

I smashed fists against my thighs to stop myself from hurling them at his face. My mouth clamped shut and I was biting my tongue so hard, I tasted the blood boiling inside me. "How long?" I managed to utter.

"None of your business what I do with my money," he said. "You dropped out of school and have been running around and when I stopped providing for you and your brother, you straightened up and worked and finally started contributing."

Raven held up a hand between us. "This isn't the time for this. Wil is still gone."

But the revelation struck me hard. My father had lied to me. Lied about having money. He lost his job, and didn't even try to look for another one. It's why I'd dropped out of school. I'd started working part time jobs where I could get them. And when it wasn't enough, I started stealing what I needed by picking pockets at the mall. Even then, we got kicked out of our old apartment and Jack convinced us we should stay at the hotel until we found another. But this whole time, I had been the only one paying the bills and contributing. Jack left nearly every afternoon when the bars opened to drink and pay for hookers out of the money I'd brought home for rent.

And now he tells me he's been getting government assistance all along. Possibly using me and Wil the entire time as the state helped pay for what we needed. Only the

money went to Jack. He must have drank it all. Gave it away
to those hookers.

My rage bubbled over. I lunged at him. I wailed. I
screamed. Marc tried to pull me back, but I wrenched myself
free. Raven dropped my bags and wrapped an arm around my
waist and pulled me back, but not before I clawed at Jack's
face with a good swipe. Even then, it wasn't enough.

"How could you?" I screamed at him as Raven started
carrying me to the door. "We needed you and you kept it all
to yourself? We were starving!"

"Get out!" Jack bellowed after me. "Ungrateful little
shithead!"

A slew of curses fell from my lips as Raven towed me
out. I fought him, but not as hard as I could have because he
wasn't the one I wanted to kill.

I was a mess, upside down, eyes seeing red and choking
on sobs as Raven brought me to the parking lot. Marc
followed, carrying the book bags that Raven had dropped.
His head was down as he stared at his feet as we left. He
opened the truck and threw my bags into the back seat.
Raven put me down in the passenger side and then shoved
me over until I was in the middle.

Raven got inside, slamming the door. "*Skatert'yu
doroga.*"

"Good riddance is right," Marc said. He jammed the keys
into the slot and started the truck.

I sat back against seat. My eyes were open and I was
staring at the windshield, but I wasn't really looking at
anything. I was trying to contain the anger that now
threatened to consume everything inside of me.

I'd been gripping Raven's thigh after he got in. As he
settled, he snatched up my hand and squeezed. Then he
opened up his arm and pulled me into him until I was leaning
against his chest. He gripped at my shoulder, clutching me.

I let him. And in a way, his strength allowed some of my
anger to flow away. Marc drove and then glanced at us. His
hand drifted out, and he gripped my knee.

None of us said anything. We didn't need to. We all

knew.

I'd never see Jack again.
But what about Wil?

The Academy

The Ghost Bird Series

Push and Shove

♥

Book Six

♥

Coming June 2014

Written by C. L. Stone

Published by

Arcato Publishing

♥

FIGHT, FAINT, FIGHT

*T*he fight started with a shout further down the hallway. The words were slurred and the dialect was too different for me to understand, since this was South Carolina, and I was from Illinois. The shout was angry and threatening, which was enough for me to understand something was terribly wrong.

Victor must have understood what was said, because instead of continuing to the staircase, he turned, scanning the crowd with his fire eyes lit up to a brilliant roar, aware and focused. I followed his gaze to a thicker part of the crowd that had stopped.

Two boys punched each other. One of them had very red skin, like he had a terrible sunburn. I didn't know their names, but recognized both of them. They hung out together in the courtyard. I had thought they were close friends. Now the red kid swung a fist at his friend's face, and the other retaliated by slamming his book bag at him, full force.

"Victor?" I asked, though my voice had disappeared amid the noise of the crowd.

Victor squeezed my hand. He had a lean figure, slim in the hips. His brown wavy hair was swept back in a stylish way that suited him: an almost-famous pianist and local celebrity. His arching eyebrows capped his brown eyes, lit up with a fire from within and warming when he gazed at me. "Go to gym class, Sang," he said.

"Don't get into a fight," I said.

"I'm just going to watch unless someone gets too hurt." He leaned in and kissed my cheek quickly before anyone noticed. My heart warmed a little. "Let me do my job. Don't stop until you get to class."

I nodded, wanting to stay with him, but knowing my interfering could make things worse. I distracted them enough from their Ashley Waters job, part of which meant school security. The fighting boys didn't seem to be interested in anyone else, but I was glad Victor was going to watch over it. Victor was going to time to see when teachers and administrators reacted to this fight, monitor who started it, and turn in a report to Mr. Blackbourne.

I left Victor to the fight, knowing he had his cell phone and could call in assistance if he needed it. I crossed my fingers he didn't need to.

Cell phones had become a problem for us lately. The boys had gotten a security update that they included me in on. We were to avoid using them if possible, and absolutely no Academy business, in code or otherwise, was to be conducted by phone. We had to appear as normal as possible. Normal was uninteresting to anyone who might be listening in.

I weaved my way around gawking students and headed down the stairs. I tried to move quickly and not be noticed. I was having a hard time being invisible and not getting noticed lately. I didn't think I was anything out of the ordinary. My hair had a slight wave, was dirty blond, a color that Gabriel often said was chameleon-like, as it changed depending on the lighting. I was a little short, which made things easier dodging around students. I did my best not to attract attention.

My fingers hovered over the phone planted in my bra. Touching the cell phone made me feel like I wasn't too far away from any of the boys. I waited for a chance to get through a narrow point in the hallway.

A bony shoulder jabbed hard against mine, striking with enough force to knock me back. Unbalanced, I fell, landing in an ungraceful mess on the tile. My book bag slid off my shoulders, and the skirt I was wearing skidded up high on my hips.

"Oh," a female voice said. I glanced up, spotting a familiar pair of disapproving eyes and dark hair. "It's you." Her tone implying that she had been fully aware who she'd bumped into.

"Jade." Jay materialized next to her. He had a shaved head and a hulking figure. I remembered him being on the football team. He frowned at her. "Don't be such an ass. It's ugly."

"Excuse me," Jade snapped at him. She glared, nearly baring her teeth. "I was trying to get to class. She stepped in my way."

"She's Rocky's girl." Jay stooped, and without asking, he took my arm. His eyes were cold with distrust, but something lingered behind them. Respect? Loyalty? Responsibility?

I let him pull me to my feet. My cheeks were on fire. I wanted to correct him about being with Rocky. I hadn't seen either of them in a while. Rocky was handsome, but he was assertive and, to me, too assuming. And the last time I'd seen him, he'd had Jade in his lap. I thought *they* were together.

Still, Jay was being nice, so I didn't want to contradict him. "Thank you," I said softly.

Jay's head tilted, quietly studying my face as if trying to determine if I was being sincere or not.

"She's not Rocky's girl," Jade uttered with a coolness. "She's with Silas. Or that muscular guy with the red hair. Or that punk kid with the gay earrings." She raked her fingernails through her hair, as if trying to make sure it wasn't out of place. "Honestly, I can't keep up with which one of those courtyard retards she's dating."

"Two of which are on the team," Jay said. He turned to her. "You're a cheerleader. So stop talking shit about the team."

Jade's eyes flashed at his face. If I ever thought someone could throw daggers with a look, she could do it. She squared her shoulders at me. "Just so you know, the football team's Friday night party is at my house. I want to keep it a small party. Cheerleaders and football players only. No friends or

3

girlfriends." Her thick, ruby lips parted into a cold smile. "No offense."

I blinked at her, unsure of what she expected me to say. "Okay," I said softly again. I broke my gaze with her, trying to appear unconcerned about the obvious rejection to something I hadn't even known about.

Only, I realized her decision meant North and Silas would be there alone. And North and Silas didn't know my suspicions about Jade and how she might have spiked my water at the last party, the one North ended up drinking and had reacted so badly from.

"It's my house, too," Jay said.

"And it's my party this weekend," Jade snapped back. "My party, my rules. I only support the team, not their bitches."

Jade and Jay moved on up the stairs. They were siblings? I didn't catch the family resemblance. Jay wasn't exactly the warmest person I'd ever met, but Jade was most certainly one of the coldest. I couldn't believe they were related.

The bell rang, and I started jogging to get to the locker room. The lucky thing about having gym class was if I happened to be a few minutes late, no one noticed as long as I was dressed and ready when class started.

"There you are," Karen said. She sat on a bench between the lockers and was tying on her tennis shoes. Her brown pixie hair was a little messed up in the front. Karen's eyes swept over me once. "You okay? Your skirt's all messed up. Or is it a new fashion I don't know about?"

"There was..." I paused, still feeling rattled about Jade. I blushed. I didn't often attract attention and I wasn't sure what to do about Jade. I never talked to her. I didn't even try to. But she seemed determine to single me out. "Do you know a girl named Jade?" I asked.

Karen's soft brown eyes widened. "Don't tell me she's trying to talk you into joining the squad."

I shook my head. "No. She doesn't really like me."

"She doesn't like anyone who isn't a cheerleader. I don't think she likes most of the cheerleaders, either. And the feeling is pretty much mutual for everyone."

I took my gym clothes out, and out of a need to use the restroom and to get two things done at once, I dashed to the stalls on the other side of the locker room. When I was finished and returned to my locker to put my clothes away, Karen was still there, dressed and waiting.

"How come you always go into a stall?" Karen asked.

"I don't always," I said.

"You do it before and after gym."

"I had to use the restroom," I said, though now when I thought about it, perhaps I did use the stalls to change. "It's a habit."

Karen shrugged and stood up. She was taller than me, and with her lean, athletic body, I thought she'd join a sports team, but she told me she was too busy for that sort of thing. She nudged at my shoulder. "Let's go before we're late."

At her touch, I clammed up. I don't know what came over me. I hurried, as though doing as she told so we weren't tardy. In reality, I just wanted to keep a distance from her for some reason. I wasn't sure what it was, but I noticed it as the weeks into school progressed. While we did talk, we never became close. I often ran out of things to say and we spent time staring at other students in class and not talking at all. I had a rough time with making friends, but it was better with Karen who was sweet and friendly; this was about as close I'd ever gotten to a friendship with a girl.

I tried to relax with her, but I clammed up every time. I internally sighed, wishing I could get over this shyness. I just needed to stop thinking about it so much.

I followed Karen into the gym and to our spots on the floor to wait with everyone else. The gym at Ashley Waters High School felt surreal with the onslaught of rain tapping at the wide windows. The clouds were so dark, it felt like night even though it was still around two in the afternoon.

I scanned the gym for Nathan and Gabriel. They were sitting and talking while other boys found their designated spots, and waited for instructions from the gym coaches. They wore matching black sport shorts and T-shirts that were the guys' uniform.

Gabriel's gym T-shirt looked a little snug against his long, taut body and his angular collarbone stood out against his broad shoulders. The three black rings that aligned along the crest of his right ear contrasted with the red crystal studs, one in each lobe. His angled face turned to me, catching me staring at him. He waved and then ran his fingers through the blond front locks in his chin-length hair, mixing it with the russet brown in the back as if trying to make sure his hair was in place. The tips of his hair were starting to hang below his ears. He didn't need to fix anything. The punk style seemed perfect for him.

The movement of his hand drew Nathan's attention and he waved, too. His reddish hair looked a little scraggly and stuck up in the back. He'd been complaining about it getting too long and wanted Gabriel to cut it for him. The locks reached around his ears and sometimes hung in front of his deep blue eyes. The sight was often stunning. And since it capped his statuesque figure, with his broad shoulders and acutely defined muscles, my breath caught often just looking at him.

But then all of the Academy boys looked good to me.

I yawned. I'd been tired all day. I would have been happy if we ended up being excused from any kind of activity for gym class. I'd put up a brave face for the guys today, but I was exhausted.

I didn't really have a reason for being tired. I'd slept the night before. I'd been busy with the guys, of course, but lately it had been harder to keep up with them. I thought maybe I just wasn't used to the constant Academy activities, plus school, plus dealing with my parents being gone. I felt like before I met the boys, I'd been in a holding pattern and now I was flying at breakneck speed and still wasn't even close to catching up with them.

I did my best. I just wanted a little break. Like not having to do any exercise today.

But Coach French was unrelenting. I saw it in her eyes as she marched across the basketball court with her whistle in her hand. She blew sharply into it, even though the rest of the girls had already started to get up in preparation. "On your feet," she said.

I summoned up my energy, hoping I'd find additional reserves after I started moving. Maybe that was my problem. I'd been sitting still all day because I was so tired. At lunch, I was half leaning against North just trying to stay awake. Maybe if I got up and got moving, I'd find I'd just needed a jump start.

I stood with the others, ready to get exercising over with.

Coach French bellowed her commands. "Start stretching."

I swayed back and forth, bending my arms and shoulders and my back. I followed the others in the usual routine.

The others lifted their arms over their heads, I lifted mine.

The others stretched down to touch their left toe, I did the same.

That was when I felt the first pang of something surging through my head, like I was being swallowed up by molasses.

When the others straightened up and got ready to bend toward the right toe, I was right there with them.

At first.

After that point, everything went dark and murky like the overhead clouds.

❤❤❤

I woke up to Nathan's voice calling my name. I felt like I was in a deep, thick sleep. I wanted to push him off of me, because I was sure he was just telling me I was in another nightmare and had woke him up, and I didn't want to wake up. I was too tired and too out of it.

But he was insistent.

"Sang," he said, though his voice sounded distant to me.

"Sweetie, wake up."

"What's wrong with her?" Karen asked.

It was Karen's voice that roused me further, forcing me to wake up. What was she doing here? Something was wrong with me? What now?

My vision was splotchy at first, revealing Nathan's deep blue eyes and serious expression. He hadn't shaved in a couple of days, although because of his deeper tan and the hair color, I didn't usually see it until I was up close. His tight lips made me wondered if I was in trouble again. Did I sleep in?

My memory returned in stages. I was on the ground. I was at school. Why was I asleep at school? On the gym floor? Nathan and Gabriel hovered over me. Karen was nearby. Other students looked on from behind them.

"What happened?" I whispered. This seemed wrong to me. My eyelids were so heavy, and the wave of sleep that had taken over had been so strong, that this felt like a dream. Everything was out of sync.

"Boys," Coach French shouted from behind them. "Get back to your class."

"I'm taking her to the doctor," Nathan said. He bent over and slid his arms under my back and thighs. He lifted me into the air, cuddling me to his strong body.

Coach French blew a whistle at him. "Stop. One of the girls will take her to the nurse. Put her down."

"I can take her," Karen offered.

"I've got her," Nathan said. I sensed Gabriel running ahead, holding open the gym doors.

There was more talking, more shouting from coaches, but Gabriel and Nathan were out into the hallway and no one came after them.

"Nathan," I said, though my voice felt small and thick. "I can walk." I thought I could. My head felt a little fuzzy.

"Shush, Trouble," Gabriel said. He walked alongside Nathan and reached for my face. His rough-skinned fingertips caressed against my forehead as if trying to ease away whatever had come over me. "You've been looking ragged for days now. I thought maybe you were on your period, but I guess you're sick or something."

My cheeks heated. "I'm fine, guys. I was just lightheaded and then tripped or something. We can go back."

"She doesn't feel hot. No fever," Gabriel said, ignoring my protests. He dropped his hand.

"Text Dr. Green," Nathan said. "Tell him we'll meet him at his office."

After a minute, Gabriel responded. "He said meet him in the nurse's office. Where is that?"

I closed my eyes, feeling disoriented as Nathan carried me through the hallways. He clutched me to his body. My hand landed on his chest, and I felt the swell of muscle. For a split moment, I thought about Karen and how she'd touched me and I wondered what the difference was. From Karen, I cowered. From Nathan and the boys, I craved. I waved the thoughts off. My mind had a hard time staying on task. I blamed my tired state.

I didn't open my eyes again until he stopped in front of an office door with a glass panel. Nurse's Office was marked in black lettering along the bubbled surface. Gabriel held the door open, and Nathan angled me inside.

Dr. Green's face swam into view the moment we got inside. His light green eyes had darkened with worry, but lit up when I faced him. Sandy-colored hair hung in front of his eyes and heart shaped face. "Hello there, gorgeous. Didn't I just see you in class?" he asked, his voice soothing.

"Hi Dr. Green," I said. I blinked heavily, trying to swallow back the dizzy feeling.

"She passed out," Nathan said. "During warm up exercises."

"I'm fine," I said. "I don't feel sick. Just a little lightheaded."

Nathan planted me on a cot. I sat on it in the middle. I flinched at seeing Mr. Blackbourne standing off to the side, quiet but focused on me.

Mr. Blackbourne was perfection in a gray suit and red tie. His short brown hair was brushed away from his face and his lips were solidly pursed. His trim figure was leaning against the wall, his arms folded over his chest. Nothing in his face or steel-colored eyes behind those black-rimmed glasses revealed what he was thinking.

It made me embarrassed to be there in the first place. It was like showing him I couldn't keep up. I wasn't good enough for the Academy.

The nurse's office was a big room, but we were in a section that was cut off by a movable standing wall. Other cots were positioned across the room, mostly masked by similar short walls. Some cots were occupied. I couldn't see faces, only the feet and part of the legs. From what I could tell from the shoes, there was a girl and a couple of guys, though I could have been wrong as nearly everyone was wearing sneakers.

Where was the regular nurse? If kids were sick, is that why Dr. Green had been in here? Is this what he did at Ashley Waters when he wasn't teaching the Japanese class? It seemed wrong to draw Dr. Green's attention if there were others who were really sick.

Even as I thought about it, my body quaked and I felt a wave of dizziness coming over me. I swallowed back those feelings, not wanting to worry anyone. What was wrong with me?

Dr. Green had a flashlight in his hands. He examined my eyes one at a time. "Tell me what happened," he said in a soothing voice.

"I was just doing warm up exercises," I said. "The next thing I know, I'm waking up on the ground."

"She fell over," Nathan said.

"Yeah," Gabriel said. "I thought girls fainted all graceful. She just crashed."

I tried to make a face at Gabriel but Dr. Green's hands spreading my eyelids apart made it difficult.

Dr. Green put his flashlight down. "Were you up late last night?"

"I was in bed by ten," I said. I looked at Nathan to help me confirm.

"Yeah," Nathan said. "She tosses around for a couple of hours, though. She does that every night, before she goes to sleep."

Heat rose to my cheeks at his revelation. "I do?"

Nathan nodded, his face grim. "It's usually not an issue with you, though. You've done it for a while. Like you can't sleep for a couple of hours and then you settle down and sleep. So if you want to be technical, you're not really deeply asleep until after midnight."

Nathan slept over more than anyone else, so I suppose he would know. When I thought of it now, I realized I probably did stay awake for a while after I went to bed. I thought it was normal. Like relaxing before you actually slept. How long does it normally take people to fall asleep?

"Yeah," Gabriel said. "Now that you mention it, she does do that. Unless she was worn out that day. Then she passes out real quick."

I sighed. "I've been tired today. That's all. I just need to go to bed earlier I guess."

Dr. Green took my hand, his comforting fingers massaging my palm before he turned it over. He examined my fingertips closely. "When's the last time you ate something?"

I opened my mouth to reply but stopped short when I realized I couldn't remember. I turned to Nathan to help. That was embarrassing, too, that I had to look at other people to answer for me. I blamed my tiredness for my memory temporarily not working.

He seemed perplexed, too. He scratched at the back of his neck. "You had coffee this morning, didn't you?"

That jogged my memory a little. "Yeah, I had coffee. One of those bottled Frappuccinos."

"What else?" Mr. Blackbourne asked sharply, surprising me. Was he angry? "When did you last eat something?"

"Luke and I split a bag of potato chips yesterday," I said. I paused for a long moment, not wanting to reveal the truth. "And another coffee that morning. But last night I was up late with homework and--"

11

"So you haven't been eating," Mr. Blackbourne's voice rose a notch. He unfolded his arms and started forward until he was standing behind Dr. Green. He nudged the doctor out of the way so he could plant a palm on either side of my thighs, bending over a little so that his face was level with mine. "Why?"

Heat spread over all of my face. I wanted to look at Dr. Green, or Nathan, or anyone else for help, but Mr. Blackbourne's steel eyes were unrelenting, holding me captive under his silent demand for a response. "I don't know. I wasn't hungry. I forgot. We've been busy." As I said the words, I knew it was the completely wrong answer. I was rattling off excuses. They were my reasons, but I should have known better. Why hadn't I realized this before? It seemed obvious now that he pointed it out.

His eyes steeled and he turned on Nathan and Gabriel. "Why haven't you made sure she eats?"

My mouth popped open. Why did he make it sound like it was their fault?

"I thought she was," Nathan said.

"Yeah," Gabriel said. "But ... I guess now that I think about it, I only really see her at lunch time during the week, and then she'll say she's not hungry or she'll split food with people."

Nathan sighed. "She was in the bath when I ate last night. I thought she'd already eaten when I was out."

Mr. Blackbourne sliced his hand through the air to silence the excuses. "I want everyone on task to make sure she eats, and to make sure she gets to bed an hour earlier for a while." He turned to me again, standing fully. "Miss Sorenson." His tone this time was clear. He wanted my complete attention.

"Mr. Blackbourne?"

"I'm going to have Dr. Green write an excuse for you to be relieved of gym class for the rest of the week. No Academy tasks for a while. No strenuous activity. If I hear you're not taking it easy and eating like you should now and through the weekend, I'll have Dr. Green put you on bed rest for a week and I'll ground you myself."

He might as well have said he'd command lightning to strike me down where I stood if I didn't obey. If he had said so, I would have fully believed it. "I will."

Dr. Green dug through a drawer and found a white bottle. He checked the label. "I'd like to give you these vitamins, but they expired two years ago." He slammed the drawer shut, tossing the vitamin bottle into the trash can. "This school is ridiculous. Yesterday I ran out of bandages."

"Mr. Griffin," Mr. Blackbourne barked.

"I'll get her new vitamins," Nathan said.

Mr. Blackbourne nodded. "And Mr. Coleman, if you don't have anything pressing..."

"I'll keep an eye on her," Gabriel said, sounding as if he was planning to anyway.

A rough cough started up from one of the other beds. One of the other sick kids, who I thought was male, twisted where he was laying. His feet picked up off of the edge of the cot and it jerked out. It slid against the tile and crashed against the side table and the wall. The movable wall tilted. Dr. Green dashed over, but the wall tumbled before he got there and it crashed to the ground.

The kid on the cot rifled through the side table's drawers. I recognized the beet red face. It was the boy who had gotten into the fight earlier. What could be wrong with him? Did he get that hurt?

"What are you doing?" Dr. Green asked. "Stop it." He tugged at the corner of the wall, trying to lift it, but it was big and awkward. Gabriel and Nathan sprinted over to help him. The three of them managed to move it on top of another empty cot, but it was awkward to correct.

The boy ignored Dr. Green. He yanked a syringe out of the drawer and examined it in his hands, like he was trying to figure out how to use it. He ripped the cap off.

"Wait!" Dr. Green shouted. He let go of the wall, jumping over at the boy and trying to grab his arm. "Nathan! Don't let him use it."

Nathan and Gabriel released the wall and it fell back.

C. L. Stone

They climbed over it, grabbing at arms and legs. The boy went wild, grunting curses. The hand with the needle waved around, avoiding capture. The boy aimed it at his own chest, and when Dr. Green blocked it, the boy aimed for his own arm.

"Everyone out," Mr. Blackbourne shouted to the others who were in the nurse's office. I turned my attention, realizing several people had gotten up from their cots. They had been staring idly at the commotion, but with Mr. Blackbourne's command, they turned, running for the door.

I started to get up. I wanted to help. What was he trying to do with an empty needle? I started forward, ready to at least grab a leg.

Mr. Blackbourne stepped in front of me, blocking me. His hand went up to my shoulder and he pulled me back. "Wait," he said.

"What's going on?" I asked. "What's wrong with him?"

Before Mr. Blackbourne could respond, the wild boy cried out in a rage. Dr. Green had the arm with the needle, but the boy wrenched it away.

The boy lifted his arm. Gabriel splayed his hand out to stop him. The boy jerked and the needle plunged into Gabriel's palm.

"Fucking shit." Gabriel swung his arm back, taking the syringe with it. He yanked it out, tossing it away before he dove back in.

Without the threat of the needle swinging, Nathan and Dr. Green dropped down on top of the boy like rocks, holding him down.

The boy started moaning, and then let out a loud grunt, as if he were in pain. He was thrashing but with Nathan and Gabriel on top of him, he barely moved.

"I need a sedative," Dr. Green said.

Gabriel scrambled up and replaced Dr. Green to hold the boy down.

Dr. Green dashed around, disappearing behind another wall. He came back with another syringe, and a bottle of liquid. He measured out a few milliliters. He withdrew the needle from the bottle.

"I need his arm," Dr. Green shouted.

Mr. Blackbourne released me. He nudged at Gabriel, who shifted slightly. The boy's arm whipped out, punching toward Nathan's face. Mr. Blackbourne snatched it and with a twist of his hand, he singled out the boy's pinkie finger. He forced the finger to curl forward. Mr. Blackbourne pinched it tight and held.

The boy howled but stopped thrashing. He tried bending his body to stop the pressure on his finger, but Mr. Blackbourne didn't release.

"Sang," Dr. Green called, snapping me to attention. "Is there an alcohol wipe in that drawer?"

I leapt up, sliding the drawer in the table open. I found a wipe, and dashed over to them, opening the package.

Mr. Blackbourne lifted the sleeve of the boy's shirt. I rubbed the wipe against the boy's bicep and Dr. Green followed up by planting the needle into the boy's arm.

The boy wailed, starting to thrash again as if trying to avoid this needle. He ripped his hand away from Mr. Blackbourne.

"Back up, Sang," Nathan said.

I stepped back, and the guys kept themselves planted on top of the boy. It took a couple more minutes but soon, he slowed. His howls became cries. His cries turned into soft whimpers. Soon, he was still.

"What the hell was he trying to do?" Gabriel asked, finally releasing the boy when it was clear he was passed out. "It was like he was trying to kill himself."

"He was doing a horrific job," Dr. Green said. He wiped at his brow. "He's watched too many medical dramas. He didn't even bother with a big enough bubble to cause an air embolism." He looked at Gabriel. "How's your hand?"

"Tingly." Gabriel rubbed his thumb over the spot on his palm. "At least he used a clean one."

"Is he sick?" I asked, gazing at the boy. Even in his drugged-induced sleep, he moaned and looked strained.

"Something's wrong with him," Mr. Blackbourne said.

"Several other students have picked it up. A strong fever that lasts for about ten hours, heavy vomiting, with delusions and paranoia."

"Is it a flu?" Nathan asked. "Is it going around? Are we going to catch this? Should we be wearing masks?"

"I don't think so," Mr. Blackbourne said. "I think there's something the students are taking. Some new drug, although the students who are sick aren't talking about it. The students who have come in don't seem to know each other, and some of the symptoms are different depending on the person. This is the first one I've seen that has been suicidal."

"Have you put any of them through drug screening?" Nathan asked.

Mr. Blackbourne nodded. "The results show nothing unusual. I don't think our tests are picking up whatever drug they're taking."

I straightened, pulling back. "He was in a fight upstairs. Victor was watching it. I've seen him before in the courtyard, too. The fight he had was with his friend. Where is he? Maybe we should talk to him."

Mr. Blackbourne turned to me, his lips parted as if he wanted to ask but he caught himself. "Miss Sorenson, I told you no Academy activities this week."

"I was just mentioning it," I said, unsure how to take a break from Academy work when they were around me all the time and they were Academy. For someone who wasn't in, I still somehow felt like part of their private school for... investigators? Security force? I wasn't sure what, but the more time I spent with them, the more I was diving deeper into their circle. "If I'm still going to school, whatever they are taking, what should I be looking out for? How am I supposed to not get involved if I don't know what it is?"

"Just stick with the boys, for now," Mr. Blackbourne said. "Family first."

My lips clamped shut at his reply, not wanting to question Academy rules. Although I would keep my eyes open, for no other reason than I didn't want to end up like the boy across the room.

ABOUT C. L. STONE

Certification

- Marvelour of Wonder

- Active Participant of Scary Situations

- Official Member of F.A.M.E.

Experience

Spent an extraordinary number of years with absolutely no control over the capping of imagination, fun, and curiosity. Willingly takes part in impossible problems only to come up with the most ludicrous solution. Due to unfortunate circumstances, will no longer experience feeling on a small spot on my left calf.

Skills

Secret Keeper | Occasion Riser | Barefoot Walker Strange Acceptance | Magic Maker | Restless Reckless | Gravity Defiant | Fairy Tale Reader | Story Maker-Upper | Amusingly Baffled | Comprehensive Curiousness | Usually Unbelievable

45357842R00247

Made in the USA
San Bernardino, CA
06 February 2017